BOUND BY BLOOD AND SORROW

J. M. WALLACE

Works by J.M. Wallace

A Legacy of Darkness Series
A Legacy of Darkness
A Legacy of Nightmares
A Legacy of Destruction
The Princess of Sagon (Novelette)
Claiming Elfhame Series
Heir of Shadows and Ice
Heir of Embers and Ash
Heir of Starlight and Truth
Born of Fire and Love (Novelette)

Cover Art by Etheric Tales
Map by J.M. Wallace

ISBN 978-1-7378806-9-1

BOUND BY BLOOD AND SORROW

J. M. WALLACE

For my Chaos Corner (Danielle, Emily F, Emily H, Jes, Kate, and Samantha) who always knows the right thing to say when I'm spiralling.

Contents

Trigger Warning

This novel contains mature content recommended for ages 18+

- Mention/Thoughts of Suicide and Self Harm

- Vampirism (detailed images of drinking blood and effects on victims)

- Light profanity

- Intimacy (on page spice)

- Kidnapping

- Battle Violence

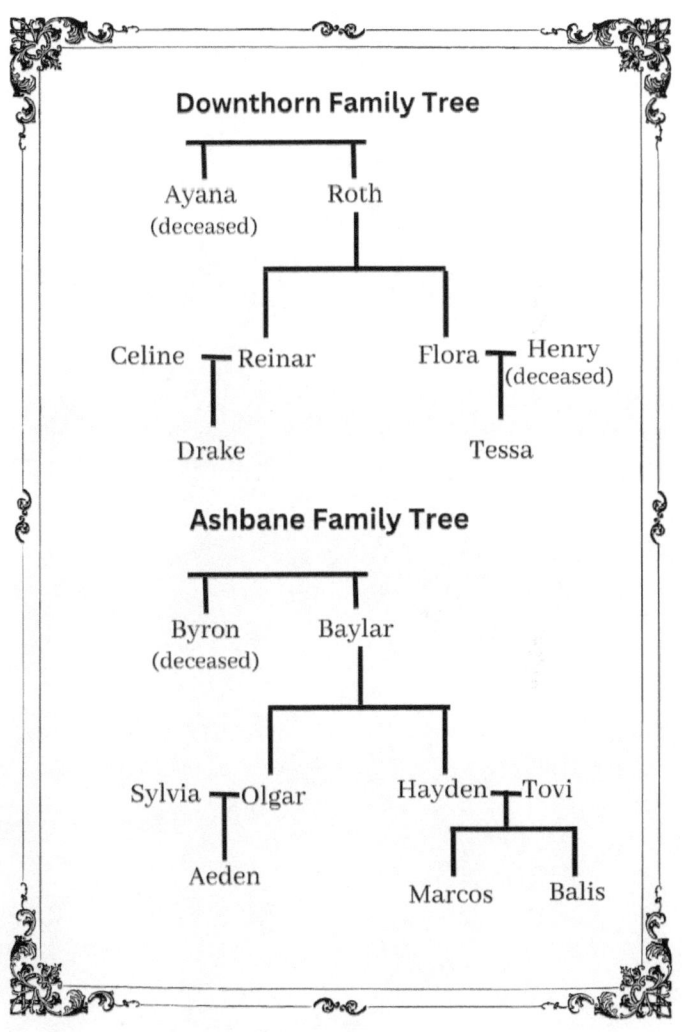

Downthorn Family Tree

Ayana
(deceased)   Roth

Celine ─ Reinar   Flora ─ Henry
                                    (deceased)

Drake   Tessa

Ashbane Family Tree

Byron
(deceased)   Baylar

Sylvia ─ Olgar   Hayden ─ Tovi

Aeden   Marcos   Balis

One

Tessa

Every kingdom has its monsters. For some, it comes in the form of creatures who lurk in the shadows, waiting to devour wayward souls. For others, the beast resides within man's own heart. But in Gwyar, where the Crimson Forest blots out the rest of the world—where the sun never fully rises, and where ancient bloodthirsty beings rule over all—it is both.

Though Tessa Downthorn's family liked to pretend otherwise, she had always known the truth. She had known it from the time she was a young girl running the halls of the family chateau. And the realization only blossomed as she grew into womanhood. Even at this moment, staring down into her reflection on the lake's surface, she did not find herself admiring her porcelain skin, or the way her eyes burned like fiery flames—as so many others often did. No. Beyond the long, rich brown hair and blood red lips, she saw what lurked beneath.

A huntress. Driven by an unnatural thirst to sink her delicately pointed fangs into any prey who dared stray too close to the forest's edge. A demon. Doomed to hide in their small corner of the world. Haunted by the sins of her kin. It was her fate. And her curse.

Tessa rose, dusting off her once pristine white gown. The one her uncle, Reinar, had ordered to be placed on her bed. It wasn't a color she would have chosen for herself. Wearing white didn't make her pure. Not in heart or body. But it was all part of his great facade. He would be cross with her for walking down to the lake in it before the guests for her party arrived. She smiled to herself, delighting in her subtle rebellion.

A soft melody drifted across the water, stopping her in her tracks. Its notes danced over the surface like ripples and echoed through the trees. She stopped to listen for a moment. It wasn't the first time she had heard the beautiful sound of the violin. Since she was a girl, she'd come to the lake for solitude, only to find that she was not there alone. It was a secret she held close. Something for just her. And years later she still delighted in the idea that the musician always seemed to know which song her heart needed.

Blood red leaves crunched beneath her feet as she swayed softly to the melody. Before the curse, she never had much rhythm, struggling to learn the dances with the other young girls in the Winter Court of their native land in Elfhame. But now she maintained the agility and grace that allowed her to move effortlessly to the rich harmony. Raising her hands above her head as if she could reach through the trees and touch the sun she longed for, Tessa soon lost herself to the music.

She didn't know who the musician was, of course. The other side of the lake was forbidden to her. It was Count Ashbane's territory, and she was a Downthorn. What started as an alliance between the families and their supporters had been tainted by bad blood and betrayal during their arrival in the mortal realm. But whoever was across the way, holding that bow must have been a kindred spirit. On days when just a little more sunlight sneaked through the trees, they would play a lively tune in celebration. Tessa, in turn, would dance to the beat with her face tilted to the sky that she hadn't been able to fully see since she was a child. The sky she had mourned and dreamt of for years since.

Other times, it was a tense harmony, mirroring the frustration at being trapped. Trapped in a life of duty. Stuck with a family who expected too much from her. But today, it was melancholy. Like something one would play when their deepest desires were stripped away. It was a ballad saying farewell to the safety of being unattached—unmarried.

What must the musician be going through to be playing a song filled with such sorrow? She couldn't imagine the Ashbanes or any of the other families living amongst them longing for anything. They did things on their own terms. That much had been made very clear.

A frustrated tear drifted down her cheek as she turned away, ready to present herself to the many suitors her uncle eagerly called forth. Tonight, at the masquerade, she would choose a man to court her until the next full moon. A man who would become her husband. But she would make sure it would be in title only.

That, at least, was something she could control. Love, after all, only ever ended in heartache.

The music stopped all too soon, leaving her empty inside. Thoughts of returning to the chateau made her queasy, and she tried to quell the uneasiness in the pit of her stomach. Part of her wanted to call out to the musician and beg for just one more song.

A twig snapped behind one of the tall oak trees and a woman peered around, meeting Tessa's eye. Sweat glistened on Scarlet Whitebrook's round face and her silver hair was disheveled. She stumbled over a fallen tree in an effort to reach Tessa. Scarlet didn't have the same appreciation for the great outdoors as her, and Tessa fought the urge to tease her about it. If her best friend had come all the way out here to look for her, then she wouldn't be in a playful mood.

Tessa's suspicions were confirmed as Scarlet huffed and said, "They're looking for you."

Tessa shrugged. "They can wait. It is *my* party, after all." Although she'd voiced her objections to it, as always, her pleas fell on deaf ears. Reinar would see her married, whether she liked it or not. Her uncle was nothing if not a stickler for the rules. *His* rules.

"The Count will not be happy." Scarlet tsked in disapproval, but the sly smile spreading across her lips said otherwise. She had always been Tessa's ally. Just as restless as she was, and dissatisfied with her lot in life.

"He'll live." Tessa scoffed. "Besides, exactly what will he do about it?" She winked. Her family believed in tradition, though she wasn't sure why they went to such lengths to uphold it. For ages, they had been living in a land that was not their own. Banished from their home for the sins of their forbearers. Cursed in blood. They foolishly clung to what they lost long ago in hopes that they could return someday. But if they asked her—which they never did—it was pathetic to hold on so tightly.

"He could send Drake to drag you home." Scarlet picked at some tree bark. Maroon sap trickled down like blood, and Tessa's stomach growled. She hadn't fed since yesterday, and it was making her irritable.

"Drake can try," she challenged. Her older cousin, Reinar's only son and heir, had a wicked streak in him. The man preferred to hide behind his expensive garments and broad smiles, but below hid the deadliest monster of all. She saw it in the way he looked at the humans brought into the chateau. The hunger in his eyes went beyond the need to feed on blood. Even his treatment of the servants made her uneasy. Striking them when they irritated him or cornering pretty naïve women in the stairwells. He thought he masked his animalistic instincts well, but she'd seen it with her own eyes.

When Scarlet gave no reply, Tessa sighed. "I need to feed first. Let's sneak in the back and grab a bite." With the viscounts and their sons coming for the party, the kitchens would be buzzing with servants preparing for the feast. They wouldn't mind if she snuck in to have a little taste.

Tessa took a step toward her family home, but a familiar tangy scent wafted past her nose. Sniffing in the air, she turned to follow it. Animals were becoming scarce in the forest—knowing predators more powerful than any coyote or wildcat were stalking in the darkness. But perhaps the day wouldn't be a total loss after all. An injured deer might be just the thing to turn her mood around.

Scarlet jogged to keep up as Tessa followed the aroma of blood. Judging by how strong the smell was growing, there had to be a lot of it. She was so eager to reach it, she didn't realize when she crossed the boundary marked with pearly sheen moonstones.

Scarlet cried out to her, "Tessa!"

But it was too late, Tessa was standing in Ashbane territory. She would have turned back immediately had it not been for the horrific scene before her. Scarlet joined her at her side and began to shake.

Tessa peeked at her friend to find her hands trembling and her shoulders rising and falling heavily. Tessa's own heart hammered in her chest as her gaze fell back to the forest floor. A human body lay on the ground a few feet away. Something... or someone, had mangled it. The sharp scent of blood filled her with uncontrollable hunger and the gums above her fangs ached.

It had been a long time since she'd seen a fresh body like this. Heat rose to her face, and she hissed, turning her back on it. Scarlet didn't seem to have the strength to do the same. She took a bold step toward the mortal, who had met a horrible end.

Tessa reached out and snatched her arm. "No." The word came out as a growl, reminding her of the beast she was. Downthorns and the cursed Fae that lived on their side of the lake did not take such a violent approach to feeding. They believed it was safer to snatch mortals from the roads closest to the forest to keep for short periods of time. It was effective in not drawing attention from the human villages.

During that time, the cooks would drain a reasonable amount of blood from their veins to serve in a civilized manner. Allowing them all to pretend that they were not monsters. Only the Ashbanes and the few families that had sided with them would feed directly from the humans. Cursed Fae who lived by their own rules...

Although this was the first time Tessa herself had come across a body in the woods, it was not the first time this had happened. The Ashbanes had become more and more careless throughout the years. Showing no attempt at exercising caution like her family and their loyalists did.

With a hungry growl, Scarlet pulled away slightly, but Tessa held firm. If she took part in feeding on the mortal out in the open this way, she would face consequences. Exile being the worst. Reinar made no exceptions for those who broke his rules.

Tessa's voice was low as she warned, "Not here. Not like this. We need to leave before someone sees us."

Reluctantly, Scarlet did as she bid. Even once the body was out of sight, Tessa could still smell it. Her tongue tingled at the thought of warm blood filling her mouth. But rather than give into her instincts, she focused on putting one foot in front of the other.

Scarlet's voice shook with hunger as she said, "Damn those Ashbanes. Your uncle will not like this. They're going to draw too much attention. What if the hunters come?" she paused, then added quickly, "I'm sorry. I shouldn't have..."

Tessa bit her cheek as memories of her father came rushing back. His warm smile and the strong hands that used to swing her onto her horse. Fond memories used to be all she had left of him. But with age they faded, leaving her with only the last moments she'd spent with him. She pinched the bridge of her nose, willing the memory of her father falling with a hunter's blade through his heart to go away.

When their people were first banished from Elfhame, they hadn't known how to control their bloodthirst. Mortal men were snatched from their fields. Women were taken when hanging laundry on the line. The rabid massacres had drawn too much attention from the humans. Once the mortals realized what was lurking in the shadows, they banded together to form *The Six*. The small, but skilled group of hunters began tracking down the cursed

Fae who they'd coined as the *Dearg-Due*—the *Red Thirst*. The *Vampyr*.

Many Downthorns, Ashbanes, and others from families who stood with them, were lost to The Six. It was why her people had created their salvation in the forest. Her people had transformed the oaks into a barrier between them and the mortal world using the last ounce of their birth-given magic. It created a veil around and above the tree line to deter humans from entering the woods on their own accord. Named for the leaves that had turned blood red from the magic which had been spoiled by the curse, the Crimson Forest was the only thing that stood between them and war with the humans.

Tessa shook her head, determined to rid herself of the dark thoughts. She had enough weighing on her with the prospect of tonight. She would leave it to her uncle to worry about the Ashbanes.

The chateau was in view now, towering high with glistening white stone. What her family called home; she called a prison. Tessa took a deep breath, preparing herself for a tedious night of parading herself around like a prized pony. She bumped Scarlet in the shoulder and quipped, "Maybe Reinar will be mad enough to postpone his matchmaking."

Scarlet laughed, the tension receding from her shoulders now that they were far enough away from the body. "Don't count on it."

Tessa frowned. She wouldn't. When it came to her family, the only thing she could rely on was that they would do everything within their power to get her in line. The thought alone was stifling. Love was something that wasn't in the cards for her. But despite her opinions on the matter, her family thought it was time for her to marry. She sighed. It was going to be a long night of evading suitors and coming up with excuses. But just because her family had finally worn her down, it didn't mean she wouldn't do things on her own terms.

Two

Aeden

Aeden Ashbane tucked his violin safely into its case, placing it under the bed and away from prying eyes. It was, after all, a piece of his life from before. And according to his father, Ashbanes shouldn't waste their time with such things. He'd given it up for a while when they were first cursed, but as years passed, he felt drawn to it again, longing to hear the music of his childhood. Putting bow to string was like magic to his ears.

Before their exile from Elfhame, he and his mother had spent countless hours practicing. His fingers were smaller back then, but that didn't stop him from choosing the most challenging pieces to learn. All for a chance to play at one of the grand balls in the Winter Palace. It was a childhood dream, but his life in the Crimson Forest had no room for such novelties. Survival had no regard for dreams.

Still, he never *could* give it up completely. Instead, he played alone in the forest where the music could flow freely without judgment. Emptiness washed over him now. Putting his instrument away always felt like parting with a piece of himself—the part of him that could reveal what he was feeling deep down.

He shook his head as if to stave off the melancholy that threatened to consume him and shrugged off his old jacket so he could replace it with something more suitable. His cousin, Marcos, had done well in charming one of their tailors into scrounging up attire for the masquerade without alerting anyone. He could have just as easily compelled a human in the village outside of the forest to do it, but leaving the Crimson Forest was becoming trickier. Aeden's father was starting to notice their absences.

He stared down at the fabric, admiring the craftsmanship that went into making it. His melancholy was slowly replaced with excitement at the prospect of what the night would hold. Tonight would be a night to remember, or so Marcos promised. Ashbanes crashing one of the famous Downthorn parties. The plan was ludicrous and incredibly exhilarating. It seemed his cousin had finally lost his mind... and Aeden along with him.

Aeden covered the tattoos that reached from wrist to shoulder as he shrugged on a black jacket trimmed with shimmering gold embroidery. The markings would make him stand out in the crowd, making it hard to blend in. He'd gotten the work done during one of his and Marcos' secret visits to a human village. The ink intertwined in a wild pattern of blackthorns—like the veil back home in the Autumn Court that separated Elfhame and the mortal realm. Sharp thorns like the ones that now stood between his people and their homeland.

Next, he pulled black gloves over his calloused hands. Spending the afternoon by the lake had been a good idea. It was better than listening to his mother bark orders at everyone in the manor. Even though he was a grown man, she would wallop him if she knew what his plans were for tonight. But he couldn't help himself. The chance to find out what went on during a self righteous Down-thorn ball was too good to pass up. Ashbane parties consisted of ill-lit rooms filled with too much smoke and men who liked to play with their food. Seeing how they did things on the other side of the lake would be interesting, to say the least.

His reflection in the gilded mirror caught his eye, and he pulled his near shoulder length, dark auburn hair back, securing it with a rough leather strap. Finally, he carefully placed the gold and black mask on his face. It left only his mouth and his golden red eyes exposed. The mask was fierce in the likeness of a wolf. It was fitting for the predator that he was, especially when he'd be entering the greener pastures of the Downthorn estate. Best of all, nobody would recognize him in it.

They would have to tread carefully tonight, though. They were there for fun, not trouble. Even so, it would be up to him to make sure his cousins didn't get out of line. Especially Marcos. His cousin suffered from a short temper, always eager for the rush of a fight. Aeden only hoped he'd be able to cage the beast inside long enough for them to have a few drinks and dance with a few women.

The door clicked open, and he turned in surprise as a lithe woman dressed like a peacock slipped into his room. Her bright red hair was striking against the deep blue and purple gown she wore. Rose Dewrun raised her slender hand to adjust the beaked mask on her face, and she gave him a sultry, full-lipped smile.

"Like what you see?" She spun around slowly, running her hands down the sides of her hips and making a grand show of the outfit Marcos had picked for her.

In all the anticipation, Aeden nearly forgot they had invited her along. But seeing her now reminded him why they had. Grabbing her by the waist, he pulled her into him, inhaling the scent of roses. She tipped her head back, leaving her neck exposed. His eyes sharpened, allowing him a clear view of the vein pulsing at the side of her throat. As much as he craved to sink his teeth into her, he resisted. A few of their people—Vampyrs like him and Rose—fed on one another for the sheer ecstasy of it. Their blood was like a drug, sending one another into a deep trance. But Aeden preferred to keep a clear mind.

He released her gently, sitting on the enormous four-poster bed so he could pull his shoes on. Rose gave a small, disappointed whine, sticking her lip out in a pout. He wasn't sure which fellow Vampyr she'd allowed to feed on her before, and to be honest, he didn't care to ask. She had always been a vicious little thing, and they'd known each other all their lives. The Dewrun family were amongst the loyal supporters of the Ashbanes. But Aeden had no intention of allowing himself to be blinded by emotion. When it came to Rose, convenience and proximity were the only things that kept them gravitating toward each other.

She slinked back, resting her head against the maroon wall. Desire rumbled in his chest, as he thought of the things he had done to her against that wall in the past. Her fingers trailed against her collarbone as she said, "You know, we have a little more time..."

Marcos chuckled from the other side of the door. "Not if we want to get around the lake in time for the ball."

Rose rolled her eyes as Marcos stepped into the room. A fox mask covered his face, leaving his clean-shaved mouth visible. It gave him a menacing, up to no good sort of look. It suited him well, especially with his fiery red hair. Blood dripped from his lips, a sure sign that he'd had luck finding game within the forest. Something that was becoming harder to do as both humans and creatures from the mortal realm realized it wasn't safe to venture into the dark and foreboding woods.

Rose asked, "Did you get it?"

Aeden raised an eyebrow, feeling out of the loop. "Get what?"

"The carriage." Rose pulled up her dress, revealing dangerously sharp heels. "You didn't think I was going to *walk* there, did you?"

Marcos licked his lips in satisfaction. "Of course I got it."

Wrinkling his brow, Aeden asked, "How did you find one at such short notice?"

News of Count Reinar's ball had only just reached them yesterday when one of their folk had gone to the border looking to trade furs. A rare, but not forbidden thing. Trading at the Ashbane-Downthorn border was acceptable, so long as each loyalist stuck to their side of the territory. It was also necessary as supplies dwindled.

Reinar had kept his plans to marry off his eldest niece close to the vest, telling only the most prominent families on Downthorn territory. Families who would be falling over one another to gain favor with their leader.

Rose shrugged and picked at her neatly manicured nails. The red polish on them glistened in the light as if she had painted them with actual blood. Maybe she had. It only added to his suspicions.

Whenever she and Marcos kept secrets, it usually meant trouble was near.

Marcos helped himself to the bar tray on Aeden's table and handed him a crystal glass of scotch. Smiling slyly, he said, "Don't worry cousin, some of us are willing to get our hands dirty."

"That's what worries me." Aeden drank the scotch in one gulp and refilled the glass. "And just who did you have to kill to get it?" There was no way Marcos would have had time to go into one of the mortal villages to buy a carriage. Besides, it wasn't his style.

Marcos puffed his chest out. He was larger than Aeden in both height and build. And that was saying a lot, considering Aeden towered over most of the Vampyrs on their side of the lake. Aeden didn't let it intimidate him, though. He and Marcos had been close since childhood and were taught to fight together. They had used each other to master the speed and agility that came with the curse. Aeden knew if it came down to it, he'd best his cousin in combat blindfolded.

Marcos bragged, "Some poor fool who took the wrong fork in the road."

Aeden gritted his teeth. The roads that ran past the forest were dangerously close to the Downthorn's side of the lake. And since he didn't smell any new bodies in the home, he could only guess, "You left him for dead? Not in the forest, I hope."

Marcos bared his fangs. "So what if I did?"

Aeden stepped up to him, raising his chin until they were nearly nose to nose. "Then I would call you a bigger fool than the human."

If the Downthorns found a mangled body near their territory, Count Reinar might finally decide to act on his threats of exile. They didn't need that kind of attention from them. More than a few times, the Count had threatened to expel them from the forest if they didn't behave. He had done it before, after all. The man was a warrior, born and bred. Trained for combat in the Unseelie Court itself. If successful in forcing them out, then Aeden's family and their supporters would have nowhere to go. Unable to return to Elfhame and hunted in the mortal realm.

Although Aeden's family didn't recognize him as the authority over all their people, Reinar's threats weren't completely empty. He had the numbers and manpower to do it. And Aeden had no doubt his own father would put up a fight. Things would be bloody. And not in the delicious sort of way.

Aeden rubbed his temples. "Maybe we should reconsider sneaking into the party tonight."

Marcos patted him on the chest, smoothing his jacket down. "Don't worry, cousin. Nothing is going to spoil this night for us."

Aeden wasn't exactly known for his restraint, but at least he attempted to think things through first. The same couldn't be said for Marcos. Aeden shook his head, but didn't push the matter any further. He'd been looking forward to this. Restlessness and boredom were getting the best of him. And mixed with the hunger that had been building with food so scarce, he needed to blow off some steam.

He gestured toward the door. "Alright, let's see this new carriage of yours then."

Marcos grinned ear to ear and led the way out the door. The carriage was finer than Aeden expected. Its rightful owner must have been a man of means. One whose absence wouldn't go unnoticed. He tried to ignore the empty pit in his stomach as he climbed in after Rose and Marcos.

A shadowy figure sprinted across the lawn, and Aeden held his breath, expecting one of the servants to bust them on their attempted escapade. He squinted into the night, sharpening his eyes to see better in the dark. Marcos' younger brother, Balis, slipped up to the window and Aeden cursed out loud. The runt was getting sneakier. Shock faded quickly as Balis came into the dim moonlight. His mask resembled a chipmunk, and Aeden burst out with laughter. His little cousin gave him a dirty look as if it would shut him up, then he hopped into the coach's seat.

Balis shouted over his shoulder in disdain, "Marcos is an ass!"

Marcos closed the bottle of wine he'd swiped from the cellar. "Just be glad I didn't think of a jackass when I commissioned the masks."

Balis snapped the reins loudly in response and Aeden sucked in a sharp breath, glancing back at the house to make sure no one had heard. The windows to the manor were hauntingly dark, with no signs of the creatures that dwelled within. A breeze carried the scent of blood down from the attic, where their mortal captives slept.

His stomach screamed in hunger. It would have been wise to eat earlier instead of slipping away to play his violin. He hoped his cravings would be sated at the ball. It would be interesting to see how the haughty Downthorns served their guests. Rumor had it that they refused to drink from the vein, even after all these years in safety. There hadn't been any sign of hunters in decades.

As the carriage rumbled down the narrow road, Aeden leaned back and looked out the window. He wasn't sure what tonight would bring, but that was the exciting part. Living in the Crimson Forest might have been a punishment, but that didn't mean they couldn't make their own fun.

Three

Tessa

Tessa couldn't remember what it was like to be satisfied by actual food. Anyone else in the world would have delighted in the grand feast her uncle had put together. But scanning the crowd of Vampyrs, she found dissatisfied frowns while they politely ate the fare. Their people had fled the Unseelie realm in Elfhame when she was only a child, but the memories of their old life lingered behind every thought she had. And although she still liked to indulge in the delectable meals prepared by their cooks—particularly the cinnamon fritters topped with cream and berries—it never compared to the way blood sated her.

So, she continued to pick at her plate, pushing roasted potatoes into the rare venison. Red juice from the meat seeped into the vegetables. Tainting them. Just as the blood curse tainted her people's hearts. Finally, she shoved dinner aside and picked up a tall crystal flute. The blood—sourced from one of the humans who was nearing the end of their stay—splashed up around the edges. Normally, she would have salivated at the sight of it, but not tonight.

The presence of several suitors and their families had taken away her appetite. She squirmed in her seat, uncomfortable with the pressure of so many eyes on her. It didn't help that they dressed her as a doe of all things. The mask was feminine and sweet. They'd certainly done a fine job of making her appear innocent and ready for the taking. Everything she was not. The white dress, laced with brown ribbons, threatened to suffocate her. Worst yet, the bodice was digging into all the wrong places, pushing her breasts up unnaturally high and tightening to make her waist seem smaller than it was. And in turn highlighting her wide hips. Her mother, Flora, had done a thorough job of grooming her for her future husband, whomever he may be.

Even Tessa's hair, pulled back tightly and secured with two sharpened pieces of metal, felt like shackles. They jabbed at her skull, reminding her that there would be nothing but agony throughout tonight's events. How in the world was she supposed to marry a man without falling in love? Most women would have been giddy at the prospect of having so many gentlemen line up to present themselves, but Tessa wasn't looking for what they had to offer. Companionship was nice, yes. But love? Now *that* was a curse in and of itself.

Drake sat on one side of her, separating her and Scarlet from one another. Tessa peeked around him to try to catch her best friend's attention, but a scraggly man wearing a hawk mask was already in her ear. She knew she should save her friend, but it was too amusing to watch Scarlet squirm a bit.

Drake stabbed his knife into a bloody piece of venison and tore into it with his fangs. With a mouth half full of food, he asked, "See anyone you like so far?"

Tessa grimaced. "Not in the slightest." Her nerves loosened a bit. There was her answer. A room packed with men she wouldn't fall in love with. Wouldn't that make each of them the perfect suitor for her?

Drake laughed as he took a loud sip of his ale. "I hear Angus Whitebrook is in the market for a new wife."

Tessa snorted with laughter. Angus was Scarlet's cousin, a plump little man who had neither skill with a sword nor with words. Even if he had been the most handsome man in the Crimson Forest, Tessa never would have been interested. Even in friendship, she needed someone who would stimulate and fascinate her. Actually, that might make him the perfect option. A safe choice. She reached for her wine, longing for an escape.

Drake shook his head. "No. He'd never do. I imagine he'd squeal like a pig in bed."

Tessa spat her wine onto the pristine tablecloth. The purplish liquid seeped into the linen as she choked down her laughter. The lady's maids standing against the wall near their table shot her irritated glances.

Drake downed the rest of his ale and slammed the cup on the table, seemingly unphased by Tessa's not so lady-like reaction. As usual, it seemed he was talking more to himself than to her. He licked his lips and declared, "Well, I'm off to find some company. Maybe Tilda is feeling particularly frisky tonight."

Tessa shook her head at the thought of anyone from the Steelhelm family being frisky. They were a proud and uptight bunch. Decent hunters and fighters, but not big on letting loose. Tessa raised an eyebrow as Tilda giggled at something Drake whispered in her ear and they disappeared into the hall. Maybe she was wrong about that last part.

With Drake gone, Tessa noticed men masked with the likeness of hounds, predatory birds, and bears all gazing in her direction. Her uncle no doubt had his own favorites for her to pick from. The Steelhems perhaps? Or the eldest Greyson? The weight of their expectant stares made her slink further into her seat. If only their curse came with the side effect of invisibility...

Beside her, her mother and uncle argued in hushed tones, giving Tessa a delightful distraction from her discomfort. Whatever disagreement they were having would be well worth listening in on. Anything was better than catching the eye of one of the eager men sitting at the long tables. She peeked at her mother and uncle to find them tense, gripping their silverware with white knuckles. It wasn't unusual to see them quarreling as siblings often did, but the heat of their conversation clued Tessa in on something more. She leaned in, pretending to reach for a warm roll so that she could hear them better.

Flora hissed at Reinar, "We have kept these humans long enough. In two nights' time, they need to be released unless we want to draw more attention from the villages. And then what?"

He griped back at her, "We will find others."

"Where? Travelers are scarce, and with the attack in the forest, we are vulnerable. Word will spread that the man did not return.

The mortals will avoid these roads, afraid that danger awaits them, too. And the hunters..."

Reinar turned to Flora with a red face. "Hunters have not been seen in these parts for many years."

"If the Ashbanes continue on as they do, then it will not be long before they return."

Tessa raised an eyebrow but pretended to be interested in the embroidered bluebirds on the tablecloth. She traced the detail with her finger as she waited for her uncle to respond.

Reinar huffed in frustration and then drained his glass to the last drop. His way of ending a conversation when it wasn't headed in the direction he wanted it to be. Tessa leaned back in her seat, pretending to be none the wiser about what she'd just heard.

Her mother was right. If word spread about the more frequent disappearances, then humans would stop traveling past the forest. And with so little sunlight and the lack of cleared land within the woods, keeping enough livestock to feed each family was next to impossible. A few measly goats did nothing to fill the Vampyrs. To make matters worse, the few animals who still braved the Crimson Forest wouldn't be enough to sustain them all.

She wasn't sure which was worse... starvation or being found by the hunters. Her father's handsome face flashed in her mind, giving her an answer. The hunters were a far worse and bloodier fate. This time, she grabbed hold of her wine. It was bitter and burned her throat, but it was better than being sober for all of this.

At Reinar's cue, his Master of Ceremonies—a gentleman whose age only showed in his peppered hair—called out for couples to join on the dance floor. Two by two, they gathered beneath the golden chandelier and formed a neat line. Men and women stood apart from one another, stiff and rigid.

All except for a man in a wolf's mask. He staggered in with a redheaded woman by his side. Confidently, she leaned in and kissed his neck. Tessa's eyebrows shot up, and she leaned forward for a better look. It was bold. Confident.

A wolfish grin spread across the man's face as he reached down to grab the woman's bottom. Something he said made the redhead laugh, drawing stares from others near the dance floor. As if having actual fun was a scandal. Tessa rolled her eyes at them. They judged the couple while she envied them. The man was clearly there for a good time. If she'd been there looking for love, Tessa might have judged him more harshly. But right now, the thought of letting loose if she could guarantee nothing would come of it seemed rather appealing.

Suddenly Tessa tensed, feeling her mother's eyes on her.

Sticking her nose in the air, Tessa said, "I am not going out there."

Flora leaned in and whispered gently, "Your uncle is relying on you. I know you were eavesdropping just now."

Tessa opened her mouth to deny it, but her mother held a firm, silencing hand up and said, "I know you, daughter. In times like this, it is important to remind our friends how important it is that we stand together."

Stubbornly, Tessa argued, "I have no intention of giving my heart to any of these men."

Her mother's solemn stare reminded her precisely why. Before The Six murdered Tessa's father, Flora had been a woman in love. It had shown in every smile and every laugh. There had been a glow about her. But in the years following the loss of her greatest love, Flora withered away.

She was a shell of what she'd once been, with hollow cheeks and silver hair that had lost its luster and shine. Even when she was able to feed to her fullness, no amount of blood would put color in her cheeks or a true smile on her face. Tessa couldn't imagine going through life like that. Like a ghost. As if half of your very soul was missing.

Flora shook her head sadly. "What are you so afraid of?"

Tessa gave her a pointed look. Her mother knew very well how Tessa felt about giving her heart to another just to have it ripped away. Love came at too big of a cost. Her parents had proved that. And before them, Tessa had witnessed the world shattering heartbreak that led them to their lives in the Crimson Forest. The love that had caused her people's downfall.

Flora bit her lip, showing a dainty fang. "Just one moment with your father was worth every moment of heartache I feel now." She took a tired breath. "Just give tonight a chance. You may find some enjoyment in it."

"Mother, I—"

A tall and what many would call, dashing, man wearing a stag's mask, stuck a gloved hand in Tessa's face. "Care to join me, Lady Tessa?"

The stag's mask that could have easily been a matching set to her own was a little too on the nose if you asked her. Had her uncle and this man's father planned that? Or was it just a strange coincidence? Judging by Reinar's eager gaze pointed in their direction, it was the former. Tessa looked to her mother for help, but Flora's crimson eyes bulged, and she tilted her head toward the man. Tessa's mouth twitched in a downward frown. Their community in the Crimson Forest was a small one, and even before that, the families had all been reasonably close. The Downthorns were once a powerful family in the Winter Court of Elfhame and had overseen the territory of five slightly less wealthy families.

Lord Peitor, the man standing before her—waiting like an eager pup for his treat—was the son of one of those families. Some of Tessa's earliest memories were of playing at the Greyson estate. But that didn't mean she was fond of Viscount Greyson's heir. More than anything right now, she wanted to smack the charming smile off of his face.

Flora nudged her in the side. Tessa should have known better than to think she would get through the night without having to entertain at least one or two suitors. Mustering an agreeable smile, she took his hand and followed him to the dance floor.

The other couples had already started in on the dance, circling around one another like birds in a mating ritual. They flowed in perfect harmony to the music, each following the steps with expertise. Tessa and Peitor joined in and it wasn't long before she was nearly bored into tears.

Dancing at these things was never the same as when she danced alone in the woods to the violinist. There, she was free to move her body in whichever direction she pleased. Decorum didn't hinder her like it did here. There was no feeling or emotion to this sort of dancing.

And Lord Peitor, as handsome as he was, didn't help to liven things up. A genuine smile stayed plastered on his face while he led Tessa around the dance floor. As he spun her around and back to him, he said, "Tell me, what do you enjoy doing in your free time?"

She could reply with a lie. Something like embroidery or journaling. Hobbies befitting a nice little wife. But he was staring at her so intently, with genuine interest, that she faltered. If she told him what he wanted to hear, he might try to get to know her even better. No. She needed to keep him at arm's length. It was safer that way.

Tessa opted for the truth, hoping it would deter him from inquiring about her further. "I enjoy hunting, practicing with the bow, and horseback riding." *And dancing to an unknown musician's music in the woods*, she wanted to add, but held her tongue.

Peitor's mouth popped open in surprise. "Interesting." Something about the way he said it startled her. Is that the sort of thing he was searching for in a woman? She let him continue uninterrupted. "You're not quite what I expected. Perhaps we could go riding sometime?"

"Maybe." Tessa bit her lip and set her mind to nit picking things she might not like about him. As of now, she couldn't find any. To be frank, she was afraid of spending time with him. If she was to go through with her uncle's plan, then she would have no choice. There was no avoiding that. Especially once married. What if time wore away the wall around her heart?

Her mouth went dry as she tried to think of a response to deter his interest. She could not deny that he was dashing, and if he kept staring at her like that for much longer, she feared she might fall under his spell. So, instead, she turned to plotting her escape.

Spotting a server carrying a rather wide tray of tarts, Tessa turned to the music, taking the lead away from Lord Peitor and pushing them closer to the server. Confused, Peitor scrambled to find his footing and keep in sync to the music, but before he had the chance, Tessa slipped her foot behind his. In one swift moment, Peitor slammed into the server, sending them both tumbling to the ground in a blur of strawberries and whipped cream.

Peitor wiped the tarts from his jacket while Tessa conveyed her deepest apologies. She stomped her slippered foot onto the strawberry jam, and said, "Oh, it seems I've made a mess of myself as well, excuse me."

Before Peitor could call her back, she slipped away into the crowd and headed for the door. Distracted by her escape, she slammed into someone. The man cut her apology off with a low growl... or was it just her imagination running wild at the sight of his fearsome wolf mask? The same one she'd spotted earlier across the crowd. He was taller and more muscular than she'd realized.

Heat bloomed along the bridge of her nose. "No need to be rude about it."

Surprise flickered in his eyes, but a small smirk crept across his face. His hand brushed against her arm, sending unexpected shivers up her spine. Smoothly, he replied, "Point taken. If I didn't know any better, I'd think you were trying to evade danger?"

She gulped, desperate to break away from the crowd before Peitor had a chance to catch up to her. *Only the danger to my heart*, she thought to herself. But out loud she said, "Something like that." Before the stranger could respond, she veered around him and picked up her pace.

Free of the crowd, she dusted off her dress and marched up to the door, proud of how easily she managed to end the dance. Distracted once again, she didn't realize her uncle was there until it was too late.

He was tapping his foot and looking as fearsome as a bear as he towered over her. "Quite an unfortunate accident." He nodded to the tart collision.

Tessa watched as ladies fawned over the poor lord and his ruined jacket. She put a hand on her hip and scoffed, "Looks like he's in excellent hands." The server, on the other hand, was being ignored, piling the ruined desserts onto his scuffed-up tray. Tessa felt a tinge of guilt for involving him.

Reinar inched closer to her, and under his breath, said, "This is an important night, Tessa. You are well enough past marriageable age."

Tessa stifled a laugh. She did not want to anger her uncle, but she also didn't know how to respond to that. Fae aged much slower than mortals did. She supposed the human equivalent to her own age would be something like twenty-five. Which she guessed placed her in the category of "old maid."

On top of that, the curse slowed their aging process down even more. She supposed the King who cursed them would have thought it delightful to know that this particular side effect of the blood curse would only prolong their suffering.

Reinar huffed. "I mean it, Tessa. You are a desirable match for any man here. And Lord Peitor would make a fine husband."

She scrunched her nose, knowing her uncle wasn't wrong. Peitor seemed thoughtful enough, and it was clear he wouldn't expect her to give up on the things she enjoyed doing. And he was well liked in their circle. She watched as he tried to deter the attention he was getting over his misfortune. Women were bringing him drinks and food, surrounding him like a small army of devotees.

"But he's so..." She couldn't think of anything terribly wrong with him. As far as suitors went, he was a catch. But that was the problem, wasn't it? What if his charms cracked open the gates she had closed around her heart?

"Loyal," Reinar finished for her. "His father was the first to jump to your Great Aunt's aid when the King ordered her execution."

Ah, Great Aunt Ayana. The curse bringer. Tessa had been hearing the story for ages now. The woman who snubbed the Unseelie King and set all their fates into motion. Just another love story gone awry. But the Greyson's were not the only families to answer their call during that ill-fated time. She jested, "If you recall, Uncle, the Ashbanes also stood with us. Would you have me entertain their litter of pups as well?"

She regretted mentioning them immediately. Her uncle's face turned as red as his eyes, and he took a thunderous step toward her. It drew looks from all directions and Tessa's face burned with embarrassment as he scolded her, "Olgar Ashbane is a coward and a troublemaker. After what happened to your father..." His breath hitched in his throat and Tessa put a comforting hand on his shoulder.

"I know, Uncle, it was a poor joke."

His shoulders slumped as he sighed. "Never mind. I'm going to get a drink." He sulked away sadly without another look in Tessa's direction, leaving her with a large pit in her stomach.

Her uncle had always done his best to keep them safe. He had defended his family with dignity and strength. And through it all, he had never asked much of Tessa, allowing her to join them on animal hunts and gifting her with her beloved horse. If he thought it was time for her to marry, then what good reason did she have to resist?

Looking out at the families that had come tonight, she noted a few of the older couples. Lady and Lord Ravenbloom, and the heads of the Steelhelm family. Even the heir of Featherton and his sour looking wife... Each had entered into marriages arranged by their families. None of them seemed particularly in love with one another. At least, not like Tessa's mother and father had been. Maybe a good marriage could work without love being involved. She certainly had no intention of falling in love with Peitor. But perhaps she could tolerate him. If that's all it took, then she could give the match a chance. So long as he didn't charm her to death first.

Four

Aeden

Aeden chuckled as the woman disguised as a little doe galloped away from him. He straightened his jacket with a smirk on his face. The last thing he had expected to find when he arrived at the ball was a beautiful woman causing a tart catastrophe. It was just the sort of trouble he enjoyed. What was a party, after all, without a bit of chaos?

He snatched a glass of wine from a nearby table and looked around. The masquerade was nothing short of extravagant. The very epitome of everything the Downthorns stood for. Pomp and circumstance with all the trimmings. Count Reinar was the ultimate showman, but Aeden saw through it. He sneered in the direction of Reinar decorated in all his finery and was surprised to see the doe arguing with him. Their mouths were both down turned. Was she in trouble for the scene she had caused? Personally, he thought she'd been very slick about the whole thing and didn't think anyone, aside from him, had noticed how her foot shot out at just the right moment.

Aeden narrowed his eyes. Reinar looked nothing like he remembered. The once proud warrior had withered a bit. His clothes fit loosely, as if he was losing his once muscular frame. As a child, when Aeden had first seen him, he'd been in awe. Reinar had led the charge against the Unseelie guards, who had been sent to bring them all in for their part in the rising. And again, when the hunters came for them, he had torn them apart with his bare hands. Now he appeared as if he wasn't capable of tearing a piece of cloth.

Aeden's father would be interested to hear that his adversary didn't seem to be the man he once was. But Aeden wouldn't be the one to tell him. Not unless he wanted to reveal that he'd snuck into enemy territory.

Marcos bumped into Aeden and handed him a cup. "Drink up."

Aeden—distracted from Reinar and the woman—stared down at the thick, dark substance. The tangy scent of blood drifted up to his nose. "Blood? From a cup?"

Marcos shrugged. "Better than nothing."

With a shake of his head, Aeden drank. The blood was cold and bitter. He grumbled, "I beg to differ." His stomach turned as the stale blood reached it and he fought the urge to gag.

Marcos clapped him on the shoulder and grabbed the woman closest to them. She yelped as he pulled her onto the dance floor.

He whispered something to her and in the blink of an eye, the two of them were laughing and spinning around the dance floor.

Rose sauntered through the crowd, leaving a trail of drooling men in her wake. Once she reached Aeden, she jutted her bottom lip out in a pout. "I'm bored. How about you take me for a walk in the garden?" She trailed her manicured nails down his chest suggestively.

Aeden's gaze wandered back to Reinar and the doe, but the woman was gone. Had she finally succeeded in her quest to escape? He peered around the room, but there was no sign of her. The stag she'd tripped had moved on to dancing with a thin woman in a feline mask. The cat-like woman didn't hold a candle to the curves of the doe. If it had been Aeden who'd had the chance to capture a woman like the doe's attention, then he would have done anything to keep it. She was lovely and judging by her little stunt; she was rather clever. The stag was a fool.

Rose huffed at Aeden's lack of response. "It's so stuffy in here."

On that, they could agree. The ballroom was massive, but between the stale scent of blood from his half-empty cup and the heat emanating from the crowd, he was suffocating. Though he did not remember many details about the revels the Downthorns had thrown in the Unseelie Court, he did have vague memories of their annual Winter Ball.

It had been the event of the year, drawing even the Unseelie King, himself, to their halls. It was where his royal highness had met Ayana Downthorn and decided he would make her his. But it was also where Aeden's great uncle Byron had captured Ayana's heart. Love made people do foolish things. Things that hurt those around them.

Rose's roaming hand stopped but remained on his chest. More seriously, she said, "I was hoping we might talk."

"About what?" He was almost reluctant to ask. A sinking feeling in his gut told him he wasn't going to like the answer.

She pursed her lips, a sure sign that she was going to make things difficult for him. "About us."

"Rose—"

"You and I have been playing games with one another for years." She winked as if trying to lighten his mood as she added, "Anyway, we know the sex is good. Why not take things another step?"

Suddenly Rose's hand felt like a shackle trying to close around his heart. He grabbed it firmly and removed it. Eager to avoid the topic, he suggested, "Maybe you should go dance with Balis. He needs a distraction from the wine." He tilted his head in the direction of his younger cousin, who was sneaking his third glass.

Rose rolled her eyes. "What is your problem? Why are you so afraid of giving something like this a chance?"

"What's bringing this on?" Aeden scrutinized her. She had never been interested in making things more serious between the two of them. She, too, liked her freedom.

With a huff, she answered, "My father thinks it's time I stop playing games. And if I have to choose, then it's you that I want."

Aeden shrugged as he said, "Love, marriage, a family... It isn't in the cards for everyone. Why ruin a good thing?"

The two of them had fun, but it usually included chaos. Even if love was something he was open to, he couldn't imagine attaching himself to a woman who tended to bring out the worst in him. She could be vicious and petty. They'd fought on more than one occasion over miniscule things. Once, a fight had even resulted in the destruction of one of the estate's barns.

Seething silently, she stalked off, giving Aeden his own chance of escape. With a quick glance around to make sure no one noticed him, he slipped out the door where the woman dressed as a doe had been standing. She'd had the right idea if she had been looking for an escape.

The hall was empty. Muffled voices from the ballroom echoed in the quiet corridor. Tall candles stood on marble podiums, giving him enough light to see the art on the cream-colored walls. Paintings of winter landscapes and regal Fae set into intricate gold frames lined the hall on either side. He shuffled his boots on the pristine, pale blue carpet as he explored.

Part of him had hoped to find the doe waiting outside of the ballroom. Seducing a girl from the Downthorn side of the lake would make for an interesting story to tell Marcos and Balis later. He wandered further down the hall until it came to a bend. When he rounded the corner, he came face to face with a large painting of a stunning woman. Her lips were soft and full. The detail was so lifelike, it was as if she might step out of the artwork at any moment.

Her hair was long and silver, a common trait of Fae from the Winter Court in Elfhame. Her eyes—with rings of varying frosty blues in the irises—bore into him. There was something guarded about them. Full of secrets, and utterly captivating. The name at the bottom, engraved into a gold plate, read: *Ayana Downthorn*.

Aeden thought sarcastically, *they should add, 'destroyer of families.'* He couldn't help but wonder how someone so beautiful could inspire such violence and ugliness. With a scoff, he pivoted to face the painting across from her portrait.

This one was larger, spanning along several feet. It was made up of different scenes, all telling the story of their downfall. Of their curse. Starting with the lovers, Ayana and Byron, meeting in secret. Ayana's shimmering silver hair blowing in the winter wind as her lover, a man with dark auburn hair, knelt at her feet. At first glance, the man could have been mistaken for Aeden. Many often spoke of how similar he and his great uncle Byron were. In both appearance and demeanor. Byron hadn't been one for rules either. He had been reckless and wild. The epitome of what an Autumn Court Fae should be. It was why he hadn't let the King stand in his way.

Aeden sidestepped to get a better look at the next scene playing out in the painting. The Unseelie King, a fierce warrior with a crown of dark, twisted metal resembling horns, was cornering Ayana in the winter forest. His possessive hands wrapped around her full hips, drawing her into him. Aeden's stomach constricted, knowing what came next. Thankfully, the artist who had painted this depiction didn't delve into the graphic details.

His eyes shifted to the next scene. Ayana and Byron, meeting clandestinely with their families assembled. The couple's hands were bound by blue and orange ribbons that represented each of their courts.

He narrowed his eyes, attempting to gain a sharper look at the woman binding their hands together in matrimony. There was something eerily familiar about her pale, graying skin. He racked his brain and jolted as a flat, feminine voice came from behind him. "I hate these paintings."

Before turning to face her, he adjusted his mask, being sure that it was still keeping his identity a secret. He wasn't quite ready to be kicked out of the party yet. A smile crept across his face as he turned to find the woman masqueraded as a doe.

Crossing his arms over his chest, he regarded the painting and said, "I can't say I love how it ends."

She sidled up beside him. Her arm brushed against his, and he couldn't resist watching her as she looked at the scene above. Long, dark hair cascaded down her back, no longer held tight by the pins she'd had in earlier. But her doe mask remained. It was delicate, contrasting with the confident way she carried herself. There was something familiar about her, but he couldn't put his finger on it. So much time had passed since their people had placed the moonstones on the border, separating the rival families and their supporters. But there was a chance they had met as children.

She tilted her head and narrowed her eyes.

He followed her gaze to the painting. It was the part he remembered all too well. The King coming to claim the woman he wanted as his own. Byron Ashbane stepping in to defend his wife with their families by their side. The Downthorns were on one side, with other prominent Winter Court families loyal to them, and the Ashbanes were standing nearby with an army of Autumn Court families that had agreed to stand against the malevolent King and his reign of terror.

Aeden's chest constricted at the last scene. The King standing triumphant in a bloody battlefield over a stone table. In his hands, he held two hearts. Below, Ayana and Byron's bodies were slain in front of the table, still holding each other's hands with open wounds where their hearts used to be. And a cup on top of the table, where the blood of the lovers dripped from the hearts, filling it to the rim.

Although Aeden had no knowledge of what specific spell the King had used, he did know the result. He winced and averted his eyes, unable to stand the sight of the downfall of his people any longer. That was what happened when people opened themselves to one another. Love too often hurt the people closest to you. Rose's suggestion still echoed in his mind, and he shook his head. There might be times when he was willing to make impulsive and reckless choices, but he drew the line at love. At putting his family and people at risk.

The doe turned, too. Following him a few steps down the hall. He felt a tinge of sympathy for her having to walk past this sickening remembrance of their curse every day. To him, it would serve as a reminder of the sort of destruction love caused. Did she see it as a warning? Or as a symbol that true love was worth fighting for?

Hoping to lighten his sour mood, Aeden asked, "Not much of a dancer?"

A delicately pointed fang peeked out at him as she bit her lip. "I don't mind it. But it was a tad stifling in there."

Aeden couldn't take his eyes off her mouth. It was full and soft, like Ayana's lips in the painting. Would they feel as soft as they looked? What would she taste like if he pressed his own against them? Something stirred in the pit of his stomach and he took a bold step toward her, curious if she would back away like a frightened deer in the woods.

To his pleasant surprise, she didn't. Her eyes darted around the hall, then settled on him. She scoffed. "I suppose you're here for the same reason as everyone else?"

He chuckled. "Not quite."

"Well, I know you can't be here for the wine. It's terrible." She placed a hand on her hip and jutted it out.

Aeden followed the hourglass curve of her body and his hands itched to grasp onto her. Would she let him run his calloused fingers over that innocent white gown? She didn't strike him as uptight, but she also didn't carry herself like Rose, who craved attention as much as blood.

Eager for the fun he had come looking for at the ball, he stalked around the doe, circling her like a wolf on the hunt. "Well, since your distaste for the wine is clear, and since I'm assuming *you* are not here to offer your hand to Reinar's niece, what is it that you were hoping to find tonight?"

She turned with more grace than he'd witnessed earlier, so she stayed facing him as he circled. With a mischievous grin, she said, "I was hoping for a moment alone, but then I stumbled upon you."

Aeden stopped circling. "Two times in one night. What a happy accident."

She clucked her teeth and scoffed. "You think highly of yourself, don't you?"

He spread his arms wide and then bowed at the waist. Referring to his mask, he said, "Well, I've heard that mortals hold wolves in high regard." He ticked off each finger as he said, "They're intelligent, strong, and have impeccable family loyalty."

She hummed in response and gestured to her mask with a perfectly manicured finger. "Since you seem to know so much about these matters, tell me... how do the humans regard deer?"

Aeden inched closer to her and ran his hand over the mask on her face. "They're graceful, gentle, the embodiment of femininity." When his fingers reached the snout, he flicked it lightly. "But mortals regard them as a source of food. Ultimately, they are nothing more than beautiful creatures waiting to be devoured. Easy prey."

The woman raised her defiant chin. "Something I am not."

Aeden licked his lips, and his heart pounded in his chest. She smelled of the forest. Bittersweet and earthy, like the tall, proud oak trees. "Then perhaps they should have given you a wolf's mask."

A smile flickered on her lips. "Perhaps they should have."

An overwhelming desire to touch her drew him closer. He leaned down, moving slowly so he could read her body language. He didn't want to overstep and spook her off. There was something mysterious about her. Most women behaved like school girls around him, or threw themselves at him like Rose. But not the doe. Yet, she didn't retreat from him, either.

Instead, she tipped her head back to look up at him with challenging eyes. Her lips parted slightly and he could hear her heart beating rapidly in her chest. With a light whisper, she said, "I should get back to the party. It might cause quite the scandal if someone finds us alone like this."

Not yet ready to let her go, he teased, "In that case, the doe seems to be a good fit for you after all."

She pursed her lips together and her eyes hardened. "Careful, sir, if I didn't know better, I'd think you were insulting me."

"I wouldn't dare." He continued to lean down close to her, just inches from her face.

Her gaze swept across his mask, then stopped to linger on his lips. The sound of her heartbeat reached his ears. It pitter-pattered like a rabbit kicking the ground, and he resisted the temptation to tease her some more. Instead, he reached out to touch her. He half expected her to call him a rogue, or to run away from him, but she held as still as a deer caught in a hunter's sights. Her jawline was soft under his calloused hands and a sudden flush of warmth ran through him.

Her lips parted in invitation. Aeden pressed his body into hers with every intention of accepting. But a thud from around the corner of the hall forced them apart. The doe's eyes went wide, and her hand flew to her mouth. Aeden stepped away, giving her a respectable amount of space befitting an unmarried woman.

A flash of blue and purple satin topped with a striking mass of red hair darted out of view. Aeden had a sneaking suspicion that he was about to get an earful from a very angry Rose. Aeden sighed in pent up frustration and ran his fingers through his hair. As much as he wanted to go back in for the kiss, the moment was lost.

The woman pressed her hand to her chest and laughed. "I should probably be going. The hallway doesn't seem to be as safe as I thought it would be." She offered him a sly smile. "If you'll excuse me."

Before he could stop her, she dipped into a little curtsey and opened the first door she could reach. As she slipped away, out of sight, Aeden was left with an unfulfilled ache. Heading back to the ballroom, he shook his hands out, trying to rid himself of the way her porcelain skin had felt under his touch.

A frazzled servant and several large men in masks gave him just the distraction he needed. The servant's face was flushed as he ran down the hall after the others, headed toward the ballroom door. With each running step he took, he shouted, "Oh no! Oh no! Oh no!"

Aeden grabbed him by the jacket before he reached for the golden door handle. "Hey, what's going on?"

The man's hands flew around erratically as he said, "A-Ash-banes."

Shit. Aeden's mouth went dry. Why should he be surprised? As he followed behind the man, his only thought was, *here we go*.

Five

Aeden

The band's music did little to drown out the shouts coming from the middle of the dance floor as Aeden entered the ballroom. He followed behind the frantic attendant, who was fluttering around the crowd like a frightened sparrow. Partygoers staggered around. Some were too deep in their cups of wine to bother with the commotion. Others kept their distance, craning their necks to get a peek from afar.

Aeden shoved his way through the crowd, trying to reach the center of the ballroom. Two voices rang out loud and clear above the rest. Only one of which he recognized... Marcos. A few of the younger men who were circled around shouted, reminding Aeden of the bare knuckle boxing matches he and his cousins had seen in the mortal court. The first time he had attended one, the savagery in which the mortal men beat on one another surprised him, but it was nothing compared to how vicious his own people could be. Even then, he hadn't expected to see it here amongst the uppity Downthorns and their friends.

An older woman in a bluebird mask stuck her snooty nose in the air and pursed her lips in disapproval. There was no sign of the woman in the sweet doe mask, and he supposed he should be grateful to not have her there to witness whatever was happening.

Aeden stumbled between the men who had rushed past him in the hall and found the cause of the commotion. Balis was standing on top of one of the tables with an empty cup in hand. The table shuddered every time he moved. It seemed one wrong step and his cousin would go tumbling.

With Balis out of the way... for the most part, Aeden's eyes fell on his other unruly cousin. Nearby, he spotted the woman Marcos had led to the dance floor earlier. She was cowed a few feet away and hugging herself. It looked as if she might shrink into the shadows at any moment. There was no sign of assault or injury, only fearful glances in the direction of the men.

Meanwhile, Marcos was arguing with a beast of a Vampyr with silver hair tied back in a low ponytail. The man shouted profanities, throwing in the Ashbane name every so often. Even that sounded like a curse word in the way he spat it.

It wasn't surprising that someone from this side of the lake would speak of his family in such a brazen manner. But it didn't make it any easier to stomach. Aeden clenched his fists tightly, trying to weigh his options. He could join in on the fight and show this pompous ass what the Ashbanes were really made of. Or he could play peacekeeper and maybe salvage what little chance they had left of leaving the party without further incident.

Marcos threw his hands in the air and grinned at the man. "Maybe if you lightened up a little, friend, it wouldn't look like you had a stick shoved up your—"

The man shoved Marcos, knocking him into Balis' table. Aeden's younger cousin swayed on his feet with a green face. The table creaked under the shift in weight. How much had he drunk?

Marcos, as lithe as ever, squared back up with the monstrous man. Someone in the crowd shouted, "Show him who's in charge, Drake!"

Aeden recognized the name immediately. It was no wonder he didn't realize this was the heir to the Downthorn estate. The last time they'd seen each other was in a training field, when they were no more than boys wielding wooden swords. Drake had nearly tripled in size since then. But now that Aeden put the name to the man, he recognized that arrogant sneer.

Drake snarled, "You and your filth aren't welcome here."

Marcos feigned offense, clutching his chest in hurt. "You cut me deep." Spotting Aeden, he shouted. "Welcome, cousin! Drake here was just giving us a taste of that warm Downthorn hospitality."

A few laughs bounced around the room, drawing Drake's threatening glare. Aeden side-stepped over to Marcos, careful not to turn his back on Drake. "Perhaps it's time to call it a night, huh?" He swung an arm over Marcos' shoulder and began to steer him away.

Drake called out to them, "And *you*," he roared with a finger thrust in Aeden's direction. "Don't think I don't know what you were doing in the hall. You are a no good savage."

Aeden gritted his teeth at the insult. "Pot. Kettle. Friend." He tried to play off the unsettling feeling in the pit of his stomach, but Drake's comment was bothering him. How could he possibly know what Aeden was doing in the hall? Moreover, what business was it of his?

Drake's words were laced with venom as he said, "I am not your friend."

Aeden shrugged and continued to lead Marcos and Balis away. The sooner they stepped foot back on Ashbane territory, the better. But Drake wasn't ready to let go so easily. He loped after them and grabbed Aeden roughly by the arm, tearing him away from Marcos.

Drake leaned in close to Aeden and spoke under his breath. "You think you have a right to come into *my* home? To put your feral paws on *my* kin?"

"Wait. What?" Aeden laughed awkwardly. "What do you mean, *your kin?*" His mouth fell open as he processed Drake's words. "How did you even know about..." he trailed off as Rose approached. With her arms crossed over her chest, she gave him a satisfied smile. The jealous little wretch.

Aeden tore his arm away from Drake. Then to Marcos, he announced, "We're leaving. Now." He swaggered back a few steps, running his tongue over his fangs. He wasn't about to let Drake believe he was running away out of fear. If he wanted a fight, he would get one. The only thing keeping Aeden from striking Drake was the little voice in his head that typically tried and failed to keep him out of trouble, saying it would be better for all of them if he just walked away. He had come for fun, not a war.

To Drake, he said, "My deepest apologies." Unable to help himself, he folded his arm over his stomach and bowed at the waist sarcastically.

Drake clenched his fists and moved as if he would pounce on Aeden. With Marcos and Balis securely behind him, Aeden squared up to Drake. Sensing the larger man's intention, Aeden ducked as a fist barreled in his direction. Drake stumbled forward a few steps and Aeden raised his fists to protect his face from the next blow that was sure to come.

As Drake advanced on him with renewed rage, Aeden struck. His fist connected with Drake's cheek. His knuckles stung as he pulled back. He shook it out, hoping it wouldn't affect his grip on the violin bow tomorrow.

A few voices from the crowd shouted in Drake's favor, and he straightened with a curse. He reached into his boot and pulled a silver dagger. Aeden clenched his jaw. Drake never did like to play fair. But before Drake could make his move, an older woman placed her hand on his shoulder. The attendant from earlier stood beside her, quaking in his shiny leather boots and biting his nails. He must have panicked and gone to get someone to quell the storm in the ballroom.

Drake froze, looking down at her, and she shook her head. Her voice was smooth like honey as she said, "That's enough, boys." To Aeden and his cousins, she warned, "It wasn't wise for you to come tonight."

Defensively, Aeden responded, "We meant no harm. We just wanted to see the party." It was the truth, even if he had known the consequences of being found out.

"Even so," her voice was steady, showing no emotion or hint of what she really thought as she continued, "these are dangerous waters to tread, especially after the body that was found on your side of the border today."

Aeden's stomach dropped. Soon suspicion replaced it. "How could you know about that unless one of yours entered our territory?" It wasn't like Reinar to break one of his own rules.

The woman's jaw twitched. "It seems both sides have overstepped today. That is why we will let you and your kin leave with a warning."

Drake grumbled. "You can't be serious."

She raised an authoritative hand. "Let it go, Drake. This is neither the time nor the place."

Aeden raised his eyebrows as Drake turned in a huff and walked away.

The partygoers proceeded with their festivities, no longer interested in Aeden and the rest. But the woman lingered. He cocked his eyebrow at her, trying to place where he knew her from. There was something familiar about her in the nose and the shape of her mouth... she resembled the doe. Drake's kin. A laugh bubbled up from Aeden's throat as he pieced it together. The woman in the hall. She was Reinar's niece. The one so many had come there tonight to see. He was such an idiot. He'd flirted with the enemy. Had almost kissed her.

Heat crept across his face from the embarrassment and he quickly turned to help Balis stand on steadier feet. The youngster hiccupped loudly and whined, "Aw, I didn't even get a chance to show them my new shimmy move." His hips waggled in unpredictable directions, completely offbeat to the music that had started back up.

Aeden huffed in frustration as he led his cousins far away from the party and even farther away from the Downthorns. It didn't take them long to reach the courtyard. Theirs was the only carriage present. Most had come by horseback or walked to the estate.

Balis stopped to heave with his hands on his knees. Aeden rolled his eyes and placed his hands on Balis' shoulders to steady him. To Marcos, he asked, "How much did he drink?"

As he waited for an answer, he eyed the door of the manor, checking to make sure no one was bold enough to follow them out. The coast was clear... for now.

Marcos shrugged. "I lost track of him. I was dancing with that beauty in a filly mask when ham hands started shoving me."

Warm shivers up Aeden's neck, accompanying his rage. "A nagging feeling tells me we may have Rose to thank for that." He shot a dagger filled stare in her direction.

Rather than cower, she placed both hands on her hips. "Serves you right."

Aeden abandoned Balis and stormed up to Rose. A pounding in his head was arising, and his stomach rumbled in dissatisfaction from having only one cup of stale blood. He ignored it all, focusing his remaining energy on Rose's smug face as he asked, "Are you really so quick to jealousy that you would put us all at risk? Why not just confront me in the hall?" Dropping his gaze to the bite marks on her neck, he laughed bitterly and continued before she could answer, "It's not like you aren't entertaining others as well." The thought of her with another didn't make him jealous. But it seemed she thought she was free to do as she pleased while he was not. And that irritated him more than anything.

Rose tapped her toe on the ground and gave him a self-satisfied smile. Aeden squeezed his eyes shut, resisting the urge to smash something. He pinched the bridge of his nose. "Do you have any idea what you did? You could have gotten us killed."

Now she had the good sense to look unnerved. With a frown, she said, "Aeden, you always do what you want. You wouldn't have listened to me if I had confronted you. And besides, I had no idea she was his cousin. I only wanted to get us booted from the party. How could I have known it would go so badly?"

Aeden was speechless. He threw his arms in the air and scoffed. Rose reached for him, but he backed away. The last thing he wanted to feel were her hands on him.

She implored, "She had a mask on for star's sake! I thought Drake would throw us out. I didn't think—"

"That's right. You didn't think! You never think. You just act." Aeden's shoulders rose and fell hard and fast, and his pounding heart was nearly all he could hear. As angry as he was with Rose and her impetuous actions, he was more angry with himself. He'd been so intrigued by the girl that he hadn't considered that he might be putting his family in danger.

Balis had stopped heaving, and he and Marcos were watching the fight in uncomfortable silence. Aeden took a steadying breath before he spoke. "Marcos, get Balis and Rose back to the manor. See them to their rooms safely. Rose can stay in the guestroom for the night, then you can escort her home in the morning."

Rose reached out, but stopped before touching him. "What about you?"

"I need some air. I'm going to walk."

Reluctantly, she followed Marcos and a hiccupping Balis to the carriage. Balis struggled to climb into the cab and it took Marcos crouching under his butt to shove him in with his shoulder. Normally Aeden would have laughed at the pair, but all humor had been drained out of him. He waved as Marcos climbed into the driver's seat and snapped the reins. The carriage jolted as it took off and disappeared into the forest.

Aeden's knees were weak now that the adrenaline was wearing off. Reluctantly, he strolled down the driveway with his shoulders slouching. He was in no hurry to get home, so he kept a slow pace, ambling down the path. Pushing the stray hairs that had escaped his leather strap, he started to laugh. It was a bitter sound, devoid of joy.

Wind blew through the trees, and the bittersweet, earthy scent filled his nose. It brought visions of the woman in the doe mask. He reached into the depths of his memory, trying to recall the last time he had seen her—before tonight. Her name still evaded him. But if his memory served right, the young Downthorn girl had been a spitfire of a child, always looking for trouble. Back then, she had resembled her father more than her mother. With rich brown hair tied in a ribbon. Time had matured her features, turning her into a striking woman.

He tensed as the memories flooded back. A little girl, tagging along with the boys, begging them to let her play with the wooden swords they used to practice with. Small, but fearsome. A daughter of the Winter and Autumn Courts. The doted upon darling of the Downthorn family.

Tonight, the attraction between the two of them was undeniable. And admittedly, he had always liked and admired her when they were younger. But that was before things went sour, tainted by mistakes and blood. Before their families declared that their alliance would no longer stand.

He groaned as the name came back to him. His voice was a mere whisper as he spoke it out loud. "Tessa."

Six

Tessa

Tessa leaned against the large oak desk in the study. The open window gave her a chill as the cool night air blew through the curtains. Her mother's favorite attendant, Talos, paced in front of it, unbothered by the brisk breeze. Something more pressing was clearly on his mind. Every few seconds he stopped and muttered to himself rather than to the family gathered together in the room. Even though he was a Vampyr, like the other attendants who had worked in their home before the curse—who had followed them to battle and thus received the same punishment—he was a nervous creature. And now his anxiety was spreading to her like a terrible cold.

Tessa's uncle, however, hadn't spoken a word to her when he walked into the room, accompanied by a furious Drake. As usual, her mother was quiet, staring intently into the fireplace. But at the rate she was downing her wine, Tessa knew something was wrong.

Maybe if she had gone back to the party after leaving the wolf behind in the hall, she would know what had her family and Talos so frazzled. Her face flushed, thinking about how she had nearly kissed the stranger. At first, she didn't see what harm a little flirtation could do. The mask had made it impossible for her to pinpoint who he was, and it seemed harmless enough. She'd actually been having... fun. But she had nearly let things go too far.

She reached up to touch her jaw where his hand had rested. Banter was one thing. But a kiss? That was something entirely different. To her, such a thing was an intimate act. One that opened doors to feelings. Now *that* she couldn't allow.

A bottle clinked against glass as her mother poured another drink. Tessa folded her arms across her chest and scrutinized each member of her family. She hadn't been nervous when the lady's maid found her in the kitchen—a place Tessa had assumed she'd be safe to clear her head of the wolf—insisting that her uncle wanted a word with her. But now it seemed that everyone knew something she did not.

She pushed off of the desk. "Will someone please tell me what is going on?" She glanced at each of them, but no one would meet her eye. "If this is about Lord Peitor, I'm sorry, okay? I let my worries get the better of me and—"

Her uncle finally spoke. "It's not Peitor."

Tessa walked to the velvet sofa he was sitting on and knelt by his side. "The argument you and I had, then? I didn't mean what I said. I'm just not ready yet to make a decision." Her stomach twisted in knots. She touched his sleeve gently, hoping to soften his resolve. The last thing she wanted to do was let her family down. And it wasn't like her options were limited.

Peitor, or even the man in the wolf mask, would make a decent husband. The thought came unbidden, surprising her. The stranger was a bit brash. He had proven that with his forwardness with the redhead in the ballroom. And judging by his wolfish grin in the hallway, she had no doubt that he was a rogue with the ladies. It was why she had lingered there for so long.

Before tonight, she never put much consideration into what she would look for in a partner. But those traits weren't exactly what she would call ideal. Maybe that was the key to keeping her heart safe. She'd felt a physical attraction to him, but it didn't have to go beyond that. Heat crept across the bridge of her nose at the memory of his body so close to hers and she shook her head to rid herself of the thoughts.

Drake huffed as he gulped down his drink. Tessa noted a growing bruise on his cheek and wondered who had been brave enough to leave it there. Wiping his face with the back of his sleeve, he looked down at her in disgust. "Do not play innocent and act like you don't know what this is about."

She crinkled her nose at him. "I'm not playing anything, *cousin*," she spat the word, as she often did when he was in one of his moods. When she was young, he'd easily intimidated her. But she wasn't a child anymore. She was a woman and her teeth could cut just as deep as his.

Drake snarled under his breath and took a step in her direction. The hairs on her arms stood on end as she rose to meet him face to face. He towered over her as he taunted, "The wolf and the doe." He flicked the mask that she'd pushed to the top of her head some time ago.

Her stomach did a somersault. How did he find out about that?

Her uncle pressed his fingers against his temples. "Do you deny it? That you were found alone in the enthralls of an Ashbane?"

Tessa balked. "Did you say Ashbane?" A laugh bubbled up from her throat. "What would an Ashbane even be doing here?" The solemn looks from her family made her laughter die out. This was no jest. They were serious. By the stars, she had almost kissed one of *them*.

Drake reached for the bottle her mother had already put quite a dent in and took a long swig from it before saying, "Three Ashbanes and one of their tarts, to be exact. And it doesn't matter what they were doing here. They knew they weren't welcome. And you should have known better than to put yourself in that sort of position."

Tessa looked down at the floor. Had the wolf known who she was? What a laugh he and his lot must be having at her expense. Her skin prickled with anger.

Drake sneered down at Tessa's mother. "You should have let me take care of it."

Tessa grew sick with embarrassment. Had the wolf been the one to take a swing at Drake? Normally it would have made her glad, but the fact that she'd been with him beforehand ruined any chance of finding joy in her cousin's dismay.

Flora stuck her nose in the air. "There's a time and a place for all that and this was neither." She rolled her eyes at Reinar. "So, they crashed a party. Is that really worth starting a war over?"

Reinar pursed his lips. "They know the rules. They stick to their side of the lake and we stick to ours."

Flora's laugh was like a wind chime. It was a rare sound, and Tessa couldn't help but raise her eyebrows in surprise. Her mother leaned toward Reinar. "Has it really been so long since you were young that you've forgotten what that restlessness feels like?"

Reinar huffed in response.

Drake was right about one thing, at least. The Ashbanes had overstepped their bounds. It didn't matter why they had come. What mattered was that the bastard had humiliated her. And now her family, Talos, and likely the entire ball, knew about it.

Tessa pursed her lips. "You have to know that I had no idea. I would never have put myself in that position if I had known."

Her uncle looked at her with a searching gaze. "It's not like you to put yourself in that position with anyone at all."

She suddenly felt like a silly little girl subjected to her family's disappointment. Even though she was stifled at times, and pushed back with minor rebellions, she had never caused any actual harm. Sneaking into the woods to hear the mystery musician or coming home disheveled were small victories. But when it came down to it, she knew her family's expectations of her were only meant to keep her safe.

"I know. I'm not sure what got into me." Her nerves were blazing like fire under her skin. Between the scrutinizing gaze of her uncle and the one filled with pity from her mother, she was becoming angry with herself and even more so with the wolf.

She snatched the mask from her head and let it clatter to the ground. "Will you all please excuse me? I need a moment alone."

Her uncle waved an exhausted hand at her and rested his head back against the chair. With the exception of Drake, they all seemed more defeated than angry now. There was nothing more for her to say or do here. But there was certainly something she could do to make herself feel better. It was quite a trek back to

Ashbane territory, and the party crashers couldn't have gotten far. With the way she was feeling right now, Tessa didn't intend to let the wolf crawl back into his hovel without giving him a piece of her mind first.

With her family resigned to stew in silence, she bolted from the room, letting the door close gently behind her. She took the stairs two at a time, careful not to slip on the smooth marble floors. She dodged partygoers as she crossed through the foyer. They staggered on unsteady feet with cups brimming with blood. It seems they'd had enough of suppressing their appetite for the night and had dipped into the barrels in the cellar. Her uncle wouldn't be pleased about that in the morning.

The large double doors creaked as Tessa swung them open to reveal the shadowy carriage way. Lamp posts lit her path as she loped down to the rocky road that formed a circle in front of the chateau. They flickered, trying to hold steady against the soft wind. It wasn't long before her eyes adjusted to the dark, allowing her to venture toward the tree line.

She wasn't sure what she was going to say to the wolf, but she had no doubt a few choice words would come to her when the moment arose. She picked up her pace as she jogged down the dirt path, wondering how far ahead of her they would be by now, and peered into the dense forest.

This was foolish. She had enough self awareness to know that. But the heat in her cheeks and her chest wouldn't allow her to go back in and face her family. Not yet. Not until she let the shame and irritation out.

It wasn't long before a lone figure came into view. He was wandering slowly with one hand in his pocket. In the other, he carried a wolf mask.

She shouted to him unceremoniously, "Hey you!"

He ignored her, but stopped walking, allowing her to come within a few feet away from him. She slowed to a halt, trying to collect herself before he had time to turn to her. She straightened out her hair, then quickly let her arms fall to her sides as he faced her.

Feeling more put together, she raised her chin. All the anger rushed back as she took in the tall man with an impeccable jacket trimmed in gold and the wolf mask resting in his gloved hand. Her nostrils flared as she growled, "You have a lot of nerve."

He raised his hands defensively and took a step back. "I take it you figured out who I am."

She gritted her teeth and her fangs ground against the bottom row. "I almost kissed you!" True, it likely had more to do with the fact that he had implied that she was timid, and at the time, she wanted to prove him wrong. But still...

"Keyword, *almost*." He flashed dazzling white teeth at her, fueling her anger.

"You made a fool out of me." More than that, he had toyed with her. This is what she got for even entertaining the idea of enjoying a man's company.

The dashing, dimpled smile he gave was disarming. Now that his mask was gone, she could see how truly handsome he was. His aristocratic nose had a small scar along the left side, but it did nothing to distract from his charms.

The breeze ruffled his dark auburn hair, and she wished it would blow him away from her altogether. The snide words she hoped would come to her when she faced him were nowhere to be found. Instead, she opted for glaring.

"You think I made a fool out of *you*?" His smile dropped. "I came here tonight looking for a few drinks, a bit of blood—which, *by the way*, is not meant to be served cold—"

Tessa skewed her face. "Are you serious right now? You're upset that the blood was served by the glass versus what? By the vein? You Ashbanes will never change."

His mouth fell open for a split second, before he retorted, "That's something our families seem to have in common. I see you're just as haughty and hard-headed as you were when you were a pipsqueak of a thing."

Tessa readied a retort, but stopped short. "Wait, what?"

Crossing his arms over his chest with an air of arrogance, he said, "To be honest, I didn't realize it was you until I thought about what your cousin mentioned while he was running his mouth."

Her eyes narrowed as she studied his face. There was something vaguely familiar about him, but a name eluded her. He didn't appear to be much older than she was, but then again, it was difficult to tell with their kind.

His eyes widened, and he placed a hand over his heart with mock offense. "Wow, really? You don't recognize me at all?"

She threw her hands up in exasperation. "According to you, you didn't recognize me either!"

"That's because you were wearing a mask." He flicked the air by her face.

Fighting the urge to slap his hand so hard that the glove flew off, she suggested, "Well, care to share with me the name of the man who tried to *kiss* me less than half an hour ago?"

He shook out his shoulders and straightened his jacket as he answered, "Aeden. Aeden Ashbane."

Tessa's stomach dropped. "Olgar's son?" She dug her nails into her palms to keep from taking him by the throat. Images of one of The Six striking her father down while Olgar ran for his life flashed in her mind. She would never forget the emotionless face of the man who had led them into that village. The one whose ravenous hunger put them all in danger, leading them right into the hunter's clutches. "Your father got mine killed."

Aeden narrowed his eyes. "That wasn't his fault."

Her lip curled in disgust, revealing one of her razor-sharp fangs. "You should leave. You don't belong here."

He pushed back the side of his jacket and put a hand in his pocket. The other raised in the air like a gesture of defeat. Tessa crossed her arms over her chest and tapped her foot on the ground, waiting for him to disappear farther into the forest and out of her sight forever.

But something rustled in the trees beside the path. Whatever it was froze, making no more sound as she and Aeden peered into the shadowy thicket. Tessa's voice was low as she asked, "Did your friends double back for you?"

He sidestepped closer to her and shook his head. "They're long gone by now."

Instinct made Tessa inhale sharply to identify what caused the noise. The scent of sweat and grime drifted through the air, and she wrinkled her nose. It was the smell of grueling labor. Of someone who toiled in the fields or the workhouses all day to get by. It was close... and human. The hairs on the back of her neck rose as the rest of her senses heightened. Her eyes sharpened to better spot whoever was foolish enough to venture this close to the predator's den.

Careful not to spook the human away, she leaned close to Aeden. The urge to hunt overshadowed her resentment of him and his family. "It's mortal."

Although she knew she was a monster capable of defending herself, she couldn't ignore her unease. The veil around the Crimson Forest was meant to dissuade humans from stepping foot into

BOUND BY BLOOD AND SORROW

it. Making it appear far more menacing and unwelcoming than it was. What sort of mortal would be brave enough to enter?

Aeden knelt to the ground, pretending to adjust the laces on his boots. Rather than tighten them, he placed his hand on the hard dirt-packed path. With a curt nod, he told her what she needed to know. The lurker was large enough to give off vibrations when he or she moved.

Insatiable hunger set her on edge, overpowering her nerves. The human might be healthy and sizable enough to handle blood-lettings. Enough to feed her family for a few weeks if handled delicately. With as worried as her uncle and mother had been during the feast about their dwindling blood supply, this might also make up for the fact that Tessa had embarrassed them.

Overwhelmed by the sneaking suspicion that they were being watched by the intruder, Tessa turned her back on the tree line and grabbed Aeden's hand as he stood. If they could keep the prey from realizing they'd noticed its presence, then she and Aeden would have a better chance of catching it off guard.

Aeden gave her a scrutinizing look. "What are you—"

"Shh." She pressed herself against him with the familiarity of lovers. Then she whispered, "Can you sense how many of them there are?"

The red in Aeden's eyes darkened and a sly smile spread across his face. "You want to hunt. With me."

"Don't let it go to your head." She frowned. It had been a long time since she'd had to participate in a hunt. Drake and his friends were typically in charge of monitoring the forest border for signs of weary travelers. But they were too far from the chateau to call for them now. That left her with Aeden. Wary of hunting with an Ashbane, who was rumored to do things a little more brutally, she added, "And we do things *my* way."

He whispered back in annoyance, "What is that supposed to mean?"

"It means I don't trust you to do this gently."

He rolled his eyes. "I'm not the monster you think I am."

She simply stared at him until he complied. And was relieved when he said, "As you wish." Then, in answer to her earlier question, he added, "There are two that I can sense for sure. One for your family and one for mine?"

"Deal." She could no longer hear rustling in the forest, which meant the mortals hadn't yet fled. Perhaps they were lost and trying to discern whether this was a safe place to ask for help. There was a twinge of guilt in her stomach, but she ignored it. If what her mother and uncle had said was true, then they needed this. And although she felt sorry for the mortal who would end up in the Ashbane's clutches, she had to think first of her family and their survival.

Hoping Aeden would control his impulses, she offered, "I will go first. They'll be less frightened if a woman approaches them. If I can get close enough, then I can compel one of them while you get the jump on the other."

When the Unseelie King cursed her people, he hadn't taken into account what consequences there would be for using such powerful blood magic. Though it had hindered their Fae power, replacing it with something sinister, marking them as outcasts amongst their own people, it had also made them stronger, giving them abilities beyond imagining. Although Vampyrism had ruined their lives as they knew it, it had also granted them sharper senses, the gift of mind control through compulsion, and incredible physical strength and speed.

Between her and Aeden, taking two mortals in alive would be simple. As long as he stuck to the plan, that is. He nodded in agreement, then looked pointedly down at their hands, which were still intertwined. With a smirk, he said, "You'll have to let me go first."

She snatched her hands away as if she'd touched fire. Embarrassment drove her a few steps away from him. She hadn't realized she was still holding onto him. Ignoring the stupid grin he was giving her, she turned and casually strolled toward the trees.

Leaves crunched under her slippered feet as she neared the brush, and her ears perked as a tiny twig snapped. The mortals likely didn't realize they were making so much noise. If they had stumbled upon a human household, then they would have been quite unnoticeable.

Innocently, she called out, "Hello?"

Someone sucked in a breath and she could hear the rush of blood as their pulse quickened. Beside them, a heartbeat pounded. Aeden was right, there were two. Neither answered her call, though.

She tried again, stepping over a log and into the wooded area. "Is someone out there?" From here, she could make out a tall, slender frame. And beside it, a stout, burly one. A few feet to the side, Aeden stalked through the trees. He was as stealthy as an actual wolf, light and quick on his feet. The mortals would never notice his presence. The only thing alerting her to him was his distinct scent of sandalwood and new leather.

She wasn't close enough yet to use compulsion, so she gently cooed, "It's alright. My name is Tessa. If you need help, then I'm happy to assist."

One of the mortals—a man with a gruff voice—responded this time. "It is not us who need help."

Puzzled by the vague threatening tone, she stopped in her tracks. Suddenly, something slammed into her from behind. There was a hard crack, and she crumpled to the ground in a daze. A new heartbeat thudded in the clearing. A third attacker. She and Aeden were outnumbered.

Seven

Tessa

T essa's head throbbed. Her attacker was strong. Too strong. Dark spots clouded her vision, and it felt like her limbs were filled with heavy stones. She needed to move. To get up and fight. Adrenaline and instinct sharpened her awareness of her surroundings. Decaying leaves crunched loudly as she stirred and her ears rang as she tried to regain her bearings. Gingerly, she reached for the back of her head to find blood in her hair.

Her gums throbbed where her fangs rested, and the urgency to fight brought heat to her chest. A third man stood over her with a wooden stake sharpened at the end. She hadn't seen a weapon like that since The Six descended on her family in the mortal village. Memories of the ambush on that fateful day flooded her. It fueled her with the fear she needed in order to duck out of his aim. The stake dug into the ground where her chest had been only seconds ago.

Heavy hands clamped onto her ankle, dragging her to the assailant. She burrowed her fingers into the ground and kicked out as hard as she could. The man cursed, holding tighter. His strength should have been no match for hers, but still, he continued to pull her toward his friend.

Where was Aeden? Panic twisted in her gut, not just for herself, but for him as well.

The gruff man who had answered her call sneered at her. He took a step forward, stake in hand, but grunted as something snatched him from her view. Fatal gurgles echoed in their vicinity and the strong, sharp scent of spilled blood filled Tessa's nose. *Aeden.* Who else could it have been? Knowing he was there in the shadows like a dark guardian angel renewed her courage. The entire area smelled like human blood now. Her stomach growled as she turned her attention back to the man holding onto her. The one that just tried to kill her.

The confidence in which he'd faced her with only a moment ago dissipated as she curled her top lip, flashing her razor-sharp canines. He stumbled back a step and a third companion yelled out to him, but it was too late. Tessa lunged for the stake wielder's throat, tackling him to the ground.

Instinct reared its head as she abandoned any intentions she had of bringing food back for her family. Was this how her father had felt when the hunters came for him? This time would be different, though. This time, the Ashbane involved wasn't fleeing for his life. She wasn't on her own.

Images of her father falling to a hunter gave way to rage. It blinded her, turning her into something feral. Teeth met flesh as she tore into the man's throat. Her fangs did their job, cutting through the skin with ease. It was like taking a silver letter opener to paper. The blood was steaming hot. It filled her mouth and flowed down her throat. A satisfied growl escaped her as her belly filled with what it craved most.

Beside her, Aeden took on the last two men. How long could he hold them off for? He dodged their strikes with grace and ease, but Tessa couldn't ignore the gnawing pit in her stomach. Killing these humans should have been quick and simple. But they fought with an agility she hadn't seen since The Six. And they were armed for a fight. This was no chance encounter. They had come to the Crimson Forest with purpose.

The woods quieted. No longer filled with the sound of the other two men's heartbeats. Only the ragged breathing of Aeden and the smooth hum he released as he claimed his victory. Tessa ripped her teeth from the man who had gone still and stiff in her arms. Her vision sharpened, giving light to the forest as if someone was shining a giant lantern on it. Aeden approached her with glistening eyes. She'd never thought the red that replaced their irises was a beautiful thing. Rather, it was a reminder of the monsters they'd become. But now she could see the different flecks of gold and orange, like an ember in a fire. It was dazzling.

Aeden looked her over carefully. "Are you alright?"

"I feel..." She drifted off. There were no words to describe it.

"It's the blood. Feeding from the vein is what we're meant to do, Tessa. It makes us whole."

She wanted to deny it, but couldn't. Not when she felt as if she were floating on air.

He took her face between his hands, grazing his thumbs along her cheekbones. "Are you sure you're okay?"

Every nerve where he touched her buzzed, and she leaned into it, craving more. The relief at having him standing before her unharmed surprised her. She swayed lightly, feeling dizzy, like she'd had too much wine. "I–"

Aeden's voice cut through her ecstasy as he shouted, "Tessa! Behind you!"

He shoved her to the side and struck the unexpected assailant with ferocious force. With fresh blood fueling her, she recovered from the surprise and planted her feet firmly on the ground. Every muscle and nerve in her body vibrated with a vitality she'd never experienced. It was as if the world was alive with a million tiny dancing stars.

She should have heard him coming, known there was another beating heart out there with them. But he'd been as silent as a wraith. It didn't make any sense. As the attacker struggled to right himself, she honed in on his movements, sensing each step he took without having to look at him. With newfound vigor, she ducked beneath his arm as he swung low. He stumbled forward, but righted himself quickly.

Aeden made a grab for the man, but he slipped through his fingers. Her attacker advanced on her, attempting to get close enough to lash out with his expertly carved weapon. His speed rivaled her own as he jabbed it at her. But his aim was off. The stake grazed her arm and wood splintered against her skin. It stung more than she would have thought and she hissed, stumbling against a branch and tumbling onto the ground.

Instinctively, she placed her arms in front of her to protect her chest, but just as the man reared back for another strike, Aeden catapulted into him.. He grappled with the only man left standing, each grunting as they attempted to kill one another.

The man pushed his weapon closer to Aeden's heart, and Tessa's stomach dropped. The only thing stopping it was Aeden's strong grip holding it back. Sweat beaded on his brow and he bared his teeth. Fear for him gave her a rush of adrenaline. Without hesitation, Tessa aimed low, thrusting her weight into the man's legs. There was a snap as one of his bones broke.

With him on his knees, close enough to her and trapped under her gaze, Tessa compelled him, "Drop it."

She'd practiced compulsion many times before. And had seen her family perform it on each mortal before being released from their custody. That's how she knew the pupils in her eyes were dilating now, replacing most of the menacing red with large black pools. The man's arm buckled, and he unclenched his hand, dropping the weapon to the ground with a light thud.

She inched closer to him. "Tell me who you are and why you are here."

His face softened and his eyes were like blank slates, devoid of emotion. With a stone-like voice, he said, "Your kind killed my brother. He was coming to see me. Should have arrived yesterday, but he never made it."

The body left in the forest. The one left there by the Ashbane's carelessness. Bile rose in her throat. Their heedlessness had drawn trouble to her family's door.

Aeden scrambled back and kicked the stake away from the man's reach.

He joined her at her side and remained silent, but she could sense he was holding his breath as he, too, realized why the men had attacked.

She pushed further. "How many of you are there?"

Anger flickered in his eyes as if he was fighting the compulsion. Still, he answered through clenched teeth as he replied, "Four."

Three were dead already. That left only him.

She continued to interrogate him. "How did you find us? And how is it that you can fight as you do?"

The man squeezed his eyes shut, making it clear he *was* fighting her compulsion. She'd never had trouble with it before. It was the ability she used most often. Relying on it with any mortals that were brought into her home as feeders. Once their allotted time ran out, her people would use their compulsion to make the mortals forget they were ever there in the first place. Sending them on their way with memories of getting lost on their travels. There had never been a human who could resist. Not even The Six had been immune to it.

Again, she tried, "Answer me."

The Adam's apple in the man's throat bobbed, and he grimaced, doing as she bid. "The disappearances. On the road. My brother took this route. We..." His voice was strained as he said, "made a deal. A witch."

Aeden nudged her in the arm. "He's marked."

She followed his gaze to the man's neck. Peeking just above his collar was a red brand. The twisted symbol was one she didn't recognize. Admittedly, because of their location in the mortal realm, she didn't have much experience with the solitary Fae like witches. But she did know they were rumored to find weak spots in the veil between Elfhame and the mortal realm. They would peddle their wares on the outskirts of mortal villages, offering answers to human's problems. Usually at a deep cost that they didn't quite understand. A man might offer his first born in exchange for riches, thinking he would never have children, only to realize the witch also granted his wife fertility.

Tessa gasped. Or a grieving brother might trade anything for the ability to slay the monsters who killed his kin. What price would this man be expected to pay?

More questions nagged at her as she stared into his defiant eyes. It was strange for mortals to stray so far from the roads, and she'd been so distracted by the ambush that she hadn't considered that these men might actually be hunters. Nor had it crossed her mind that they might have abilities to rival her own.

This was the reason they had their rules. So the humans would never again come looking for them with stakes in hand. She side-eyed Aeden. It seemed his people had forgotten the danger a mortal posed.

The hunters who had hurt her family so long ago hadn't been seen in decades. The Six were long gone by now. Dead or too old to wield a stake or sword as they once had. At least, that was the hope she and her family held on to. They'd been careful not to draw attention from humans who might once again band together against them. This was the price they paid for being reckless. Only it wasn't just Aeden's people who would suffer for it. It was hers as well.

Aeden surprised her by asking, "What do you want to do?"

Tessa clenched and unclenched her fists. They could keep this man to feed on him, but with his resistance to compulsion, it would put them all in danger. If they killed him, more of his friends or kin might come looking for him. But if they let him go, then he would definitely lead them right up to her front door. There was no safe choice here.

Decisively, she said, "Kill him. Either way, we run the risk of someone coming for him. But at least this way, there will be one less to face."

In one swift movement, Aeden grabbed hold of the man's head and twisted. There was a sickening snap and then the hunter hit the ground. For a moment, she wondered if they should take him back to the manor. Drain what blood was left. But as she eyed the witch's mark on him, she thought better of it. Best to rid of him altogether. Who knew if the mark would draw more of them to their door?

What a waste. Tessa turned to Aeden. "This is our worst nightmare. What if others know about us?"

"We'll cross that bridge when we get there."

Tessa was immediately annoyed by his flippant response. "It's just like an Ashbane to look at a threat like this with such disregard. To not think ahead..." She trailed off as he flinched at her words. As mad as she was, he had saved her tonight. Had fought beside her without hesitation, and for that, she owed him.

With a sigh, she said, "You need to go. I'm not sure how my cousin and my uncle will react if they find you here."

Aeden's shoulders visibly tightened with tension. But he didn't argue. Instead, he dipped his head to her and turned to leave. She watched him go, slipping into the shadows as if he were a part of them. Then, with a deep breath, she looked around at the carnage.

Something warm and thick dripped from her mouth and she wiped at her face with the back of her hand to find it was covered with blood. Realization of the rule she had broken caught up with her. It didn't matter what the circumstances were. If they thought she had fed out of hunger and not just survival, her uncle might see no other choice but to set an example with her. She scrubbed at the blood furiously with her sleeve. What would her family think if they found her like this?

Her stomach was full and content from the feeding. But her mind was in turmoil. She had never fed from the vein before and never imagined it would feel so good. Guilt nestled heavily in her stomach, weighing her down and making her feel as if she was being dragged underwater.

Coupled with Aeden's absence, she felt like she was losing her mind. Would her uncle punish them both for this? Would he blame Aeden for the attack? If so, where did that leave her? Defending him didn't feel right. But neither did condemning him.

The absence of Aeden's body near hers sent cold shivers down her back. With him gone, she felt unbelievably alone. But that was how she liked it, wasn't it? Taking a deep breath, she trudged through the forest and back to the confines of her family home. It was time to face the consequences of the night.

Eight

Tessa

Tessa sat at the wide, white vanity in her room with a pounding headache. Muted sunlight drifted in through the lace trimmed curtains, casting a gentle glow on the elegant walls. Their soft hue of sage green clashed with her dark mood.

She reached down for her hairbrush, trying to untangle the knots from a restless night's sleep. By now, the intense sensations of drinking blood from the source had worn off, leaving her with an empty feeling settled deep in her stomach. Coupled with gnawing guilt, she struggled to work up the courage to leave the room.

Abandoning her usual morning routine, she didn't bother powdering her face or adding any blush to her pale cheeks. It seemed like a lot of work when all she'd be doing was having breakfast with her family. She stifled a groan and stared at herself in the mirror. Intricate carvings of birds taking flight framed it, and suddenly she wished she was one of them.

Unfortunately, she had no such luck. Knowing her mother would send someone for her if she didn't join them soon, she tied the blue velvet bow on the top of her gown. The bright yellow dress did nothing to help her complexion. It was a well-meaning gift from her uncle—who knew little about women's fashion—and she hoped that wearing it to breakfast would soften him toward her.

He'd been the epitome of understanding when she'd told them about the attack. More concerned for her wellbeing than the mangled bodies he would have to take care of, Reinar had patted her on the shoulder and instructed her to go home and clean herself up. It seemed punishment for the rule she broke had been the last thing on his mind. Would it be the same now that he'd had a night to sleep on it?

There was a light rap on the door and Talos called out meekly, "Tessa, your family is waiting in the parlor."

She shut her eyes tight, silently willing Talos and the day to go away. His feet shuffled in the hallway and she imagined him reaching his hand up to knock again, only to lower it and repeat the jittery process. He'd been this way since she could remember.

His father had been Tessa's father's footman, and when he passed, he'd handed the position over to Talos. By now, he was practically a member of the family. All the household staff were. They had followed the Downthorns into battle and beyond. Had been turned into Vampyrs, just like her family had. That created a bond that could not be broken.

She sighed, "Talos, just come in here, won't you?"

She turned toward the door, still in her seat. Talos peeked in with his head before opening the door fully to step inside. It looked as if he'd been up for hours with his disheveled hair and tired eyes. But his jacket was pressed and pristine as if it was fresh from the laundry.

"Tell me," Tessa implored, "how is my family this morning?"

"They're uh... hungry."

Tessa grumbled and rose to meet him in the doorway. "Very helpful," she teased. Then, grabbing his hand, she pulled him with her down the hall.

The chateau had fallen back into its usual steady rhythm. Attendants moved around at a perfected pace. Their day started much earlier than Tessa's, and she noted the subtle color in their cheeks. Proof their bellies were filled with enough blood to perform their daily duties. Normally her stomach would have growled at the thought of blood first thing in the morning, but last night's feeding had done more than enough to sate her.

Guilt twisted like a knife in her chest. Here she was feeling good—stronger and more alert—while everyone else was getting by on the bare minimum. She shook her head. It did no good to think like that. There was a reason for her uncle's rules. She knew that.

Two lady's maids stood at the doorway of the parlor room. Their chin cropped hair was nearly identical with a silvery blue tint.

Something more interesting than morning tea must have been on their minds, because they didn't notice when Tessa and Talos approached. Their efforts to gossip in a whisper were fruitless. Their excitement was ill contained as their voices carried to Tessa's ears.

One leaned close to the other as she exclaimed, "She fed on a man. A man! From the vein."

The other swatted at her. "Who cares about that? Did you *see* the Ashbane man? I heard they were in the woods together when those humans attacked."

"I don't care what family he comes from. I'd let him do terrible things to me."

The girls fell into one another with scandalized laughter.

Talos gasped, placing his hand over his heart. "Ladies!"

The women practically toppled over each other when they spotted Tessa.

They apologized in unison, turning a shade of red that rivaled that of their eyes. Tessa pressed her lips together to keep from laughing. Being gossiped about wasn't how she wanted to spend the day, but she didn't blame them for their reaction to the previous night's events. It was actually the most interesting thing to happen in their half of the forest since... well, she couldn't really remember when.

Talos, however, was not so forgiving. He scolded, "Don't you two have bedrooms to attend to?"

They dipped in a curtsey and began to scuttle by Tessa. To her surprise, one of them stopped beside her and whispered excitedly, "Do you think he'll offer himself up as a suitor?"

Tessa's mouth gaped open. These women really had to be exceedingly bored to have imagined something like that. Let alone speak it out loud. Rather than respond to the ludicrous suggestion, she called out, "Talos?"

His wide, alert eyes darted to the girls, and he waved his hands at them erratically, shouting, "Shoo! Shoo!"

The girls scurried down the hall and out of sight, allowing Tessa the room to breathe. She didn't know Aeden well enough to understand his intentions, but she was *positive* he hadn't crashed her ball so he could throw his hat in the ring. He was thoughtless. A rake. Definitely not a man looking for a wife. In enemy territory, no less.

Talos poked her in the arm. "Should we go in?" His eyebrows scrunched together as he added, "You look a bit flushed."

She tossed her hair behind her shoulder, hoping to swing away any lingering thoughts of the pompous wolf with it. Then, with any dignity she could still muster, assured, "I'm fine. Let's go."

The parlor curtains were drawn, giving way to soft rays of sunshine. Even though it was a sunnier day than usual by the Crimson Forest's standards, there were shadows cast around the corners of the room.

The atmosphere of the room was darkened, too, by Reinar's mood. He sulked in his seat across from her mother. Flora quietly nursed the mug in one of her hands and held onto her head with the other. It seemed she couldn't handle a night of excessive drinking as well as she used to.

Drake stumbled in behind Tessa, shoving past her without a word. He grabbed an apple from the table and tore into it. She noted a dark stain on the front of his shirt. The bold scent of fresh blood lingered in the air where he had rushed by her. Staring at the droplets on his shirt, she opened her mouth to let him know, but thought better of it. Intently, he stared out the window by his father's side. He was quieter than usual, which gave Tessa an uneasy feeling in the deep pit of her stomach.

Since the death of Drake's mother, Celine, he had become more and more difficult to talk to. Though he had always been prone to outbursts and foul moods, it seemed that the Ashbanes had worsened his disposition.

Her gaze drifted to her uncle. His hand trembled ever so slightly as he raised jam covered bread to his mouth. Was it nerves or something else? Tessa approached the table. It was set with piles of food grown on their land. Freshly polished plates shimmered in the light from the window. It was impressive what the household staff could accomplish with some effort. The dishes had to be a few decades old. When they'd first come to the forest, they had taken as much as they could from the villages and trading posts in order to rebuild a home for themselves.

Once things quieted down, Reinar allowed excursions outside of the forest for only a select trusted few. He sent women mostly. Ones who appeared less threatening than their male counterparts and who could easily hide their fangs from the general public. But they all did their best to stock up and make these comforts last as long as they could. Caring for them with a delicate touch and putting as much time between these trips as possible in an effort to keep them safe.

Talos pulled a seat out for Tessa to sit. She accepted with a grateful smile in his direction. Like a mouse running back to its sanctuary, he hurried into the decker's room that connected the parlor to the hallway leading to the kitchen.

No one bothered to greet her, so she broke the silence herself. "Good morning."

Her mother's eyes flitted to her and the corner of her mouth perked up in a halfhearted smile. "Morning, darling." She stared back into her cup and swirled it around absentmindedly.

Tessa clucked at her teeth, trying to think of something else to say. When they returned to the chateau the night before, Reinar had gotten every detail out of her about the attack. Once she'd gone over the series of events several times, he'd gone straight to his large solid oak desk and set to work. Wielding his quill as if it were a warrior's sword, he'd written news of the night to every family on the Downthorn side of the lake, warning them to stay vigilant.

Now he appeared drained. Like he hadn't slept a wink. Tessa reached for the mug that was set out for her. The blood inside scarcely hit the halfway point. Their morning feedings seemed to be smaller and smaller every time she sat down for breakfast. It would soon be time to release the current feeders. But if they didn't find someone to replace them, then they faced the dangers of bloodlust setting in. She couldn't remember a time when they'd had to ration so heavily.

Guilt nagged at her for not bringing any of the mortal men back alive. Even if they were able to fight the compulsion, maybe her family would have found a way to lock them up somehow. At least until new feeders were located... Tessa's stomach twisted into knots. How could she even be thinking like that? Their feeders lived in comfort during their time at the chateau. They were treated with respect, kept calm with compulsion, and never truly harmed.

She took a sip and cringed. The blood was more bitter than usual and made her cheeks pucker. It was nothing compared to what she'd tasted the night before.

Her mother's brow creased with concern. "Is something wrong?"

The studious glances she was getting from everyone made her jittery. It was like they were all waiting for her to turn into some raging beast. When she had come back from the forest covered in mortal blood, they hadn't bitten their tongues. Drake, in particular, subjected her to an interrogation about how she was feeling. Did she crave more of it? Were her abilities sharpened? And other questions to that nature.

Hoping to ease their worry now, she replied, "Not at all."

Then, setting the mug back down, she reached for a sliver of warm bread with a pad of butter melted on top. There was a small jar of fig preserves within reach, so she scooped it onto the bread eagerly. When she bit into it, she was sorely disappointed, like always. Figs were a favorite of hers as a child, but its flavor didn't taste as vibrant as she remembered.

Still, she ate. The silence seemed to swell in the room, leaving barely enough air to breathe. When Reinar finally spoke, she was relieved. That is, until she realized the topic he had chosen.

"The Ashbanes are to blame for this, you know." He threw his fork down, and it tinged against one of the serving plates, leaving a little dent in it. He lowered his voice, but Tessa could still sense the contempt in it as he said, "Something must be done about them."

In a way, she agreed. Those mortal men never would have come into the forest if it had not been for their kin; killed at the hands of the Ashbanes. She said a silent prayer to the stars that others like them wouldn't come.

Drake's snarl broke through her prayer. "Say the word and I'll take care of the lot of them."

Tessa shivered. Even though his words were foreboding, his eyes sparked with excitement. Just by hearing him, one might think he valiantly wanted to protect his family, but she had a sneaking suspicion that he simply wanted to do it for fun.

Tension was heavy as her uncle weighed his options. He slinked further down into his seat and pressed at his temples as he spoke, "Our numbers may be greater than Count Olgar's, but do not underestimate him, son. We must tread delicately. There is no room for error here."

Drake argued, "Ceasing to do anything will make us look weak." At his father's whip-like stare, Drake shrunk a bit. He continued, "You made the terms clear when we came to the forest beaten and desperate. Still covered in the blood of those who were lost to us."

Tessa shifted at the implication. Drake knew what her father's brutal death had done to Reinar. They all did. He, like her mother, had barely survived the loss and carried it heavily on his shoulders to that very day.

Drake continued, taking no care to spare anyone's feelings. "Each and every family here has the responsibility to keep us safe. To snatch humans only when given the opportunity and to send the feeders back to their lives once they have served their purpose."

Reinar's voice thundered so loudly, Tessa swore the room itself quaked. "I made the bloody rules! Do not think to lecture me, *boy*."

Drake shut his mouth promptly and she couldn't help but feel warm satisfaction. It might have been a precarious situation they were in, but she didn't like the idea of anyone being harmed over it. Her uncle often threatened exile, but he had only ever followed through with it once.

No one liked to talk about it. But she'd heard enough gossip in the kitchens to know the key details. Before the families and those loyal to them split from one another, there had been an incident. The man had captured a caravan of women. It was in the early days of their curse, and the bloodlust was nearly impossible to control. He'd slaughtered them. Just outside of the forest, far too close to the border.

Anyone who might have happened upon the carnage would have known immediately that it was not an animal attack. The bodies had been drained of every drop of blood. Left gray and rotting for anyone to find.

Reinar and Olgar cleaned the mess up together. The loss of Tessa's father had been the first fray to the thread of their alliance. But that day—as they covered up the evidence that had been left so close to their home—was the day it had been severed. Olgar Ashbane insisted that the man be forgiven. Believing that the only way to survive was to accept what they'd become.

Reinar disagreed. If the hunters had caught wind of what happened, they would come for them all. For that the man needed to face consequences. Rules needed to be established so that they could live undetected. Furthermore, so they could maintain any dignity they still had if they hoped to ever return home one day.

Tessa's mind snapped out of the past and she watched Reinar carefully, wondering how far he was willing to go to keep their people a secret. Personally, she was grateful none of it fell on her shoulders. She couldn't imagine how much pressure came with protecting Vampyrs who didn't even want to protect themselves. Surely the Ashbanes and their loyalists knew what was at stake.

She bit her lip, wondering if Aeden returned home to tell his family about the wreckage their carelessness had caused the night before. Would his father, Olgar, listen? Even if he was aware how close his son had come to death?

Her mother's dainty voice rocked her from her thoughts. Flora's brittle hair hardly shifted as she rose from her chair. "The answer, dear brother, is right in front of us." She gestured slowly to Tessa.

"W-what?" Tessa stood and took a defensive step back, genuinely confused about why her mother was looking at her with large, hopeful eyes.

Flora tilted her head to the side slightly. "Tessa's match was meant to strengthen our connections to our noblemen. But perhaps we were focusing on the wrong men? What if we could offer a match that bound the two families together as we once were? As we were always meant to be? The Ashbane boy may very well be able to persuade them to stay in line. How better to strengthen our position than to have Olgar's heir in our own household?"

A hiccupped gasp came from the other side of the decker's door. Tessa wondered how many of the household staff had their ears pressed firmly against the oak, listening in as her world was flipped upside down.

Flora twisted the wedding band on her ring finger. "Our families came together against a common threat once before. We could do it again. You know I am right in this, brother."

Reinar shook his head vehemently. "It's out of the question. Our allies would never agree to this."

Flora raised her chin, reminding Tessa of the proud, confident woman she had once been. She once again looked like a High Fae from the Winter Court rather than the broken bloodthirsty creature she had been cast down to as she said, "They will if they understand that it is for the greater good. If you tell them it was your idea, then they will fall in line."

Reinar raised a skeptical eyebrow. "And the Ashbanes? Why would they agree?"

Flora shrugged. "You, dear brother, will make it clear that it is in their best interest. That it is a far better alternative to the exile of whichever one of them drew those mortal men to our door last night." Her mouth tugged into a deep frown. "You are not the warrior you once were. I do not mean this as an insult. It is simply the truth. We may have more Vampyrs on our side, but they grow hungrier with each passing day. Even if those men had not attacked Tessa and the young Lord, a dispute with the Ashbanes might be catastrophic for both sides of the Crimson Lake."

For a moment, Reinar looked thoughtful. Like he might actually be considering such an outlandish thing. A laugh bubbled up from Tessa's throat. But it died the moment her uncle's eyes met hers. He valued her mother's opinion above all others. Of course, he would heed her advice now.

Drake's words struck like a bolt of lightning. "You can't possibly be considering this, father!"

Reinar warned him in return, "I am the head of this family and I will decide what I will and will not do."

His son pushed back as he exclaimed, "You would have history repeat itself? The communion of our families ruined us all. An Ashbane and a Downthorn can never be together. Or have you already forgotten the misfortune such a union brought us?"

"I have forgotten nothing. Ayana Downthorn and Byron Ashbane were foolish. Young lovers willing to risk *everything* to be together, even the King's wrath." Reinar sighed as he turned to her. His skin sagged around his mouth, evidence of the hardships he had faced in his countless years of life. He shook his head regretfully. "I am old, hungry, and tired. I do not know what else to do."

"No," Tessa whispered as she shook her head.

Her uncle rose from his seat and urged, "Let us invite him here. The two of you will court until the next full moon. If and only *if* I see in that time that this might actually work, then you will marry him." He took hold of her hands and she could feel the strength slipping away from them as he added, "For the good of our family. You will do this for us, won't you?"

It was as if her stomach had become a viper's den. The twisting pain accompanying the horror of what she was being asked to do nearly knocked the breath from her. She fought the urge to pull away from her uncle and flee.

She thought of her father. Of the others who had been struck down by the hunters. And she recalled the men in the forest who fought with more strength than she could have expected from mortals. If she could help keep the people she loved safe, then she had to do it. Right? Even if it meant marrying Aeden Ashbane.

Forcing a small, agreeable smile, she nodded. There was no relief on her uncle's face as he released his hold on her and called for his papers and quill. Tessa looked down at the floor, avoiding her mother's gaze. She sucked in a long, steadying breath.

There was only one thought, giving her the strength to remain still and in place. Despite the spark she had felt in the hallway and then again in the forest, Aeden was not the right match for her. Not only was he a rake, but he was the son of the man who had left her father at the mercy of The Six. She inhaled sharply through her nose, accepting her fate. At least her heart would be safe. She would never have to know heartache like her mother. Because there was absolutely no way she would *ever* love an Ashbane.

Nine

Aeden

Aeden was grateful for the healing powers of the curse as he walked out to the balcony that overlooked the common room. After the brawl the night before, he should have appeared beaten and bruised. The mortal men's strength both surprised and unnerved him. More shocking was how grateful he was that Tessa had been there. If it had been only him, then he wasn't sure he would have fared so well.

His family waited below in the spacious sitting room. They were already dressed for the day in their usual dark, moody hues—silks and fabrics stolen from the mortal ports. He resisted the urge to roll his eyes. His father, Olgar, was quick to refuse Aeden and Marcos' requests to venture into the human's territory, yet he was always willing to send out a few of his loyalists. Typically, second sons who were considered slightly more expendable. Aeden would have been happy to go in their stead.

As he descended the stairs, the tangy aroma of fresh blood drifted up to him. He quickened his pace, eager for his fill. For a brief moment, Tessa's face coated in steaming blood crossed his mind. The mortal had easily gotten a hold of her. Too easily. Aeden suspected he knew why. Clearly, the Downthorns had strict rules about drinking from the vein. It was no wonder Tessa had struggled against the unnatural strength of the mortals. It also explained why she had seemed like an entirely new woman when she finally fed the way the curse intended.

It could also explain why her mother had looked so frail in that ballroom. Even Reinar was a shadow of his former self. For all Count Reinar's precautions to keep them safe, it seemed he was ignoring the one thing his people needed most... To be ready for a fight. Blood from the cup wouldn't give them the strength they needed if hunters came for them.

Marcos was waiting for him at the bottom of the stairs. His face was flushed, and he held the hand of a pretty mortal girl. Her honey blonde curls bounced as she dipped into a small curtsey. The long sleeve on her flowery blue dress was pushed up, revealing two bite marks on her wrist.

Aeden didn't recognize her. Which meant his father had sent scouts out to bring in fresh feeders. Poor sods who were down on their luck and easily lured in. Once they were within the Vampyr's grasp, there was no fighting the compulsion. Until the men last night, that is.

He glared across the room at his father. Bringing new mortals into the forest was always a risk. One worth taking to sustain themselves. But the run in with the witch-blessed mortals gave him pause.

Marcos smiled broadly. "Heard you had a rough walk home, cousin."

Aeden tipped his head back. Apparently, it hadn't taken long for his father to spread the news of the attack. With a grumble, he replied, "I managed."

"You mean you and *Tessa* managed." Marcos wiggled his eyebrows up and down suggestively, then he added, "Who knew the Downthorn darling had such spunk?"

I did. The thought was so fleeting that Aeden didn't dwell on it. Instead, he shrugged and crossed the room to where his feeder was waiting. Her soft yellow dress clashed with the mahogany bookcase behind her. Her long, cascading brown hair reminded him of Tessa's silky strands, and suddenly the idea of sinking his fangs into her arm made him queasy.

Though her eyes were as wide as a deer, she didn't flinch when he came closer. It seemed someone had already compelled her to stay still and do as she was told. Aeden glanced around at his ravenous family, too consumed by blood to notice him talking to the mortal girl. "What's your name?"

"Annie," she squeaked.

"Well, Annie, my name is Aeden." He locked eyes with her, summoning the intense gaze that would allow him to reach into her mind. Then he compelled, "You have nothing to fear from me. It feels like scarcely more than a bee sting. I promise."

Her face softened instantly, eyes glazing over as his words took their place within her mind.

Olgar humphed from a deep forest green armchair. "Get on with it, son. We have business to discuss."

Aeden grabbed Annie with a gentle touch and led her to the couch where his mother and an incredibly hungover Balis were sitting. Their feeders must have been dismissed. Sent back to their rooms on the top floor of the manor. Although Olgar confined them to their quarters, Aeden, Marcos and Balis made sure there were pleasantries stashed in the nooks and crannies of the old attic for them. Cards, books, dice. Things to entertain them throughout the day. Since Aeden was little, he had always stocked it full of entertainment. Anything to help the feeders pass their time.

Annie stared at him with blank eyes and a passive expression on her heart-shaped face. The footmen made sure to compel the feeders first thing in the morning, never allowing a chance for it to wear off. But they didn't always take away the fear. To some of the Vampyrs on the Ashbane side of the Crimson Lake, fear was like a drug. Intoxicating and delightful. To Aeden it was sickly sweet and turned his stomach. Some preferred it, but he couldn't stand it.

Not only that, but using compulsion was the only thing keeping these mortals from going mad with fear. Some, like the ones his father and uncle fed on, did in fact lose their minds. When one was driven past their breaking point, Aeden had desperately tried to compel them back to normal. But to no avail. All he got in return was a bloody lip and a swollen eye from the heavy hand of his father.

Olgar tore his fangs from his feeder's arm and cleared his throat expectantly.

"What business?" Aeden asked as he pulled Annie's sleeve back and lifted her wrist to his mouth. He salivated as his fangs pressed against her flesh, puncturing her vein with expertise. She winced slightly, but stilled as the blood began to flow from her and into his mouth. His stomach warmed as the blood filled it.

Olgar grabbed his feeder again—a man who appeared to be no more than in his twenties—and pulled him roughly into him, biting into his neck. The man didn't make a sound, but his eyes bulged in a desperate, pleading sort of way as Aeden's father took one last deep drink. When he was done, he shoved the man away and smoothed down his maroon morning jacket.

Haughtily, Olgar said, "A letter came by way of a Downthorn courier this morning."

There went Aeden's appetite. He patted Annie's arm, signaling that he was finished with her for now. Obediently, she rose and went to join the others upstairs. Trying to maintain his cool demeanor, he asked, "And what is the Count threatening us with this time?"

Balis gagged, drawing everyone's attention to him. He covered his mouth, looking green in the face. "Apologies." He gagged again. "I just... excuse me!" He ran from the room and Aeden shook his head. Poor lad. Marcos really should have cut him off earlier the night before.

Olgar's lip curled in disgust as Balis ran to the hall to throw up his breakfast. Then back to the issue at hand, he drawled, "It seems yours and your cousin's recklessness has gotten you into quite the predicament this time."

Aeden should have seen it coming. But he didn't want to hear any more. His fingers itched to feel the smooth wood of his violin under them. Would Olgar stop him if he left now? His father had no love for Reinar and his rules. Why not just brush it all under the rich woven rug?

Olgar held the letter up. The broken Downthorn seal—golden wax imprinted with a sparrow taking flight above blackthorns—glinted in the firelight. His father's chest puffed out as he said, "You've been invited to stay at the Downthorn estate."

Aeden scrunched his face. "Stay? Like a prisoner?"

Olgar shot him a scrutinizing gaze. "As a suitor."

Marcos barked with laughter from across the room. When Olgar nailed him with a seething look, red faced with fangs bared, Marcos stopped laughing and said, "You're serious?"

Marcos' father, Hayden, strode in from the other room. Aeden watched him carefully, noting the blood on his collar. Had he overfed again? Out of the lot of them, Hayden had the least self-control. He snarled at Marcos as he passed him, taking a seat beside Aeden's mother.

Hayden's voice dripped with disdain as he said, "Seems you're to be leashed to the girl like a young pup."

Olgar grunted and gave a curt nod. "You leave tomorrow morning."

Aeden scoffed. "Absolutely not."

Olgar's nostrils flared, sending warning shivers down his back. His father was not a kind man by any means. He was quick to anger and, before the curse, had been one of the Unseelie's punishers. Carrying out the King's orders in the Autumn Court. Born and bred in darkness and blood. Still, Aeden would not cave on this.

He treaded carefully, feeling the tension in the room rise. "Why is it so important all of a sudden to get into Reinar's good graces? Agreeing to court his darling niece is hardly going to make up for years of bad blood between us."

It was a strange choice of punishment. Did Reinar expect Aeden to come eagerly with flowers in hand? Ready to offer up his sincerest apologies for his family's misbehavior? He wasn't one to grovel, a lesson taught to him by his father. Besides, it was Marcos who had killed the man in the woods, drawing his kin to them.

"Father, tell me straight. Why agree to this?"

Olgar puffed from the tightly rolled tobacco in his hand. For a moment, Aeden believed they would be kept in the dark. It wasn't unlike his father to keep secrets. After all, when Olgar's own father—Aeden's grandfather Roth—had joined in the uprising against the King of the Unseelie Court, no one had known until it was too late to object.

To Aeden's surprise, his father ordered, "You, my boy, are going to charm the girl."

Aeden stood. It felt as if his jaw might hit the ground. Was this some sort of joke? He laughed as he said, "The niece? You can't be serious. She would sooner see me skinned alive than *marry* me—"

"Enough!" Olgar stood, causing everyone in the room to still. His father was quick to violence. Even in adulthood, Aeden knew better than to speak against him publicly. With his uncle's family present, Aeden was stepping on dangerous ground.

Olgar straightened his jacket and smoothed back his peppered hair. "Marcos is facing expulsion for the body left in the woods. The one that drew those damned vengeful men here last night."

Aeden clenched his fists. The men were filled with more than the need for vengeance. They were branded with magic. The witch's involvement meant trouble. It meant they were desperate and knew more than they should about the Vampyrs.

Olgar continued, "If Reinar won't prepare his people for the threat, then I will take matters into my own hands." He waved the invitation in the air. "We are lucky this opportunity has presented itself. That is why you will do precisely as I say."

Aeden's stomach rolled, and he opened his mouth to speak, but his father held up a silencing hand. His words were firm as he said, "Before you give me some loose-lipped argument on the matter, allow me to finish." He held his hand out to help Aeden's mother,

Sylvia, from her seat. Her deep red and golden gown swished along the ground as she straightened it out.

Olgar continued, "Food is scarce here in the forest. Fewer mortals travel these roads. We are nature's ultimate predator. You know very well that we should not be hiding away. If we are to take what is ours, then we will have to tip the scales of power in our favor."

Aeden suppressed a sigh. He'd heard this all before. Many times, his father and uncle had talked in hushed tones about how the Downthorns had wronged them. It had been Reinar and his family's decision to hide their people away in the forest. To feed not from the vein, but from the cup. Aeden was usually inclined to side with his father on these matters, but he couldn't imagine how offering himself up to the enemy family would benefit his own.

Not only that, but the Downthorns believed in etiquette. Feeding from the cup to spare whatever indignity they found in drinking from the vein. Keeping their prey for short periods of time and wiping their minds afterward. Aeden knew from his own experience that taking only enough blood from the source to survive left one weak. It also dampened their powers. It was dangerous.

But the majority of their people had followed the Downthorns, placing Reinar on a pedestal and turning their back on the Ashbanes and any of the other Vampyrs who decided to stay with them. The decision had been a bloody one with neighbor turning against neighbor. Until both families and their followers conceded, content to stay on their own sides of the lake. Until now...

He shook his head. "Even if I could convince her to choose me amongst the other suitors, marrying her won't make a difference. They will merely expect us to play by their rules. Surely you see that this is just a way to placate us into submission."

Olgar curled his upper lip in disgust. "How can a son of mine be so shortsighted?"

His Uncle Hayden laughed and Aeden fought the urge to leap across the short table between them.

Marcos finally spoke up again. "Tell us what you plan to do, Uncle." He shrunk under his father's silencing look.

"A change is coming," Olgar sat back down and crossed his leg, resting his ankle on his knee. "For years, I have not had the power to build an army or turn their followers to our side. This offers the tiniest chance to rectify that. If done right."

Aeden had overheard his father's musings about gathering enough of a force to leave the forest and take control of the mortal kingdom beyond it. But they had been drunken ravings. Mentioned only in the night when he and Hayden had overfed on the feeders and emptied many bottles of wine from the cellar. And whether Aeden shared in his father's dream or not, the plan was flawed.

Hayden cackled. "See, brother, I told you he wouldn't have the stomach suited for the job. Why not offer Marcos in his stead?"

Olgar snarled at him. "Marcos does not have the tact nor the charms for such a task." Then to Aeden, he said, "You will get close to the girl, no matter what it takes. You will leave in the morning. Reinar has given you and the girl until the next full moon to court one another. During which time, the brat may make her choice." He rose, stepping dangerously close to Aeden. Stale smoke and bitter alcohol drifted off his breath as he added, "And while you are there, you will do what needs to be done."

Aeden kept his hands steady at his sides, careful to show no fear in the face of his father. "And what might that be?"

"You will kill Reinar and his son."

Ten

Aeden

Aeden picked up his pace as he walked down the rocky drive. Marcos called out behind him, but he ignored him, eager for the solitude of the lake. He could still hear his father's voice echoing in his mind. *You will kill Reinar and his son.* Aeden was no assassin. He clutched the violin case tightly in one hand and balled the other into a fist.

There was no love lost between him and the Downthorns. But to enter their home and commit such a vile act was a line he never expected to cross. Hunting... fighting... those were things he was more than comfortable with. But lulling their own kind into a false sense of trust only to stab them in the back? That was downright cowardly.

Marcos jumped in front of Aeden, forcing him to a halt. Holding his hands out, Marcos said, "Slow down. Just wait a minute."

"For what? You heard them in there. They've lost their minds."

"Maybe they have a point."

Aeden shoved him aside. "And I guess you've lost yours, too."

Marcos jogged to keep up with him. "Listen, the attack last night changes things."

"An attack that you caused," Aeden corrected.

"I know. I fucked up." Marcos took hold of Aeden's shoulders, forcing him to look him in the face. "But those mortals wouldn't have gotten close enough to attack if Reinar wasn't so weak. We're predators, but this forest is a cage."

Aeden narrowed his eyes. "He wants me to charm my way into that house. But no amount of charm is going to make them forget about the past. Even if I can make Tessa fall for me, make the rest of them trust me... What's to stop them from suspecting us when Reinar and Drake turn up dead?"

Doubt clouded Marcos' face and Aeden thought maybe he'd see sense. To his disappointment, Marcos sighed and said, "Your father has a plan. He always does. Whatever it is, it will put us all back on top, where we belong. Not just our family, but everyone, on both sides of the lake. This is one small sacrifice for the good of the whole."

"One sacrifice turns into another. What happens if getting rid of Reinar and Drake isn't enough?" Aeden knew as well as any that they were prisoners of this forest. Doomed to live out their days in solitary, like the Fae who wandered aimlessly around Elfhame. Just because they had built homes and found a way to live comfortably, did not make them less barbaric. It did not restore them to what they once were. But even if his father had a plan that could work, how much trust could Aeden put in it? And just how far was he willing to go?

Marcos didn't answer, but this time when Aeden pulled away, he let him go. Every step toward the lake felt weighed down by the task his father had thrust on him. When he reached the water's edge, rather than take the violin from its case, he sat in the sand.

Soft ripples kissed the toes of his boots. He laid back, resting his hands behind his head, and stared up at the full canopy of trees. The tiniest sliver of sunlight cut through the symphony of fall colors. Side effects of Annie's blood still lingered, sharpening his vision enough that he could see oranges and reds reflecting in the sun's rays.

He cringed as a voice as soft as the breeze blowing through a field of flowers rang out. "You look troubled."

Aeden didn't bother to sit up. The witch who drifted through the water, going between realms using her powers, often showed up at the worst possible time. He wasn't sure where she called home, but he knew she'd been haunting the lake since his family had first come to Gwyar.

"I'm not in the mood," he grumbled, hoping she'd take a hint and sink back to where she'd come from.

To his disappointment, she didn't. "The waters are stirring with troublesome gossip."

"Are they now? Then I take it you heard about our visitors last night?" Aeden tried to ignore the uneasy pit in his stomach. The witch always seemed to know things she had no business knowing. But he did his best not to dwell on it, since she had never shown herself as a threat to him and his own. It was easier to believe that she was just lonely and looking for gossip to pass the time.

Her voice was like a whisper on the wind as she said, "Very unfortunate." Her bare feet didn't leave footprints in the wet sand as she walked over to him. It was eerie, as if she could come and go without ever leaving a trace. He'd never seen her leave the lake's edge, though, and wasn't sure her magic permitted her to do so.

Still, perhaps she knew of another witch who did walk beyond the lake's edge. "Do you know of the witch who aided them?"

"I know that more will come if you do not act." The long, nearly see through dress she wore dripped as she sat beside him. He tried not to stare at her bare arms, which were a strange tint of gray. Like she'd been in the damp, dark depths of the water for too long. Even her hair was a dull blonde, tangled with seaweed. And tiny shells and pieces of something that looked like barnacles stuck out of her skin.

They'd been running into one another by the lake since he was a young boy. By now her unsettling appearance, as well as her vague responses, had grown on him. Though he wouldn't call her a friend, she was something close to it. There were a few times when she'd offered him counsel. From dealing with his father, to navigating the rocky waters of his on and off again thing with Rose.

The paintings hanging inside the Downthorn chateau lingered in his mind. More specifically, Ayana and Byron's wedding scene. Where a strangely familiar woman stood with them. Had this witch known them? She never spoke of her past during their visits together. Perhaps she was older than he thought...

She quirked her head to the side. "You want to ask me something else?" she guessed.

"Did you know them? The curse bringers, I mean."

Something like grief washed over her face. It was as brief as a wave lapping into a ship. With a soft sigh, she answered, "I have crossed paths with many over the years. Some have taken my advice, while others have cast it aside."

Aeden knew he would get no more out of her. But it didn't stop him from wondering if they had done more than cross paths. Why else would she still show signs of grief at the mention of them? Those feelings didn't linger this long for those you only met in passing.

Deciding he would be better off focusing on his troubles at hand, he sighed and admitted, "I don't know if I can go through with this."

Quickly—as if eager to change the subject—she asked, "What's holding you back?"

"It's..." He recalled the heat of Tessa's body close to his. "Complicated."

What *was* holding him back? He and Tessa were nothing to one another. He owed her no loyalty. But the prospect of seducing her just to get close to her family was wrong. It twisted his stomach into knots. Facing Drake in combat or challenging Reinar publicly sat well with him. It was true that Olgar had tried it once before. After the murder of Tessa's father, Reinar had gone after Olgar in a fit of rage. Olgar had nearly been killed in the process himself. Aeden didn't have the experience that the two older men did, but he'd still rather take part in a duel. It was upfront. Honest. An assassination felt... dirty.

The witch shrugged. It was odd to see such a normal gesture coming from the ethereal creature. "I think you should go."

Aeden propped himself up on his elbows. "You do? Why?"

She drew circles in the sand with her finger. One inside another. "I have been to many realms. In all my time, I have seen men betray one another for far less than this. Perhaps you should be worrying less about your decisions and more about what fate might have in store for you."

"You're saying it's already decided?" Aeden scoffed. "Men make their own fate." It certainly wasn't fate that had gotten them cursed. It was Byron Ashbane's decisions. The choice to marry a woman coveted by the Unseelie King himself. And it was Aeden's family's decisions that had led to this moment. Their resolve to join forces with the Downthorns to stand against the King when he came for Ayana. And then their determination to avenge Ayana and Byron's deaths when the King cut their hearts from their chests.

But now it seemed it was Aeden's turn to choose.

The witch flicked sand off of her finger. "I'm saying that it is love that destroyed all of you, and perhaps it is love that will save you."

Love. A simple four letter word. One that held more power than all the magic in the world combined. But like fate, Aeden didn't believe in it. But that wouldn't matter, would it? He just needed Tessa to believe. He recalled of how fiercely she fought at his side the night before. The way she'd looked at him after she'd drank the man's blood. As if she were seeing the world for the first time after all these years.

If he did this. If he made her fall in love with him, only to kill her family, she would never forgive him. But wouldn't it all be worth it if Reinar and Drake's deaths made their lives outside of Elfhame more bearable? If it kept them from starving and scraping for every miniscule comfort that they could get their hands on?

If his father could give their people power again. A place in the world. The gift of not having to hide anymore. Then the betrayal would be for her own good as well. There was nothing more to think about. He owed his loyalty to his family. To their people. Woo the girl. Save them all.

Eleven

Tessa

Tessa's boots were too tight. They pressed her toes together in such a way that made her squirm and writhe. As if to add to the discomfort, Drake stood too close beside her on the gravel drive. Far closer than she liked. She crossed her arms and huffed, sending a small frosty cloud of breath into the early morning air.

"Stop fidgeting," Drake grumbled. It seemed the sour mood was going around this morning.

Tessa pressed her fingers down on her arms. She hadn't realized she'd been tapping them incessantly. Her shawl—expertly

BOUND BY BLOOD AND SORROW

crocheted by one of the lady's maids—was soft and she stroked it slowly, trying to quell her nerves. Drake frowned at her and walked away.

Her uncle immediately took his place. Tessa sensed him watching her, and it only made the silence between them more awkward. He cleared his throat loudly. "I uh. I just wanted to tell you that what you're doing for this family is more than I ever dreamed of asking of you."

She tensed. What could she say to that? Did he want her to assure him everything was going to be okay? She could lie. But the words wouldn't come. The wolf would be entering her den soon. Goosebumps rippled along her arms. Courting an Ashbane, even one as handsome as Aeden, was horrifying. Her family was practically laying her out as bait for him. What would her father say if he were alive to witness it?

When she didn't respond, Reinar continued, "You know, your mom was the biggest bundle of nerves anyone had ever seen when your father came to call on her." The smile spreading across his face at the memory brightened and drew Tessa's attention.

Part of her longed to hear more about her parents' romance. But the sensible side of her knew she shouldn't. Trudging up old memories of times when her family was happy and whole was too painful. She swallowed the lump in her throat and stroked the shawl faster.

Reinar's voice was wistful as he said, "Theirs was a love for the ages. One that many of us will never be blessed enough to find." He turned to Tessa and more firmly said, "But this. What you're doing. It is the noblest of sacrifices. I am growing old, darling girl. And my strength fades with each feeder we release."

Tessa's own stomach rumbled in response to his words. Yesterday she'd been sated the entire day from the mortal's blood during the attack. Now that it had worn off, the rationed blood with her breakfast had done little to fill her. And now that her uncle pointed it out, she could see how thin his face was becoming and how he slouched slightly after standing for long periods of time.

It was her turn to clear her throat uncomfortably. "Uncle, I will do my duty as you have asked. But I don't understand how forcing the Ashbanes to behave themselves is going to fill our bellies."

Reinar grunted as he straightened his shoulders. "Mortals forget much faster than the likes of us. As long as we continue to release feeders back to their villages when their allotted time is up here, then there will be no reason for other humans to steer clear of the roads running along our borders. There will be nothing to draw hunters to our door. And more than that," his eyes welled with tears as he continued, "if we are good... If we can prove ourselves to still be who we once were, then perhaps the King will put an end to our banishment."

Tessa sighed. She'd heard this many times before. The dream. Her father's dream. That if they served their time, eventually the King would allow them to return to their rightful place in Elfhame. The few memories she had of the ruler of the Unseelie realm were not fond ones. He was cruel. Without remorse, easily slighted, and downright evil.

It wouldn't matter that they maintained their homes, or drank blood from polished silver cups as if they were drinking an expensive port. The King would never let them return. The belief might be the one thing she and the Ashbanes had in common. They had voiced their disdain for her father's—and now her uncle's—hope.

Reinar scratched the back of his neck. "I'm trying my damndest to hold on to your father's dream, but it feels like it's slipping away with my strength."

Tessa reached deep for the words to comfort him. "Then I will help you hold on to it." She might not believe in the dream, but she wouldn't be the one to snuff out her uncle's hope. She would take the threads and hold tight when her family could not.

Reinar leaned down and kissed her on the top of her head. Tessa's heart warmed at the gesture. It was the affection of a father. That, after all, was the mantle he had taken up when her own was lost to her.

"Darling," Flora, flitted toward Tessa. Her cheeks were sunken and the circles beneath her eyes were more prominent this morning. She stepped to the other side of Tessa as she spoke. "The carriage is approaching."

Tessa's ears sharpened and sure enough, there was the rumble of wheels on a packed dirt road. Her stomach was knotted up worse than the vines that snaked up the balcony to her room. In her short time around Aeden, it had felt as if someone was tugging her in a million different directions. One minute, she was enjoying his company. The next, she was humiliated, and feeling the violent urge to break his nose. And then there was the moment during the ambush... She had spent the entire night chalking it up to the blood she'd drained from the mortal's neck. It had done something to her. Amplified every sense in her body.

So when Aeden had touched her, it was no wonder she'd felt like her skin was humming. Combined with how dangerously attractive he was, it had to be nothing more than a moment of lust. A *fleeting* moment. One that had no deeper meaning.

The carriage came into view, riding smoothly along the road. A young man with a head full of rich, red hair sat in the coachman's seat. His freckled face was pinched as he caught her eye. At least she wasn't the only one battling nerves today.

Reinar left her side to greet them, and Drake stepped into place next to her. He clenched and unclenched his fists and she sensed the hatred rolling off of him in waves.

When the carriage rolled to a stop, the young man swung down from his seat and stumbled slightly as he hit the ground. Drake snorted beside her. "Not very graceful for a Vampyr, is he?"

Ignoring Drake's obvious disdain, Tessa whispered back, "Do you know him?"

"Ashbane runt. Balfour... Baldric..." Drake's brow furrowed.

Flora cut in. "Balis. The young cousin of our Viscount Aeden."

Tessa looked him over, trying to decide what to make of him. He didn't appear to be a brute like the other Ashbanes she had met in the past. If anything, he looked as innocent as one of the humans in the village. It was hard to imagine him ripping into human flesh for the fun of it.

The carriage door swung open, and Tessa sucked in a breath, preparing herself for Aeden's appearance. Instead, a taller, *much* broader version of young Balis hopped out. He smoothed his flaming hair away from his face and smiled mischievously at her. Then, in Drake's direction, he raised his hand to his head as if he were tipping a hat. Baiting her cousin was never a good idea, but she had to give this man credit for the courage to do it.

Drake snarled in response, but Reinar was there, blocking his path before he could do anything unsavory. Oh, how splendidly this was already going. She rolled her eyes. This would never work. Already, the men were agitating one another.

Her uncle plastered a cheerful expression on his face. But Tessa didn't miss the twitch of his eye as he said, "Lord Balis. Lord Marcos. Welcome."

Marcos stepped aside, and finally, Aeden hopped down from the carriage. His maroon jacket was fitted, doing nothing to hide his strong, muscular arms. His hair was let loose this time. Dark auburn waves stopping above his shoulders. He pushed it from his face with a swagger that told her he was used to things working out the way he wanted. It was utterly irritating.

Still. She stared. Whatever sunlight managing to peek through the treetops shined on him. In the dark, his hair had looked brown, but the sunlight highlighted the reddish tint to it. She tried to focus on something else, but her gaze drifted to his face. The smile he gave her seemed genuine enough, with deep dimples on both cheeks.

Her gaze shot quickly to the ground. She might have agreed to this courtship, but she would not let him charm her. They could be pleasant to one another, but she wasn't about to let herself fall for his flattery.

Aeden's smile stayed firmly in place. It didn't even falter as Drake stepped in his way, blocking his path to Tessa. She eyed the two men curiously, wondering if either would be humble enough to stand down. Or would their pride keep everyone there throughout lunch, watching them stand toe to toe in a stubborn challenge?

To her surprise, Aeden was the first to break. He folded into a shallow bow as he said, "Viscount Drake. It is nice to see you looking well."

It didn't escape Tessa's notice as Aeden's gaze flitted to the fading bruise on Drake's eye. It must have been quite the hit to have left a mark like that. Especially considering how quickly their people healed. For a moment, she wondered whether it was the lack of blood slowing Drake's ability to heal, or if it was the strength that Aeden got from drinking from the vein that allowed him to leave such a serious mark.

Something to consider later when she was alone. Every footman and lady's maid in the chateau had gathered outside to welcome Aeden. Even Scarlet had ridden in that morning to catch a glimpse of what was sure to be the spectacle of the season. A few women from the other families were there too, giggling like schoolgirls as Aeden strode by them. All he had to do was look their way and blushes bloomed along the bridges of their pretty noses.

He was like a wolf on the prowl. Tessa crossed her arms tighter across her chest. He was certainly giving them plenty to gossip about for years to come. As he approached her, she lowered her arms to her sides and took hold of the skirts of her dress to stop from fidgeting some more.

Aeden reached out for her hand, but she hesitated to give it to him. The steady smile on his face twitched slightly, and she had a brief sense of satisfaction at catching him off guard. Perhaps he had never had a woman deny him before. Well, it was something he'd have to get used to now.

Her mother urged through her teeth, "Tessa, greet the gentleman, if you please."

Mustering a tight lipped smile, Tessa placed her hand in his. His leather gloves were rough, but part of her couldn't help but be thankful for the thin layer standing between the two of them. The feeling was short-lived as he leaned down and brought her hand up to his lips.

The kiss was quick and to the point. Butterflies didn't flutter around in her stomach. There was no heat of a blush coming across her face. It was very dutiful and business-like. Perhaps this would be easier than she thought. She took a tiny step back as he released her hand. Tucking it behind her, she wiped it softly on her dress.

Her uncle cleared his throat again. Was he coming down with a cold? Tessa's brow furrowed with concern until he said, "Yes. Well." He scanned Marcos and Balis with suspicion. "Welcome to our home. We, uh, weren't expecting an entourage, I must admit..."

Aeden swatted behind him in the direction of his cousins. "They're only here to see me settled. I can assure you they won't be any trouble."

Marcos crossed his heart with his finger and bounced on his feet. "Aye. You won't even know we're here."

Her uncle grunted in response and pursed his lips. Tessa shared his disposition. If the night of the ball were any indicator, it seemed no Ashbane could go anywhere unnoticed. Having one of them in her home was bad enough, but three? That was downright distressing.

But her uncle, ever the gentleman, relented. "Very well. Talos has been kind enough to arrange lunch in the gardens for you. He and Miss Scarlet will join you." He paused, looking at Marcos and Balis as if they were stray dogs who had wandered to his door with fleas. "I suppose you may wish to accompany them as well?"

Marcos swept into a dramatic bow. "Nothing in this world would make my life feel more complete."

Her uncle grunted with his lip curling slightly. Then, without any further fuss, he returned to the chateau. Drake backed away a few steps with his hand resting on the hilt of his dagger. Tessa wondered if he'd strapped it to his side as a threat. He rarely relied on weapons. Maybe he'd finally met his match in the Ashbanes, though.

Tessa breathed a small sigh of relief as he spun on his heel to follow his father. Her mother took her leave next. She shooed away the bystanders with her usual air of authority. Then, as she passed Tessa, she patted her gently on the shoulder. If she intended it to be a comforting gesture, it didn't do any good. Tessa shivered as she watched her mother disappear in the doorway. Not only had she gotten her into this, but she was now leaving her to fend for herself amongst a pack of wolves.

Marcos' eyes trailed up and down her. "You sure grew up good."

Like she thought. *Wolves.* Mustering false enthusiasm, Tessa turned to the other two men, who were staring at her expectantly. Gesturing to the path beside the chateau that led to the gardens, she asked, "Shall we?"

Aeden stood frozen in place, looking dumbfounded, which gave Tessa another jolt of pleasure. Scarlet shuffled her feet on the ground awkwardly, drawing Marcos' attention to her. As quick as a cat, he leapt to her side.

"Watch carefully," he purred, "this is how it's done." Scarlet yelped as he plucked her hand from her side and looped it through his arm. He strode ahead, tugging a frazzled Scarlet with him.

Aeden chuckled as he sidled up to Tessa. "Ready when you are."

Tessa froze as he held his arm out in a gentlemanly fashion. Reluctantly, she placed her arm through his and rested her hand on his forearm. Something stirred in her chest and she silently chided herself for acting like such a coward.

He was a man, just like any other Vampyr who lived in the Crimson Forest. She was perfectly safe with her uncle and cousin nearby. And with Scarlet leading the way and Talos taking up the rear beside Balis. So why was her body vibrating with unease?

She risked a glance at Aeden from the corner of her eye. He was well built. Even through his jacket, she could feel the hardened muscles in his arms. Like a statue made of stone. Yet his touch was soft. Gentler than she believed someone from his side of the lake would have been capable of. Heat pulsed through her at the memory of his hands on her face. And the way the effects of the mortal man's blood had made it seem as if stars were reaching down for them.

She shook her head, cursing to herself inside her head. When he looked down at her, she froze again. He narrowed his eyes as he teased, "Am I making you nervous?"

"No," she answered too quickly. *Idiot*, she thought to herself. She was supposed to be charming him. Luring him into liking her enough to persuade his family to change their ways. Yet so far she'd acted like a frightened little deer in the woods being tracked by a hunter. This was not her. *She* was the huntress. The monster prowling through the forest.

With newfound resolve, she straightened and said, "I'm just new to this, that's all."

"I see." His voice was filled with doubt.

Sweet florals filled the air as they approached the gardens. White rocks crunched beneath the many pairs of boots as the group strolled to the elegant setup. Talos had outdone himself, placing pristine ivory tables and chairs under a canvas awning. Each table had enough room for two and was set with platters of pastries and tea sandwiches.

Marcos opened the lid of a teapot and sniffed at it. "No blood?"

Scarlet's face scrunched as she replied, "Not for elevenses."

Marcos raised a dark eyebrow at her. "You're a strange bunch."

Scarlet's mouth popped open and Tessa interceded before her friend could offer a smart retort. She pushed a plate toward him. "Try the sweet cakes. You'll find they're a suitable substitution until lunch."

Marcos scrunched his nose, but took a seat as Tessa bid, leaving the plate untouched. Scarlet sat across from him, but turned away, making her disdain clear. Balis and Talos took their seats at the second table, quietly picking at the food while keeping a watchful eye on Tessa and Aeden.

With a heavy sigh, Tessa caved to her fate and sat down at the third table. It was closest to the rose bush, and the scent was so overpowering it made her queasy. Or maybe it was the man sitting across from her. She wasn't sure at the moment.

Unceremoniously, Aeden asked, "What now?"

Tessa glanced down at the table. She didn't have much of an appetite, and tea would only make her sleepy. So she opted for the cards sitting to the side. "We could play," she suggested.

Aeden nodded and pulled his gloves off. Black ink snaked along his hands and Tessa tilted her head to see that it wound up his wrists. Tattoos weren't common amongst their people. It was a very... human thing to do. But there was something beautiful about the sharp edges of the thorns and the soft curve of the vines. Without meaning to, she continued to stare. How far did the ink go? Her eyes drifted up his arm and to his chest. Where did it end?

Aeden's voice cut through her thoughts like a dagger severing a very frayed rope. "Your turn." Something like amusement glinted in his eyes.

Her own practically popped out of their sockets when she realized he caught her staring. She quickly snatched up the cards he had dealt and focused on her hand. She wasn't even aware of what game they were playing. Had he told her? She bit her lip, too foolish and stubborn to ask.

"If you don't feel like playing after all..." He trailed off and his eyes widened as they met his cousin's. As if he were silently begging him for help.

Tessa folded her arms over her chest and settled back in her seat. "May I ask you something?"

Aeden hummed in response.

"Why are you here?" She couldn't imagine what he was getting out of the match. He didn't strike her as someone who cared about marriage and alliances.

Aeden's brows popped up in surprise. "You invited me."

"True. But why have you agreed to it?" Her eyes roved over him. At the confidence in the way he sat. Like everything in the world had been conveniently laid at his feet. "Surely, there are women on your side of the Crimson Lake who would trade their finest jewels to gain favor with the son of their bold Count Olgar."

Aeden snorted. "And?"

She narrowed her eyes. If he was trying to bait her on purpose, then it was working. "And I just don't see why someone like you would agree to something like this."

"Someone like me?" His brow furrowed, and he pressed his lips together as if to keep from laughing at her.

By the stars. He was irritating.

Their many chaperones quieted. It might have been better if she'd kept her mouth shut. To avoid insulting any of the men. But she couldn't help herself. She knew exactly why she was committing to this. But why was he? Was it really the threat of his cousin being expelled from the forest? Admittedly, the prospect of being cast out would have frightened her as well. Without the option to return to Elfhame, they would have to wander the mortal realm. Living in constant fear of being found out and struck down like rabid dogs. It had been hard enough living outside of the forest when all the families had been united. But going out alone, or with only half the force they once had, would be devastating.

With a twinge of guilt, she tried to fix the direction the conversation had gone. "I just meant. Someone attractive and—"

He grinned. "You think I'm attractive?"

She ignored him. "I would imagine that you have more experience in..."

"In what? Love?" His grin widened. "Sex?"

Talos cried out, "Oh, by the stars!"

Aeden laughed, but kept his eyes solely on Tessa. She shifted uncomfortably under his gaze. She wasn't a prude. At least, she didn't think she was. But she'd never really let anyone close enough to experience that sort of thing. And her uncle would have lost his mind if she had. If they were to be good, upstanding members of the little society they had created, then it was important to maintain decency.

Aeden placed his hands over his heart as if he'd been wounded. "Why, Tessa Downthorn! Do you think I'm some sort of rake?"

She didn't know him well enough yet to decide. But she had her suspicions. Instead of voicing them, she opted for glaring at him.

He leaned forward and his knee brushed against hers. The heat that had been blooming in her chest earlier slinked down below her naval. Something fluttered in her stomach, but she ignored it.

With his leg still pressed up against hers, he asked, "What gave you this impression of me? Or are you always so quick to judge someone you just met?"

The accusation was offensive. Maybe a bit true, but offensive, nonetheless. She leaned forward now as well, and hissed in a whisper, "For starters, you nearly kissed me the other night in the hall when you were clearly there with another and then there was that... that moment in the forest." She gestured erratically toward the woods where the men had attacked them.

She froze, turning to see that their little party was watching her in shock and awe. How incredibly foolish she must appear to them right now. This was all Aeden's fault. How in the world could one man make her feel so flustered?

Scarlet balked. "He tried to *kiss* you?"

Marcos chimed in, "Nice."

Aeden shot him a dirty look. Then his face fell as he turned back to Tessa. At least he had the decency to look sorry for the turn this had taken. Even though it was as much her fault as it was his. Her cheeks burned with embarrassment.

Suddenly, Scarlet popped up from her seat. She grabbed Tessa under the elbow and dragged her up. "If you will all excuse us. We'll be just a moment." Then, tight lipped, Scarlet pulled Tessa further into the gardens.

They came to some overgrown rose bushes. It wasn't like the gardeners to allow their prized flowers to go unattended for so long. Even with Scarlet tapping her foot expectantly, Tessa took a moment to worry the gardeners weren't feeling well.

Finally, Scarlet spoke. "I have been here all morning. How am I just now finding out about this?"

"It was stupid." Tessa tried to find the words to explain. But how could she? She had been the one to allow him close enough for the near kiss. Had even encouraged it. With a huff, she said, "I just wanted to have a bit of fun. No strings attached. To see what it would be like. I didn't know who he was at the time. If I had, I never would have—"

A laugh bubbled up from Scarlet's throat. It soon turned into a howl and Tessa couldn't help but laugh, too.

With a hand pressed into her side, Scarlet quieted enough to say, "At least things are finally starting to get interesting around here."

"No doubt there will be plenty to entertain the gossips."

Scarlet swatted at the air and looped her arm around Tessa's. "Don't worry about them. They act as if life before the curse wasn't filled with debauchery and scandal. They forget too easily what life was really like in Elfhame's Unseelie Court. How the parties raged until morning. How the Elfwine would knock even the most prestigious lady and lord on their butts."

Tessa couldn't remember much of life before the curse. Only glimpses and glimmers of starlit rooms and music that played until sunrise. But she'd heard stories. Tales of her uncle and father wreaking havoc in the countryside. Drinking and dancing in the town square. Charming women as young men. Had her father been similar to Aeden in that respect? A strapping man with a dimpled grin? Any laughter she'd been filled with a moment ago faded.

"I don't know how to do this," she admitted.

Scarlet shook her head and her shining silver hair rippled around her. "I'm not sure either. But I do know that I will support you. No matter what happens." She paused as they turned back to the awning. "At least he's not unbearable to be around. His cousin, on the other hand..."

"Is most *definitely* a rake." Tessa choked down a laugh. "But you're right. With some effort, I can learn to deal with Aeden."

As they walked, she watched him and his cousins closely. They had dragged Talos into some sort of stepping dance. Aeden drummed on the table, keeping a steady, but fast paced beat that the men could move their feet to. Talos looked paler than usual and he stumbled as he tried to keep up. When he looked up, he caught Tessa's eye and mouthed *help me*.

Tessa couldn't keep her lips from turning up into a smile. Maybe this wouldn't be so bad. There hadn't been much laughter in their home as of late. She had to admit, the Ashbanes knew how to let loose. And she'd be lying if she said she wasn't a bit envious of that.

Aeden would keep her on her toes, but he was frustrating enough that her heart would be safe. What sort of daughter would she be if she fell in love with the son of the man who got her father killed? Aeden's eyes met hers and locked on tight. She promptly wiped the smile from her face and scowled at him. Still, he grinned at her. Cheeky bastard.

Twelve

Aeden

Aeden tugged his collar up to hide the tattoos as best he could. Count Reinar didn't strike him as the type to approve of such things. And according to his father, the entire fate of their family was resting on Aeden's shoulders.

Olgar was clear in his instructions. *"Make nice. Win them over. I will tell you when the time comes."*

Aeden's mission was simple. Gain their trust publicly, so when the opportunity presented itself to get rid of Reinar and Drake, no one would suspect the Ashbanes had anything to do with it. It was the only way to allow his father the opportunity to step forward as a leader. If anyone thought for a moment that the Ashbanes had orchestrated the whole thing, then the families on the Downthorn side of the lake would never follow them.

He clenched his fists in irritation. Until his father gave him instruction, Aeden was in the dark. Making it look like an accident would be difficult. Would he have to make it appear like another human attack? He shivered at the thought of driving a stake through the heart of a fellow Vampyr. With a sigh, the tension in his shoulders released slightly. Either his father wasn't sure how they were going to accomplish this yet, or he wasn't willing to share the entire plan with Aeden so soon. In the meantime, he needed to focus on the task at hand.

He glanced around the room. His room. At least for the time being. The contrast to his family's manor was striking. Soft rather than bold. Light instead of dark. Even the bed was littered with pastel blankets. Not his style. But it was nice enough. He imagined he wouldn't be spending much time in it, anyway.

Rather, he would be spending his days with Tessa. At least she wasn't dull with her sharp tongue. There had been a number of times in the garden when he had caught her studying him with that intense gaze of hers. At least he knew she was intrigued by him. Even if he did have a knack for getting under her skin.

Eager to explore a bit, he slipped from the room. Dinner would be served within the hour, which gave him just enough time to wander. If nothing else came from this experience, at least he would find some adventure in it.

The halls downstairs were loud with the bustling of household staff. They flitted around like little birds tending to their nest. In Elfhame, the Downthorns had owned a much larger estate than his family did. And it appeared every single one of their staff had followed them into battle and beyond. How was it that Reinar was able to inspire such loyalty?

As he rounded the corridor, the scent of fresh mortal blood wafted past his nose. A plump woman in her forties bumped into him. His body reacted instantaneously. The gums where his fangs rested throbbed and his senses sharpened.

As she offered her apologies, he gazed down the hall. There was no one there. Only the unaccompanied human. His mouth salivated. Lunch had consisted of a mere cup of stale blood. Why were they serving that, when there were perfectly healthy feeders wandering the home freely?

The woman didn't look at him with fear. Instead, she had a soft smile plastered on her face. There was a slight daze in her eyes. A sure sign of compulsion. He gulped. If he could have just a small taste...

Tessa's voice echoed loudly through the hall. "Odessa." She was peeking out of the little divot in the wall that led to the kitchen doors. Had she been there the whole time?

The woman's attention snapped to her. With the same authority Tessa's mother had used in the ballroom the other night, she announced, "You are excused."

Aeden watched in disappointment as his snack waddled down the hall and out of sight. He strolled over to Tessa, preparing himself for a tongue lashing. She was pressed into the little alcove. The stern glare on her face clashed with the demure white gown she wore. It had a simple blue sash tied around her waist, accenting the fullness of her hips.

She crossed her arms as he reached her. Ignoring the embarrassment of nearly being caught breaking her family's biggest rule, he asked, "Why are you hiding?" His eyes drifted down along the hourglass shape of her and settled on her bare feet. "And where are your shoes?"

Quick as a whip, she snapped back, "Why are you asking so many questions? And what were you doing with Odessa?"

He leaned his elbow on the wall above her head. "We were just getting to know each other."

"Right," she drawled.

Glancing at the closed kitchen door, he tried again. "Seriously, what are you doing?"

She raised her chin. "I'm listening."

"To?" He resisted the urge to smirk at her. There was no need to get a rise out of her when she just caught him with the feeder. If she told her uncle, it might ruin everything.

She sighed heavily, leaning her back against the wall. "Gossip. I just wanted to see if they were talking about... us." She rolled her eyes. "It's childish, I know."

"Not at all." He shifted, so they were standing face to face in the confined space. Then, he pressed his ear to the door. Though he couldn't hear a thing other than dishes being pushed about, he gasped. "They're saying that I am the best looking man to ever step foot in these halls."

That earned him a small laugh from Tessa. So he continued, "Now they're gushing about how lucky you are to have found such a great catch."

Another laugh. Less restrained this time. Then she said, "They are not."

He grabbed her by the shoulders and steered her toward the door. "Listen for yourself."

She was quiet for a moment before whispering, "I don't hear anything."

His voice was husky as he said, "How odd."

He felt his face flush and his pulse quickened. They were close. As close as they had been the night of the masquerade.

With a knowing smile, she replied, "Very."

They stayed that way, side by side. He tried to think of something charming to say. Anything to make her laugh again. But the dinner bell interrupted the moment.

Doing the gentlemanly thing, he offered his arm. "May I escort you to the dining hall?"

To his surprise, she accepted, looping her arm through his. "Considering you don't know where it is, perhaps it should be *I* who escorts *you*."

"Fair enough."

There was no more banter between them as they walked. But the closer they came to the aromatic scent of a home cooked meal, the tighter her grip on his arm became. A better man would have found something comforting to say to her. But Aeden wasn't that sort of man. Instead, he enjoyed the way she was clinging to him. There was something contradictory about her. A woman who was quick to tell him off. One who would bravely face mortals wielding expertly carved stakes. Yet she trembled at the prospect of attending a dinner with him.

He suspected her family had sent him the invitation as some sort of desperate peace offering. Hoping to make things right between them in the event that more mortals came into Gwyar's Crimson Forest. Perhaps Reinar and his people were even weaker than they looked. It would make sense that they would be frightened and looking for help in case more witch-blessed humans attacked. But what was Tessa's agenda? Family loyalty meant a lot to him, so he supposed he could understand if that was why she, too, had accepted. But surely, she'd had different hopes for herself and who she would gain as a future husband.

They entered the dining room side by side. It was far more extravagant than the one at home. But the silver mirror above the fireplace and some of the candle holders had lost their luster. Though the staff had done a meticulous job of keeping away cobwebs and dust, it wasn't enough to hide the impact of time.

When he and Tessa approached the table, the thin, shaking man—the one they called Talos—scurried to pull Tessa's chair out for her, but Aeden shooed him off. The man hopped back and looked as if he might cry. Aeden recognized him from the masquerade. He'd been so frazzled that Aeden thought Marcos had done something unspeakable. Turns out it was just Talos' nature. Honestly, it made Aeden tense just to look at him. Maybe he should slip the poor man the flask he had hidden in his jacket. Anything to calm those nerves.

But he didn't get the chance. Everyone's eyes were on him, even Tessa's. He swiftly pulled the chair out for Tessa himself, then took the seat beside her. Marcos grinned at him from across the table and Balis sat stiff as a board beside him.

Reinar, of course, was at the head of the table with his son to his left and Tessa's mother at his right. The right-hand side was a place of immense honor. How strange that his son wasn't the one sitting in the position of an adviser. It brought Aeden a warm sense of pleasure. Drake was a scoundrel, there was no denying it. And his own family seemed to agree, even if they didn't realize it.

Reinar raised a glass. "A toast. To our esteemed guests, who have accepted our invitation in good faith. Let us view this as a gift. One that will bring our families together after so much time apart."

"Here! Here!" Marcos laughed as he drained his cup.

Aeden wished the table wasn't so wide so he could kick him. Being a sarcastic ass would only make their task that much harder.

Reinar frowned in Marcos' direction, so Aeden redirected the attention to him with a clink of his glass.

He stood, smoothing his jacket down as he spoke. "To our forgiving hosts. The past is a dark path. Let us look to the light of the future." He paused, casting a smile down at Tessa. "And to the lovely Miss Downthorn. I am honored to have the chance to get to know you over the next few weeks."

Tessa watched him with an arched brow. Her eyes never left him as he sat back in his seat. He shifted under the scrutiny. Luckily, his efforts weren't lost on everyone.

Reinar smiled broadly as he announced, "Let us dine!"

Staff drifted in and out of the room during the span of two hours. Each course that was set in front of Aeden smelled and tasted delicious. Not quite how he remembered food tasting before the curse. But still, he marveled at the spices and care that went into each dish and devoured every one of them. It was rare that his family's cook put this much thought and effort into the food they prepared. Especially when it didn't provide vitality for them like blood did.

With each new food displayed before them, Aeden took care to serve Tessa first. He picked the best of everything to offer her, and she accepted it graciously. Still, there was something gloomy about her mood, like a dark cloud was hanging over her. So, he racked his brain for witty things to say.

How was he expected to seduce her if he couldn't even get her to smile? He dug into his food, using his best table manners. Each bite was like a small reward. At least if his father's plan turned out to be a flop, Aeden would have spent the month dining like this.

Tessa, on the other hand, shoved her food around with her fork in sullen silence. Was he the cause of her lost appetite?

He swallowed a particularly tender piece of venison and opened his mouth to say something to her, but Reinar clapped his hands together loudly. He boasted, "If I may, I want to take a moment to honor our guests with a gift."

Vampyrs carried in several large crates. The scent of fresh meat drifted through the wooden slats, but more intriguing was the sharp scent of blood. Even though Aeden's belly was full, his mouth still watered.

Reinar went on, "We would like to show how serious we are about this union of our people. Starting with this offering. Our hunters had some luck today and came across a family of deer. It is spring outside of these woods, so I believe we may see some new game traveling through these parts." He nodded to Marcos and Balis. "We would like for you to take this to your uncle to distribute amongst your people. An example of the sort of partnership we hope to have in the future." With a stern look in Aeden's direction, he added, "To keep us all safe here in the Crimson Forest."

Aeden glanced at Marcos in an unspoken warning. He pressed his lips together and gave a barely noticeable shake of his head. There was no reason to say what they were thinking. Not when Reinar believed that this was a gift. In truth, his father would be annoyed by the gesture. They didn't want stale animal blood. They wanted fresh human blood. And this gesture would feel more like a slight than anything else. Whether Reinar meant it as such, it would seem to Olgar like he was trying to convince the Ashbanes and their loyalists that the way they did things was wrong.

Marcos was silent as Aeden spoke. "A truly kind gesture, Count Reinar."

With unfortunate timing, the staff brought wine glasses filled to the brim with blood. After going all day without feeding, Aeden craved it. But it was cool and bitter as it touched his lips. It was like eating soup that had been left out overnight. This was not the way his father did things. He knew when those crates arrived, he would butcher the carcasses for the meat and let the blood drain into the grass. He would not bottle and serve it to his people. He would not risk them becoming weak.

It seemed like such a waste when it was clear that the Down-thorns and their loyalists needed it to survive. His father would get more humans to feed on one way or another. Olgar was always willing to take bigger risks than Count Reinar was. Happy to break the rules if it meant keeping themselves in peak condition. But between Reinar's rules and how scarce game and travelers had become in the forest, the Downthorns needed to stock up when they had the chance.

Aeden wasn't here to see to it that they were fed right, though. He was there to gain their favor. Keeping his thoughts to himself, he did his best not to breathe through his nose as he gulped down the blood. It barely did any good, but he was at least able to stomach it with a straight face. Marcos and Balis followed suit.

After that, the rest of the dinner passed by quickly. Aeden enjoyed the quiet relief that they had gotten through several courses without incident. Once the dessert plates were cleared away, Reinar announced that they would retire to the library for drinks.

The thought of mixing his cousins and alcohol didn't sit well with him. Not when they would be in close quarters with Drake. But there wasn't much he could say without offending Reinar, so he followed them to the door.

He was the last to reach it, and before he could step into the hall, Tessa stopped suddenly. He nearly slammed into her, but she didn't shrink away. Instead, she placed a firm hand on his chest. Raising her chin with authority, she said, "This is going to be a long month. So I think it's important for us to be honest with each other."

Aeden gulped. Had he done something during dinner to indicate that he was being dishonest? His cousins had behaved themselves. Much better than Aeden anticipated. And he himself had done everything in his power to appear charming.

He assured her, "I agree."

The others must not have noticed their absence, because no one called for them or came looking. Still, Tessa lowered her voice as she said, "Good. It's just... I can't go any further in good conscience without telling you that I have no intention of this being more than an arrangement benefiting both of our families."

Tension dissipated from his shoulders. So, she didn't suspect him after all. This was about *her* being honest. Not him. Now that he knew he wasn't in trouble, he processed her statement. "You mean you have no intention of this being a romantic match?"

"Exactly." She bit her lip.

Was she afraid he would react badly to the news? It might be a good idea to appear disappointed in order to keep up the ruse. In truth, though, it might pose a problem if she was completely closed to the idea of falling in love. After all, what better way to make a woman trust a man? But if she was already willing to go through with the courtship, then maybe he wouldn't have to worry about making her fall for him. He would simply have to shift his plans. Gain her trust through friendship.

"The prospect of being in a loveless marriage doesn't deter you?" he asked, needing to know just how closed off she was going to be over the course of their courtship. It's not like he had any intention of coming there to find love. But he needed to know if she would stand in his way as he tried to insert himself into her household.

"Love only leads to heartbreak." Her words were raw, and he knew without a doubt that she believed what she was saying.

It was surprising. What could have left her so jaded? He tucked the question aside for another time. At least their view of love was one thing they could agree on. He just wasn't sure yet if that would be a good or a bad thing.

Thirteen

Aeden

A eden ambled along the corridor. The others had already reached the library, leaving him with his spinning thoughts. He knew he should take advantage of every opportunity to charm the Downthorns, but spending time with the entire family also meant ample time for him to slip up. Wooing Tessa was one thing, but the rest of them? It seemed Reinar was good at presenting himself in an agreeable manner. But when taking the history between their families into account, it left Aeden with a bad taste in his mouth. Almost as bad as the aftertaste of the blood they served.

Tessa's mother was pleasant enough, too. But each time he caught her eye at dinner, it had felt like she was peering into his very soul. Like she might see right through his act if she looked hard enough.

The hallway was quiet, with most of the household staff dismissed for their own dinner. The doors to the study were closed, but two figures at the end of the hall grabbed his attention. Aeden's eyes struggled to sharpen enough to see through the dark shadows—an unsettling side effect of not feeding from the vein since that morning. But as he neared, he could make out Drake's massive frame towering over a smaller, plump woman. The mortal from earlier... Odessa.

She stood with her back pressed against the wall, as if hoping to shrink away into the shadows. Aeden was too far away to catch what Drake was saying to her, but the hairs on his arms rose on end. The woman trembled from head to toe.

Aeden picked up his pace, getting close enough to hear Drake say, "You'll do as you're told. It wouldn't be wise to cross me." He shoved her hard in the shoulder and she let out a tiny whine.

Still a bully. Drake was twice the size of Odessa and the disgust dripping in his voice was enough to set even Aeden on edge. "Is there a problem?" he interrupted. He might have wanted to sink his fangs into her earlier in the hall, but Drake was clearly taunting her simply because he could. It wasn't as if Aeden's family treated humans any better. But seeing Drake behaving in the same manner got under his skin. This was a man who pretended to be *better* than him. Yet here he was, mistreating those who were under his care.

Drake glared at Aeden and drew back from Odessa. Wordlessly, he turned and stalked into the library. The sniffling woman mustered a smile in Aeden's direction, but as she walked by, her legs visibly trembled.

Aeden understood the importance of feeding on mortals to maintain their vitality. Because of that, it was easy for Vampyrs to dehumanize them. To view them as nothing more than walking supper. That didn't make it right, though. And in this instance, it seemed like Drake was actively going out of his way to pick on those he deemed smaller and weaker than him. For what? Entertainment? It certainly wasn't for his own survival.

Aeden grumbled to himself as he pushed open the door. The library was the darkest room in the Downthorn chateau. It helped the tension in his shoulders dissipate. He breathed in deeply, reveling in the musty smell of old books that reminded him of home. He decided immediately that this was by far his favorite room in Tessa's house. It must have been one of her favorites too, because her face had brightened, making her seem much more comfortable than she'd been in the dining room.

Flora was already hard at work, serving drinks to everyone. As she handed Marcos a glass, he said something that brought a smile to her lips. Aeden wasn't sure he had seen a genuine smile from the cold woman yet. It made the resemblance between her and Tessa more evident. They had the same full lips and a sparkle in their eyes when they deigned to grace everyone with it.

Aeden followed the tall bookshelves around the room, noting the titles. Books on the histories of Elfhame and the Unseelie Courts, stories about love and romance, even a few about the mortal realm, lined the shelves. But what really caught his eye was the grand piano in the corner of the room.

Shadows were cast over it, even though it was near the moonlit window. And a thin veil of dust settled over the once polished wood. He ran a gloved finger over it and his heart ached for the abandoned piece. Something this beautiful should be put to use, not left forgotten. He itched to lift the cover and reveal the keys, but Flora fluttered over to him with a drink in hand.

She offered it to him and softly said, "It's beautiful, isn't it? It belonged to Tessa's father."

"Oh, I didn't realize." He snatched his hand away from it. Tessa had accused his father of being responsible for his death. But Aeden admittedly didn't remember much about what happened. He knew the Downthorns blamed them, but wasn't sure why Tessa thought it was Olgar's fault directly. And he wasn't about to ask. Not when he was there to make them forget the animosity.

Flora's eyes grew hard and distant as she stared down at the piano and Aeden shifted uncomfortably. There was nothing he could say to make her feel better. That sort of grief wouldn't be cured with a few smart remarks or thin words of sympathy.

Snapping out of her daze, Flora asked, "Do you play?"

He thought of the violin tucked safely in the bottom of his trunk upstairs. "No," he replied. It was a lie. He had practiced piano as a child. Although he'd enjoyed it, it didn't come close to the way he felt with a violin bow in his hands.

"Oh," was all she said before excusing herself to join Reinar by the fire.

Aeden ignored Drake's seething gaze as he walked over to Tessa. Marcos and Balis flanked her, making her look very small between the two towering men. There was a pleasant mask of indifference on her face as she listened to Marcos drone on about how fascinating he thought the masquerade had been. Balis chimed in with a word or two every once in a while. It was hard to get a word in when Marcos wanted to be the center of attention.

As Aeden approached them, he noted the slight, grateful smile from Tessa. He might not be able to make her fall in love with him, but he could at least save her from his kin. He placed himself between her and Marcos and asked, "What did I miss?"

Tessa spoke up. "Marcos was just telling me what a talented dancer he is."

Aeden joked, "Ah, so he's over here telling tall tales."

He was rewarded with a laugh from her and a scowl from Marcos.

Aeden continued to goad him. "Now little Balis, on the other hand..." He gestured to his younger cousin, who took the opportunity to place his hands on his hips as he moved like a squirrel shimmying up a tree.

Tessa barked with laughter, drawing the attention of everyone in the room. Even her own mother looked as shocked as Aeden felt at the sudden outburst. Drake's face reddened as if the simple fact that his cousin might enjoy herself in Aeden's company filled him with rage. Noticing all eyes on him, Balis blushed deeply and stilled. Placing his hands behind his back, he took a bow.

Tessa dipped into a courtesy and before anyone stopped him, Balis took hold of her hands and drew her into a lively dance. The ones Aeden and his cousins had witnessed in the mortal villages. He looped his arm around Tessa's and began to spin her around the room. Her face was soon flushed as she tried to keep in step with him. Aeden couldn't take his eyes off her. She was beautiful.

Not in the dangerously mysterious way that Rose was. No. Tessa's beauty was something truer. Something that required little effort on her part. It came as naturally to her as it did to the flowers in the garden. Like she was meant to shine. If she could just shake that storm cloud that seemed to follow her around, sullying her mood. Aeden bit his cheek at the rising tinge of guilt. Would he be responsible for bringing a larger storm into her life?

He glanced at Reinar. The Count gave the impression of a genuinely nice man. A little high-strung, but there was a softer side to him when he was around his family. Even now, he clapped to the beat of Tessa and Balis' steps, encouraging the fun.

Aeden's gaze fell back to Tessa, who seemed to be genuinely enjoying the dance. A grin spread across his face. If she had belonged to any other family, Aeden could picture her fitting in just fine with the Vampyrs on his side of the Crimson Lake. She and Balis appeared to be having the time of their lives, and he found himself admiring it. Regardless of her prenotions about his family, she was putting in an effort.

This might be more difficult than he thought. There was no doubt he would charm her and the other Downthorns if given the time. But how was he going to make it to the next full moon without befriending them in return? He cursed his father under his breath. To send him into this home with ill intent seemed cruel now that he had spent some time with them. And when the moment presented itself, would he really have the stomach to go through with the assassination? Was he clever enough to think of an alternative to murder?

Drake growled from across the room, breaking through Aeden's thoughts. Killing Reinar might give him pause when the time came, but Drake might be a different story. The Downthorn heir watched Tessa and Balis with disgust.

As if unable to stand the sight of his cousin enjoying herself with an Ashbane any longer, Drake shouted, "Enough!"

Balis and Tessa skidded to a stop. Drake crossed the room on a rampage, knocking over a small end table and a chair. Tessa's face paled, and she shouted at him as he shoved Balis away from her.

Blinding, red rage filled Aeden. Before he could stop himself, he was shoving Drake into the wall. There was another crash as they knocked furniture out of their path. And then Marcos was there. Aeden spotted the swing coming from the corner of his eye as he held Drake in place by the collar. He ducked, and Drake's fist connected with Marcos instead.

Swiftly, Marcos reared back and slammed his head into Drake's face. The crunch of bone turned Aeden's stomach, and then the stench of blood filled the room. It poured from Drake's broken nose, but it didn't slow him. Tessa's cousin tackled Marcos to the floor, and he wrapped his massive hands around Aeden's cousin's throat.

It took all of Aeden's strength to pull Drake off of him. Where did this strength come from? Drake was a colossal brute, but Aeden didn't expect him to be as strong considering the way they fed. Marcos' eyes rolled in his head as he was freed of Drake's grip and he gasped for air. Before Aeden or Drake could react, Reinar had them both roughly by the collars. He shoved them in opposite directions, sending Aeden stumbling into Tessa. She caught hold of his arm and kept him from falling to the floor. Her rapid breathing reached his ears, but he wasn't sure if it was her fear for her cousin or his that had her in such a panic.

Drake shouted in a rage, "You are all imbeciles! Dancing and frolicking like we're all old friends." He pointed an accusatory finger in Tessa's direction. "You're making a fool of yourself. Acting like a trollop and throwing yourself at this scum."

Tessa pushed Aeden aside, facing her cousin with a courage that he admired. She pushed her hair back from her face. It was tangled, but still flowed beautifully down her back. Aeden held his breath, eager to see how she would deal with Drake.

She spat her words like venom as she said, "The only fool in here is *you*, dear cousin." She gestured to Aeden and his cousins. "They have done nothing today but try to show respect and decency.

Aeden is here in good faith. And, still, you let your temper rear its ugly head. It is an embarrassment."

Drake bared his fangs, and for a moment, Aeden thought he might attack her next. Instinct moved him and placed him in front of Tessa. Surprise flickered in Drake's eyes as he sized Aeden up.

Then Reinar commanded, "Drake. Leave. Now."

With one last sneer in Aeden's direction, Drake spun on his heel and stormed out of the room. The door shook on its hinges as he slammed it shut behind him. Reinar was apologizing profusely, but Aeden paid him no mind. He turned to Tessa, who was trembling with anger.

"Are you alright?" he asked her.

Her nostrils flared as she stared him in the eye. "What do you think?" Then she was gone. She fled the room with her mother in tow, leaving Aeden feeling like he had dug himself into a hole he might not be able to climb out of.

So much for a night without incident.

Marcos and Balis left for home immediately after the scuffle with Drake. With a carriage loaded full of crates, they had bid Aeden and Reinar farewell. They'd overstayed their welcome. It seemed Drake's temper had been stretched thin. Having more than one Ashbane in his presence proved too much for him to handle. Aeden wished Marcos had broken more than his nose. But at the same time, it did them no good to challenge Drake at the moment. He'd get what was coming to him soon enough.

Hours later, Aeden was still restless. It had been a long time since he had slept anywhere other than in his own bed. Once he was sure everyone had gone to sleep, he ventured back downstairs. It wasn't long before he found himself back in the library alone.

It was quiet and dimly lit by the candelabra he had brought down with him. He shivered slightly and chided himself for not putting a night shirt on. His room had been warm with the fire going, but the library was frigid as the late night breeze slipped through the old window panes.

Just when he considered creeping back upstairs, the abandoned piano caught his eye. He hadn't had a chance to play his violin all day, and after such a rough end to the night, he longed to hear music. Any music. With the doors shut, he wondered if anyone would hear him if he played a few notes.

The chateau was large, and the doors were made of thick oak. So, he crept toward the bench. The wooden cover was cool under his touch as he lifted it. It creaked softly when he opened it to reveal a row of pristine ivory keys. They glistened under the glow of the candles, calling to him like a very old friend.

The first chord he played was sloppy. Its sound was striking and jarred him. But as he closed his eyes, the memory of playing in his childhood home came flooding back. It reminded him of cool autumn days and leaves crunching underfoot. A few notes from the music his mother had played with him came to mind, and soon he was recreating the haunting tune.

The melody became full and round. It warmed him, replacing the icy chill of the room. He kept his eyes shut, allowing his muscle memory to take control as he channeled everything he had into the song. Soon his body relaxed, releasing the weight of his family's plans and the fear of befriending the very people he had been sent there to destroy.

His fingers picked up their pace, running from one end of the keys to the next. But a voice echoing in the darkness caused his hand to slip and a long, deep note rang out from the piano. He drew back quickly, jarred by the sudden ugly tune, and opened his eyes.

Tessa's face was filled with shock. She looked out of place in the middle of the dark room, dressed in her white nightgown. Almost like a ghost who had wandered in unknowingly. The only thing covering the soft curves of her body was the embroidered wrap that hung loosely around her shoulders. He stood abruptly, realizing how strange him sitting at her father's piano must have looked to her.

Her voice was small as she asked, "What are you doing?"

"I couldn't sleep." He gently closed the piano's cover and shuffled around to the side. "I didn't mean to wake you."

"You didn't." She crossed her arms stubbornly. "I was looking for you, but you weren't in your room."

Even though he knew she wasn't implying anything scandalous, it would be fun to tease her as if she had. "Oh?" He raised a suggestive eyebrow.

"I... you..." He loved when she fumbled for her words around him. There was something deeply satisfying about it.

He took a few steps toward her. Her gaze ran from his chest to his waist and a bright blush formed on her cheeks. He bit back a smile.

She cleared her throat and glanced away. "Could you maybe put a shirt on?"

Aeden smirked and stepped even closer to her. "Why?"

Her nightgown was thin and through the gaps in the wrap, he could see how it clung to her. Heat filled his chest, and now his fingers itched to play her instead of the piano. Had she ever been alone with a man like this before? The prospect of her and another gave him a small pang of jealousy, but he ignored it.

She shook her head, and her eyes snapped to his. "Because I am trying to tell you how furious you make me. How you didn't need to lower yourself to Drake's level and how tonight was a total disaster, but this," she paused with a huff and gestured wildly at his body before continuing, "is distracting."

"Distracting?" Aeden took another step and was surprised when she didn't move away. She might be closed to love, but would she be closed to other things? Would it be so wrong to find a little enjoyment in one another during his stay?

She faltered at her words with her mouth gaping, and finally, he relented. "I don't have a shirt down here. I didn't expect to have company."

Tessa crossed her arms over her chest. "Fine."

"And since you've basically said what you came here to say, why don't you join me for a drink instead?" She shot him a skeptical look, so he added, "You can berate me while we drink if you'd like."

With a sigh, she headed for the small green sofa by the fireplace and flopped down on it. Aeden started the fire, stacking three perfect logs on top of one another. Then he poured a drink for the two of them and joined her. She released a startled gasp as he sat beside her instead of taking up one of the other chairs.

The sofa was cozy, made for only two. Which left them sitting close enough for their legs to touch. She was stiff as a board beside him as he reached behind her to rest his arm on the sofa's head. He, on the other hand, was feeling more relaxed than when he'd arrived. The whiskey he had poured was strong and smooth, burning his chest as it went down.

He followed her gaze to the large painting over the mantle. It showed the destroyers—Byron and Ayana—hand in hand on the border of the Winter and Autumn Courts in Elfhame. Behind Ayana was a blanket of sparkling white snow, and behind Byron was a leaf strewn field, vivid with oranges and browns. The artist had somehow found a way to convey love in the way the two of them stared at one another. It twisted Aeden's stomach into knots.

With a grimace, he asked, "There seem to be a lot of paintings of them here in the house. Why is that?" There wasn't a trace of Byron and Ayana in his own home. The curse was enough to remember the ones who had caused it.

With her eyes still fixed on the painting, Tessa replied, "It serves as a reminder of what we lost and what we hope to reclaim one day."

Honest. He'd give her that. If not a little naïve. He gulped down the remainder of his whiskey. "If not for being stuck in this forest, the curse wouldn't be so bad, would it?" He stopped to study her reaction. Her pursed lips told him she disagreed. So, he elaborated, "I mean, we have strength, precision, abilities that place us high on the food chain. If we accepted what we are, then we would have more power than we ever did in Elfhame."

Even though she was quiet, her silence said enough. Her uncle's views were engrained in her. Making her ashamed of what they were. Or maybe it was that she didn't fully understand what the curse had to offer her because she had only ever experienced its full effects once—when she fed on the human after the masquerade.

He shrugged. "It could have been worse."

Tessa scoffed and turned to him with an incredulous look. "Worse than being expelled from our home and having our magic twisted into something ugly?"

Aeden winced as flashes of a memory tucked away long ago came to mind. The King with a horned crown on his head, casting his shadows out at the men trying to flee. Aeden riding on horseback behind his father. His mother shouting at him to not look back at the ones lost to them.

With a heavy sigh, he said, "We could have been enslaved like the others who didn't make it out. I saw what he did to them." He leaned forward, resting his elbows on his legs and gazing into the fire. Bits of memory continued to spark in his mind. Shadow magic striking the men in their chests. Burrowing into their hearts and twisting them into something far worse than a Vampyr. Darkening their souls until there was nothing left of who they once were.

Finally, he said, "At least we still have our souls."

Tessa leaned in close to him until her arm brushed against his. The thin, soft fabric of her nightgown kissing his bare skin sent shivers down his back. Pulling his gaze away from the dancing fire, he looked at her. There was pain and sympathy reflected in her eyes, but there was also something hard in the way she pressed her lips together and set her jaw.

She spoke gently as she said, "Do we? Just look at how easily we turn to our murderous instincts."

Aeden pitied her for seeing things that way. It was true that they'd been cursed, but they'd also been given an opportunity. One where they might thrive if given the chance in the mortal realm. His mouth was dry as he guessed, "You feel bad about feeding on that man in the woods. And you're ashamed of what we are. I get it. But is that how *you* feel or how *they* have made you feel?"

She frowned as he gave a quick nod to the family portrait hanging to the right of them. In one swift movement, she downed her whiskey, then flopped back against the sofa. "Perhaps you're right. Maybe I did enjoy how drinking blood from that man's neck made me feel. But I don't want to live like that. Putting what I want before everything else. What matters is that we keep our families safe and hold on to any shred of dignity we have left." The next words came as a whisper. "It's what my father would have wanted."

Aeden didn't know what to say to that. He was too drained from the day and lack of acceptable blood to engage in another argument with her. Nor could he bring himself to defend his father at the moment.

"Can I ask about it?" Tessa gestured to his tattoos and bit her lip.

Aeden chuckled. Of course, she was curious. Having ink pricked into your skin was a very human thing to do. When you lived as long as his people did, marking your body was a risky commitment. He shrugged, thinking back to the day he'd decided to do it. "The easy explanation... Marcos and a *lot* of poorly brewed ale."

Tessa smirked. "And the not so easy explanation?"

Aeden raised his arm in front of him, turning it over to reveal the way the vines twisted all the way around, snaking up his arm to his neck, shoulders and chest. He'd never shared the meaning behind them. When Marcos had asked, he'd simply given some flippant response about it looking interesting.

But Tessa's interest and the heat from the fire sparked something in him. "It's so I don't forget." She remained silent, as if giving him the room he needed to muster up the courage to explain further. It worked. And he finished, "So I don't forget where we came from. And what keeps us from returning."

Boldly, she reached out, tracing her finger along the thorny vines. It was like lightning flashing across the sky. Exhilarating. He held his breath and was disappointed when she stopped as she came to his upper arm.

Her voice was wistful as she asked, "Do you wish we could return?"

Truthfully, he answered, "Sometimes."

"Do you think we could?"

The hope in her eyes was almost more than he was able to bear. He didn't want to be the one to snuff it out. But he also did not want to lie to her. "For a time, I did. I believe it less than I used to, though. I have my father to thank for that." He winced at the memory of Olgar doling out punishments to him and Marcos whenever they spoke of going back to Elfhame. And how adamant his father was that they adapt to what they were now.

He shivered as she removed her hand from his arm. The silence settled heavily between them. The fire crackled, casting a warm glow onto Tessa's face. In such a short time, he'd seen different sides of her that he could appreciate. Fierce in the forest, fun and light when she danced with Balis in the library, and reflective here tonight. What could she do with her life if her family would release the hold they had on her?

After a while, Tessa stood and smoothed down her nightgown. Aeden followed quickly. Part of him wanted to ask her to stay. But how could he? It wasn't like he could explain to her that her presence was a pleasant distraction from his own thoughts. That it was the only thing drowning out the sound of his father's voice telling him he would soon have to kill in order to save them all.

Voiceless, he watched her walk to the door. With her hand resting on the handle, she turned back to him and the corner of her mouth quirked up slightly. "Please don't stoop to Drake's level next time. The two of you can at least *try* not to kill each other."

Aeden struggled to smile at the jest. If only she knew. His heart raced as he nodded and said, "Good night, Tessa."

Fourteen

Tessa

A n entire day and night had passed, and Tessa hadn't seen
Aeden. After the fight with Drake, she supposed he was attempting to give them some space. But she couldn't help wondering if it also had something to do with their midnight rendezvous.
He hadn't seemed put off when she asked him to play nice with
her cousin. She tried to replay the night in her mind, but couldn't
think of anything else she might have done to offend him.

Yet, it was another new day and once again, Aeden wasn't at
breakfast. And he was absent again for lunch, which disappointed

Tessa more than she expected. They were supposed to spend time together, after all. Even if she didn't have any designs to fall in love with him, she still intended to get to know the man she would be saddled with for the rest of her immortal life.

Reinar walked with her through the hall leading away from the parlor. He shrugged. "Maybe he's allowing you your space. Waiting for you to come to him."

"Well, do you know where he is?" Tessa twisted her hair around her finger. It appeared she'd have to track him down herself.

"Talos said he's been coming to the kitchens to get his meals. Says he's taking them down to the stables." Reinar raised his eyebrow, and a smile crept across his face. "Were you looking forward to seeing him today? I admit I wasn't sure how you would be feeling after the other night's events."

Tessa scrunched her nose. "That night was unfortunate..."

She knew her uncle was referring to the fight in the library because he had no idea she'd been alone with Aeden later in the night. Honestly, she hadn't intended to stay for as long as she did. The only reason she had gone searching for him was because she hoped to settle things between him and Drake. Her cousin was uncontrollable. So asking Aeden to try to keep the peace seemed like the more reasonable route. As far as Ashbanes went, he appeared to be willing to at least listen to what others had to say.

"But?" Her uncle narrowed his eyes, waiting for her to continue.

"But you have asked me to make an effort, and that is what I intend to do. We have a limited amount of time for the courtship." She bit the inside of her cheek. What if he was avoiding her because he was no longer interested? It wasn't a heart breaking scenario, but where would that leave their people? Most likely with another dead body in the woods and more witch-blessed humans sniffing around.

Parting quickly with her uncle, Tessa headed down to the barn. A woman in the enthralls of the idea of love and an engagement would have opted to bring him some baked goods or something. Wasn't that what people did? But not her. She strutted with determination. Intending to make it clear to him that this wasn't going to work if they avoided each other like a bad plague.

The stables were a short trek down the hill and were normally one of her favorite places to spend the day. The stone building was larger than the ones most of their loyalists maintained. Her family had always taken pride in their herds and doted on the horses they kept. Even when the bloodlust cramped their stomachs, the horses were off limits. To drain blood from creatures they considered family was too barbaric.

Galahad—the tall shire horse her uncle had gifted to her—was out of the pasture, drinking from a large trough. Tessa's temper rose, seeing her horse out when she wasn't around. He was a temperamental steed, and most of the stable boys were nervous around him. Especially since he towered over even the tallest Vampyrs on the estate. With a look in all directions, she prepared to scold whoever had been foolish enough to leave him standing alone in the open like that.

Seeing no one, she sidled up to Galahad. "Hey old boy, what are you doing out here?"

A whinny was the only response she got. She scratched at his midnight black coat and he pulled his head from the trough, splashing the entire front of her dress with water from his mouth. She jumped back, patting at the light blue fabric, but it was no use. The water had soaked her, leaving the dress nearly see-through.

She cursed at the big oaf and took a deep breath to control her temper.

There was hearty laughter coming from the other side of Galahad, and Tessa ducked under his neck to see who it was. Aeden was holding a bale of hay with a stupid smile plastered on his face. The inky black pattern of blackthorns showed through his shirt, which was unbuttoned. Couldn't the man just stay fully clothed like the rest of them?

"I see he got you too." Aeden chuckled and pointed to her chest.

The light, wet fabric did little to hide the chemise she wore underneath. The low cut one with tiny yellow flowers. Was it possible for a blush to spread across one's entire body? Heat flooded all the way to her toes as she stood totally exposed.

She turned to leave, but Aeden stopped her. "Wait, don't go. Here..."

Tessa froze in place as a jacket was placed over her shoulders. She pulled it around her, covering her chest, and turned back to Aeden. He looked very pleased with himself, but she wouldn't give him the satisfaction of thanking him.

Instead, she inquired, "Was it you who let him out?" She nodded to Galahad, who was grazing on the nearby grass.

"He was marching along the fence line. Figured he wanted to join me."

"And he didn't give you any trouble?"

"Should he have?" Aeden's voice dripped with genuine confusion.

Tessa failed to hide her surprise with a raised eyebrow. Galahad would have taken off or made a mess of things around the barn if anyone else had given him this much freedom. Anyone except for her.

"It's just odd for him to behave for anyone other than me." She hugged Aeden's jacket tighter around her. What did Galahad's opinion of Aeden say about the man? Typically, it would have been an honor. But she wasn't keen to grant it to him. Not until she knew why he was avoiding her.

"You were missed at breakfast." She walked back over to the trough, eager to put some distance between her and Aeden's bare torso. His pants hung low along his waist, and she did everything in her power to keep her eyes from trailing down. "And at lunch," she added.

"You missed me?" He practically purred.

She spun to face him again. "No. I mean... We're supposed to be courting one another. I figured that meant spending time together."

"Aren't you afraid that too much intimate time between us might lead to deeper feelings? You said yourself you have no intention of falling in love." There was nothing negative in the way he said it. Just open curiosity. He studied her face intently, and she looked away, trying to avoid his stare.

"That doesn't mean I want my husband to be a stranger to me."

Aeden stepped closer to her, and she took an evasive step around the trough, keeping the container between them.

There was a glint in his eye, like he thought this was some sort of game, and he asked, "Am I making you uncomfortable?"

Her foot itched to kick him in the shins. He was lucky the trough was standing in her way. She tried to come up with something witty, yet uninsulting to say, but her mind was blank.

Instead, she said, "This whole arrangement is uncharted terri-tory for me. You might have the experience in this sort of thing, but I—"

He clucked his teeth as he interrupted her. "I have never court-ed a woman, per se."

The implication was clear. He had experience in other areas when it came to women. Again, heat crept along her arms and back. This wasn't a game to her.

"Can't you be serious for just one minute?" she snapped.

With his hands on the trough, he circled around until he was beside her. "Seriously, I didn't know how much of me you wanted to see. I thought yesterday I would give you some space, and then today at breakfast and lunch, I was honestly just trying to avoid another run in with Drake. I don't know him well enough to know how long it takes for him to cool off."

Tessa rolled her eyes. "Longer than most, actually." Drake had been sulking for the last two days. He hadn't spoken a word to her or the others. And after each meal, he retired to his room, demanding not to be disturbed.

"See, then there is nothing for you to take offense of where I'm concerned." His proximity to her became shorter and shorter with every word he spoke.

Tessa fought the urge to flee. It was becoming painfully clear that Aeden was unpredictable. A few weeks didn't seem nearly long enough for her to bond with him.

His hand brushed along her arm, and she flinched at the unwel-come butterflies fluttering in her stomach. Her voice was strained as she asked, "What are you doing?"

"You said you want us to get to know each other." He leaned down until he was only inches away from her.

"You misinterpret my words."

"Or maybe you, like your Galahad, just need to be let loose for a bit." Those dimples presented themselves again as he smiled, making it hard for Tessa to step away like she knew she should.

"Did you just compare me to a horse?" Her pulse quickened as Aeden's eyes trailed down to her lips.

With a mischievous whisper, he teased, "Better than a timid little doe, is it not?"

The statement struck her deeper than she expected. Who was he to insinuate that she was timid? Tessa's shoulders rose and fell quickly with each breath. Aeden's intentions were clear. So why was she still standing here entertaining it? This was too forward. Too inappropriate. It was bad enough that they had shared a drink and a moment in the library the other night. But was she really about to let him kiss her?

Between the brisk breeze outside and the warmth of his body so close to hers, her head spun. Thoughts warred in her mind. Would kissing him be so bad? What if he was right, and she needed to let loose a bit? After all, it might be fun. Except that he had spent the last day and a half ignoring her. And his big grin made it seem like this was all some grand joke to him.

Just when she thought things couldn't get more confusing, he leaned in for the kiss. Alarm bells rang out in her head and she jolted back. "What are you doing?"

Aeden's expression was smooth as he asked, "Aren't you curious what it would be like?"

Her body was screaming yes. She tilted her head back slightly and then chided herself. This was wildly inappropriate. But what harm could one little kiss do? Overcome with trying to decide between right and wrong, she eyed him warily. As he went in again, she pulled away.

Aeden's laugh was similar to the deep notes on the piano he had been playing the other night when she walked in and, to her dismay, he asked, "Would you just hold still?"

She steadied herself. He was quite possibly the most frustrating and intriguing man she had come across. There hadn't been an ounce of judgment from him since she met him at the masquerade. Not when she fed on the mortal man and not when she unleashed her temper on him.

Uncertainty clouded his face, and for a moment, Tessa thought she saw fear. Was he worried he had gone too far? It dawned on her that she was, in fact, curious. She'd never kissed anyone before. And in this moment, she wanted to be bold. Longed to do the unexpected. Before he could pull away, she reached up on her tippy toes and pressed her lips to his. As if he were afraid to move too fast for her, he gently ran his hands through her hair, tangling his fingers in the silky strands.

Her fangs scraped against his mouth as she clumsily dragged her teeth along his lower lip. But he must have taken it as her permission to deepen the kiss. They stumbled toward the watering trough, and he pressed his body against hers. They fit together like a puzzle. Heat rose between her legs, and she suppressed a small moan.

Galahad's loud, angry snort startled her out of the moment. In a panic, she pulled back with nowhere to go but into the trough. Instinctively, she grabbed onto Aeden's shirt. There was an abrupt sound of fabric tearing, and then the splash came.

Icy water filled her mouth and her nose as Aeden's body toppled on top of hers, pushing her further under. Their limbs tangled together as they both tried to get up. Finally, sitting upright, Tessa pushed her hair from her face. Water dripped from her nose and lips. But as Aeden shook his soaked head, her embarrassment set in. Hard and fast.

This was what she got for trying to let her hair down with someone like him. Her first kiss and it was a total disaster. She climbed from the trough, ignoring his offer to help her. Once they were both standing on solid ground again, soaked to the bone, Tessa's irritation rose.

She twisted the bottom of her dress, attempting to get as much water out of it as she could. Without looking at him, she declared, "This was a mistake."

Aeden argued, "I wouldn't go that far."

Tessa gestured to herself. "Look at me." Then, gesturing wildly at him, she added, "Look at you!" She twisted her hair next and water fell from it like a faucet. "I wish you would stop pushing my buttons. Just because I'm not as experienced as you does not mean I'm *timid* or don't know how to let loose. I've made it this far in life following the rules, and the second I listen to you, everything falls into chaos."

Aeden scoffed. "Oh, please. I saw you at the masquerade. You tripped that wait staff on purpose. Caused plenty of chaos just to get out of a simple dance."

She shook her head defiantly. "That's different. Nobody gets hurt when I do those things."

"Surely what I do is not that bad." Aeden had the good sense to look a tad bit remorseful as the smile fell from his lips.

"How is this ever going to work when we're so different?"

Panic flickered in his eyes. "It will work, Tessa."

Still skeptical, she pressed her lips into a firm line. This would have been easier with someone like Lord Peitor. Someone who knew their ways and followed the rules. She tapped her wet boot on the muddy ground. "No. Aeden, you are," she paused. *Pompous, self-centered...* which word should she pick to finish that sentence?

He spoke before she could choose. "I think you're scared. Because there's a spark of something here. Why else would I get under your skin so easily?" He smirked at her. "Personally, I think this tension between us could be quite beautiful if you gave it a chance."

Tessa scowled. Frustration turned to anger boiling in her veins. He wasn't taking her seriously. He strolled over to Galahad. With a pat on the neck, he started to steer him toward the pasture. Tessa shivered in the cool breeze. She needed to change before she froze.

"Joke all you want. This isn't over." She stomped away in her wet, squeaky boots.

Aeden's voice echoed through the field as he shouted to her, "Thank the stars! I don't think my heart could take it if it was."

She let out a low, frustrated growl. He knew very well that she was referring to the conversation. *Infuriating.* That was the word she should have used to describe him. If they were to spend a lifetime together, it was unlikely they'd both make it out in one piece.

Tessa couldn't make up her mind. Did she want to kiss the man or gouge his eyes out? She paced in front of her balcony door, dressed down to her undergarments. No one was able to see her from there, but she could discern the distant shape of Aeden still down at the stables.

If only she had the self control to keep calm and collected around him, rather than making a total and utter fool of herself. She'd gone to search for him. Yet she was the one who ran away. She had one task—charm him—and she couldn't even do that.

Instead, he baited her, and she showed him a clumsy, frightened version of herself.

She groaned. Storming off and hiding in her room wasn't going to help her family. It wasn't going to convince him that she was someone worth listening to. Where would that leave them? With more bodies dropping in the woods. More mortals sniffing around.

Trying to ignore her embarrassment, she pulled on a fresh dress and tied her hair back in a low bun. It was still damp, so she tied a silk scarf around it. Then, with all the class and grace she had left, she marched back down to the barn.

Aeden was leaning against the stables with that same swagger that said *the world is my playground and you're here for my amusement.* Something that had intrigued her at the masquerade when they first met. But now reality set in and that sort of fun wasn't her style.

He didn't even have the good grace to appear at all surprised that she had returned.

Tessa gritted her teeth. *You're doing this for your family,* she reminded herself. Mustering a forced apology, she huffed, "I was wrong for storming off. Can we try this again?"

He raised a suggestive eyebrow. "The kiss?"

"No. The spending time together."

"Alright then." He spun on his heel, heading into the barn.

"Alright what?" She called out to him, but all she got in response was the sound of buckets being thrown around in the stables. An excited nickering echoed down the rows of stalls. Each horse was eager to be picked for whatever it was that Aeden had in mind. Far more eager than she was.

With her arms crossed, she tapped her foot impatiently. Galahad nudged her gently in the arm. Ignoring him would only result in more bad behavior, so she scratched beneath the thick forelock, pushing the hair aside so she could get to his favorite spot. His coat was shining and smooth. She wondered if Aeden had brushed him. Most of the stable hands weren't brave enough to try.

Aeden returned a moment later with Reinar's stout horse, Sunny. He was a gentle soul with a gorgeous coat of white and big inky black spots. It looked as if someone had splashed paint on him by accident. Sunny was so easy to ride that you didn't even need a harness or saddle. Which, by the looks of it, Aeden sensed as well. He wrapped a soft rope around Sunny's head, creating a non-abrasive head piece. One that would give him control if needed, but not so much that Sunny couldn't take a bit of it back for himself.

Tessa watched Aeden as he mounted the horse with an expert swing of his body. She grabbed a nearby harness, placing it on Galahad, and inquired, "No saddle?"

Aeden graced her with a boyish grin. "Didn't think we'd need them. If you want, I can—"

"No," Tessa said quickly. If he wanted to ride bareback, then she would do the same. She, however, was far too short to mount Galahad from the ground, even with Vampyr abilities. She pulled him over to the stump that her uncle had placed there for her and used it to get a leg up.

Galahad whinnied in satisfaction. Ready for adventure, as always. Tessa ran her fingers through his mane and gave him a gentle warning. "Go easy. Just a little stroll."

With his usual sass, Galahad kicked at the dirt with his hind leg. Then, with a jolt, started a nice and gentle walk. Aeden and Sunny joined at their side and they rode in comfortable silence for a while.

Tessa swore she could feel Aeden's eyes on her, but she was desperate not to let him catch her stealing a glance. Instead, she trained her eyes straight ahead. It was a nice enough day, and she felt immensely better now that she was in dry clothes.

Aeden challenged her, "Care to race?"

Tessa scoffed. Sunny would never beat Galahad. No matter how capable a rider Aeden might be. She was ready to deny the request, that is, until she caught the cocky smirk on his face. Galahad knew her well. No words needed to be spoken. All it took was a squeeze of her thighs and they were off. Galahad took his cue and literally ran with it. His hooves trumpeted across the ground like he was a steed stampeding through the sky with the Wild Hunt.

Aeden shouted, "Cheater!" Then, with a whoop, she heard Sunny's easy gait pick up.

Tessa let out a joyful laugh. Now this was the sort of fun she enjoyed. She loved riding this way. But it was rare she had someone join her. And even rarer that she had the chance to show up a confident man like Aeden. Just before they came to a small, curved path in the woods, she turned and blew a sarcastic kiss in Aeden's direction. His voice bellowed behind her as he encouraged his poor horse to try to keep up with her and Galahad.

Tessa ducked and dodged branches with familiarity. This particular path wasn't well traveled. It was her little secret. One that, if traveled in the opposite direction, led down to the lake where she could listen to the musician play on lazy afternoons. There was a small longing in her chest as she realized she hadn't heard the violin in a while. Maybe she could sneak away one day soon.

Aeden shouted at her, "Okay! I concede!"

Tessa commanded Galahad, "Woah." Reluctantly, he skidded to a stop. She turned him to face a sweating Aeden and a heavily panting Sunny. Feeling sorry for the poor things, she said, "Well tried, boys."

Aeden tipped his head to her. "I am outmatched, I admit." With a wink, he added, "If Marcos asks, at least tell him I was only a tail's length behind."

She made a crossing gesture over her heart. "Of course."

Still wild with the excitement of the run, Tessa inhaled deeply, basking in the scent of the forest. Rich soil, moss, and wildflowers. Smells she now associated with home. And a hint of something else...

She whipped around, twisting on Galahad's back to get a view of the large animal she sensed. She whispered, "Aeden."

"Yeah, I smell it, too." He peered around slowly, moving carefully like a hound when it hunts.

Tessa narrowed her eyes, trying to see through the thick of the forest. *Damn* the stale blood she had that morning. If she'd had something fresher... She pinched the bridge of her nose. It didn't do any good to think like that. Blood from the cup had been fine every other day of her life. She had to make do with the powers it gave her.

White fur caught her eye. It was a few feet away, hidden by a thick, vine covered trunk. She waved a hand, signaling to Aeden where the movement was coming from. Neither of them dared move. Something she was grateful for. They couldn't afford to spook such a fine catch.

The creature came into view, nibbling leaves off the branches. Tessa's breath caught in her throat. It was the most incredible stag she'd ever seen. Tall and proud, with fur the color of freshly fallen snow. Snow like they had back in the Winter Court. It was breathtaking. And the antlers on his head were so large she couldn't imagine how he wasn't toppling over.

More enchanting, though, was the call of his blood. Thudding in his veins like war drums drawing her to battle. Tessa licked her lips. Focused only on her prey, it was as if everything else in the forest fell away. Nothing existed except her and the extraordinary creature.

Carefully, she began to slide from Galahad's back, but Aeden stopped her. "No, Tessa. Let it be."

She stopped. Her fangs ached, and her hunger screamed at her to keep going. But the concern in Aeden's voice gave her pause. Seating herself firmly back on Galahad's back, she turned toward Aeden. His brows were knit together, but his mouth softened when his eyes met hers.

"Why?" Her question came out as a mere whisper. Almost pained. She couldn't ignore every nerve in her body compelling her to seize the beast. To drink just a bit from the vein and take the rest back to her family. She would feel strong again. Like before with the man.

But Aeden reached across, turning her chin toward the stag. "A thing of such unique beauty shouldn't be struck down. Let it live. As an act of grace."

Tessa looked at him in astonishment. He was defending the creature? Asking her to let the nourishment they needed walk away? She sucked in a breath as she watched the magnificent beast forage along the forest floor. It was oblivious to how close it was to danger. To death. It nearly broke her heart. She knew it sensed her. But it didn't think she was a monster. If he had, then he would have been long gone by now. Instead, he trusted her to watch over him as he ate. To leave when she'd had her fill of his beauty.

With a tear drifting down her cheek, she turned Galahad away. Aeden followed quietly on Sunny. She waited to speak until they were far enough from the stag that his blood no longer taunted her. "You surprise me."

Aeden chuckled. "I could say the same to you. But since we're talking about me, I'd love to hear what it is that surprises you so."

Tessa gave an exasperated sigh. Of course, he was happy to talk about himself. "You saved that creature. For no reason other than it was beautiful."

"That's not enough reason?"

She pursed her lips. In her opinion, it was. If she hadn't been so consumed by bloodlust, she wanted to believe she would have spared it. But Aeden... He was an Ashbane. If the stories were true, then they didn't care who or what they sank their fangs into.

Finally, she replied, "It is. It's just, with your family background..."

"We're not animals, Tessa." His face fell into a frown. It was unsettling to see on a face that so often had some variation of a smile on it.

"I didn't mean to suggest that."

"We eat the way we do because it keeps us strong. Survival means making hard choices. Killing is a preferable alternative to dying. And while I admit that my family and our friends can let their impulses get the better of them, I take great care not to. The mortals I feed on do not feel any pain. They are treated well enough. Better than they were on the streets."

The hairs on Tessa's neck stood on end. "What do you mean?"

Aeden ran his hand through his hair as if trying to search for the right words. "My father takes mortals who were already weak and dying. Forgotten by society."

She had no idea. It never occurred to her that the Ashbanes and their folk would pick and choose their feeders. Not when her family grabbed anyone who happened to travel by the forest. She thought for a moment, mulling his words around in her head.

For a time, she had admired the Ashbanes and their defiant nature, wishing she could be more like them. Brave enough to decide her own fate. To go after what she wanted without worrying about how others would view her. But the way they fed on the mortals until there was nothing left was barbaric.

Aeden stared at her with an honest, open expression. Either he was masking his deceit when he told her about his restraint, or he was being truthful. He *had* been on his best behavior since coming into her home. Had drank blood from the cup without complaint. And just now, he had stopped her from killing the stag. To find out that she might have been wrong about him intrigued her.

"You said the humans you feed on don't feel any pain, but that the rest of your people don't exercise the same restraint? Why?" If Aeden was capable of mercy, then surely, he could convince his family to follow Reinar's ways and drink from the cup after all.

Aeden's jaw twitched in response. "I don't know that I can give you an answer that will satisfy you." He turned to her now. "My father is not a kind man. He never has been. Our people have had a hard lot in life. Some harbor resentment with nowhere to channel it. Others were never good to begin with. So I can only speak for myself, Tessa. And I hope that will be enough."

She couldn't hide her disappointment. Her shoulders slumped at the realization that Olgar wouldn't be so easily swayed. Not even if she were to marry his son. Was it something she should bring up to her uncle? Surely, he should know whether his plan to use Aeden to their advantage would work. Would he send Aeden home if he thought Olgar wouldn't fall in line?

She twisted her fingers through Galahad's mane. The thought of Aeden leaving gave her an empty feeling in the pit of her stomach. Something that frightened her. She glanced over at him. Watching Aeden was becoming a common pastime of hers, it seemed.

Whenever he was near, her gaze gravitated toward him. And he wasn't unpleasant to talk to...

They neared the tree line leading back to the stables and disappointment set in at the thought of their ride being over. Before they cleared the woods, Aeden waved at Tessa to stop and jumped from Sunny's back without warning. The horse whinnied angrily and sidestepped away. But Aeden ignored him, kneeling down to shove some sticks and shrubbery out of the path.

"Tessa," his voice shook, "these footprints. They're human." He sniffed at the air. Frustration was prevalent in his voice as he said, "We should have caught the scent of them sooner." It seemed he was talking more to himself than to her as he went on. "My senses are dulled."

Tessa slipped from Galahad immediately and joined Aeden at his side. "How do you know they're not from one of us?"

He gestured toward the heel of the boot print. "It's possible. But these markings here look as if they've come from a custom shop." There was an outline of a sparrow imprinted in the dirt that she didn't recognize.

"Unless your people are shopping in town, these are mortal. And they stop here." He pointed to the left. "Then turn back."

Tessa tensed. If he was right, then the humans had returned. Ones that might very well be witch-blessed like those she and Aeden had encountered before. She whipped around, trying to catch a shadow or anything else that might not belong. There was no sign of the trespassers and only the faintest scent of human lingered in the air. Whoever it had been, they were long gone by now.

Aeden pointed to the ground again. Tessa leaned over to see the boot print he was pointing to. He grumbled, "Another set of prints. There were at least two of them here." He exhaled loudly through his nose. "We need to alert your uncle. There needs to be a patrol. One made up of your strongest men."

Tessa didn't miss the doubt in his words. It was clear he didn't think her family was up to the task. As angry as she wanted to be about that, she found she wasn't. Instead, she couldn't shake the unsettling feeling that he might be right. If she hadn't fought the witch-blessed mortals herself then she never would have doubted her people's ability to defend themselves. But those men had fought with such strength and ferocity. They had caught her off guard. And had it not been for Aeden's help or the blood she drank from the man's neck, she might not have fared so well in the end.

Tessa grew hot with anger. If more men had come, it was because of Marcos. Because of the body he had irresponsibly ravaged. If he had followed the rules—if the lot of them had—then this wouldn't be happening. Her head spun, and she rose. Needing to put distance between her and the Ashbane heir at her side, she took a few large strides back.

Aeden held out a hand to her. "Tessa—"

"Don't," she snapped.

Hurt flashed across his face, but he reassured her, "We'll get the defenses we need. Send trackers out to see for sure. Don't get upset until we know exactly what we're dealing with."

"Don't get upset?" she scoffed. "Look at what's happened." She pointed furiously at the boot prints. "Look at the position you've put my family in. The danger your family has put all of us in. If these belong to mortals like the ones from the other night, then we are facing a threat of the likes we haven't seen since we first came to this realm." Since her father. A threat like the hunters who struck him down so brutally right in front of his own child.

Aeden closed the gap between them, taking her face between his hands. "Tessa, I will do everything in my power to make sure that doesn't happen. Do you hear me?"

The sincerity in his voice and the way his eyes bore into hers helped her catch her breath. There was no doubt in her mind that he meant what he was saying. The words caught in her throat as she said, "Then get your father to agree to my uncle's terms. Persuade your people to change their ways. To keep us all safe. Convince him to help us *protect* this forest and *all* the Vampyrs inside it."

Aeden rubbed his thumb along her cheek as he promised, "I will do what I can."

Fifteen

Aeden

Aeden stalked back and forth in the garden. The chilly night breeze did nothing to settle his nerves like he'd hoped. The sweet scent of flowers only tightened the knots in his stomach. Finding the boot prints in the forest shook Tessa more than he'd expected. He desperately wanted to blame them on wayward humans. A couple, perhaps, who had stumbled into the forest by chance and decided to turn back. But even *he* couldn't help the nagging feeling that it might instead be hunters scouting the area. Watching the Vampyrs to determine how they might attack.

Reinar was vigilant, setting patrols up immediately. Careful not to leave anything up to chance or speculation. But Aeden's faith in the Downthorns and their friends was in short supply. He and Tessa had struggled to fend off the witch-blessed humans before. And lately, with each cup-fed meal he had, Aeden sensed his Vampyric abilities growing weaker.

Aeden kicked at the dirt and considered going up to his room. There was nothing else to be done tonight. Besides, Tessa and the others had already retired to their rooms. Earlier, Aeden politely excused himself from after-dinner drinks in the library. In part hoping to avoid Drake's grumblings, but also to send a letter to his father. Olgar needed to be aware that things had escalated. That it was in the realm of possibility that the mortals might be planning something.

The messenger delivered the carefully drafted note detailing what he and Tessa had found. A naïve part of him hoped his father might call off the assassination because of it. Now was not the time for discord between their people. If this was a legitimate threat, they needed all the manpower they could get. But the realistic part of him feared that it might instead speed up his father's timeline. No doubt, Olgar would be eager to lead everyone against the threat himself.

Aeden stopped pacing, lingering near the large rose bushes. Between the kiss with Tessa and finding the prints, the day had been a whirlwind. And that *promise* he'd made. What was he thinking? Although it wasn't a lie that he would do everything in his power to make sure their people were safe from the danger the mortals posed, his father would never agree to live by Reinar's rules. No matter what Aeden said to try to convince him. She had no idea just how far Olgar was willing to go. That he was already orchestrating the death of a man she loved deeply. Like a father.

Aeden couldn't shake his tingling nerves. He groaned, thinking of how their first kiss had gone. What was he thinking, kissing her like that? She wasn't like the other women he'd come across. Jokes and flattery didn't move her. So he switched tactics, but he hadn't meant to push her. After all, *she* had kissed *him*. When they were in the moment, he never expected her to actually do it. He'd been trying to lighten the mood. To show her that there could be something between the two of them. It was why he was here. But she was impossible. There was a wall between them of her own making. And try as he might, he couldn't break through it.

He sighed through his nose, looking up at the night sky. Even in the clearing around the estate, the stars didn't shine brightly. The magic his people used to create their safe haven in the forest had been weak. A dim flicker of the power they once held. It had run them dry, too. Somehow, their sloppy work had cast a shadow around them, keeping the sun, moon, and stars from shining on them fully.

He missed those stars. The ones that had sparkled like laughter in a child's eye. And the sun. Which had once kissed his face. It might be why he was so taken with Tessa when she smiled. When her eyes glittered and her face shined, like the very best parts of night and day were radiating from her.

Unexpectedly, he felt another wave of guilt. And it wasn't from failing at his family's mission. It was *her*. The thought of her being angry or frightened was like having an itch he couldn't scratch. Avoiding her yesterday had been the wrong move. It should have made her want to pursue him. To be interested in him. What was the mortal saying? *Absence makes the heart grow fonder?*

And if he was being honest, he'd hoped it would give him a chance to collect his thoughts. To focus on why he was there.

Allowing himself to feel sorry for her and what he was going to do to her family would be his downfall.

A rabbit scurried by and his stomach grumbled. His eyes sharpened, but only slightly. Drinking from that damned cup was dulling his senses. Making him slower. Going for a ride earlier had left him with aching muscles. Something a decent feeding would have rectified.

The rabbit stopped, sensing its predator. Its velvety brown ears twitched, but Aeden made no move to snatch it up. Such a small creature. Innocent. Helpless. He shuffled his feet on the path, sending the rabbit scurrying into the finely manicured bushes.

"Dammit." What had gotten into him? First Tessa, now the rabbit. Was he really becoming so soft? If only his father could see him at this moment. He shut his eyes tight, knowing Olgar would call him a fool. A coward. Unworthy of his position as the Ashbane heir.

Aeden shuffled around the winding garden path until he came to a candlelit balcony. Vines twisted up the trellis, leading to a warmly lit room. He peered up and spotted long, silky brown hair. It looked nearly raven where the shadows cast down on it. Tessa.

She was pacing the stone balcony and muttering to herself. If he'd been eating well, then he would have been able to hear what she was saying. But no matter how hard he strained his ears, it didn't do any good. He crept closer to the trellis, staying light on his feet.

The vines were thick, and the stones jutted out just right. Before he knew it, he was climbing. With stealth and precision, he grabbed hold of the divots in the stone and found his footing as he scaled the wall. He wasn't sure why he was doing it or what he was going to say to her. But he knew sleep would never come tonight if he didn't act.

Tessa's slippered feet pattered on the stone and her voice was low as she muttered, "It's fine. Fine." She groaned. "Who am I kidding? This isn't going to work."

After a few unsteady minutes of climbing, Aeden reached for the edge of the balcony, but his foot slipped. A yelp escaped him as he caught himself on a vine. His feet dangled, and he made the mistake of glancing down. It was higher than he'd realized.

Tessa called out, "Is someone there?" Her voice was closer now, and he suspected she was peering over the edge. "Aeden! What in fate's name are you doing?"

He grunted as he swung himself back toward the wall. "Just... wanted to... talk..."

Tessa rested her forearms on the stone railing. "I have a door, you know."

Sweat beaded on his forehead as he flung himself again. "Really?" He grunted harder this time, running out of breath. "Hadn't... occurred to me." Finally, his feet met solid stone once more, and he shimmied until he had enough of a grip to climb the rest of the way.

When he reached the railing, Tessa's face was as smooth and unmoving as the stone. Face to face now, he caught the scent of rosemary scented soap on her skin. Her hair was damp, as if she'd just gotten out of the bath. And she was wearing a different nightgown than she had been the other night. It was a deep blue. The darkest color he'd seen on her yet. Something stirred in his chest. Though he wasn't sure if it was her appearance, or the last of his strength leaving him after the climb.

She didn't bother to move so he could hoist himself onto the balcony, nor did she offer an invitation, so he clung to the railing like an idiot. It would have helped if he had come up with something to say to her before popping up outside of her room.

He gulped and focused on the cold stone. "I was out for a walk."

"Hm." She frowned. "And then you decided a climb might suit your needs better?"

Inching closer to her, he shrugged and said, "I noticed you were up and thought I'd come see you."

She glanced down at his arm, which brushed against hers. Her eyes snapped back to his. "Aeden. This is wildly inappropriate. Whatever it is that you have to say to me can wait until tomorrow." She leaned forward and added, "After all, you had no problem waiting a day and a half before." There was no bite to her voice, which was a relief to him.

Fair, he thought. Then out loud he said, "I'm sorry about the kiss and about how this day ended. That's what I came here to say. Believe it or not, I'm new to this, too, and I admit I haven't handled it well."

Her face softened slightly at that, giving him a tiny sliver of hope. This wasn't going so badly. A strand of his hair fell from the strap he'd tied it back with, but as he reached up to push it out of his face, his foot slipped again.

He shouted a profanity and scrambled for a better hold on the railing. Tessa's eyes went wide and she leapt forward, but she stopped before reaching out to help him. The stone was smooth and cool and his palms were slick. When did he start sweating? *This*. This was what she did to him. Got him all jumbled up and made him nervous. Never in his life had anything like this happened.

"A little help," he pleaded.

Tessa bit her lip, leaning over the balcony. Her eyes trailed past him to the ground.

The muscles in his arms screamed as he tried with all his strength to hold on. In genuine horror, he shouted, "Are you seriously considering whether or not you should let me fall?"

Tessa's mouth tipped into a smirk. "Maybe." She tilted her head to the side. "Doesn't look like that big of a drop."

He grunted again. "Trade me places, then let me know what you think."

She groaned and rolled her eyes. "Fine. Come on." She offered her arms to him. He sucked in a worried breath as he transferred his grip from the railing to her. Her embrace was stronger than he'd expected. She dragged him up with ease. Once he was on the railing, he let go of her, but the toe of his boot caught on the edge and he tumbled forward. Onto her.

She cried out as they both crashed onto the balcony floor. Something stirred deep in his stomach as he lay on top of her. The nightgown was shifted up, revealing her bare thighs. No sign of a chemise. Which meant there was next to nothing standing between him and her soft, supple skin.

"Aeden," she said flatly, and she raised her eyebrows at him.

As if he'd been burned, he rolled off of her and shuffled back, trying to put space between him and the thoughts of what he would like to do to her. Apparently he wasn't hiding it well, because she pulled down her nightgown, curling her knees into her chest so it reached her ankles.

Aeden cleared his throat. "I uh, didn't mean to..."

Laughter bubbled up from Tessa and her face reddened. "Who climbs a lady's balcony in the middle of the night?"

He laughed, too, realizing how crazy he looked. "I don't know. I thought maybe it was a romantic gesture."

"You did not." She barked with laughter this time, and Aeden couldn't help but join in. It was contagious.

"No. But it could have been if done properly." His body warmed, despite the chill in the air. It was good to hear her laugh. Especially after everything that had happened.

She quieted, but her beautiful smile remained. "You didn't have to use a grand gesture to apologize. A few words before breakfast would have sufficed. Especially considering the tracks. There's a lot more on my mind than that kiss."

"Ouch. I thought it might have left more of an impression than that." He joked, "Is it because I lost to you in the race? Because I can do better, I assure you. Maybe if we traded horses."

"You are *not* riding Galahad." She pursed her lips, but he caught the laughter in her eyes.

He scratched at the back of his neck. "I admit, I was worried about you. I know seeing those boot prints shook you. That it might be bringing up a lot of feelings about the past."

She winced at the implication, but didn't deny it.

Aeden fought the urge to reach for her. To take her hand and promise that everything would be alright. But he couldn't. Not when things were about to get much worse before they got better. There was another stab of guilt, but he did his best to ignore it. Instead of more promises, he said, "I don't mean to brush aside the severity of what those prints might mean." He wiped his sweaty hands on his pants. "I tend to take things too lightly. Something my father wishes I would have outgrown by now."

Something in the way Tessa nodded told him she could relate. She stood, offering a hand to help him up. He took it gladly, then followed her into her room. It was exactly as he would have imagined. Pristine and very ladylike. All pastels and flowers. But he couldn't resist thinking it didn't quite suit her. There was something more to her. A wildness and rebellion that she tried to hide. A facade she had dropped when they rode together. It was as mesmerizing as witnessing the snow white stag in the woods. Awe inspiring. He longed to see more of that side of her.

As Tessa led him to the door, he called to her, "Do you think we could start over? Try to do this whole courting thing the right way? I know there is a lot happening right now, but at the very least, we can do this for our families."

She turned, leaning against the heavy oak, with a contemplative look on her face. "You haven't been doing *that* bad of a job. It's not like I've made it easy for you."

With a tender smile, he leaned in slowly. Her gaze dropped to his mouth until his hand met the doorknob. A blush bloomed along the bridge of her nose as the door clicked open. Aeden chuckled. "Good night, Tessa."

Breathlessly, she whispered, "Good night."

As he slipped from the room and into the hall, he smiled to himself. Once again, his palms were slick with sweat and he wiped them vigorously on his shirt as he wandered back to his own room. The day had taken a turn, but this thing between him and Tessa had been salvaged. Tomorrow, he would be the very epitome of a gentleman. That is, if he could control himself around her.

Sixteen

Tessa

essa tapped her foot impatiently against the breakfast table.
Her mother had opened all the windows in the parlor and
the smell of fresh grass filled the room. It was an exceptionally
warm day as summer approached in Gwyar. A muted version of
the season, though, with the magic permanently placing them
inside their own bubble. The weather attempted to mimic that of
the mortal villages surrounding them, even though the trees in the
Crimson Forest never changed from their enchanted blood red
shades.

It seemed Aeden had once again decided to take his meal elsewhere. There was no sign of him. Judging by the boiling rage rolling off of Drake, it was a wise choice. He'd spent the morning begging his father to allow him to put together a hunting party to go after the mortal trespassers. But her uncle was adamant that it would only attract more attention. That the best thing to do was fortify their defenses.

With Drake in this sort of mood, it was probably safer for Aeden to stay away. Best not to give Drake someone to take his frustration out on. Aeden, after all, was not one of his favorite people. He had offended her cousin. Had struck and humiliated him. And Drake wasn't quick to forgive. There was no telling what minuscule thing Aeden might do to set him off.

Reinar assured her it would be best for the time being not to push the two of them together. The mood of everyone else in the room was one of false ease. Reinar and Flora spoke with tight, forced smiles about the recent appearances of critters in the forest. And although the humans had trespassed on their land, the Ashbanes had been quiet. No more mangled bodies were left on the forest floor. Something her uncle and mother were eager to attribute to Aeden's presence. Everything, according to them, was going to work out in the end.

If only they knew how rocky it had been between her and Aeden. Her family's excitement was blinding them from what was staring them in the face. It was way too soon to determine whether her uncle's plan was working or not. Even Aeden didn't seem to have much faith in his father's ability to be persuaded. Especially by him. It didn't evoke a lot of confidence. What would happen if the mortals really were banding together to form a hunting party? If they returned with a larger force, would the Ashbanes stand by her family? Or would they see it as every Vampyr for themselves?

Not eager to add to the stress, she kept her troublesome thoughts to herself. For the time being. Flora's eyes scrunched at the corners as she smiled at something Reinar said. Tessa's stomach twisted into knots. Their faith in this union might have been the only thing getting them through the day. And that was something Tessa didn't want to strip away.

Reinar boasted, "Drake and the others patrolled early this morning and found no signs of the humans. They're gone for now, and with our people patrolling the borders, I am confident that no more mortals will make it through the tree line. It seems we might have been quick to jump to conclusions. It was likely just a couple taking a stroll."

Tessa frowned. A stroll in a forest that was veiled to appear ominous and unwelcoming to any who stumbled upon it? Surely her uncle didn't really believe that. Something told her he was trying to comfort them while shouldering the fear on his own. She tapped her foot nervously on the ground.

Reinar cleared his throat and continued, "And the Ravenbloom family brought back three more deer. It seems they are coming in from the north. Babies from early spring that are finally large enough to harvest."

Tessa's stomach turned some more. She stared down at her half empty cup of blood. The last of their human supply. It was time to wipe the feeders' minds clean and send them on their way. Back to their lives, believing they had taken a long and relaxing trip.

It was bad enough that the blood her family served her had a stale taste to it. Like drinking cold soup that was left out overnight. But now she was looking at sustaining her appetite on drained animal blood. It would be far too dangerous to risk taking humans from the road.

She thought again of the white stag she had seen in the woods. The one that had left her dizzy and salivating. It had been like a beacon of innocence. Unsuspecting. Easy prey. She propped her arm on the table and rested her chin on the palm of her hand as she stared out the window. Drinking that man's blood was like cracking open a door that she'd kept locked up tight. One that stood in the way of her morality and the monster she could truly be.

Maybe Aeden and his family could control themselves. Perhaps he was telling the truth when he said the mortals that he fed on didn't experience pain. But draining them meant taking a life, nonetheless. It was something Tessa wanted no part of. No matter how good it would make her feel.

Talos bounced into the room. Even he was in high spirits today. The hunt must have been leaving everyone, but her, with a full belly. He slipped an envelope from his pocket and handed it to her.

"Master Aeden asked that I pass this along to you."

Tessa hesitated before taking it. Everyone's eyes were on her. Flora and Reinar with wide, hopeful stares, and Drake with a pinched mouth. Turning it over in her hands, she admired the elegant script written across the front with her name on it. Tucking it into her chest, she rose from her seat.

"If you will all excuse me." She hurried to the door. It was impossible to predict what Aeden had written to her, and she didn't need an audience there when she revealed it.

Once she was alone in the hall, she tore it open, careful not to rip the delicate paper inside. The handwriting was beautiful. Not at all what she expected from a man like Aeden. It read:

Dearest Tessa,

I thought a walk this morning would do me some good. I do hope you won't hold last night against me. I can assure you I'm not usually such a klutz. I also humbly ask that you join me for a picnic lunch. Just the two of us?

Yours,

Aeden

Dearest Tessa. So, he had opted for flattery today? Tessa fanned herself with the letter, unsure if the heat blooming along the bridge of her nose was from the note or the hallway. The windows were still closed and suddenly the heat felt stifling. An afternoon. Alone. With him. There was no reason to deny him. With merely a few short weeks left in their courtship, she supposed it was time for her to play her part.

But every time she was alone with him, she got this strange buzzing under her skin. Like lightning before it strikes. Just last night, when he'd leaned in to open the door, she'd thought he might try to kiss her again. Yet she hadn't moved out of the way, wondering what it might be like to kiss him this time without retreating. Whenever he was close, her body betrayed her, while her head screamed at it to stop being so foolhardy.

But if they weren't alone... She popped back into the parlor. "Talos!"

He nearly knocked over an end table when he spun toward her.

More calmly, she asked, "Would you mind sending word to Whitebrook manor and ask Scarlet to come for lunch?" Her best friend would be just the buffer she needed. That way, she could still spend time with Aeden and get to know him without the danger of doing something she might regret later on. With Scarlet there, she and Aeden were sure to behave themselves.

"Of course, Miss. Consider it done!" He fumbled with the buttons on his jacket, then tipped a hat—that he was not wearing—to Reinar and Flora before scurrying off.

Feeling very pleased with herself, Tessa smiled and returned to the hall. There was still a bit of time before lunch. And in the meantime, she could use a walk as well. Aeden was likely strolling through the gardens again or spending time down at the stables, so she headed for her favorite place in the forest. The one place she knew for certain that she would be alone.

Well, sort of. Deep down, she hoped to hear the familiar sound of music drifting across the lake to her. This was the longest she'd gone without hearing her private concert from the mystery musician. Maybe a few sweet notes would help clear her head and prepare her for a day with her soon to be betrothed.

Tessa mindlessly wandered down by the lake like she'd done countless times before. She memorized the precise location where the music flowed over the water's surface just right. The exact spot where it would wind itself around her like a familiar embrace.

Even without the sun shining directly on her, a thin veil of sweat beaded down her back. As she took a seat on a nearby stone, she shed her soft cotton wrap, leaving her arms exposed to the gentle breeze that rhythmically drifted past.

She laid against the stone, turning her face toward a skinny ray of sunshine, and closed her eyes. Then she waited. A few birds chirped at one another high above in the trees. Their little feet scratched against the bark each time they moved. And the lake rippled softly against the bank with each breeze that blew by. They were subtle sounds. The sounds of nature. Everything moving in harmony and working together to sustain life.

Life that she craved to take. She grumbled to herself. Wasn't taking her mind off of things the whole point of coming down to the lake? She said a silent prayer that her musician would arrive at their designated place on the other side to carry her off with the perfect melody.

In the absence of the music she hoped for, her traitorous thoughts turned back to Aeden. He brought something out in her that she couldn't quite understand. It went further than the urge to prove him wrong when he implied that she was sheepish or pampered. Something about him made it seem like the world was big. As if it was hers for the taking.

The sudden screech of the violin made Tessa's heart skip a beat. It was like someone had torn into the strings without thinking. She shot up, looking around wildly. Again, bow met string, sending the birds above fluttering away in a flurry. The sound of their wings flapping was drowned out by the music.

This wasn't the soft echo of a song coming from a distance. It was close. Very close. Tessa's heart raced and before she knew it, she was following the sound. It had never come from this side of the lake before and excitement brewed in her, driving her toward the mysterious musician. The one that had unknowingly played for her for years.

Eager to unveil them, Tessa scrambled along the water's edge and up a slight hill that led further into the thick of the woods. The violin's jolting melody would begin, only to come to a screeching halt every few notes.

It grew louder with every step she took. And she could practically feel the hesitation of its master. Never before had she heard anything but perfection coming from their fingertips. But now they seemed unsure. As if something were weighing as heavily on them as it was on her.

The melody slowed, and she realized she had made it. She peered around a large tree, careful not to reveal herself too soon. Was it one of her uncle's loyalists all along? Or maybe this wasn't her musician after all. It could be that a Vampyr on their side of the lake had decided to take up a new skill. That would explain the difference in what she was hearing.

It was like her heart stopped beating all together when the mysterious musician came into view. Aeden's hair wasn't tied back like usual. Instead, the strands blew freely in the breeze. Sweat dripped from his brow as he put the bow to the string again. He started off slow this time, playing a few expert notes. But then he slipped.

Tessa ducked quickly behind the tree, pressing her back to the sturdy, rough trunk. Grasping for something—anything—to hold on to, she dug her fingers into the bark. Never in her wildest dreams would she have guessed Aeden was the man who had been playing for her all these years. Well, not necessarily playing for *her*. Not as far as he was aware. But she had been there. So many times, listening to his music. Resonating with it deep in her bones.

Curiosity got the better of her as she peeked around the tree once more. With her mouth gaping open from the shock, she watched him try again. The note came out as another wild shriek, and he cursed loudly.

She gripped the trunk in silent encouragement. Something was bothering him. He just had to figure out a way to let it out. To release it through his song. She gulped heavily. It wasn't right to spy on him. To be here for such an intimate moment. But she couldn't turn away. Couldn't find it in herself to leave now.

This time, he shut his eyes tight. His face hardened with determination as he began to play once more. What came out next was breathtaking. The notes obeyed his every command. He sucked in a heavy breath, eyes still closed. And soon the tempo picked up, turning into a sound that was so smooth and rich it brought tears to her eyes.

She'd been too hasty to judge him. To think that he was flitting through life, making decisions based on a whim. She knew she was wrong because of the countless times she'd listened to him play before. Pain, heartache, longing, joy, happiness. It was all expressed through his music.

Feelings that had often matched her own. She and Aeden had been sharing these moments together for years without even knowing it. Goosebumps pricked along the back of her neck. They were more alike than she realized.

Leaning forward, aching for more of his song, she didn't realize that she was pulling the bark from the trunk. It snapped off under her grip and she fell face first into the brush. With twigs tangled in her hair and thorns cutting into her skin, she panicked, flailing around until she was free to regain her footing. She shot up straight, filled with red, hot embarrassment, to find Aeden standing a few feet from her.

The bow and violin hung in his hand and his eyes were wide red pools. Tessa was frozen in place, wishing she could crawl back into the brush and live there for the rest of her life. She shrugged, "I, uh... decided a walk would do me good, too."

Aeden's jaw ticked. Then he said, "I see that." And with a shake of his head, he extended his free hand.

With a sorry sigh, she took it and allowed him to graciously help her to the small clearing. She couldn't bring herself to meet his eyes and was surprised when he reached up to pull a leaf from her hair.

As he tossed it to the ground, he asked, "How long have you been hiding there?"

She grumbled, "Longer than I'd like to admit."

As if sensing her embarrassment, he forced a laugh. "Well, tell me what you think." He took a step back and opened both arms to her. "Don't hold back."

The smile on his face couldn't hide the uncertainty in his eyes. Had he ever played for anyone before? Tessa tugged at her hair. "Honestly... it's magnificent."

His brows knitted together, creasing his smooth forehead. And he bit his lip. Had no one ever told him how brilliant he was?

With a step toward him, she continued, "The way you play... I can *feel* how you get lost in the music. It comes alive through you. It's like nothing I've ever heard before." A small lie. She had listened to him do this many times. More than she could count. But she was already so embarrassed she'd been caught listening and watching, that she couldn't find the nerve to share the whole truth.

His shoulders slackened, and he scratched nervously at the back of his neck. Then jokingly again, he said, "High praise. You flatter me, Miss Downthorn."

"I mean every word." Tessa reached out and touched his arm before she could second guess herself. "You have a true talent."

His eyes flitted to her hand. The joking demeanor melted away, and he met her eyes with something she thought was appreciation. Withdrawing her hand, she gestured through the trees in the direction of the house. "Care to escort me back? You did promise lunch, after all."

"Of course!" He scrambled a few steps back, bending down to secure the violin in its case.

Tessa bit back a chuckle as he stumbled toward her and offered his arm. As they walked arm in arm, she couldn't stop stealing glances at him. He looked forward, but every few seconds, she caught him staring at her, too. This time, the heat blooming across her face wasn't from her own unease. Seeing him nervous for a change was actually fun.

"You should really play for a crowd," she suggested. "It's a shame to keep such a talent to yourself."

He was quick to respond. "No. I couldn't. Not here."

Tessa frowned, "Why not?"

He sighed through his nose and his grip on her arm tightened ever so slightly. "It just doesn't feel right. Not when I always imagined myself playing in..."

When it seemed like he wasn't going to finish that sentence, Tessa asked, "Playing where?" She thought of his admission that he had dreamed about returning home to Elfhame a time or two. Of the blackthorn veil standing between them and where they truly belonged that were permanently inked on his body. Her voice was barely louder than a whisper as she guessed, "Playing in Elfhame."

He grunted in response. "My mom always wished I'd have a chance to play in the Winter Palace. Where only the most renowned musicians were invited."

Tessa's heart hurt for him. Thinking of the young boy who had big dreams. Only to have them stripped from him along with everything else he'd ever known. She knew the pain of it. Had felt it right alongside him, even if she hadn't realized it.

"I remember the celebrations back home." She added, "Faintly, of course. But sometimes memories come back. They're fleeting like a shooting star. But I can remember how they made me feel. How everyone came together to share in these incredible moments. I remember standing on my father's feet as a child while we danced. I can recall the way the music filled the room." Music that touched her soul like his own did. Working up the courage to tell him that she'd been his audience all these years, she turned to him. "Aeden, I—"

Footsteps shuffled up ahead in the driveway. Breaking the moment, Scarlet's voice carried from the house in singsong, "Tessa!"

They'd come to the edge of the drive now and Scarlet waved at her excitedly. She lifted her skirts and ran toward them, jumping into Tessa's arms. Scarlet whispered breathlessly, "I can't wait to hear *everything*. Don't leave anything out." Then, pulling away, she beamed up at Aeden. "Hello."

Aeden let out a strained laugh and replied, "Hello." He bit his lip as he gestured to the gardens and added, "Shall we?"

Tessa's heart grew heavy with regret for having asked Scarlet to tag along. As she passed Aeden, he caught her eye. The look he gave her seemed to be filled with words left unspoken. The feeling sank deeper, forcing the smallest crack in that wall she had built around her heart.

Seventeen

Aeden

I t wasn't the afternoon Aeden envisioned when he invited Tessa to lunch. Scarlet sure enjoyed listening to herself talk. She commanded most of Tessa's attention throughout the picnic—gossiping about the other families and how some bloke named Peitor felt slighted about Aeden's presence in the Downthorn home. Not that it bothered Aeden. He didn't have the time or energy to waste on some stranger's chipped ego.

Not when he was trying to sort through what he was feeling at the moment. Tessa knew his secret now. One of them, at least.

He hadn't played for anyone in so long, and it felt as if she had seen the barest parts of him. And she had liked it. Told him it was magnificent. The praise caught him off guard. It stirred something in him, and he hadn't wanted the moment to end.

But what did that mean for his father's plan? Time was fleeting and the full moon would be there before they knew it. There was no question that his father would call on him soon, with plans on how to get rid of Reinar and Drake. And although he'd had a few hiccups when it came to charming Tessa, it seemed she was finally giving him a bit of trust. His ribs tightened with doubt. Would any of it be enough to keep the suspicion from falling on him if he went through with the plan?

More worrisome than that, Aeden was having trouble fooling himself into thinking he would be able to go through with the assassination without regret. He still hadn't thought of a way to change his father's mind. What he needed was a worthy alternative to murder.

The time passed quickly with a few stolen glances between him and Tessa. It wasn't all that bad. Scarlet was nice and included him in their talks where she could. But leaving his and Tessa's conversation at the edge of the woods the way they did left him with a sense of longing he wasn't entirely comfortable with.

The look on her face when she'd told him what she thought of his music had been so open and honest. It touched his heart. Stirring feelings that he wasn't sure he'd ever experienced before, nor wanted to.

Even now, as Tessa lounged beside Scarlet with their heads pressed close like they were in a secret club that he wasn't fully inducted into yet, he couldn't take his eyes from her. All rosy cheeked and easy laughs, Tessa was stunning. He preferred her this way. Free of the prim and proper mask she wore at dinner with her family. Or the way she clammed up when her boorish cousin was near.

Aeden shot up when he spotted Talos jogging in their direction. He was always sort of a nervous wreck, but he looked especially frazzled, with his silver hair jutting out in all directions like he'd been tugging at it.

When he reached them, he keeled over, trying to catch his breath. Raising a finger in the air to signal that he needed a minute, he sucked in loud, heavy breaths. Aeden wanted to snap at him to just spit it out. Had they found the trespassers? Or had another attack occurred? His father had been clear with his instructions—directed mostly at Marcos—that there were to be no more slip-ups. Not while Aeden was staying with the Downthorns.

Finally, Talos straightened and spoke in Tessa's direction. "Your uncle. He's invited the Ashbanes." With a wheeze, he added, "Here. Tonight."

Aeden scrambled to his feet. Reinar hadn't mentioned any of this to him. "Why?" He couldn't help the suspicion rising. Reinar and Olgar had not been in the same vicinity since they made their home in the forest.

True, at some point, it was bound to happen. But he didn't imagine it would take place so soon. At least not before the courtship was over. This might change things. His father had a rotten temper and a tongue sharper than his fangs. It was one thing for Aeden to come to the Downthorns and insert himself in their good graces. But if his father came and couldn't control the feelings of bad blood between the families, then he would ruin his own plans. He would undo everything Aeden had done to mend things between him and Tessa.

Tessa, however, was calm and collected as she stood. "Well, then. We should all prepare to welcome our guests." It sounded as if there was a tightness in her throat and Aeden wondered if she was holding back tears.

He didn't know the extent of it, but she blamed his father for the death of hers. He couldn't imagine having to stomach being in the same room with the man you believed was responsible for tearing your family apart.

Reaching for her, he started, "Tessa, are you—"

"Fine." She gave him a tense smile. Then, turning to Scarlet, said, "Let's go."

Aeden watched as they walked to the house, huddled together. The sun would be setting in a couple of hours. And Aeden wondered what sort of terror the night would bring.

Aeden paced outside of Tessa's room. So much so that he feared the light grayish-blue carpet under his feet would start to fray. In the last thirty minutes, he had reached up to knock only to second guess himself and lower his hand back to his side in a closed fist.

His father would be arriving soon. Along with whatever relatives decided to accompany him. Marcos for sure. It was fruitless to hope that he would remain behind. His cousin would never miss a chance to be a part of the fun.

Sweat beaded under Aeden's evening coat. Fun was the wrong word for what tonight would be. The only thing he could hope for was that there would be no murder attempts. Something twisted in his gut. Another bad choice of words. Murder was exactly what his father had on the agenda. It was just a matter of finding out when and how.

Aeden jumped as Tessa's door creaked open. With as much grace as he could muster, he turned toward it, smoothing his hair back and adjusting the lapels on his jacket. He'd chosen a maroon one. So dark that it looked nearly black.

Tessa revealed herself on the other side of the threshold, stealing his breath away. The dress she'd chosen for tonight was a stark difference to her usual attire. A striking midnight black dress embroidered with bold red roses. Words escaped him as his gaze roved over the fabric that clung to all the right places.

Her eyes—darkened with red from the curse—widened. "Aeden! I didn't expect you to be here."

"I thought I'd escort you." He whistled. "You look..."

She scrunched her nose as she finished his sentence, "Strange?"

"No!" He shook his head vehemently. "Incredible."

The corner of her mouth quirked up. "Really? It's not too much? Too different?"

Grabbing onto her hand, he assured her, "It suits you. Much better than the white."

Her long, thick lashes fluttered, and she tightened her fingers around his. "Thank you. I thought I'd try something new tonight."

To his enjoyment, she walked hand in hand with him down to the dining room. Even when they entered to find both of their families standing tensely on opposite sides of the room, she didn't let go. Instead, her grip tightened, and he gave her a light, reassuring squeeze.

He leaned down to whisper in her ear. "It'll be fine."

Uncertainty weighed in her words. "If you say so."

Admittedly, the families did little to give him confidence in his own reassurances to her. Downthorns and Ashbanes stood divided as if an invisible force were pushing them apart. No one conversed, and it seemed they couldn't even bring themselves to make eye contact.

At the sight of Aeden and Tessa with their hands embraced, Reinar brightened and gestured grandly to them. He was dressed in his finest. Likely in an attempt to show Aeden's father how well they were doing on their side of the lake. And to serve as a distraction from the aging furniture and worn amenities.

Reinar boasted, "Ah, the happy couple is here at last."

Olgar scowled with his eyes lingering on Aeden and Tessa's hands locked together. His lips were puckered like he'd eaten a lemon, then he said, "Son. It is good to see you."

Yeah right. Aeden plastered a pleasant smile on his face. One he'd have to hold in place for the rest of the night. "You as well, father." Then to Sylvia, he added, "You look lovely tonight, mother."

Sylvia beamed at him. It appeared both families had pulled out all the stops tonight. The jewels around her neck glistened in the light of the chandelier and her manicured nails were painted gold. Still as sharp as claws.

Aeden glanced at Tessa to find her staring at his mother in fascination. Quickly, he remembered his manners. "Tessa, I would like to introduce you to Count Olgar, my father. And Countess Sylvia, my mother." Then, nodding to Marcos and Balis, who remained in a shadowy corner, he said, "I suppose I don't need to reintroduce you two."

He scanned the room for his uncle, Hayden, but there was no sign of him. Instead, fiery red hair caught his eye. His stomach dropped. Rose crept out of the shadows and dipped into a mocking curtsey. The glare she shot him could have cut through armor.

He could practically feel Tessa's discomfort through their hands, which were still wound together. Or was it his own? It was hard to distinguish between the two when he felt like the room was closing in around him. Why would they allow Rose to accompany them? It was idiotic.

He cleared his throat, trying to ignore his rising frustration with his family. "Tessa, this is Rose Dewrun. Her family has been friends with ours for..."

Rose intercepted, "Ages." She stuck her nose in the air, looking Tessa directly in the eyes, as she said, "Aeden and I were practically raised together. Isn't that right, love?"

Tessa gently pulled her hand from his. The absence of her touch was jarring. But as much as he wanted to reach for her, he remained still. They needed to move this dinner along and get Rose and his family out of there as soon as possible.

To Reinar, he suggested, "Should we get started?"

Reinar gestured to the table. "Yes, please, if you will all take your seats."

Tessa and a few others strolled to the table. She walked confidently, clearly unwilling to let Rose get to her. Or at least she must have been trying. Aeden couldn't resist admiring it. He started to follow her, but his father grabbed him roughly by the arm.

Aeden bit back a snarl as his father's fingers dug into him through the coat. Olgar narrowed his eyes and uttered, "Me and you need to talk, boy."

"Later." Aeden shook him off so he could join Tessa at the table.

He took a step, but Rose bumped into him roughly. In a mocking tone, she said, "Someone's in trouble."

Aeden chided, "What are you even doing here?"

With a shrug, she answered, "I had to see what all the fuss was about. Oh, excuse me, I believe there's a seat beside Lord Drake." With a wink, she sauntered off.

Aeden tried to shrug off the twitch he felt coming on with his irritation, when a tall Vampyr—the one who had been covered in dessert the last time he'd seen him at the masquerade—began to pull out the chair beside Tessa. Aeden approached before he could sit and clapped him heavily on the shoulder. He gripped it, digging his fingers in, and pushed the Vampyr back just enough to take the seat for himself.

"Thanks, friend."

The lord's eyes bulged as Aeden sat down next to Tessa. With every other seat already taken, he had no choice but to sit to the right of Aeden. Tessa leaned forward, eyes flitting between Aeden and the other Vampyr.

Worry creased her brow. Cautiously, she said, "Aeden, meet Viscount Peitor. Heir of the Greyson estate."

Aeden sized him up. He didn't look like much with his tightly buttoned vest and soft hands. It would be a shock if the man had ever done manual labor in his life, let alone taken part in a hunt. *This* was the Vampyr her family had chosen for her first?

He stifled a laugh as the image of Tessa being married to such a dandy flashed in his mind. She would be bored senseless. Poor Peitor would never have known how to keep up with her. Or satisfy her, for that matter. The last thought made the hairs on Aeden's neck stand on end.

It was a welcome relief when the household staff marched in carrying fine dishes. A creamy squash soup, followed by fresh-caught fish from the lake, adorned with sprigs of rosemary and thyme. In true Downthorn fashion, a parade of both delicate and hearty dishes were brought before them.

After the last few days, Aeden knew this was all for show. The family rarely ate this extravagantly, but he supposed this could be considered a special occasion. Little did Reinar know, Olgar wouldn't be impressed. Actually, quite the opposite. The opulent feast would be offensive in its uselessness. They needed blood not just to survive but *thrive*.

Aeden cringed as the star of the meal was finally brought out. Jugs that had been kept over the hearth to maintain some semblance of warmth were placed on the table. Aeden watched his father like a hawk, praying he wouldn't snub the offering. Vampyr servants made their way around the room, inching in between the guests in an effort to gracefully pour the blood into crystal chalices.

Olgar sniffed at it, then set it down without taking a sip. Aeden stiffened, waiting for some snide words to leave his father's mouth. When none came, he sat back in his seat. Still, he watched his family and waited.

Tessa huddled close and whispered, "Are you alright?"

Aeden gave her a tense smirk. "Of course, why wouldn't I—"

Across the table, Rose laughed at something Drake said. Aeden couldn't imagine Drake having anything remotely interesting to say. Yet, the two of them seemed to be getting on well enough.

Rose reached across Drake for a butter dish and Aeden wasn't the least bit surprised when the bloke's gaze fell to her exposed neck. Aeden shook his head. If Rose thought flirting with someone else was going to get under his skin, she was mistaken.

Tessa's warm presence beside him was the only thing getting him through the dinner. It was *she* who he looked forward to spending time with when it was over. The sudden thought surprised him, and his eyes shifted to her. She, too, was watching the interaction across the table. And doing a fine job of appearing indifferent to the whole thing.

Drake remarked, a bit too loudly, "Those marks on your neck, Lady Rose. Are those from—"

"Fangs?" She gave him a sultry smile. "Surely, you've dabbled in that guilty pleasure before?"

Beside him, Tessa choked on her drink. Rose shot her a venomous glare, then turned her attention back to Drake. "If you'd like to try sometime, I'd be happy to—"

Reinar slammed his cup down. Aeden held his breath in anticipation. All eyes fell on the head of the household, but rather than voice what Aeden knew would be disgust, he gave a tight-lipped smile and began to ask Sylvia how she had been. The families fell into courteous conversation and Aeden finally began to breathe freely again.

Until Lord Peitor leaped up suddenly. He sauntered over to Drake and whispered into his ear. The men exchanged a few words and then Peitor returned, looking as if he were holding onto some grand knowledge Aeden did not have.

He tensed as Peitor passed his seat and leaned between him and Tessa. The jackass could have whispered, but instead he made the bold move of speaking loud for Aeden to hear. "I've been meaning to offer you my sympathies. It is quite the unfortunate predicament you're in. A better man would have kept his station in mind and politely declined this absurd invitation for courtship."

Tessa recoiled away from Peitor, but Aeden wanted nothing more than to slam the imbecile's head into the table. It was as if all thoughts of assassination and betrayal were forced from his mind. Over the last couple of days, his feelings for Tessa had grown complicated. He knew the engagement wasn't real. That it was a means to an end. But in his heart, those lines were becoming blurred. Forgetting himself, and all the eyes that were on him, Aeden slapped the table with both hands. Diagonal to him, his father's nose flared.

To hell with him and the rest. Aeden stood, forcing Peitor away from Tessa. Drake stood too, with bared teeth. The chandelier light caught on his fangs to reveal them dripping like a venomous snake ready to lunge.

Aeden raised his glass, looking at him and then each one of the others in the eye. His voice carried through the large room as he proclaimed, "A toast! To knowing one's place." The last bit was directed at Peitor. Aeden smiled savagely, showing his own fangs. Fangs that would slice through the ridiculous cravat tied around the young Lord's neck.

Peitor raised his glass to his lips, but just as he opened his mouth to drink, Aeden gave him a heavy pat on the back. It forced him forward and blood slipped from his cup, dribbling down his chin. Aeden grinned, pleased with himself, and sat back down beside Tessa.

He wasn't sure how she would react to the little display, so he peeked out of the corner of his eye. Her hands were placed over her mouth as she hid a giggle. The rest of the table—aside from a sulking Peitor and fuming Drake—fell back into polite conversation. Olgar and Reinar only spoke one or two words here and there, but Flora and Sylvia seemed to be getting along splendidly. The two leaned into one another like lifelong friends.

Aeden tried to think back to before the curse. The two families had come from different territories, but had frequented the same annual events. Maybe the two women had been more familiar with one another than he remembered.

Tessa pushed a plate in front of him. Its citrus scent was strong, mixed with subtle notes of vanilla. He eyed her suspiciously. "What's this?"

In a hushed and mysterious tone, she said, "Don't worry, it's not poisoned."

Aeden laughed uncomfortably and glanced at his father, who was watching them intently. Olgar's seething presence was making him nervous. He never did anything without a hidden agenda, so why had he come here? And if he had sent Aeden there to win over the Downthorns, then why did he seem so bothered that it was working?

Tessa rested her elbow on the table, still looking down at the cake. Aeden scooped up a bite with his fork and offered it to her. "Want to share?"

She wrinkled her nose. "The cake is too sweet. I only like the lemons."

Aeden discarded the fork. "Well, in that case..." He plucked a slice of candied lemon from the top and dangled it under her nose. "You eat the lemons and I'll eat the cake."

She flashed him a dazzling white smile and held her hand out eagerly. The lemon plopped onto her palm, coating it in flakes of sugar. She ate it, licking bits of the sugar from her lips. Aeden took a bite of the cake, unable to take his eyes off her. The cake was rich and soft, and he wondered if Tessa would taste just as sweet.

Rose snorted from across the table, and he shot her a warning glance. But it only seemed to fuel her. She clinked her knife on a glass, meeting his look in a silent challenge. Once everyone's attention was on her, she stood. "I'd like to propose a toast as well. To Aeden, who sowed his wild oats and finally settled down." She smiled sweetly, but it reminded him of a viper.

His eyes drifted to Tessa, but her face was unreadable. The easy going joy that had been on it a moment ago was gone. Replaced with indifference as she listened to Rose politely.

Rose tipped her glass to Tessa and continued, "Don't worry, Lady Tessa, I've taught him a thing or two. And let me tell you, he was an excellent student." She laughed deeply, leaning forward so both Tessa and Aeden could see down the front of her dress. "He's going to make you *very* happy."

He opened his mouth to chide her, but his father snapped at her first. "That's enough of that."

Aeden turned to apologize to Tessa, but she was already standing. She shoved her hair back, shocking everyone at the table. He swore he could feel the heat of her anger as she brushed by him. With murder in her eyes, she scoffed, "Thank you for enlightening us, Rose." Then to the rest of the group, she said, "Excuse me, I need some air."

Aeden jumped from his seat, nearly knocking it over. Tessa was lightning fast, slipping through the door and out of sight. He took long strides to follow her, but Drake blocked his way. Through clenched teeth, Aeden warned him, "Out of my way. I'm not in the mood."

Drake gave a curt shake of his head and nodded for Aeden to sit back down. Instead, Marcos and Balis took it as their cue to join Aeden at his side. They faced Drake in a show of force. Lord Peitor, however, did nothing to offer support to his friend. *Coward*.

Reinar's voice was thunderous as he roared, "Enough!"

Drake stared Aeden and his cousins down, sizing each of them up. Aeden clenched his fists. He didn't want another fight, but if Drake left him no choice, then he wouldn't hesitate. Drake huffed. And to Aeden's amazement, he stepped aside. Marcos and Balis flanked Aeden's back, positioned to stop Drake if he changed his mind.

Rose called out, "I was just teasing! Poor thing can't take a joke."

But Aeden was already bolting from the room. He didn't pay her or anyone else any attention. He was too focused on finding Tessa. Desperate to fix what Rose had just tried to break.

Tessa hadn't made it far. He jogged to catch up and called out to her, "Stop, please, let me explain!"

Without looking at him, she responded over her shoulder, "No need. I think she spelled things out pretty clearly."

Aeden grabbed her by the elbow, forcing her to stop and look at him. "Rose is a petulant schemer. She is jealous and petty, and you shouldn't listen to a thing she has to say."

Tessa raised her chin, staring him directly in the face. "Are you trying to tell me that you and her never—"

Aeden groaned. "No. We did. But it was nothing. Just childish antics."

"I'd hardly call what she was insinuating *childish*." Her nose flared. "For star's sake, did you *feed* on her, too?"

"No. Not that. Not ever." Aeden's stomach turned at the thought.

"I need to know now if you're in this with me. I will not be humiliated by marrying someone who is still entertaining other women on the side. If she can give you what I cannot, then maybe calling this off is for the best."

Aeden took hold of both her hands and squeezed firmly. She needed to understand that it was different with Rose. That it had been a fling. Albeit a long one. But there had been no love. No connection. "Tessa. Rose and I are over. There is nothing between us. It was never love."

Fear flickered in Tessa's eyes. "This isn't love either, Aeden. That is something I cannot give you."

Guilt churned in his stomach. It was something he didn't want to give her, either. But he couldn't deny that the spark was growing between them since accepting her invitation. Call it affection. Call it friendship. Whatever it was, went beyond what he and Rose had shared.

He sighed softly, still clinging to her hands. Afraid that if he let go for a second, he would lose her. "Please. Believe me when I say that I am in this with *you*. That there is no one else."

Tessa's hands relaxed in his grip and her resolve seemed to soften. "I'm not going back in there." She frowned. "I might slap that haughty grin off her face if I do."

"Fair." Aeden chuckled. He actually wouldn't mind seeing that.

"I think I'm just going to go to bed."

"I'll see you in the morning?" Absentmindedly, he ran his thumb over her knuckles.

"Yes." Withdrawing her hands slowly, she added, "Good night, Aeden."

He waited, watching her walk gracefully down the hall that led to the stairs. There was no point in him returning to the dinner either. He'd had quite enough. Enough food. And more than enough time with his family. They would be going home tonight with Rose in tow. And he'd be free of the weight of their judgment and poorly controlled attitudes.

Leaning against the wall to collect himself, he shut his eyes tight. Tessa's face filled his thoughts. Beautiful cascading hair and sugar on her lips. Suddenly, rough hands were on his shoulders, pressing him firmly against the wall. He opened his eyes to find his father.

"Listen close, boy." Olgar's dark red eyes blazed like a flame in the night. "I don't like what I saw tonight."

"What a shock," Aeden drawled. Olgar never liked anything when it came to him.

"I sent you here to woo the girl. Not the other way around."

"I'm not—"

"I saw the two of you together. Walking hand in hand like two young lovers. You're letting her get to you. I'm cursed. Not blind. I see the way you look at her." His father's hands were brutally strong as he pushed Aeden harder against the wall, forcing a small crack to form up to the ceiling. Normally it wouldn't hurt this much, but Aeden was weak after days drinking from the cup. It unnerved him more than the hateful gleam in his father's eyes.

Aeden's voice was strained as he argued, "I'm doing what you sent me to do. If you don't approve of my methods, then get someone else to do your bidding."

Olgar snarled, pulling a vial filled with a dark purple liquid from his jacket pocket. "In two day's time you will slip this to the Count and his son. Put it in those cups they enjoy drinking from so much."

"So soon? It's hardly been enough time to gain their favor, and make sure the blame doesn't fall on me." The vial was bitterly cold in Aeden's hand. He whipped his head around to be sure no one had seen, but they were alone. Swiftly, he shoved it into his pocket. "Surely, there's another way to get the Vampyrs over here to follow you."

Olgar snarled and leaned closer. The strong scent of whiskey wafted off him. "Human scum are skulking around *our* territory and you choose tonight to challenge me and the decisions I make? You said it yourself in that damned letter. Reinar is too weak to defend his people on his own. And tonight, I've seen for myself how far he's fallen. He is a shell of the warrior he once was. Slow, weak, and aging."

"Then what? What will happen to the others?"

"You will play the supportive fiancé. Attempt to make sure no blame will fall on us. We will step in to help the family after their grievous loss. Then, when I have the power, the girl will be yours to do with as you please."

Aeden hissed at a whisper, "They could still suspect me. And even if they don't, how will you convince their loyalists to follow you? They're weak. If they still refuse to drink from the vein, then they won't be any use to you and your plans for the mortal villages."

His father was right that something had to be done in case the humans who left the tracks had been there with ill-intent. But what good would this plan be if Reinar's followers accused Aeden and his father of murder?

Olgar sneered, as if it angered him that Aeden wasn't putting all his faith in his plan. "Don't be a coward. Besides, it won't matter once the two of them are gone. Reinar's people will be grief stricken. We will be strong enough to force any naysayers—anyone who might accuse you—to follow us, regardless. Whether they like it or not. Once they see the extent of the threat, they'll fall into line." Joy glittered in his eyes which, coming from his father, made Aeden more nervous than angry.

Aeden narrowed his eyes. His father knew something he didn't. There was an angle of this plan that he couldn't see. "What are you keeping from me?"

Olgar finally released his hold on him. Taking a bold step back, he replied, "Just do your part. Don't disappoint me."

Aeden reached into his pocket, grasping onto the vial. It was like rocks had settled in the pit of his stomach, weighing him down with guilt, anger, and pain. Two days. His father was giving him two days until he was to destroy a family. To send Tessa's world crashing in around her.

Or... two days to make plans of his own. To find a way to bring the families together in a way that didn't involve the loss of life. Reinar and his family had welcomed him into their home. Had shown him how accepting and tolerating they could be. There had to be a way to make things right for everyone. To save them all.

Eighteen

Tessa

Tessa tied her hair back with a satin ribbon. The tailor had delivered her a handful of new dresses last night when he'd brought her the black and rose gown. Each new piece of her wardrobe was darker than what she usually wore. Deep blues and purples, even a red evening gown that was lined with lace.

Today she opted for blue. It was trimmed with silver vines and thorns, very similar to Aeden's tattoos. When she had placed the order, she couldn't wait to show him, but after last night, she wasn't so sure. Rose had gotten under her skin. Just who did she think she was, coming into Tessa's home and trying to humiliate her in front of everyone? Clawing her eyes out hadn't been an option, so Tessa had fled. It left her feeling cowardly and immature.

Worse was the confusion that settled over her like a storm cloud this morning. As much as she wanted to chalk the whole thing up to wounded pride, Tessa recognized the jealousy laying at the foundation of it. The thought of Aeden and Rose entangled together burned her throat.

Rose had probably never pulled away from his embrace or panicked after a kiss. She was experienced like he was. She'd unabashedly tried to make him jealous by flirting with Drake. And considering the history between Rose and Aeden, they were a match that made sense. Much more sense than he and Tessa made. So, what was he doing with Tessa? If he was being pressured or forced into a marriage he didn't want, then that wasn't fair to him. It was different when he had come to her wholly unattached. But even with his assurances that Rose meant nothing to him, Tessa couldn't shake the sinking feeling in her gut. Putting aside their families and their hopes for the match—what could she give him that Rose couldn't?

Her chest burned with an emotion she couldn't place. Aeden wasn't hers yet. Why was she letting this thing with Rose get to her? Determined to brush it all out of her mind, Tessa threw her door open and stormed down the hall. There were muffled sounds downstairs as the humans were being rounded up to be released back to their lives outside of the forest. The household staff were busy going through the motions, but upstairs was deserted, leaving Tessa overwhelmed by the silence.

She passed by her late aunt's room, a room she had walked by every day for most of her life. The one that Reinar had given her when she became too sick to share a bed with him. So uncomfortable when anyone even brushed against her that she would cry out.

Celine had been quite sick toward the end. Unable to sustain herself on the blood that was served to her. Most days she had been too ill to even come downstairs. Instead, spending her days in the confines of her room, reading or writing. When Tessa was young, she enjoyed sitting with her, but as time went on, Celine grew distant. Withering away to nothingness, until death claimed her in her sleep.

Since then, Reinar had kept the door closed. Too pained by the reminder of yet another loved one lost to them because of the curse. Tessa often wondered if guilt played a part in Reinar's decision to lock away any memory of the woman he loved. Ashamed that he hadn't been able to find a way to keep her fed.

Tessa narrowed her eyes at the door, which was cracked open now. Her breath hitched in her throat. A man's moan slipped through the crack, followed by a woman's whimper. Someone was in there. And they weren't alone. The hairs on Tessa's arms stood on end. She tiptoed closer, peering into the room carefully.

It was dark with the curtains drawn tight. Odessa—one of the humans who was to be released later that day—leaned on the arm of the couch, her hair cascading over her face to reveal her neck. Blood trickled down, staining her gown. Someone had fed from her. Tessa gritted her teeth as the sweet woman who she had come to know and like, whimpered again and slumped further into the corner.

A man growled softly beside her, causing bile to rise in Tessa's throat and she thought she might get sick right then and there. Someone was using her aunt's room to break the rules. Her uncle needed to be alerted immediately.

Tessa began to pull away from the door, but movement at the other end of the couch stopped her in her tracks. Drake came into view as he shoved a petite girl—another of the mortals being released—down on the cushions. He moved her like she was no more than a rag doll, grabbing her hair and bringing her neck to his teeth. Tears streamed down her face as he cut through her flesh and feasted.

No. This was wrong. It wasn't the way things were done on this side of the Crimson Lake. Even when they took blood from the mortals in their care, they used compulsion to calm them. To make them believe that they were safe. That everything was alright.

But Drake was doing nothing to lull his victims. It was like a knife twisting in Tessa's gut as she watched in horror. He pulled back, licking the blood from his lips, and he stared down at the girl.

Her eyes were wide and pleading and she begged him, "Please, don't. Please."

The smile that crept across his face was inhuman. It was as if the girl's fear was making this more enjoyable for him. Beside him and his victim, Odessa choked out a heart stopping gurgling sound. Had he taken too much from her? If he didn't stop, he was going to kill them.

Tessa grabbed the handle of the door, but just as she started to push it open, Drake growled, "Stop your crying. I've had enough." He pushed the girl away from him without remorse and stood, leaving his victims alone on the couch. "I need some fresh air." He walked to the desk, grabbing his jacket from the chair, and Tessa scrambled back.

She slammed into someone and turned to find Aeden with his brows pinched together. His eyes darted around the hall and he asked, "Tessa, what are you—"

Tessa pressed a hand to his mouth, desperate to shut him up. Drake's footsteps grew louder, and she panicked. She pushed Aeden across the hall, scrambling to open the nearest door. She shoved him inside and followed, quietly clicking it shut behind them.

Aeden's eyes sparkled with amusement. "Tessa, if you wanted to be alone, all you had to do was ask."

She had the urge to pace, but she'd shoved them into a closet. There was barely enough room for them to move with all the buckets, mops, and storage boxes crowding the small space. Instead, she was forced to press herself against him. His body was relaxed and languid compared to her rigid and stiff posture.

Ignoring his joking attitude, she whispered to him. "He was feeding from the vein. I saw him. It was vicious. Sickening in the way he seemed to take pleasure from it." The words flowed from her like a flood.

Aeden's easy going demeanor shifted into something dark, reminding Tessa of his Ashbane roots. "Who?"

"Drake." Her head was spinning. Saying it out loud made it all too real. What she'd witnessed was heinous.

"Does your uncle know about this?" Aeden's jaw twitched.

Tessa immediately shook her head. Reinar would never stand for it. Ever.

Aeden's hand brushed against her cheek. He wiped away a tear she hadn't realized was falling. Her uncle rarely concerned himself with Drake. He always respected his wishes when he asked not to be disturbed. Never questioning the hours in which his son went missing or when he came to breakfast with blood already staining his collar. Tessa wanted to kick herself. They had been blind to it. There was no telling how long this had been going on.

Tessa leaned into Aeden's touch. It grounded her. Keeping her steady. "I need to tell him about this."

Aeden put his hand under her chin and raised it to him. "You need to handle this carefully. If he doesn't already know, then he will confront him. And I've seen enough to know that Drake won't take kindly to someone ratting him out. You could get hurt."

"He wouldn't," she began to argue, but thought better of it. He would hurt her. She had no doubt. But it was Reinar who gave her pause. He, unlike Drake, would never do anything to harm her. Her uncle would protect her from his son's wrath, like he'd done many times when they were younger.

That wasn't the concern here. Rather, she feared this news would break Reinar's heart. To hurt the man who had stepped in as a father figure for her was unthinkable. Feeding like this was an offense worthy of exile. He might have overlooked Tessa's transgression during the mortal attack, but this was different.

Aeden pressed further. "Seriously, Tessa. I think you should wait. Just until everything else blows over. Think about everything your uncle already has on his mind."

She gulped heavily. Maybe he was right. The feeders were being released, after all. If she could be certain that the women made it out of the forest, then they would be safe. Drake wouldn't be able to hurt anyone else for the time being.

Aeden was quiet for a moment before he said, "I think he's gone."

Tessa's heart flipped. "The women. They need help!" She took hold of Aeden's hand and pulled him across the hall to her aunt's room. The door was shut this time and locked tight. She couldn't risk breaking the handle and tipping Drake off, so she slipped a pin from her hair, leaving only half of it gathered neatly. The other half of it fell into a tangled mess. She ignored it and shoved the pin into the lock. After a few jerky movements, she heard a click.

Aeden whistled. "Impressive."

Ignoring him, she pushed the door open and stepped into the room. It was still dark, and the scent of blood made her dizzy with hunger. Her gums ached, and she salivated. Digging her nails into her palms to distract her from her cravings, she gestured to the couch. Aeden knelt in front of Odessa and pressed his fingers to the side of her neck that hadn't been fed on.

"There's a pulse." He sounded as relieved as Tessa felt.

She blew out a sigh of relief and then checked the other girl. She, too, had a pulse. It was weak and unsteady, but it was there. Tessa pushed the girl's soft curly hair from her face and was overcome with sadness. This atrocity had happened beneath her own roof. It was scandalous and unacceptable. These women were no match for a Vampyr's strength.

It wasn't like it had been when Tessa fed on the hunter in the woods. Those men had been blessed with a vitality that rivaled her own. And the guilt she'd had for feeding on one of them... The concern she'd had that her family would be ashamed of her. When all this time, Drake was doing much worse.

He wasn't taking their pain or fear away. This was monstrous. The hypocrisy was almost enough to make her scream. Not to mention how loudly he made his disgust for the Ashbanes known. Had he been jealous of them all this time? Envied them and wanted to feed just as they did? Did that jealousy build to this—making him lock himself in his room all day so he could feed on the innocent without reprimand?

The girl's eyes fluttered open, and she wailed at the sight of Tessa. Aeden put himself between the two of them and grabbed

J.M. WALLACE

the girl by the chin. His words were soft and soothing as he said, "You're safe now. We're going to get you home."

Instantly, the girl relaxed. She nodded calmly as the compulsion took hold. But Tessa wasn't prepared for what Aeden did next. He lifted his wrist to his mouth and bit into his own vein. Two small drops of blood bloomed on his inked skin and he held it out to the girl.

"Drink," the command was gentle, and she obeyed.

Tessa grabbed him by the jacket. "What are you doing?"

"Healing her." He said it so matter-of-factly, like it was the most natural thing in the world.

Tessa sat back, dizzy with confusion. She stayed like that on the wolf fur rug and watched as Aeden did the same to Odessa. He whispered a few calm words to her and soon both women were sitting up right with color on their cheeks once more.

She'd never seen anything like it. "Can all Vampyrs heal mortals with their blood?"

Aeden turned to her with genuine confusion twisting his features. "You didn't know?"

Of course not. Tessa's pulse raced rapidly. She knew her people had the ability to heal *themselves*. But she never considered what would happen if they gave their blood to the humans. What else didn't she know? She shook her head, embarrassed by her ignorance.

But Aeden said nothing more about it. Instead, he suggested, "We should get them out of here. I can wipe their minds when we reach the forest's edge."

Tessa froze. Drake was supposed to go with a few others to release the feeders. What if he decided to keep the women? To stash them some place so he could continue to feed on them?

She bit her lip. "We need to take them all. My uncle is sending the others home today, but it needs to be the two of us who take them. We need to be sure they actually make it out of the forest alive."

Aeden nodded, helping the mortals to their feet, then gestured to the door. Admiration filled her as she watched how tenderly he handled the women. There was nothing monstrous or dangerous about him at this moment. It warmed her heart to see. Forcing herself to look away, she opened the door, glancing both directions down the corridor to be certain that no one would see them. She motioned for him to follow, and he and the women started down the hall behind her.

Before they reached the stairs, she turned to Aeden. "Take them out the servant doors in the back. I'll go talk to my uncle and tell him that you found these two wandering the hallway, so you took them outside to prepare to leave."

Aeden bowed his head to her, and she was relieved he was letting her take the lead on this. Then, with haste, she scurried down the stairs to find Reinar. He was waiting with the humans all lined up in the foyer. Their eyes were already glazed over, a sure sign that he'd started working on the compulsion to make them forget the last few weeks.

"Uncle," Tessa called out cheerfully. She clasped her shaking hands to hide the tumultuous emotions she was really experiencing. "I was hoping you would allow Aeden and I to escort the humans back to the road. I'm feeling a little cooped up today, and after last night, Aeden and I could use the time together."

Reinar beamed. "I think that's a splendid idea. And a great opportunity to let Aeden witness the way we do things here."

"Exactly." Tessa fought the urge to tap her foot impatiently. Drake could walk in at any moment to challenge her. To give himself the opportunity to keep any of the humans for his secret feedings. She sucked in a deep breath. "Aeden is already outside with Odessa and one of the others. I'd hate to keep him waiting." She gestured for the humans to follow her, and they obeyed. With their emotionless eyes and slow gait, they appeared as if they were sleepwalking.

Reinar bid her goodbye and disappeared into his office for midmorning tea. Relieved that he was fine with her interjection, Tessa led the humans out the door and to the side of the house, where Aeden waited. They walked silently, going at a pace that the recently fed on women could sustain. It wasn't long before they reached the edge of the Crimson Forest.

Tessa didn't dare say a word for fear that she would lose all control over her emotions. Now that they were here, so close to giving the women and the other mortals their freedom, the shock was setting in. Drake was a monster. One who had condemned the Ashbanes time and time again for the way they fed. When all along, he had been doing it in hiding. He was a hypocrite.

Aeden finished compelling the women and the others. Making them forget the walk and commanding them to go home, believing they had taken a long trip. The women joined hands with joyful smiles and walked calmly from the forest with the other mortals in tow. They looked like two old friends taking a stroll together. You would never guess they'd been at death's door only minutes ago.

Aeden rubbed his hand along Tessa's arm. "Are you okay?"

She realized she was trembling. "I-I don't know."

"I'm sorry, Tessa." He grabbed her hand and cupped it between both of his. "Drake won't get away with this."

Her mouth grew dry and her body burned like she had a fever coming on. Maybe it was denial and defensiveness. Or maybe she was still in shock at what she'd witnessed. And drained from the mess she had just cleaned up for her hateful cousin. But it was as if she had to unleash the anger building within her at someone. Anyone. She tore her hand from his. "He's doing no more than what you and your family have always done."

He snarled and glared at the house. "Say what you want about my family, but *I* never play with my food. Nor have I ever approved of those who do."

Tessa winced. But still, she argued, "But you do feed from them. You can't deny that. And you can't deny how ugly that is." She didn't know why she was lashing out at him, but she couldn't stop. She had to do something. Say anything. Or else she was going to lose her mind.

Aeden stood his ground, but clenched and unclenched his fists. "Yes. We feed from the vein. We need blood to survive, and this is the only way to give us the strength necessary to defend our people. But I have *never* fed like that. I always use compulsion. *Always*. And our household staff heals them the minute they leave the room. Do not dare compare me to someone like Drake."

"He's..." she trailed off, unsure of what she could say in her cousin's defense. In truth, he had none. Something about the way he'd been feeding had seemed like it was all sport to him. She inhaled sharply and said, "I'm sorry. I didn't mean to accuse you. I owe you gratitude for what you just did for those women."

"I don't want your gratitude, Tessa. I just want your trust." He broke eye contact with her, looking down at her boots. If she didn't know any better, she'd think that he looked remorseful. But why? He had done a good thing just now.

"Aeden," his name rolled off her lips, and she closed the gap between them, placing her hand on his chest. "I know you're not the same as Drake. And I do trust you. Right now, you're one of the few people in this world I feel like I *can* trust."

He shook his head. "Tessa, I..." he drifted off.

She bit her lip. "We should get back before anyone wonders what's taking so long." Worry gnawed at her. Drake would be sure to wonder how the women had gotten out of his mother's room on their own. But she doubted he would bring attention to it. Not if he wanted to keep his secret, that is.

Aeden nodded. Silently, they walked back to the chateau, hand in hand. Tessa leaned against him as they trudged through the forest. His presence was a comfort. Knowing she didn't have to carry the weight of this secret on her own. Guilt ate at her like waves chipping away at stones on the shore. Adding this to her uncle's burden didn't feel right. She would tell him when things with the Ashbanes and the possible human threat had calmed down. When she knew how to do so without putting herself at risk. In the meantime, at least she could count on having Aeden in her corner. Her shield. Her partner. The man she would trust with her family's shame.

Nineteen

Aeden

A eden spent the next two days at Tessa's side. She was more solemn than before, but only he knew the cause. Her family had no idea that the weight of Drake's secret was resting on her shoulders. They assumed it was the rationed blood, leaving her like the rest of them with the sharp pain of cravings. Her mother and uncle doted on her and attempted to cheer her up, but none of it did any good. Couldn't they see that something more was eating at her?

Through it all, he kept his thoughts to himself. Even when Drake joined them for meals, Aeden said nothing. He didn't speak out about what he'd witnessed or voice his disgust. Instead, he sat silently beside Tessa, holding her hand when the secret became too much for her to bear.

Selfishly, he was glad she'd taken his advice to keep it to herself. A part of him knew that Drake would lash out at her, and the last thing he wanted was for Tessa to put herself in danger. But the other part of him—the one that felt ill every time he thought of the dark purple poison hidden away in his violin case—was relieved she hadn't said anything because this was a secret he could use to his advantage.

Having an alternative to offer up to his father allowed him to rest easy for the time being. Of course, he still had to get Olgar to agree. But in the meantime, Aeden's mind was at ease. Allowing him to give Tessa the attention she deserved.

Alone in his room now, he took the vial from his violin case and tucked it safely into his pocket. If everything went right tonight, then he would no longer need it. An invitation had arrived at breakfast asking him and the Downthorns to join his family for dinner on their side of the lake. Aeden knew it was a ploy on his father's part to get him under the same roof as him.

If he could get his father alone to explain his plan and make him see the sense in it, then he would be free to bury the poison where it would never be found. No one would ever know how close he'd come to murder.

Three days had passed since the dinner with the two families at the Downthorn estate. And his father would be livid at the fact that Reinar and Drake were still standing. A lifetime of wrath doled out by Olgar made him grit his teeth. He had always tested Aeden. Forcing him to prove his worth to the family. Even if it was at his own expense. But the more time he spent away from Olgar, the more clearly he saw his flaws. The man was vain and short-sighted. Those things were not the makings of a great leader.

This dinner was nothing more than his father's way of summoning Aeden to explain himself. But it was tonight that he would put the secret he and Tessa shared to use. With the knowledge that the Downthorn heir was breaking the laws Count Reinar himself had created for his side of the lake, they could manipulate their loyalists. Open their eyes to see that the Downthorns weren't perfect. That even *they* were not good enough to stand upon the pedestal they'd crafted.

It was the perfect solution. And it had fallen right into his lap. His father could still get exactly what he wanted, and Tessa would still have her family together and whole. And Aeden... well, he wouldn't have to betray her. Wouldn't have to repay hers and her family's kindness with the worst deceit imaginable. It could all work out. After all, wasn't spilling a secret more forgivable than murder?

Tessa was waiting for him outside of his room. She was stunning in a deep red dress lined with black embroidery. The fine detailing consisted of tangled florals and small winged creatures that resembled bats more than birds. She was the very epitome of Vampyr. A deadly beauty.

He longed to kiss her. To pull her into his arms and make her smile again. During the past few days, they had spent all of their time together. Glued to one another's sides. Sometimes they talked. Reminiscing about their childhoods before the curse. Or swapping stories like two old friends. But he'd only gotten a handful of true smiles out of her. Whether it was from the secret weighing on her or their growing friendship, he couldn't quite tell. And he was too afraid of the answer to ask.

Opting for a kiss on her hand, he pressed his lips to her cool skin. "Breathtaking as usual." He winked.

With a half smile, she held onto his hand and pulled him to the stairs. Her family was waiting, bundled in warm jackets to battle the frigid night. Aeden greeted everyone except for Drake, making a point of ignoring him just as he had been doing lately.

Drake eyed him warily. Something told Aeden that he suspected it was he who found the mortal women upstairs. But he hadn't said anything yet, so Aeden went about his business as usual. Focusing all of his attention on Tessa and on making polite conversation with Reinar and Flora when needed.

Reinar beamed at them. "In we go!"

A rush of cold swept over Aeden, chilling him down to the bone. For a moment, he considered talking Reinar out of going. To keep Tessa and the rest of the family far from Olgar's reach. But he needed to speak with his father in person. Convincing him through a letter was too risky and would leave no room for Aeden to plead his case. No. They had to go. He had to pretend everything was normal, so Reinar didn't become suspicious.

Drake and Flora followed Reinar into one carriage, while Aeden and Tessa climbed into the other. Talos snapped the reins. The horses spooked, jolting the carriage violently, making Tessa fall into Aeden's lap with a gasp.

Her body on his summoned an ache of longing. He tugged at the collar of his shirt in an attempt to loosen it along with the hold she seemed to have on him any time she touched him. Helping her up, he pulled her into the seat next to him. Now that he'd lost confidence in Talos' driving capabilities, he thought it best to keep her close. He put his arm around her and she snuggled in nicely. A perfect fit.

"Tessa." Worry for tonight swirled in the pit of his stomach. "If this doesn't go well, simply say the word and we'll leave."

She lifted her head, shifting to look up at him through her thick lashes. They kissed the tops of her cheeks when she blinked. He warmed, though he was quick to blame it on her body heat passing to his and nothing more.

Her voice was pinched with worry as she asked, "Should I be worried about tonight?"

"No," he answered too quickly. "It's just, after the last time our families were together... I only wanted to tell you that if you get the urge to run again, I'm happy to join you."

With a satisfied half smile, she leaned into him once more.

Trees passed by in a haze of red. It was as if Aeden were trapped in a fog. His thoughts whirled with the leaves in the trees. Would his father agree to his plan? Could the two families be in the same place without someone trying to tear another's throat out? Both seemed unlikely.

The Ashbane estate came into view. Its ominous presence cast a large shadow over their carriage and Aeden's mood. It was as if his father had built the manor to be everything the Downthorn home wasn't. Dark, chipped paint coated the outside. Statues of creatures only seen in the Autumn Court of Unseelie—gargoyles with horned heads and bat wings, phoenixes with flaming tails—adorned the courtyard. They were all there to welcome him home.

Aeden helped Tessa down from the carriage, putting on a confident front so she wouldn't worry. He would be doing plenty of that for the both of them. The greetings between the families were pleasant enough, and he breathed a sigh of relief when they finally stepped into the home.

It was warm, with a fire going in the massive fireplace. As the families began to converse amongst each other, Aeden watched Tessa. She walked around the large sitting room, running her hand over the velvet armchairs and gazing up at the golden framed paintings, different from the ones Aeden had seen in her home. There was no reminder of the lovers who had set their fates on this course. Instead, his father adorned their home with vicious tales of the strong triumphing over the weak.

The paintings in the Ashbane home told stories of war and defeat. Of ancient gods who had forced men to bend the knee. Of monstrous creatures who breathed fire, laying waste to mortal cities. They were tales that the humans told in the villages. Mostly to frighten little children. But Aeden's father had taken them to heart. Had poured himself into the stories, imagining himself as one of those forces that would leave the mortals trembling at his feet.

Aeden had never paid them much mind. Preferring to spend his time by the lake or gallivanting with his cousins and sometimes with Rose. But at that moment, he had a twisting in his gut. What would Tessa think of them? He had tried to explain to her that not all of his folk were as bad as they'd been made out to be. But he wouldn't blame her if she didn't believe him now that she had seen his father's art collection for herself.

He sidled up to her. "What do you think?"

After a thoughtful moment, she cocked her head. "It's unique."

Aeden laughed. A polite answer. But a vague one.

She shook her head. "I actually find it really interesting, you know. The way their emotion is portrayed. And how the mortals never seem to lose their faith."

Aeden had never thought of it that way. In every depiction, they were being cast down. Conquered or eliminated. But now that he looked closer, he could see what she meant. Their mouths were hard set. Eyes overflowing with determination. Even the men cowering and bowing to their oppressors held a glimmer of hope in their eyes. A furrow of their brows. Expressions that said all was not lost. They would rise again.

He wanted to ask her more about what she saw and what she thought, but his father bee-lined for him. "You and I need to talk. Now." He sneered at Tessa and something deep and primal inside of Aeden made him take a step, putting himself between the two of them. His father was welcome to any feelings of disdain he might harbor for Tessa, but Aeden wouldn't allow him to make her uncomfortable. His blood boiled in his veins.

Olgar stormed into the study and Aeden placed his hand on the small of Tessa's back as he promised, "I'll just be a moment."

Concern knitted Tessa's brow, but she didn't try to stop him. It pained him to leave her like that. There was no telling what might be going through her mind. But the sooner he and his father spoke, the better.

The study was bitterly cold. Aeden shuddered as he closed the heavy door behind him. He started before his father could. "Listen, I know you're upset—"

"One job. You had one job." Olgar wagged a furious finger in the air. "I should have known you wouldn't have the balls to go through with it."

Aeden gritted his teeth. "If you would let me speak, then you would know that I have an alternative plan. A *better* one."

His father huffed indignantly. "Do share."

Aeden inched closer. He spoke low, even though the large oak door was thick enough to protect them from eavesdroppers. "Count Reinar's son has been feeding from the vein."

That seemed to pique Olgar's interest. He raised a curious brow and poured himself a drink. Aeden knew better than to expect that he'd be offered one. So he continued, "This information gives us the upper hand if used correctly." He walked to the desk, shoving his father's papers out of the way so he could sit.

An old leather-bound notebook titled *The Change* caught his eye. He'd never seen the inscription before, but he recognized the journals his father favored for personal use. Tucking the curiosity away for later, Aeden explained, "We present him with two choices. Either he steps down as self proclaimed judge of the Crimson Forest, forcing him to follow your lead. Or we expose his son for the hypocrite he is. If Reinar knows of Drake's deceit and does nothing to punish him for it, then he will be breaking his own rules. Thus swaying their loyalists to our side in the end when they all see sense." To drive his point home, he added, "Death is sympathetic. But this makes us look good and honest."

Olgar grunted. He had several variations of those grunts, but this was the one he reserved for rare occurrences when he was pleased with Aeden. After a thoughtful beat, his father said, "Your plan's not without merit. He would *never* send one of his own into exile. At least not without pause. So that leaves him with no other choice than to take us up on the offer or risk losing the faith of his followers."

"So... you'll do it? You'll exchange the assassination for blackmail?" Aeden's nerves were taut. If his father accepted, then Tessa wouldn't have to face the heartbreak of losing yet another father.

The Vampyrs loyal to her family wouldn't like Olgar's plans for them. Not at first. But he could be persuasive when he put in the effort. They would come to accept that this was a better way of life. One where they didn't have to hide and starve. Tessa would see, too, in time. This was the only way for him to help his family without hurting her or anyone else. And then maybe they could continue on the way they had been. The last thought came unbidden and Aeden couldn't help but note the fluttering in his stomach.

Olgar slammed his drink on the desk, spilling a few drops on the notebook. "I'll consider it and have my answer for you by the end of the night."

That was enough to soothe Aeden's nerves. He lingered, watching carefully as his father returned to the rest of the party, leaving him alone at the desk. With one more glance to be sure no one was lurking, he flipped the notebook open.

The sketches portrayed a ghastly beast with grotesque human hands. The elongated talons and a row of teeth as sharp as his own fangs made the breath hitch in his throat. And scratched beside it was his father's familiar handwriting: *Price? Blood Curse?*

What was this? His father never took part in artistic endeavors. He never did anything to simply pass the time. But if these drawings weren't purely imaginative, then what were they?

Tessa popped her head in the door and Aeden leapt up from the desk. "Dinner is beginning." She tilted her head and curiosity overshadowed the smile on her face, turning it into a frown. "Is everything alright?"

Aeden reached behind his back and shut the journal. "Of course." His mouth felt as dry as sand in the Summer Court beaches, but he forced a charming grin. "Let's go."

Dinner in Aeden's home was never as extravagant an affair as it was in Tessa's. Olgar saw no point in wasting resources on fancy meals when the sustenance it gave them paled in comparison to blood. The only reason he bothered to serve it at all seemed to be out of habit. Instead, rare bloody meat sat on platters at the center of the table. Surrounded by bland, undercooked root vegetables. If his father was serving such a sorry fare for the company, then he must be saving up for the main course.

Rose sauntered into the room as if she owned the place, which grated on Aeden's nerves. There was no reason for her to attend yet another family dinner. And considering what happened at the last gathering, Olgar should have known better than to allow it.

On his way to join Tessa, Rose threw herself in front of him. She ran her hands along his chest and down to his sides. Aeden dodged the kiss she had aimed for his cheek and warned, "Don't."

With a pout and her hands still fondling his jacket, she replied, "I'm just saying hello."

Aeden rolled his eyes and took a step back. When he locked eyes with Tessa standing a few feet away, he smiled.

Rose, who never liked to lose, bumped into him hard as she left to find her seat. Aeden ignored the slight. He was far too eager to be near Tessa than to allow Rose to get a rise out of him. His heart thudded in his chest as he pulled Tessa's chair out for her. The dining table was set with unpolished silver plates and tilted goblets. He sat on the edge of his seat, hands planted firmly on the table.

Rose sat across from him. She had no doubt invited herself there. Beside her, Drake leaned in close and whispered into her ear. With a tilt of her head, her hair shifted behind her to reveal bite marks in her neck. Drake licked his lips. Aeden's stomach turned.

Tessa whispered to him, "Are those—"

"Bite marks. Seems she's been busy." Who was she allowing to feed on her this time? Aeden cringed as Drake trailed his fingers along Rose's bare arms. There was his answer. He drawled, "And I would wager I know who it is."

Tessa paled. "You mean. Drake and Rose? That's..." she trailed off, wrinkling her nose in disgust.

"Yeah..." Aeden grabbed Tessa's hand under the table. "Let's just get through this. When it's over, I owe you a strong drink."

Tessa smiled warmly and suggested, "In the library."

Aeden returned the smile. A night cap in the library was just what he needed.

Once everyone was settled, Olgar took his place at the head of the table across from a very suspicious looking Reinar. With a wave of his regal hand, Aeden's father called in the servants. Each of them held a thin silver chain wrapped around the wrists of several mortals. He recognized a few as the humans who had been under his family's roof for some time now, but there were at least two fresh faces.

If this was his father's idea of appeasing Reinar in order to get close to him, then he'd lost his mind. It was like he was purpose-fully trying to make Aeden's job harder. Unless he had decided to take Aeden's advice after all. If he planned to blackmail Reinar, then there was no reason to keep up the charade.

Tessa tensed beside him as the mortals were brought around the table. There was one human to every two Vampyrs. Aeden held his breath, waiting for the outrage to come from Reinar. The mortals stepped forward, holding their arms out above the goblets. Servants inched in with them, flashing shining daggers. They placed the blades on the mortals' wrists, releasing small droplets of blood.

Drake's eyes glittered with excitement. But Reinar bellowed with anger, "Just what do you think you're doing, Ashbane?"

Olgar puffed out his chest. "Is there a problem?"

Reinar seethed. "You know damn well there is."

Both men stood. They marched to the middle, where a mortal stood behind Drake, ready to fill his cup with their blood. Reinar snatched the blade from the servant and threw it to the ground. Olgar sneered down at it. When he looked up, Aeden saw the brewing hatred in his eyes. It was a look he'd seen often as a child. Mixed with delight. Eager to inflict pain.

Aeden pressed his hands on the table and began to stand, ready to intervene, but Tessa's hand clutched his tightly. He watched the patriarchs of their families stand nearly nose to nose in an outrage. Flora fluttered to Tessa's other side. She whispered, "Aeden, perhaps you should take her home."

Before he could respond, Olgar bellowed. "We eat fresh from the vein because it makes us stronger, Reinar. You know this. We need to be at our best. This is no slight to you."

Reinar shook his head vehemently. "It is not right. There are better ways to survive."

Olgar snorted, taking a long drink from his glass of scotch. "Says the withering warrior. You're a shadow of your former self, old friend. Had you been feeding as we have all this time, then you wouldn't be in the predicament that you are. Then again, you've always been short-sighted."

Reinar snarled, his entire body trembling for all to see. "And you have always reached far above your station. Even if it means putting your own people at risk."

Flora raised her voice in warning. "Brother. Don't."

Olgar slammed his glass on the ground. The shards scattered across the aged wood floor. Then he drawled dangerously low, "Henry's death was not my fault."

Tessa sucked in a loud breath at the mention of her father's name. Aeden burned with anger for her. Olgar and Reinar were too blinded by the past to see what they were doing to everyone in this very moment.

Olgar didn't stop there. "We needed to raid that village. We had to feed if we wanted to defeat those damned hunters."

Reinar's hands shook as he declared, "You led him right into their clutches. And then you *ran*. You ran like the coward that you are. My brother-in-law would still be alive today if it hadn't been for your hubris." Pointing at Tessa, he added, "He would be here to see his daughter grown. To give her away on her wedding day."

Sarcasm dripped in Olgar's voice as he said, "*Count Reinar,* ever the martyr. You are at as much fault as I am for drawing those hunters into the village that day. Your scouts missed the signs of their presence and failed to warn us."

Reinar drew his shoulders back, reminding Aeden that he was once a warrior. A match for his own father. One that had humiliated him in battle before and looked ready to do it again. Proudly, he countered, "That is why I have devoted my life to keeping us safe. To prevent something like that from ever happening again."

Olgar spat. "You have done nothing but make us weak. The only thing you've accomplished is preventing our people from living up to their true potential."

Reinar started, "The curse—"

"Is a *gift*," Olgar finished. "One that we should embrace." The look he shot Drake sent Aeden off the edge. Was he about to announce their secret for the entire room to hear?

Reinar must have been too overcome with anger to notice the exchange. He snarled, "We're leaving!" The room turned into a blur of movement as the families shuffled and shoved around each other. Reinar passed them in a flurry, followed by Drake, Flora, and then Tessa.

Aeden took one last look at his father. Then, using his words against him, said, "You had one job." He didn't wait for a response. Turning to follow the Downthorns out to the carriages, he ignored his mother, who was calling after him.

The Downthorns had already climbed into their carriage, all except for Tessa. She waited at the bottom of the stairs, clutching her jacket close to her. The carriages creaked as they started to move and soon they were rolling down the path leading back the way they'd come. Aeden shot a questioning look at Tessa.

"I told Talos we'd walk back. I thought the fresh air might do us some good."

He offered her his arm. "You read my mind."

They headed down the path, shrouded in shadows from the thick trees overhead. Even though it was just the two of them, Tessa spoke low. "They both mean well in their own way."

Aeden scoffed. "They're both stubborn and believe they know what's best for us."

Something rustled in the trees and Tessa's grip tightened on him. "What *is* best for us? Does anyone even know anymore?"

Aeden frowned. "We live in a world of limited choices." None of which appeared to be the right one. And when it came to Reinar and his father, it seemed like their decisions were clouded by mistakes of the past.

Tessa wove her hand into his. "Maybe it's time for someone else to start making them."

It was impressive how she could read him so well. Anticipate what he needed to hear before he realized it. What if that was the answer? For both his father and Reinar to be replaced by someone who could make unbiased decisions. But who? Certainly not Drake.

And Aeden hardly wanted that responsibility on his own shoulders. Besides, for as long as their people had lived with the curse, they had followed one man. He peered down at Tessa. What sort of leader would she make if there was no one to stand in her way? She was more open minded than most. And when given the freedom to do so, she listened to her heart as well as her head.

His father would gladly take that position from Reinar by any means necessary. But he knew Tessa well enough by now to know she wouldn't be willing to do the same. What if Aeden could help her? If they wanted it badly enough, they might be able to figure out a way to do it. To at the very least, get Reinar to take their advisement into more consideration.

He opened his mouth to suggest it, but something rattled the trees nearby. Chills ran up the back of his neck and he drew Tessa closer to him. She sucked in a quick breath and wrinkled her brow. It jumbled his nerves even more. Deer never would have stumbled on them like this. Their instincts would have told them to steer clear. So, what was it?

"Tessa, something's not right." His neck prickled. An instinctual warning.

An ear-piercing screech in the trees stopped him short. Shielding Tessa was his first thought. Placing himself between her and the noise, he attempted to sharpen his eyes in the dark. He wished now that he had fed back at the house. It would have been to

Reinar's horror, but at least he wouldn't be fruitlessly staring into the shadows. He was running on stale blood from lunch and, because of that, his senses were dulled.

Tessa clutched the back of his jacket. "Do you see what it is?"

"I can't see shit. Do you—"

Something pounced on him, throwing him across the path and into the thicket of trees. It was no bigger than he was, but it was quick. Aeden struggled to get his footing. Tessa called out to him, but there was no time to answer her. The creature closed in on him and snapped at his neck with a full row of razor-sharp teeth. Teeth like fangs. But not just two. They were all like that. Images of the sketch in his father's journal flashed in his mind, and his blood ran cold.

A wispy trail of moonlight caught on the creature's body. It was human-like, but its skin was gray and thin. As if it hadn't seen the sun in sometime. He'd never seen anything like it. Not even in Elfhame.

Aeden roared, pushing the grotesque creature off of him. It recovered quickly, advancing on him again. He braced himself for impact, but it stopped just inches from his face. It croaked like a squeaky door and grappled at its chest where a long, broken stick protruded through its heart.

The beast dropped to its knees to reveal Tessa breathing heavily behind it. Her hand shook as she reached up to wipe the sweat from her brow. Her eyes were wide with shock as they roved over Aeden.

Quickly, he reassured her, "I'm fine. It's okay, come here." He inched around the creature's body, which writhed with the last few moments of life. Aeden reached out for Tessa, eager to get away from the grotesque, dying beast.

She fumbled with his hand and said shakily, "I've never seen anything like that. What is it?"

Aeden didn't know how to answer. He had never encountered something like it in person. But the illustrations in his father's notebook were fresh in his mind. The notes had read *price* and *curse*. He released his hold on her and stepped closer to the creature's now lifeless body. Its neck was clear of any marks, so he grabbed its arm carefully and turned it over. There was no need to push its sleeve up since it was already tattered and nearly falling off of it.

Bile rose in his throat at the old leathery feel of the monster's skin. When he caught sight of what he was searching for, he almost lost his balance. "Shit," he cursed as his eyes fell on the red, inky mark on its forearm. The same mark the previous attackers had donned. "He's one of the witch-blessed. This is bad." The words fell flat in describing just how big of a problem this was.

Tessa's voice was tight as she said, "I guess we know what the price of accepting the witch's help was now."

Aeden's pulse raced, and he dropped the man's arm quickly. Whatever aid the witch had offered was no blessing. It was a curse. But why had those very words been in his father's journal? How had he known before Aeden and the rest of them? More importantly, why hadn't he warned them?

Aeden grabbed Tessa by the arm and drew her close to him. His heartbeat pounded in his ears as he peered around the forest. The humans hadn't come alone when they attacked them after the masquerade. And when they'd found the tracks, there had been more than one set. It seemed they didn't travel alone.

As if fate thought of him as one big joke, several more screeches filled the air. His chest tightened with dread. With a low growl, he urged, "We need to run."

He tugged at her hand. If they could get back to the road, they'd have a clear shot to the manor. They'd gone too far to turn back to his home, so the Downthorn chateau was their only option. With weak knees, he jolted forward, but before they could break into a run, Tessa was torn away from his grasp.

Panicked ringing in his ears drowned out her shouts. Several of the witch-blessed creatures had slinked from the shadows. All marked with the same treacherous brand. Humans twisted by dark magic. And they had Tessa. Aeden bared his fangs at them. As the creatures descended on them, he prayed to the fates to spare her.

Twenty

Tessa

Searing pain scorched through Tessa. Burrowing through flesh and muscle. It came from every inch of her, making it difficult to tell where the twisted, monstrous claws were actually tearing into her. Aeden grunted nearby, but she couldn't spot him through the tangle of elongated limbs reaching for her.

One of the humans turned monster snapped at her neck. The moonlight accented its red eyes. Eyes like her own, only brighter and there were no pupils. As if fresh blood had filled them to the brim. Survival instincts kicked in, and Tessa dodged the bite with whatever little agility she had left. She hadn't fed in hours and with each heavy blow from the witch-blessed hunters, her strength faded. *Not blessed,* she corrected herself. *Cursed.*

Just as the Unseelie King cursed her people to an eternity of bloodlust, the witch's so-called blessing had turned these men into something more horrifying than she or anyone might have imagined. Dark shadows crept into her vision, but she couldn't lose consciousness. Not here. Not like this. Using all of her weight, she rolled until she was on top of her nearest attacker.

Claws continued to tear at her arms and her back, but taking out one was better than none. The monster wailed in agony as she sank her fangs into its throat. Rank, rotten blood filled her mouth, and she choked. It was nothing like the blood she drained from the human after the masquerade. It was as if it had curdled in this man's veins. But if she let go now, she'd lose her chance to kill it. So, she clamped down harder. With her teeth still latched, she pulled away, spilling enough blood to fill the air with its putrid scent. As if sensing the death of one of their own, the creature's comrades cried out into the night.

They retreated from her. Just enough for her to catch a glimpse of Aeden. He was drenched in inky black blood. It was impossible to tell if he himself was wounded. With savagery, he grabbed the creature closest to him and tore its arm from its torso. Tessa's stomach roiled at the sight, but despite that, she felt a glimmer of hope. Together, they might make it out alive.

The turned human wailed and reached for Aeden with its remaining arm. Had it still been a mere mortal, it would have succumbed to its wounds. But this was different. Although it wasn't healing the way Vampyrs did, it still didn't die. Tessa's heart dropped as it came close to grabbing a tiring Aeden.

She scrambled across the ground, dodging a few of the beasts who had snapped out of their grief-like howls. One grabbed onto her leg and she screamed as she watched his opponent's claws meet the flesh on Aeden's flawless face, leaving a long jagged gash from forehead to chin. It cut clear down his nose, narrowly missing his right eye.

Seeming to only fuel Aeden's determination and renew his strength, he snatched the creature by hair that still looked alarmingly human-like. Then, with its brittle, brown hair wrapped around his hand, Aeden yanked its neck to his mouth and bit with a disgusted grimace.

Meanwhile, Tessa tried to kick free from the hold on her ankle. Teeth sank into her calf, straight through the muscle without resistance. Rolling onto her back, she slammed her heel into the creature's face and felt bone crunch under the impact.

"Aeden!" Her limbs grew heavy as her injuries began to catch up with her. She wouldn't last much longer. Not when they were so outnumbered.

Her eyes began to flutter shut. All she could do was focus on Aeden's fearsome shouts. He was close. Much closer than before. But he couldn't fight the beasts all on his own. She needed to get up. Willing her body to give just a little more, to hold on a little longer, she began to push herself off the ground.

When she opened her eyes, the forest was no longer pitch dark. Firelight glowed above her. Were the trees on fire? No. There was no smoke. No searing heat kissing her skin. But the glow was bright enough to light the ground around her. The dirt was soaked. Covered in the darkest blood she'd ever seen. Was it her blood? Or was it theirs?

Aeden shouted, "Back! Back!" He stepped into view, holding a large branch. It burned bright at the end. Fire and the faintest hint of alcohol wafted in the air. As he thrust the flaming branch at the beasts, dry pieces of leaves drifted down around her.

Before she registered what was happening, the creatures' shrieks pierced her ears. A new flood of adrenaline rushed through her and she watched wide-eyed as the strange human-like monsters shrunk into the shadows of the forest. The smell of burning flesh covered the scent of blood. Those who weren't quick enough to escape Aeden's fiery wrath sizzled like flint lighting a new fire. And her heart swelled with joy.

Their attackers were burning. And those who weren't were fleeing. Aeden had saved them. She would have shouted for joy if she was strong enough to summon any semblance of sound. Her eyes threatened to close again, growing heavier with each ragged breath she took.

"I've got you. Tessa, you need to stay awake. Do you hear me?" Aeden's voice trembled, but his arm was sturdy as he scooped her up. The fire was warmer up there where he held her. With a few grunts and shakes, she was suddenly laying across both of his arms as he cradled her.

He never let go of the fire, though, and held the branch out like a blazing sword. Like a knight. Her knight. The one who was carrying her to safety. Her back throbbed where she rested on his arms and she hissed. Sucking in an uneasy breath, and trying to focus on the light of the fire leading their way, Tessa felt hot tears on her cheek.

Aeden's voice was like a beacon in the night, calling out to her, "Just a little farther. Stay with me, okay?"

She desperately wanted to tell him she would stay with him for as long as he wanted her to. That she would do as he said. But her voice wouldn't obey. Instead, black spots danced in her vision. Try as she might, she couldn't battle the exhaustion as it came to claim her.

Muffled voices echoed through the void that Tessa seemed to be trapped in. Her mom, uncle, and even Drake were there, but she couldn't bring herself to open her eyes.

"What in the star's name happened, Aeden?" Reinar's voice was thunderous, but Tessa didn't miss the fear laced there.

"Creatures like I've never seen before. They were... like us. But not. More twisted. More wild." With a heavy sigh, he added, "And they were marked. Like the ones that attacked us after the masquerade." Aeden spoke low, and she wanted to thank him for it. Her pounding head couldn't handle much more.

Reinar spoke again. Too loudly. "Impossible."

Aeden snarled. "All I know is what I saw. They're fast. Deadly. But afraid of fire. Or light. I don't know. Whatever power the witch granted them to hunt us has turned them into something inhuman. We barely made it out alive."

Drake's voice grated on Tessa's nerves as he bellowed, "We'll assemble the other families."

Aeden spoke to Drake for the first time in, well, Tessa couldn't even remember right now. "Take torches. A lot of them."

Tessa's mother interjected, "Maybe we should wait until the morning. The house is fortified. We're safe here."

Reinar argued. "No. We can't risk losing them."

Footsteps thudded against the wooden floors and doors in two different directions opened and shut. A gentle, icy hand pushed

Tessa's hair from her sweat soaked face. Her mother's voice was like a lantern lighting her way home as she said, "Aeden, take Tessa to her room." She paused and shouted for Talos, and Tessa couldn't stop the small moan that tunneled up through her throat. Too loud.

Flora took on a commanding tone. "Get Aeden a poultice for their wounds. And blood. A lot of it."

He stuttered, "B-but the rations..."

"Damn the rations," Flora's voice cut through the air like a knife. "Without sustenance, she might not heal fast enough."

Talos sniffled in response. Tessa would have told him it was nothing to get worked up about, but now that she was returning to total consciousness, she knew that would be a lie. Her skin felt as if it had been hacked with a hatchet. Like she'd been thrown into a den full of vipers. Everything hurt. Never had she experienced this sort of agony.

Each step that Aeden took up the stairs tore through her and she bit down so hard on her cheek she drew blood. It distracted her from the rest of the pain, but only for a moment. It was a relief when they finally made it to her room. The door creaked as it opened and the familiar scent of lavender and fresh air coming from her balcony wafted under her nose. Home at last.

Aeden cursed as he laid her down on her bed. "Damn them to seven hells."

Tessa's eyes fluttered open. "Aeden?"

Her mother gasped as she stepped beside him and looked down at her. "Oh, my baby." She knelt next to the bed and wrapped her chilly hands around Tessa's.

"Mom," Tessa croaked, "I'm okay."

Flora bit her lip. Her eyes welled with tears and she shook her head. "No, my girl. You're not—"

Reinar's voice carried up the stairs, muffled by the thick door. "Flora!"

Aeden placed a hand on Flora's shoulder. "Her body will heal itself. It will just take some time. You go. I'll stay with her."

Flora looked like she would argue, but sobbed instead. She gripped Tessa's torn sleeve and whimpered, "I can't leave her."

Tessa cleared her throat. "I'll be okay, mama. Aeden is here."

With a long look cast between Tessa and Aeden, Flora relented. "I'll be back as soon as I can."

Tessa shook her head. Her mother's frightened face was scaring her more than anything else. She couldn't bear to be watched like that all night. "No. Get some rest. I'm not going anywhere." She summoned a weak smile.

Flora bit her lip again and gave Tessa's hand a quick squeeze. "Call for me if you need me. I love you, my sweet girl."

"I love you, too." Tessa averted her gaze from the desperation in her mother's eyes.

Talos slipped in as Flora opened the door and then he disappeared into the bathroom. Once Flora was gone, Tessa released a deep sigh of relief. Aeden hovered over the bed, clenching and unclenching his fists. She'd never seen him appear so uncertain.

Talos was the next to interrupt. Nervously, he approached the bed, handing Aeden a tray with trembling hands. His eyes stayed glued to the floor as if he couldn't bear to look at Tessa and, for a moment, she wondered if it really looked as bad as it felt.

Aeden dismissed him and grabbed one of the cups on the tray. It was filled to the brim with steaming blood. Someone had heated it over the fire for her. With a gentle hand, Aeden held the back of her head steady while putting the cup to her lips.

As soon as it touched her tongue, a rogue hunger set in. She fought back an animal-like growl. Her stomach ached in longing for more. She grabbed Aeden's hand, forcing him to tip it further so she could drink faster. Blood flooded her mouth and caught in her throat. He pulled it away and set it down as she choked.

Her throat burned as she caught her breath. She likely looked like a savage, but she didn't care. The blood was already beginning to do its job. The pain became bearable as the nourishment reached her belly, filling it and her body with newfound strength.

Aeden drank from his own cup without complaint. Then, carefully, he gestured to her. "We need to get you cleaned up."

Tessa struggled up to her elbows. The pain still throbbed, but it wasn't as debilitating as before. For the first time in her life, she was grateful for the Vampyr curse. Its ability to heal them even faster than the magic they once held in Elfhame was the only thing keeping her going. Normally, a meager cut or bruise healed quickly, but whatever these things had done to her caused more damage than her powers could handle.

And then she saw the extent of it. Looking down, she sucked in a shocked breath. They had shredded her dress to pieces, revealing bits of torn flesh. Most of the blood was drying, leaving flakes all over. She raised a fist to her mouth and bit down to stifle a scream. It did, in fact, look as bad as it felt.

Aeden was at her side in the blink of an eye. "Tessa, listen to me. We need to get you washed up so I can apply the poultice Talos gave us. If these get infected, then it will take your body even longer to heal."

She nodded, too stunned to make a sound. As she pushed herself off the bed, she trembled. One shaky step toward the bathroom was all it took for Aeden to be at her side. He reached out for her, but she shooed him away. It wasn't that she didn't want his help, but she feared the pain would worsen if he touched her.

She made it a few more steps before stumbling into the door-frame. Aeden was there as quick as a fox. He lifted her arm over his shoulder and led her to the tub, which was already steaming with fresh water. Talos' doing, no doubt. She'd have to thank him later for being so attentive.

Never had she been this banged up before. She hissed as she attempted to remove her dress. But there were too many fastenings and ribbons to do it on her own. Sucking in a breath, she turned to Aeden with pleading eyes. Wordlessly, he knew exactly what she needed, helping her out of the dress. She couldn't stop studying him as he gently peeled the fabric off her.

There was a greenish pallor on his face. The claw marks from the monster had already begun to fade, leaving three long pinkish, puckered streaks. But the nagging feeling told her he didn't look sick to his stomach because of his own injuries. His eyes flitted from her neck to her belly, where she'd gotten the worst of it.

Normally, she would be horrified at the thought of him seeing her naked like this. But all she wanted was to plunge her aching body into the deliciously warm water. She went slowly, leaning on him for support, until she was submerged up to her collarbone.

Silence settled between them as he picked up a soft cloth and began wiping the dry blood from her face and neck. She leaned back, melting under his tender touch. The bath was heavenly with lavender to soothe her pain.

From the corner of her eye, she caught him dipping his hands into the ginger cream meant for her hair. His knuckles were red and bruised and she worried that he was exerting himself. He, too, needed to heal. Surely, someone else could do this for her. Her mother. Or Scarlet. It would give him a chance to rest and recuperate.

But as he began to massage the soap into her hair, she lost all train of thought. No words would come. Instead, she leaned back, closing her eyes, and relaxed for the first time since returning. Her skin tingled where the magic of the curse worked to piece her back together, and she was starting to feel better already. Though she wasn't watching it happen, she could feel the wounds repairing themselves. Relief came slowly, but surely. Turning the deep gashes into shallow ones. Fading the bruises away. Her Vampyr abilities were doing their job. And for that, she was grateful.

Once he rinsed the soap from her hair, she opened her eyes again. He was chewing on his lip with his brow furrowed. She squirmed under his worried gaze and said, "They'll heal, you know."

Aeden's eyes widened as if he'd forgotten she even knew how to talk. "Huh?"

"The bruises." She forced an uncomfortable chuckle. "You're looking at me like I'm a chipped teacup."

His frown deepened and his voice dipped low as he said, "I almost lost you tonight."

A slight flutter ran through her stomach. It was like the faintest brush of a butterfly's wing. But it was there, nonetheless. She looked down at his hands. They were strong and calloused, resting on the edge of the tub now. They were the hands that had saved her tonight. Ripping apart the horrific creatures only to later tend to her with such gentleness that it nearly broke her heart.

Attempting to comfort him, she took them with her own. Gripping them tightly, she said, "I know. But you didn't. I'm here right now. See?" She placed one of his hands on her cheek and leaned into it. He was warm. As warm as the water that surrounded her. "You saved me, Aeden."

"You fought hard, Tessa. You saved yourself."

"No." Stubbornly, she lifted her chin, moving away from the hand she still held onto. It was her lifeline. Tonight, *he* had been her lifeline. "*You* make me braver. Make me believe I am capable of so much more." With a laugh she added, "Most of the time it's the taunting that does it to me. Gives me the push I desperately need. But ultimately, it's just having you nearby. Knowing that you've got my back."

He pulled his hand away and red hot embarrassment welled inside of her. If she had gone too far, or gotten the wrong impression about what was going on between them... She couldn't have imagined the moments they'd shared lately, though. They'd opened up to one another. Confided in each other. And he'd kept her family's secret. Then literally saved her life. So why was he avoiding her eyes right now?

She shifted in the tub. Water splashed onto the floor at his feet, but she didn't care. The embarrassment was too much. Even worse than the constant throbbing pain. "That was out of line. I only meant that I'm grateful to you..."

"No." He grasped on to her arms. "You didn't say anything wrong. I care for you, Tessa. More than I ever could have imagined was possible. But if anything happened to you, I don't think I could forgive myself."

She leaned over the tub, toward him. "Nothing is going to happen to me. Our families will fix this. They'll find a way to keep us safe."

His lips parted as if he was hesitating to say what was weighing on his mind. But he didn't need to say anything at all. She didn't need words right now. Her heart skipped a beat as she realized what she did need. *Him.*

Leaning forward, the cold tub pressed against her bare breasts, sending chills down her spine. But she ignored it. She tilted her head, pressing her lips to his. It was different this time. There was nothing awkward about this kiss. Aeden's lips parted and their embrace deepened. He helped Tessa from the tub with a feathery light touch.

She gasped as he pulled away. Worried that he'd change his mind. That he would think this was a bad idea. It was bold of her to kiss him. Naked. And alone. But she needed to forget about the pain. About the horror of the night. And there was no one in the world she would rather forget with.

Her worries dissipated when he placed a warm wool blanket around her. Water dripped from her and onto the floor, leaving a small puddle. She should have been cold, but she wasn't. Heat bloomed in her chest. Deciding she wasn't quite ready to let him go, she grabbed his hand and led him to the bed.

The blankets were as soft as clouds. He laid her back carefully, but there was no need. Between her healing abilities, the lavender, and the fresh adrenaline coursing through her now, the pain was barely noticeable.

Aeden paused at the edge of the bed. His eyes darted between her and the door. He made no move to leave or to join her. So, she reached for him.

"Stay with me, please." She didn't want to be alone. Didn't want to be left to replay the night over and over in her mind. Sleep would not come easily tonight. In fact, it wouldn't come until those beasts were put down. But for now, she wanted to forget it all. To be with Aeden.

Tentatively, he climbed in, remaining above the covers. He leaned against the headboard and wrapped his arm around her shoulders. She burrowed into the safety of his embrace. Her limbs grew heavy with exhaustion. Maybe it was the dream-like state she was falling into as the shock finally wore off, or the heat of his body, but it was in that moment that the last wall around her heart began to crumble.

"Aeden," she whispered groggily, "can I tell you something?"

"Anything," he answered gruffly, sounding like sleep was threatening to take him soon. Slowly, he ran his free hand along the wounds on her arms that had already healed. Tracing the light pink lines and sending goosebumps all the way up to her neck.

"The other day in the forest... it wasn't the first time I'd heard you play your violin." The arm that rested around her shoulders tensed, but he said nothing as she admitted, "I've been sneaking down to the lake to listen to you for years. I had no idea it was you, of course."

Nerves twisted her stomach into knots. She shifted, lifting her head to meet his gaze. Needing to look him in the eye. She wanted to make him understand the significance—the impact his music had made on her life. His brows lifted in surprise, but he remained silent, allowing her to continue. "It was always the two of us out there. When things at home, or the burden of this curse, became too much, I went down there just to hear you. I danced beneath the few rays of sunlight that deign to shine down on us in this curse-forsaken forest. It was as if you were playing just for me."

His crimson eyes bore into hers, not with embarrassment or surprise, but with kindness and understanding. He parted his lips as if to respond, but Tessa hurried to finish. She needed to say it before she lost the nerve. "It has always been the two of us. Long before that night at the masquerade. There, by the lake, unknowingly together. You have always given me what I need. Even when we were too clueless or hardheaded to realize it."

She pushed off the blanket. The ache in her muscles was no match for the adrenaline coursing through her now. With a plush cotton sheet wrapped around her, she climbed from the bed.

Standing before him, she realized words weren't enough. They could never express how much he had impacted her life. And how much more they could do to enrich one another's lives.

With courage she didn't know she had, she dropped the sheet to the ground. Aeden's eyes took in every inch of her. Roving from her chest, down to her hips. Hips she'd always worried were a bit too wide. Thighs she had thought were too powerful for a woman.

But as his eyes darkened, she realized she had nothing to worry about. Not when she was here with him. The heat in her chest spread, reaching down between her thighs. In a place she'd only ever explored on her own.

Taking a bold step forward, Tessa unbuttoned the white cotton shirt he'd been wearing beneath his jacket. It was torn and bloody where the creatures' claws had met skin. But he didn't flinch as she drew the shirt away from him, dropping it onto the floor.

When she climbed back onto the bed, Aeden ran his fingers over her collar bone then down between her breasts. He went no farther, though she craved for him to do so. Perhaps it was her trembling that gave him pause. But with one subtle nod of her head, he removed his pants. Delicately, he settled over her. The muscles in his arms flexed at either side of her head and her breath quickened. He was like one of the statues in his family's courtyard. As hard and unmovable as stone. But made with such beauty that it was impossible to turn away. He was both dazzling and terrifying. And tonight, he was hers.

She reached up, placing her hands firmly on his back and drawing him into her for a kiss. They lost themselves in it. Breathlessly, he pulled away and, with a gruff whisper, asked, "Are you sure this is what you want?"

"Surer than the sun when it rises." She pulled him back to her, hungry for him and what he had to offer her.

It seemed to be all he needed to hear. Dominating fingers clung to her hips. Even though sweat beaded along her skin, shivers wracked her body as he ventured where no man had before. At first, he was gentle, easing into her with as much tenderness and care as he'd used when he had washed her. But the moment she wove her fingers through his hair, pulling him into a kiss full of longing and need, his rhythm picked up.

It was melodic, like when he played the violin. Like the days when he played unknowingly for her. A fast-paced song filled with both excitement and determination. One that she could dance wildly to with her hair down as the sun shined on her face.

In this moment, he played that song for her again, only she was his instrument. The idea delighted her as much as the building of immense pleasure begging to be released. She called out his name, her voice filled with longing.

He was everything she never knew she needed. More than a friend and confidant. It was a dangerous path to travel. One that would surely end in heartache. But for once, she wasn't sure she cared. It occurred to her that maybe—just maybe—traveling down this treacherous road might be worth it. *Aeden* might be worth it.

Twenty-One

Aeden

Aeden ran his hands through Tessa's hair. It was as soft as the blankets they were wrapped in together. The wounds on her shoulders had healed completely by now, and he fought the urge to lift the blanket to check the rest of her body.

She'd made no mention of pain throughout the night. And though they hadn't slept much, he felt well rested. The events in the woods were like a terrible nightmare. One that he'd easily forgotten with Tessa in his arms. But now that the late morning sun peeked through the windows and balcony door, memories creeped in.

There had never been a time when he'd experienced fear like that. Not since the day they'd fled Elfhame and the Unseelie King's wrath. The two events vied for first place. But Tessa was safe. He had to remind himself of that. And he did so as he nuzzled her neck. She gave a pleasant sigh, sending eager shivers through his body.

Drawing the covers further over their heads as if he could hide them away from the world, he whispered, "Tessa, are you awake?"

She moaned lightly in response, pressing herself into him. His body responded immediately, craving more of her. What he was feeling now was a thirst that couldn't be quenched by blood. It was one only she could fulfill.

With heavy-lidded, glossy eyes, she turned to him. There was a soft, satisfied smile playing on her full, red lips. He longed to have those lips on him again. But before he could lean in to kiss her, she surprised him with a question. "Aeden, what would you do if we did go back? To Elfhame I mean? Hypothetically." Her delicate smile turned sly as she added, "I'm not naïve. I know it's impossible, but *if* by some miracle..."

"A miracle as big as you taking me to bed?" He smirked and kissed her at the base of her neck.

She wiggled and laughed. "Yes, a miracle as big as that."

Giving in to her little game, he answered truthfully. "I would start playing music publicly again." It was something he'd dreamed of when he was young but had never told another soul about. Anyone other than Tessa would think he was a foolhardy dreamer. But it turned out she understood more than he could have imagined. That she knew how much playing meant to him. And that, it seemed, it meant just as much to her. He leaned back, resting his hands behind his head. "And get myself invited to the Winter Palace to play for all the most prestigious Fae in the realm."

Tessa leaned up on her elbow. A piece of her tangled hair fell in front of her face. She ignored it, whispering with awe in her voice. "I think that's a wonderful dream."

Aeden brushed the hair away and tucked it safely behind her ear. "And what about you, dear? What would you do?"

She appeared thoughtful for a moment. "Well, after I finished attending your concert, I would ride Galahad into the mountains. There is a herd of wild horses that live there. My father used to tell me stories about them. With manes of ice blue and eyes as light as the frost."

The wistfulness in her voice drew him in, yearning to hear more. But instead, sadness flickered across her face, drawing her mouth down slightly. It pained him. Sending a piercing jab into his heart. If he could take her there right this minute, he would. If given the chance, he would whisk her away to a world where she was free to explore mountain ranges, chasing creatures as enchanting as she was.

Unfortunately, it wasn't in the cards. Instead, they were trapped in the forest. Caught between their family's feud and the different ideals that tore them all apart. There was no telling when or how his father planned to confront Reinar with the ultimatum. Or what involvement he had with the twisted, cursed humans. There was little Aeden believed would dissuade his father from his quest to take control of the forest and then the mortal realm. If anything, whatever was going on with that journal would urge Olgar to enact any nefarious plans he had in store for them all.

Guilt gnawed at Aeden like a woodland creature trying to make their nest. Tessa had been so open and raw with him last night. She'd given herself to him in a way he didn't deserve. Yet he'd been unable to turn away. A better man would have. A better man would tell her everything—the whole ugly truth—right now. It would come out anyway. Better she heard it from him.

"Tessa," he started, "I'm afraid of what today will bring." He sat up and she followed suit, sitting cross-legged face to face. Aeden squeezed both her hands in his. "Before we go out there, I need to tell you that I never imagined I would feel like this with anyone. That I would find someone who understood me and who I would be willing to risk everything for."

Because that was precisely what he was doing. Risking his father's wrath. His family's safety. For her. Because he couldn't bear the thought of losing her. Not just her affection, but her respect. He could tell her here and now. Come clean about the plot to an extent. There was no need to mention the poison in his jacket pocket. He could spare her those details. Instead, he could explain what his father desired and how they could use Drake's deceit to get it without anyone getting hurt.

She listened intently, worry creasing her brow. With a deep breath, he continued, "But I admit, when I first came here, it wasn't with pure intent. My father—"

The door creaked open and Aeden shot for the blankets, bunching them over Tessa's bare chest to cover her. Talos yelped and froze in the doorway. The tray in his hands trembled like a quake in the earth. "*By the stars!*"

Tessa shushed him and then scolded, "Talos, close the door!"

The nervous attendant shut the door and leaned against it, still staring at them in shock. "Tessa," he hissed, "your mother will be coming up here any minute. If she finds you like this," he gestured wildly at the two of them and then whispered excitedly, "she will... will..."

Aeden ventured to finish the sentence, "Faint? Yell at us? Be incredibly impressed that her daughter was able to catch a man such as myself?" He hoped the last bit would lighten Talos' mood before the man shook the tray into shambles.

It didn't work. Talos set the tray down on the vanity and wagged a scolding finger in Aeden's direction. "This is no time for jokes. You need to get up and dressed. Now." The bite in his tone surprised Aeden enough that he obeyed. The jumpy man had never spoken with such surety and confidence in front of him before, so he knew he meant business.

Although he and Tessa were not the first to have engaged in marital affairs before their actual marriage, he guessed this was uncharted territory in this particular household. One where purity and dignity were held at a high standard. Above even the purest of emotions and intent, apparently.

Talos turned toward the door with his nose stuck in the air while Aeden dressed. Tessa giggled from the bed, still swathed in an enormous pile of blankets. Her cheeks were pink and her smile was bright.

Aeden teased, "Hey, you're in trouble, too."

"But I'm not the one who just got scolded like a naughty child." She threw a pillow at his face with expert aim. He caught it and tossed it back, making her fall into a fit of laughter. It was as if the final brick that made up the wall around his heart had been removed. Watching Tessa left him utterly enamored.

It was clear by the tapping of his foot that Talos wasn't leaving until Aeden did. The opportunity to come clean to Tessa was lost for now. Perhaps it was fate's way of protecting him. Of making sure he didn't destroy everything they had built in one swift confession. He gritted his teeth anxiously. If he could send word to his father to call it all off. To plead with him and promise to help him find another way to set things right...

Talos cleared his throat and opened the door just a crack. Seemed it was time to take his leave. Aeden backed toward the hall slowly and to Tessa, said, "We'll talk later. Right?"

"Of course. I'll be down shortly." She blew him a kiss, but the easy going gesture of a young lover felt instead like an arrow piercing his heart. The last thing he wanted to do was leave their little sanctuary. There was no telling what awaited him outside of those four secure walls.

Once downstairs, Reinar gave Aeden a vigorous update on the creatures that had attacked them. The only problem was that there wasn't much to go on. The tracks were erratic, leading in no simple direction. They looped around and around, weaving through the forest like a ball of yarn. It was impossible to tell where they began or ended.

Flora was tense, but silent, throughout the entire meeting. Aeden had trouble looking her in the eye the few times she chimed in. Though he wasn't sure why. It wasn't as if she could see the truth of what he and her daughter had done on his face.

It was a relief when it was all over. Reinar claimed he had already sent word to the families on *both* sides of the lake. This was a threat to them all and needed to be handled accordingly. It had been years since they all had to depend on one another, though, and Aeden wasn't sure how the loyalists to his family would react to Reinar calling on them.

There was to be a council. Each head of household and their heir would attend to decide what should be done. Reinar believed Aeden's suspicions that the creatures were human. Mortals who had made a deal with the witch from before. Only this time, the cost that came with the deal was greater. Something that twisted them into monsters even worse than the Vampyrs they wanted to hunt.

Aeden wasn't sure what should be done about them. They hadn't been easy to kill. What if the rest of Reinar's people lacked the strength they needed to put the ghastly beasts down? He wasn't willing to put Tessa at risk again, trying to find out. So he excused himself, promising to return for the meeting, and headed down to the lake. If anyone could give him insight as to where these monsters came from, it would be the woman in the water.

He trudged down as fast as his feet would take him. Even though he felt safer in the daylight, the forest still gave off a foreboding air. What little wildlife still resided there seemed to be gone. Or hiding. Whatever new predator lurked in the shadows of Gwyar had everyone on edge.

Even the water witch, it seemed. She was already there waiting, as if she knew he was coming. With her long, slender arms at her sides, she posed as regal as if she were the queen of the very lake in which she stood. The water lapped around her ankles, and she tilted her head when he reached her.

"I see you took my advice." She leered at him, making his skin crawl.

"I accepted the invitation like you suggested."

"Interesting." Water splashed as she stepped onto the shore. Slowly, she circled around him. He tensed when she sniffed at him. "You have the scent of deceit about you."

Shamefully, he hung his head. "I wanted to tell her everything this morning, but we were interrupted."

"Everything?" She drawled the word out as if it amused her.

Aeden glanced around at the thick of the forest. He couldn't shake the sensation of eyes on him. Like something or someone was watching in wait for the right moment to attack again. But he saw no one. No gray skin or red-filled eyes. No rows of fangs eager to sink into his skin.

He shook his head, trying to rid himself of the paranoia. "If I tell her about the poison, she'll never forgive me. I hoped to find a way to come clean about my father's plan without including the shameful details." He clenched his jaw, worried that he was wasting his time coming to the lake. Still, he added, "I thought if you could tell me more about the witch who made a deal with those mortals or where these predators are coming from, then I could come up with a solution where no one has to get hurt."

She stopped when she came to the front of him. Then jabbed him in the heart with her eerily long finger. "It is not *that* deceit that you reek of." She drew back with a puzzled look. "Why haven't you told the girl you love her?"

Love? Aeden cared for Tessa. More deeply than anyone in the world. But was he ready to call it love? He shook his head. "It doesn't matter. Not until I fix this mess." A chill crept across the back of his neck. He honed in on the sounds around them and heard no other heartbeats. No rustling in the leaves. So he continued, "We think these monsters are human. Or *were* human. Are we right?"

"Yes." She said it so matter-of-factly that it grated on his nerves.

Through clenched teeth, he asked, "Did they make a deal with a witch?"

"They did." Laughter danced in her eyes, though her mouth remained neutral. She offered no more than she had to. Normally, her vagueness did not bother him, but there was too much at stake. There was no time for half-truths.

Aeden wanted to ask why they would be willing to sacrifice their very souls in order to hunt his people, but he didn't need to. Hadn't he been ready to do anything for his own family? If this was revenge for the humans his people had fed on, then he could understand. Instead, he asked, "Did my father know about them?" He recalled the journal with the drawings.

Another short answer, "Yes."

Murderous rage filled him. How could his father have kept that to himself? If he was tracking down the witch-blessed hunters, then what did he stand to gain by keeping the rest of them in the dark?

"Why now? Why are the hunters amassing?"

The water witch clicked her tongue and instead of answering, her gaze flicked in the direction of the thick trees, tainted with the never changing crimson leaves. Then she answered, "Desperate men are as unpredictable and volatile as the creatures that now roam this forest."

Aeden wasn't sure if she was referring to the hunters or his father's deceit. He bit his tongue to keep from lashing out at her. He had come to her for a solution, not a philosophy lesson. "Where are they coming from? How many of them are there?"

"You are asking all the wrong questions." She twisted a lock of her seaweed entwined hair around her finger.

"How do I stop them?" It was the only real question he needed to ask.

The witch took a few steps back into the lake. She waded in until the water reached her hips and Aeden worried she would dive into the dark depths before giving him the answers he desperately needed.

The water sparkled as she ran her hands through it. Just beneath the surface, it seemed like life was returning to her cold gray skin, revealing pink, unblemished skin in its place. He wondered if it was a glamor, or if it was what she looked like when she was in the source that held her full power.

Answering him, she said, "You ask a question I cannot answer. For your troubles are far greater than *the turned*. There is only one thing that can set all of this right. One path that will lead your people to their salvation."

Aeden clenched his fists, recalling how brutal the turned hunters had been. And how close he came to losing Tessa. He could think of no greater threat than hunters who were as strong and fast as a Vampyr.

The witch continued, her voice like a strong wind on the sea, "Since I could not give you the answers you sought, allow me to offer another to a question you failed to ask." Her smile was sinister, baring razor sharp rows of teeth. Aeden thought he might be sick. It only worsened as she continued, "You and the girl hold the key to it all. Through your blood you were cursed and through that same blood you are saved."

Aeden took a bold step toward her, ready to force her to give him the answers he *needed*. But she dipped beneath the water, lingering just long enough for him to catch a glimpse of a rosy face and vivid silken hair. Then she was gone. Leaving him emptier and more helpless than before.

Twenty-Two

Tessa

Tessa descended the stairs confidently in an emerald green dress. It was loose fitting and brushed softly against her injuries, which had faded to a gentle throb by now. With her hand on the banister, she crept gently down each step, and hummed to herself.

From there, she could see the foyer. Her eyebrow peaked at the unusually crowded room. Household staff shuffled in, standing against the wall so they would be out of the way. While her mother and uncle stood at the center, Drake was nowhere to be found, thank the stars.

Tessa hadn't been able to stand the sight of him since she'd discovered his dirty little secret. Although she knew she should have told her uncle about his son's cruelty, she'd decided to wait until after their other troubles were dealt with. Besides, all the humans under their control were released. There was no one to protect from him for the time being.

She reached the bottom of the stairs just as the front door opened with a flourish. Two of Drake's friends—men from the Steelhelm family—herded a young man inside. The eldest of the Steelhelm brothers, Elric, had a ghastly bruise forming on his jawline. Meanwhile, his younger brother, Ricard, growled, trying to restrain the man between them. The man under their hold had the same sort of frailty that could only be found in mortals. Dusty hair, and trembling hands full of callouses from a hard day's work. Between that and the alluring scent of his blood, Tessa had no doubt he was human.

Ignoring the intense hunger rumbling in her stomach at the smell of fresh human blood, Tessa narrowed her eyes at him. The Steelhelm brothers were fierce hunters. They were as deadly with a bow and sword as they were with their teeth. So why did they look so disheveled? It seemed like the man had put up more of a fight than they could handle.

Reinar stepped up to them and used a kerchief to wipe at his brow with a shaking hand. Had he fed this morning? Her own stomach grumbled in response. As silent as a cold winter's night, her uncle studied the man. The entire room seemed to hold their breath in anticipation. Though she wasn't sure if it was from rumors of dangerous mortals roaming their forest, or the hope that they would keep the man for feeding.

Unable to stand idly by, Tessa joined her uncle. The man struggled under the tight hold the Steelhelms had on him. Their fingers dug into his wrists, turning his skin bright white where they squeezed. She inched closer, ignoring the sneer the mortal shot at her.

He was much younger than the men who had attacked her and Aeden after the masquerade. An angry red rash splayed across the bridge of his nose and on his forehead like a bad sunburn. Tessa tilted her head. He was almost harmless looking. Like a farmer's son or a shop keep's apprentice. But when she met his eyes, her heart dropped. Faint red lines like one would get when they hadn't gotten enough sleep slinked along the whites. Only there were no dark circles to indicate fatigue. And by the way he still resisted, he had plenty of energy.

Elric puffed out his chest and was the first to speak. "Found this one with a broken down carriage near the border."

Ricard scratched at the back of his closely shaven head and added, "Put up one hell of a fight."

Tessa's eyes flitted to the mortal's wrist. Her mouth and throat were painfully dry as she commanded, "Roll up his sleeve."

Reinar furrowed his brow, but nodded to Ricard without question. Angry red tendrils swirling into a familiar mark drew the breath from her. He was marked. That explained the strength. And the fight he had seemingly put up by the looks of the Steelhelms. And why his eyes were reddened. Was the witch's *blessing* coming to claim its prize? Coming for his soul?

With a shudder, she whispered, "He's one of them."

Gasps spread across the room, followed by concerned chatter. Reinar held up a silencing hand, but it didn't do any good. The household staff grasped onto one another. They had been there for it all before. The hunters, and the death of their own. They had lost friends and family, too, in those early days after their expulsion from Elfhame. Though it had been years ago, Tessa knew their wounds were as fresh as her own. Wounds inflicted on her mind and heart at the loss of her father.

Flora rushed to Reinar. "We need to lock him up."

"No." Tessa rubbed at her arms where claws and fangs had torn into her only a few hours ago. Locking him up would do no good. If he turned, there was no telling if locks or bars would hold him.

Flora reached for her shoulder with pity-filled eyes. Tessa drew away. She didn't want sympathy. She wasn't a wounded deer in need of comforting. The turned mortals attacked her, but she survived. With Aeden, she had fought them off.

"No," Tessa repeated, completely ignoring her mother's concerned gaze. "We don't know if he came alone. Or when the change might take effect in him."

Reinar gestured to the man. "What do you propose, then?"

Tessa raised her chin. "Kill him," she said simply. It was the only way to ensure he couldn't hurt anyone.

Her mother gasped. "Tessa—"

"It's the only way. If he becomes one of those *things*, then there's no telling who might get hurt. I know first hand what they're capable of."

Reinar shook his head sadly. "We can't be sure that he'll turn."

Tessa bit her lip. Turning pleading eyes on her uncle, she tried to make her case. "The mark on his forearm *assures* us that he will."

"We need to question him. Find out where the witch is who keeps giving his people the blessing. Make him tell us how many others there are."

"Fine," Tessa replied through gritted teeth. It wasn't worth the risk. But Reinar's hands were still trembling. He was afraid. And he wouldn't be appeased until he got answers. "Just promise me you'll do it quick. And kill him after."

She shifted uncomfortably under Flora's shocked gaze. Tessa lowered her eyes to her hands, unable to face the disappointment of her mother. She had only ever killed for survival. But things were changing. She was changing. There were only so many times she could be ambushed, attacked, and assaulted before she lost her will to fight. If protecting herself meant killing before anyone had the chance to hurt her or the ones she loved, then that's what she would do.

Ricard Steelhelm, who had always had a kind demeanor, shrugged innocently. "Questioning shouldn't take long. Besides, we could drain a bit of blood for storage."

A few of the household staff mumbled happily about the prospect of human blood. Starving bellies made for poor decision making. They couldn't honestly be willing to risk their lives for a few pints of blood.

Elric grumbled. "Once we're done, I'll kill him myself, Lady Tessa."

Her heart leapt into her throat as an inhuman snarl rumbled up from the human man. It was the first sound he had made since entering the house and sent eerie shivers down her spine. The chills worsened as he spoke. "Keep me one hour or one day. It makes no difference. They'll come for you. For all of you."

Tessa's heart skipped a beat. "Who?"

He spat at the floor. "The Sons of the Six. Kill me if you wish. But it will make no difference. Word is spreading and more join our cause every day. They're gearing up for a hunt. And they're strong enough to take down any beast, no matter how *inhuman*. Together we will cleanse the world of your kind." Laughter danced in his eyes.

Tessa flinched. Then, more firmly, demanded, "Uncle. He cannot stay here. Kill him. Now."

Reinar glanced between her and the man. His shoulders rose and fell heavily with his breath. How could he honestly be questioning this? Tessa bit her tongue. Surely, he had to know it wasn't worth the danger. They would find answers and blood elsewhere. The stag from the woods or some rabbits. Young deer from spring were still wandering into the forest. That would suffice. It had to.

Her mother's face paled to a shade of cold milk. "She's right. This is too risky."

Reinar massaged his temples. "Take him to the cell in the basement. Try to compel him. We need to know exactly how many of them there are and what their strategy is."

The Steelhelms each gave a curt nod. Her uncle's word was law, and they would obey. But before they reached for the cellar door, Reinar added, "Be careful. And make sure the compulsion takes. Do not at any point lower your guard."

"Aye, sir," was all they said as they shoved the mortal man through the door and down the stairs.

Flora's voice was pained as she asked, "Are you sure about this, brother?"

Wordlessly, Reinar stormed out of the room. The household staff murmured amongst themselves, but Tessa didn't stick around to listen. They had just dangled food in front of starving Vampyrs. There was bound to be discord.

Defeated and in desperate need of some nourishment after a long night, she slipped into the parlor and grabbed a mulberry muffin that was still sitting in a basket on the breakfast table. It was cold by now, but something was better than nothing. Admittedly, her stomach felt like an empty trough, even with each bite she took. She needed blood. Especially after all the healing her body had done through the night.

She started for the decker's room, which would lead her to the kitchens, but Drake shouted as he burst in. "Slut!"

The hairs on Tessa's arms rose. "What did you just call me?"

Drake's hands were on her and before she realized what was happening, he was pinning her against the windowsill. "You gave yourself to that swine? What else did you do, let him feed on you?"

Red hot hatred bloomed in her chest. "How dare you accuse me of that! How dare you come in here and rage at me about *anything*!" She shoved him back roughly and before he could get his bearings, she reared back, slapping him hard across his face. A thunderous crack echoed through the room, and he turned back to her, stunned.

His cheek turned bright red, but he made no move to lay his hands on her again as he said, "Talos told me everything. That the two of you were naked in your bed. Aeden Ashbane is our *enemy*, Tessa. I knew you were a twit, but I didn't think you were *that* stupid."

Tessa couldn't ignore the stab of betrayal, knowing that Talos had told Drake about her and Aeden. "Why would he tell you that?"

Ignoring her, he hissed, "An Ashbane? Of all the men to give yourself to, you chose an Ashbane."

"I am doing what was asked of me." She blew out a frustrated breath. "All I have *ever* done is what has been asked of me."

Drake leaned in and spoke as if his words were a lance that could cut right through her. "Your duty was not to bed him. It was to keep him and his family amiable."

She snapped back, "What does it matter? He and I are to be betrothed, so what difference does it make?"

Drake raised a hand in the air as if to strike her, but she held her ground. He stayed his hand and spat, "I never would have permitted my father to go through with this heinous plan of his. He would have seen reason before it was too late. The Ashbanes are not to be trusted. The moment they have the chance to seize any semblance of power, they'll take it. And that scum will use *you* to do it."

Tessa clenched her fists. "Only I can decide my fate. The lot of you allow names to hold far too much weight. But not me. Not Aeden."

Drake shoved his finger in her face. "You have no idea who you've been crawling into bed with."

She raised her chin defiantly. "It is you, dear cousin, who I do not truly know. I thought I did, but I was wrong. Aeden, on the other hand, has done nothing but stand by my side since coming here. I know exactly who he is."

"Then you know that he is meeting with a witch as we speak."

Shock and confusion rocked her. "Why would he—"

"Because it seems his father was using Aeden as a weapon against us. Don't you see? It is his family who has put us all in peril time and time again."

"You're wrong. Even if he came here for self-serving reasons, that is hardly enough to accuse him of putting us in danger. He was attacked just the same as me by the witch-blessed mortals. He saved me."

Drake's nostrils flared, but his voice was steady as he urged, "Ask him about the poison, then. Ask him about all of it."

The room was spinning. Suddenly, the walls felt like they were closing in on her. Threatening to smash her into pieces like a porcelain doll. Aeden wouldn't hurt her. But what if his father had been pushing him to do so all this time? Aeden had been trying to tell her something, but she never imagined it was this. Never thought that his family hated hers and the families loyal to Reinar so much that they'd be willing to put the entire forest in danger. If his father was capable of this, then what else were they hiding? What else was *Aeden* hiding?

Drake continued to berate her, but his words were muffled. She had to get out of there. Out of this room, out of this house. Just *out*. She needed to find Aeden. She shoved Drake aside, knocking him into one of the sofas. He shouted profanities at her, but it didn't matter. The only thing that did was finding Aeden and getting the truth directly from him.

Tessa nearly trampled Talos on her way back to the foyer. He pressed himself against the wall and called out to her as she passed, "I'm so sorry, Tessa. Drake, he... he cornered me. Told me to tell him everything I knew about how close you and Aeden had gotten."

She ignored him, uninterested in hearing his reasons. It didn't matter. Drake had decided from day one that he was against the match. It was only a matter of time before he blew it up. She kept walking.

Talos' voice grew distant as he shouted, "He was going to kill me, Tessa! Please, forgive me!"

She shook her head angrily. Hair flew in front of her eyes, but she didn't care. Drake was a son of a bitch, but was he lying about *this*? What reason would he have to make up such outlandish and dangerous claims? And she had met Olgar. He was a nasty man.

Intimidating to even his own son. It wasn't out of the realm of possibility that he would turn to despicable tactics to undermine her family.

But Aeden was different. He was kind. And brave. Tender and loving. Everything his father seemed not to be. Was it all a facade? To what end? Questions whirled in her mind like flurries in a snowstorm. The kind that whipped you in the face until it stung.

She didn't have to go far to find Aeden. He trudged up the rocky drive with a worrisome look on his face. All the bliss and joy from her morning with him seemed tainted now. By both Drake's knowledge and disdain of it and by the lies lingering between them all.

Aeden's face brightened when his eyes met hers. "I was just coming to find you. We need to talk."

Tessa planted her feet firmly when she reached him. Shoving the hair unceremoniously from her brow, she snapped, "Is it true?"

The brilliant smile that she had come to love so much, dropped from his face. He drew back slightly. "Is what true?"

"That your father sent you here to hurt us. That he plans to... to..." She wasn't sure where she was going with this. That he was planning to, what? Amass an army? That he was trying to ruin them all?

Aeden reached for her, but she crossed her arms over her chest, closing herself off to him. Like she should have been doing the entire time. Hurt spread across his face like a shadow and he said, "It is true. But please, let me explain."

"Did you know?" she spoke slow and concise. "Did you know what he was planning all along?"

He exhaled deeply through his nose. "I did. But I had a plan of my own. Something that could fix all of this."

"By the fates." Tessa ran her hands through her tangled hair.

Aeden grabbed her firmly by the waist, trying to draw her into him, but she resisted. His eyes were wide and pleading as he said, "I didn't know how to say no to him. All I wanted was to protect my family. Tessa, I never imagined I would feel this way. Not just about you, but about your family."

She listened with an incredulous smile. "How could you do this to me?" She clenched her jaw. "What else are you keeping from me? I want the truth. All of it."

His grip on her tensed. "My father wants to take control of our people on both sides of the lake. He sent me here to..."

"To *what*?" The feel of his hands on her were like a rope tightening. She grabbed them and pushed them off her. "What did he send you here to do, exactly?"

"To get close to you." He looked down at the ground and she had a sickly feeling that he wasn't telling her everything.

Her voice cracked as she said, "This was a mistake. You and I." It felt like her heart was breaking and she gripped her chest.

Aeden shook his head. "Don't say that. Please don't say that." He wiped a tear from her face. "Tessa, it was wrong for me to have allowed my father to use me as a pawn in his game."

"More like a weapon," she retorted.

"But every choice I've made, good or bad, has led me to you. I will not allow myself to regret coming here. We can still set things right, but we have to do it together."

Tessa wanted to accuse him of using her. Of tricking her. It didn't matter that she had gone into the courtship to serve her family's interests. What he had done wasn't the same. She never intended to hurt him. And it didn't matter how many heartfelt words he blurted out to her. They wouldn't make the pain go away. This was worse than anything she ever imagined. Like being buried alive under stones. She had wanted so badly to be wrong about love. To open her heart to someone without having it ripped away.

They both should have known better than to think that this thing between them might turn into something beautiful. Their families were just too different. She and Aeden were doomed from the start. And letting her guard down had only led them all to trusting the wrong people. Trusting that the Ashbanes would behave any differently than they always had was naïve and foolish.

Not wanting to say something she would later regret, she took a deep breath and said, "I need some time to think. I have to tell my uncle what I know. The council will be gathering soon, and he needs to know that he could be walking into a trap." She would tell her uncle about Olgar, but in this moment, she realized she had no choice but to leave Aeden's involvement out. It was something she would keep to herself. Even after what she'd learned, she still wanted to protect him.

"I understand. But I need you to believe that I'm not going anywhere. I will not walk away from you."

Tessa looked away, unable to handle the way his eyes shined with tears. He might not be willing to walk away, but right now, it was exactly what she needed to do. She turned away from him. But as she walked back to her family home—to the place where they had welcomed him—she could have sworn she was leaving a piece of her heart behind.

Twenty-Three

Aeden

Aeden cursed the gut-wrenching turmoil in his stomach. Watching Tessa walk away from him was tearing him to pieces. If he would have told her the truth when he had the chance, then maybe she wouldn't hate him now. But what was done was done. No matter what, he needed to protect her and his family from the coming threat. Unlike him, the water witch was still bound to the laws of Elfhame. That meant she was incapable of lying.

Vampyrs from all over the Crimson Forest would be gathering soon. It had to be stopped. No good would come from his father and Reinar coming face to face again. Not when all of their lies and plots were spilling over.

The crunch of boots on tightly packed earth made him swing around. His stomach dropped as Marcos and Balis came trotting into the drive. They were bewildered and worse... they were bearing arms. Swords were strapped to their sides and daggers swung in their belts.

Aeden shook his head firmly and strode their way. It wasn't safe to be near the Downthorn home. Not now. "You can't be here. Tessa knows everything. Soon Reinar will too."

Balis nearly slammed into Aeden as he skidded to a stop. He squeaked, "Everything?"

Aeden thought of the bit he left out about being sent in as an assassin. "She knows enough."

Dragging them further into the tree line and out of sight of the house, he eyed his cousins suspiciously. He thought of the journal in his father's office. Olgar had known something Aeden hadn't. Had known about the monsters lurking in the forest. Although Olgar didn't hold either of his nephews in high regard, it seemed unlikely that Marcos wouldn't have figured out what was happening under their roof.

Aeden added, "And so do I now. I know about *the turned*. If you knew what was happening to the hunters, why didn't you warn us?"

Marcos held his hands out in front of him as if to stop any blow that Aeden might make. "You have to understand. If Reinar knew, he would have had them all killed. We couldn't afford for that to happen. Not until we understood their curse. Not when everyone in the Crimson Forest is so weak. Your father only wanted to study them. But the cage... it wasn't secure enough to hold them. Not once they had fully completed their transformation. But we fixed it. It won't happen again. The turned give us the upper hand we need when the hunters come."

Aeden shoved Marcos' hands out of the way and hit him in the chest with open palms. "Tessa was nearly killed! I was nearly killed!"

Balis' voice quaked as he piped in, "Our fathers had no idea they'd be so raving mad. But these creatures... when they turn, it's like they've lost all sense of thought—"

"No shit!" Aeden turned on Balis. "They've been stripped of their humanity. Twisted into something unthinkable."

Marcos took a wary step toward Aeden, treating him like a rabid animal. "Cousin, listen to me. They're working on a way to kill them. Or to control them. If they can master the beasts, then we can put them to use. Last night was," he cleared his throat, "unfortunate."

Aeden scoffed. He couldn't believe what he was hearing. It seemed he'd underestimated just how far his father was willing to go to get what he wanted. Thinking he could use the turned to his advantage? Then again, that was how Olgar had always been. Ever the opportunist. "You are fools to believe that he is doing the right thing here. My father is blinded by his need for power. Is willing to do anything to harness it." There was no integrity in this. First the poison. And now, keeping them all in the dark while they were being hunted.

His cousins watched him with fallen faces. Aeden closed his eyes tight, remembering the fear and pain he'd felt the night before. And how heartsick he'd been as he tended to Tessa's wounds. "I almost lost her because of all of you."

Balis' Adam's apple bobbed as he gulped. "You really care for her."

"More than anything in this world." The truth of it weighed heavily on his heart. But there it was.

Marcos grimaced. "More than your own kin?"

Aeden opened his mouth to speak, but no answer came. Even though his relationship with his father was a strained one, he still loved him. Knew that Olgar tried in his own way to protect them all. And he loved his mother—the woman who had nurtured his love for music. Most of all, he loved his cousins. The men who had grown up alongside him like brothers. They were his best friends. But all of that paled in comparison to the feelings he was having for Tessa.

Aeden's voice was rough as he asked, "Why do you say that like I have to choose?"

Marcos sighed. "You don't. But if we do not figure out a way to understand or control the turned, then we won't stand a chance when more come. Not even Tessa."

"Reinar will never agree to it." Even if Aeden supported his father in this, Reinar would stand in their way. He would never trust Olgar enough to follow his lead. Even the hypocrite, Drake, would stand in their way. Likely out of spite more than anything else.

Marcos' hand fell to his dagger. "Reinar will not have a say."

Aeden rubbed at his eyes. He couldn't allow his cousins to kill Reinar. That is, if they were even up to the task. Starving or not, he was still a warrior. He hadn't held his position amongst their people by being feeble or untalented.

"Let me talk to him first." Aeden glanced back at the house. He hoped Tessa had talked him out of the council meeting. "Go back home. Tell my father that the meeting is canceled. Stall him for as long as you can. I'll deal with the Downthorns." Maybe if he swayed Tessa to see his family's side of things, then she would help him.

Even if she hated him, she would want to do everything in her power to protect the people she loved. Together, they might be able to convince Reinar to give his father's plan to deal with the hunters a chance. It was far better than the alternative. His eyes dropped to the sharpened steel in Marcos' hand.

Up the path behind them, Drake's voice rang out loud and clear. "Came to catch us an Ashbane scum, but looks like we hit the jackpot, boys."

A man nearly the size of a bear whistled. "Three for one. Not a bad hunt."

Aeden turned, aligning himself with Marcos and Balis. Drake was flanked by three men. Two of them were massive, sharing familial similarities with one another. And the third was Peitor. The dunce. They were unarmed, but that didn't mean much. Not when they were the true weapon.

Aeden attempted to quell what he was sure was about to be an ugly brawl as he said, "My cousins were just leaving. There's no need to cause a scene, gentlemen."

Drake snarled, flashing his massive fangs. "We have every reason, *dog*. You soil my cousin's bed and her good name. And you conspire against us. It's time to put the whole pack of you down."

"I will not shed blood shared with the woman I care for more than myself," Aeden warned. Fighting her family—even one as despicable as Drake—would only hurt Tessa more.

Peitor spat unceremoniously on the ground. "She is no longer yours to care for." The sneer on his face made Aeden's blood boil. "Don't worry. I'll make sure she's well looked after."

Aeden grimaced. Peitor, like Drake, hid behind expensive silks and cloth—living under the guise of integrity—but his true colors were showing. Just as they had at the dinner they'd attended together at Reinar's table. No wonder he and Drake got on so well.

Aeden balled his hands into fists, nearly trembling with the effort it took not to wipe the smug look off of Peitor's face. But it was Marcos who reacted. Steel scraped against the leather as he unsheathed his weapon.

The burly men hissed in response. But they made no move to attack. Aeden suspected they wouldn't unless Drake gave them the go ahead. Aeden placed a steadying hand on Marcos' shoulder. "Do not take the bait. There will be no blood shed here today." With a pointed look in Drake's direction, he emphasized, "*On either side.*"

The snarl that tore from Drake gave Aeden a jolt of adrenaline. His fight response kicked in as Drake barreled towards him. Aeden shoved Marcos out of the way, hoping to keep his sword at bay.

Drake's fist connected with Aeden's gut, knocking the wind out of him. They grappled with one another, throwing fists and elbows. Neither cared where they landed so long as they did the job. Aeden tried to anticipate each move Drake made, but he was unpredictable. Savage.

Blood trickled down Aeden's face. At some point, he'd been struck at the corner of his eyebrow, and it was bleeding profusely.

Aeden's promise to Tessa that he would do his best to avoid conflict with her cousin was one he could no longer keep. Yet another reason for her to pull away from him. But with each blow Drake dealt, Aeden's hatred for him grew.

Drake's friends began to close in, but he shouted at them, "Leave us!"

He and Aeden circled around one another like animals who had been thrown into a pit. Balis and Marcos inched closer like wolves ready to defend one of their pack. Aeden held a firm hand out. A silent command for his cousins to let him deal with Drake himself. If he subdued him long enough to get out of there, then a few cuts and bruises would be the worst of it. Maybe Tessa wouldn't add this to the list of reasons to hate him.

Drake seemed to have no such reservations as he bared his teeth and spat blood. "Perhaps the Elders of Elfhame will welcome you with open arms in the land of the dead. Either way, your time here is up."

Before Aeden could retort, Drake barreled into him. Aeden should have been stronger. He knew that. But he hadn't fed from the vein in nearly two weeks. He was no match for someone like Drake, who, up until recently, had been getting his blood directly from the source as the curse intended.

Earth crunched beneath Aeden's fall. Or was it bone? Adrenaline kept the pain at bay and Aeden jerked his head in an attempt to regain his bearings. He stood with fists raised to protect his face. But before he knew it, Marcos roared, running at Drake with lightning speed. The speed of another Vampyr who had been drinking his fill. The men clashed, rolling on the ground. Drake's lackeys shouted encouragements like Aeden had seen mortals do in the fighting rings.

Before he could take a step in their direction, there was a sickening crack of bone. It echoed in Aeden's ears and for a moment he thought it was the sound of Drake or Marcos' limbs breaking. But as Drake pulled back with a hand soaked in blood, horror engulfed Aeden.

Drake turned to him with a hideous sneer. Instantly, Aeden's gaze dropped to his cousin. Marcos was lying on the ground, blank eyes staring up at the crimson treetops as if searching for the sky he hadn't been able to fully see in years.

Aeden couldn't move. He wasn't even sure if he was still breathing. His gaze drifted to Marcos' chest where Drake's savage fist had left a gaping hole. Blood soaked the torn fabric of his shirt. The damage was like nothing Aeden had ever seen before. And though he couldn't see it, he knew his cousin's heart had been crushed.

A powerful wave of nausea overcame him, and he became both hot and cold. He blinked rapidly, willing the scene in front of him to change. To turn time back to before the fight. To go back to before he had come to the Downthorns. Or even to take back the night of the masquerade. If only he could go back before all of it.

Balis was shouting Marcos' name, but it sounded like he was a million miles away. His little cousin tried to run to his brother, but Aeden grabbed him by the collar of his jacket. Then he tossed him back, as far away from Drake as he could. He would not lose both Marcos *and* him today.

Drake's friends were shouting, too. Their blurred shapes grappled with Drake, but all Aeden saw was red. Like the leaves of the old oak trees. Like the tainted color of their cursed eyes and the blood he craved. The rage took hold of him, making him act without thinking. Drake would die for this.

Aeden charged. But Drake was faster. He caught Aeden from behind, wrapping his arm around his throat like one of the man-eating snakes in the mortal realm. Aeden gasped for air while clawing at the arm that was threatening to crush his windpipe. Taking hold with both hands, Aeden pulled down and reared up quickly. With a sweep of his leg, he threw Drake off balance, sending him tumbling back far enough to give Aeden a moment to catch his breath.

Another set of footsteps entered the small clearing. Too maddened to care, Aeden balled his fists. He would kill Drake with his bare hands or he would die trying. As the air returned to his lungs, he heard the sickening sound of punctured skin and fabric. When he looked up, Drake was on his knees. Shining steel flashed. A sharp blade stuck out of his chest. Marcos' blade.

Blood dripped down Drake's chin, and his eyes glazed over. Tessa, who was standing behind him in her beautiful emerald dress, released her hold on the sword—the one she had pulled from Marcos' scabbard—and allowed her cousin to collapse on the ground. There was no remorse on her face, but there was also no anger. Instead, she paled and stumbled back a few steps, eyes never leaving the man she'd just killed.

No. She wasn't supposed to be here. She wasn't supposed to see any of this. Wasn't meant to be a part of it. Aeden wanted to go to her. To save her from what she'd just done. But he was as frozen as the lakes of the Winter Court. Mouth dry and chest numb, he looked around at the carnage. It was a nightmare come to life. His cousin—his best friend—was dead at a Downthorn's hand. And Tessa's cousin was dead at hers.

They had let themselves be blinded by dreams of what could be. They had opened their hearts to one another. And because of that, they had destroyed everyone around them. Just like their forebears, Ayana and Byron. Just like the curse bringers.

Twenty-Four

Tessa

The Crimson Forest was quiet, apart from the ringing in Tessa's ears. Although she was aware that she was surrounded by men—their heavy stares dug holes into her like the one in Marcos' chest—they felt distant. It was as if she was floating above, watching herself standing over Drake's lifeless body which now had an Ashbane sword plunged inside.

As much as she gasped for a breath, it wouldn't seem to come. Despite the fresh air of the woods, none of it seemed to fill her lungs. With shaking, clammy hands, she pushed her hair from her face and stumbled back a few steps.

Through the ringing in her ears, she swore someone was calling her name. Still, she couldn't take her eyes from her cousin. As treacherous as Drake could be, he was her family. He was Reinar's son. Memories clouded her thoughts. A young, gangly Drake giving her a boost on his shoulders so she could swipe cookies from the counter. A teenage Drake smiling broadly as his father boasted about his swordsmanship. A grown Drake grumbling at the masquerade and making her laugh behind her hand.

But he was going to kill Aeden. She had seen it with her own eyes. Nobody was doing anything to stop them. If she had stood by and done nothing, then it would have been Aeden lying lifeless on the leaf-strewn ground.

Still, the weight of her treachery set in. Her uncle would be heartbroken. How could she have done this to him? She had taken his only son from him. It was unforgivable.

"No." The word came unwarranted. Then again, "No. No. No." She shook her head. Scalding tears streamed down her face and blurred the bleeding body at her feet.

Strong hands took hold of her, and someone drew her into them. She buried her face in their chest, leaning on them as her knees threatened to give out on her. It was Aeden's voice speaking into her ear. "It's alright, Tessa. I'm going to fix everything."

Her stomach dropped and she pulled away from him. She no longer belonged in his arms. She could no longer depend on him to make things right. The wounds of his betrayal were still too fresh. When she had come into the forest after hearing from Talos that Drake had gone looking for Aeden, she had expected a brawl.

What she hadn't expected was to find Drake choking the life out of Aeden. Something had snapped inside her. A fierce urge to protect him. But that didn't change his deceit. They were through.

Wrapping her arms around herself, she murmured, "Look around, Aeden. Things are beyond repair."

He shook his head stubbornly. "Listen to me. When your uncle comes, we will tell him *I* killed Drake."

She scrunched her face. "What? No. He'll kill you." She hadn't saved him just to watch him die at her uncle's hands.

"Not if it was self-defense. Please, let me do this for you."

Aeden's skin was ashen. It was as if the shadows of the forest were painted on his face. His cousin was dead, too. Because of hers. Would she or Aeden ever brighten again? Or would they forever live under a dark shroud?

Peitor uttered from behind her, "What have you done?"

Tessa sniffled and stepped back to look at him. She expected judgment in his eyes, but instead, he stared at Aeden with pure hatred. Heat spread through her chest. The question wasn't for her. It was for him.

Harshly, Aeden answered, "This is *all* our doing. I will not have Tessa bear the consequences of our actions. When Reinar comes, you and your friends will corroborate our story. There was a fight. Drake murdered my cousin and so I took my revenge."

Peitor's gaze darted between Aeden and Tessa. Shivers were wracking her body now, chilling her down to the bone. Aeden couldn't take the blame. It wasn't his burden to shoulder. As much as she wanted to argue, her voice wouldn't come.

Aeden pushed as he said, "Tessa doesn't deserve to be blamed for our folly. Can we at least agree on that?"

Peitor's face softened, his lips turning down as he eyed Tessa carefully. "Agreed."

The Steelhelm brothers stepped up to his side and nodded solemnly. This time, when Aeden approached her, she could do nothing but cling to him like an anchor. She pressed her face into his chest again, afraid if she didn't, then she would look at the carnage once more. Something she couldn't bear to do. Not when it felt like she was falling apart at the seams.

Shouts echoed through the trees. They were coming. And then they would see what she had done. Would her uncle forgive her? Or would he banish her from the forest just as he had threatened to do to others who committed such heinous acts? She shut her eyes tight, inhaling the blood and sweat on Aeden. It turned her stomach, but she didn't let go of him. Her fingers dug into the rough fabric of his jacket.

Her mother's cries were the first thing she heard as her family reached them. Followed closely by her uncle exclaiming, "What is the meaning of this!" He drew in a loud breath and Tessa knew it was the moment he noticed his son slain on the floor of his beloved forest. His voice cracked as he said, "My boy."

No one else dared to speak. Behind her closed eyes, everything was dark. Free of the horrific sight of her uncle, no doubt running to his only child. She desperately wished the darkness would swallow her whole. Take her far away from the forest and the nightmare that was now her life.

When Reinar spoke again, she flinched. "Who is responsible for this?"

Aeden's chest vibrated as he answered, "I am."

Tessa stifled a sob and twisted her fingers into his jacket as if they might meld into one if she only squeezed hard enough. Wishing that her grasp on him would save him from her uncle's wrath. Wrath that he didn't deserve. But only she could do that.

Shoving Aeden aside, she spoke with a quiver, "It's not true. It was me. I—" her voice broke, and a shuddered sob escaped her.

Aeden grabbed her roughly by the arm and hissed, "What are you doing?"

She tried to pull away, but his grip was too tight. She pleaded, "Let go." She wasn't sure if she was talking about the hold he had on her arm or her heart. All she knew was she needed to be free of him.

With a deadly hush, Reinar spoke. "Peitor. Tell me precisely what happened here."

Tessa stilled. Her uncle's face was darkened with grief, but mostly he looked... tired. She held her breath. It was as if the forest itself was doing the same, waiting for the moment of truth. All hope of doing the right thing was lost as Peitor exhaled loudly and told the story exactly as Aeden had commanded. The only lie—as far as Tessa knew—was the part where he described Aeden instead of her, holding the hilt of the sword.

She sensed that her mother was close as she said, "Tessa, my love, you need to come with me." There was an urgency in her voice that made Tessa's insides twist. No. If she moved, she would leave Aeden exposed.

Her words came out small and child-like. "No. I can't."

Aeden smoothed her hair down and whispered, "It's alright, Tessa, go with Flora. Please."

Facing the Steelhelm brothers with one of her hands clasping her elbow, she pleaded, "Please, tell them. Tell them the truth of what happened here." They were her last hope.

Her throat tightened at their silence. They couldn't even meet her eye. She turned back to Aeden and shook her head. "He's going to kill you." As angry as she still was with him, she would not let him die. Especially not for something she had done.

Her uncle's heavy hand tugged on her shoulder. "I do not intend to kill anyone. There has been enough death today."

She softened slightly. Reinar had never lied to her before. He was possibly one of the few people in the world who hadn't. Reluctantly, she allowed herself to be removed from Aeden's arms. She still shook like a fever was ravaging her body as her mother took her by the arm with a firm, but loving grip.

For the first time, Tessa met her uncle's eyes. Grief was painted over his face. Every feature drawn down giving hints at just how old he actually was. She swayed as the guilt gnawed at her. It was going to eat her alive.

Reinar set his shoulders back. "Aeden Ashbane. You defended yourself, but the shedding of blood—Vampyr blood—cannot go unpunished. For that, I sentence you to exile. You may bid your family farewell. But by dawn, you are to leave the Crimson Forest."

Tessa's knees weakened at the pang in her chest. With the threat of the witch-blessed hunters, exile was as good as a death sentence. He would never survive. And if he did, what sort of life would he be able to live amongst the mortals?

They would notice when their neighbors or livestock went missing or showed up with fang marks on their necks. Even if he kept his feedings discreet, they would grow suspicious when he didn't age as they did. He would have to live like the solitary Fae, traveling constantly. Never able to settle down. Unable to make a home.

Her heart raced as she silently pleaded for Aeden to argue. To say something. To tell the truth. That it was she who deserved the exile. She sagged into her mother's side. There was nothing she could do but say goodbye.

With tear-filled eyes, she started, "Aeden—"

He stopped her with a kiss. She tensed at the intimate touch. But she couldn't bring herself to resist. Not after everything that had happened. Both the good and the bad. This was goodbye. She leaned into the kiss, and for just a moment, the trembling in her limbs stopped.

When he drew back, he smiled sadly. "It was all real for me, Tessa. I'm sorry it had to end this way."

And with that, he turned on his heel, signaling for Balis to follow. Together, they lifted Marcos from the ground and carried him further into the forest with reverence. Tessa dug her nails into her palms. This wasn't right. It wasn't how things were supposed to go. Their union was meant to bring everyone together, not tear everything apart.

Tessa couldn't seem to get warm. Even with the raging fire in the library and the dozen blankets piled on top of her, the shaking wouldn't subside. Her mother had gone to get her a glass of blood. Something she claimed would calm Tessa's nerves. Meanwhile, her uncle paced the room.

Aeden was gone, and with him, any semblance of peace between the families had gone, too. What would his father say when he returned home with Marcos' slain body? It might not matter that his murderer was dead. Olgar was a proud man. One treacherous enough to send his only son into the heart of his enemy's home with traitorous intent.

Tessa shivered roughly and bit her cheek to distract herself. However, it didn't seem to be doing anything but making the inside of her mouth raw. Scarlet had come bearing dinner, but Tessa hardly paid her any mind. No one seemed to be able to figure out what to say to her. And she knew they assumed her silence was from the shock of witnessing Drake's death. They still refused to believe it was shock from being the one to put a blade through his back.

Peitor had stayed, too. Though she couldn't figure out why. She didn't want any of them there. If she'd had her way, she would have curled up in her bed and stayed there for eternity. Peitor crossed the room, looking around as if unsure of himself. Then he sat beside her. It was the same sofa she and Aeden had sat on together that first night, and Tessa couldn't help the tightening in her jaw. This wasn't Peitor's place.

She curled away from him, drawing her knees up to her chest and locking her arms around them. Keeping her eyes trained on the flames in front of her, she willed him to go away. Instead, he leaned toward her and promised, "We'll avenge Drake. Don't worry, it'll all be alright."

Her nostrils flared in response, and she bit down on her cheek, drawing blood this time. Anything to keep from snapping at him. Didn't he understand? Nothing would ever be alright again. She would have to live in silent guilt for the rest of her life because of him and Aeden. Because of their lie. Because of them, the hatred between their people had grown immensely. Two sons dead, and one exiled. This surely wouldn't be the end of it. Olgar was bound to retaliate.

Talos popped into the room, announcing more visitors. The families in support of the Downthorns were trickling in to pay their respects. Reinar excused himself. One less pair of eyes on her. She breathed a small sigh of relief.

Scarlet exchanged words with Talos. A moment later, she rounded the sofa and set a large basket in front of Tessa. Gingerly, her friend knelt down and rubbed her arm. "This was sent for you."

Tessa looked away from the gift and from Scarlet's pity-filled stare. "Who is it from?"

There was a rustling as Scarlet searched the basket. "I'm not sure. There's no note. Should I take it to your room?"

Peitor's hand brushed against Tessa's arm where bare skin was peeking through the blanket. Hastily, she pulled it tight over her shoulders and stood. "No, I'll take it." She needed to get out of there. To be alone with her guilt and heartache. Sitting in the library while everyone tried to console her only weighed down the heavy sensation in her chest. Like a stone giant threatening to crush the life from her.

Better to be alone and let all the emotions rush in. Let them drown her. She deserved it after everything she'd done. Between allowing Aeden into her home and her heart, and Drake's blood on her hands, she deserved every bit of pain coming to her.

Before Scarlet or Peitor could protest, she reached down, grabbing the basket and walked from the room. With the blanket still wrapped around her shoulders, she didn't notice the chill in the halls. Once inside her room, she shed the covers. Someone, likely Talos, had lit the fire in her fireplace. It was stifling, so she threw open the balcony doors. A soft breeze drifted in, ruffling her hair.

Then she listened. Straining for the sounds of the forest. For any sign of the turned beasts who now haunted their land. Most of all, she listened for Aeden, half expecting him to come scaling up the wall of her terrace again with that goofy grin on his face.

But all she received was silence. It settled in with the gloom. Not ready to give up just yet, she sat cross-legged on the threshold. The basket, now resting on her lap, had a lonely red rose resting on top. Beneath, it was filled to the brim with pastries. But it was the dark, dusty bottle of wine that caught her eye.

It's what Aeden would have reached for. Whoever had sent the basket must have guessed she'd need to lose herself in the bottle tonight. *Cheers*, she thought bitterly. It was just as well that Aeden didn't come. There was nothing she could say to him to fix things. Nor would she want to. It had been the two of them that set these events into motion. If they would have said no to their families, or if she would have kept that shield up around her heart, then Marcos and Drake might still be alive.

She should have known better than to believe that it would be safe to let Aeden in. To care for him the way she did. They had ruined one another in more ways than one. Her throat stung as bitter tears threatened to fall.

Desperate for a distraction, she tossed the rose on the ground, ignoring the sting of the thorns on her fingertips. Ruffling through the pastries, she grabbed the bottle, discarding the rest of the basket to the side, and stood. She tugged at the cork, using what little energy she had left to open the bottle. The burgundy wine almost seemed like a shimmery purple in the moonlight. Hopefully, it was the good stuff. A stiff drink would be just the thing to help her fall into a fitful slumber. The first swig was bitter. She grimaced, but drank more. The burn going down was almost enough to overpower the guilt and anger building in her chest.

She lifted the bottle to her lips once more, but the muscles in her arm buckled. The bottle slipped from her hands, shattering on the stone balcony floor. Bile rose in her throat, rejecting the contents of it. Heaving, Tessa stumbled to the edge of the terrace. Her fingers scraped against the stone, grasping for something, anything, to keep her steady.

She sucked in, desperately trying to get a breath, but everything was tight. Her muscles, her lungs, her throat. White dots filled the sky like the stars she missed. But these weren't beautiful. No. They were her enemy. Threatening to steal her vision from her.

Too dizzy, Tessa lost her balance and fell to the ground. Someone—her mother, perhaps—shouted her name. But Tessa was already losing consciousness. Maybe this was fate's way of punishing her. Maybe she deserved it. She gave in, embracing the icy cold that enveloped her. Ready to face the consequences of what she'd done. Of what she and Aeden had done.

Twenty-Five

Aeden

Aeden leaned back in a creaky leather chair, watching his father pace anxiously in the large family room. They had all neglected to sleep the previous night. Instead, they had laid Marcos to rest down by the lake. The pyre had burned hot, filling the forest with smoke. Aeden had watched the ashes drift in the night sky and wondered if Tessa was standing on the other side of the lake saying goodbye to her own kin.

The pain of being apart from her hit him harder than expected. Even now, with his family surrounding him, he couldn't shake the emptiness in the pit of his stomach. Not even fresh blood helped. Though it *had* sharpened his focus enough to catch his father mumbling under his breath.

"That son of a bitch thinks to exile my son. The hunger must be eating away at his mind."

Aeden did not bother trying to placate Olgar. Not when his own mind was a hurricane of emotion. After sending Marcos' eternal soul off to what they all hoped would be the land of the Elders—the hollow beneath the oak trees where the dead resided—they had returned to the manor to feed. Today, Aeden's strength was restored, leaving him full and ready to face what was to come.

Exile. The most unthinkable punishment for their people. It was hard enough to survive the curse within the forest with the support of their community. But to venture into the mortal lands alone meant new and challenging hardships. Ones that would more than likely end with a stake through the heart.

Aeden pressed at his temples. Visions of Marcos and his wide, mischievous grin danced in his mind. Tangled with memories of Tessa's hair blowing wildly on horseback. How had things come to this? Maybe death was what he deserved. He'd gotten his cousin killed, betrayed Tessa and was the reason she now had blood on her own hands. The feel of her clinging to him with all her might lingered like a wraith's touch. The scent of her still remained on his jacket, which he hadn't bothered to change. And his heart ached.

Olgar grumbled, forcing everyone in the room to lean forward so they could catch what he was saying. Aeden's mother was tucked into a corner. She hadn't stopped crying since Aeden and Balis returned with Marcos' limp body hanging between them.

Balis sat beside his father. He always seemed to shrink in the man's presence. As if trying to become invisible. It didn't matter, though. Aeden's uncle hadn't looked at him or Balis since the funeral at the lake. It was no secret that Marcos was his favorite son. Even if he barely tolerated him.

Others had come, too. Rose and the other Dewruns, the Pinegaze family with their gaggle of daughters, and even the Redborne family who rarely attended any social gathering. All had come to show their support for the Ashbanes.

Aeden shivered. It felt eerily similar to the meeting in Elfhame that led up to the curse. When the prominent families of the Autumn Court previously gathered to offer to stand with Aeden's great uncle, Byron. Only back then, they were united with the Downthorns and their Winter Court loyalists. Banding together to defeat a common enemy.

Today, when Olgar spoke of war, it was aimed at those very families who had stood with them so long ago. The ones who had suffered the same consequences of raising their magic against the King of the Unseelie Court. To fight together as one...

But now, Aeden couldn't figure out who the true enemy was. The witch-blessed hunters, surely. Remnants of the infamous Six. But after the prior day's events, they were not the imminent threat. They were not the topic of this gathering. Reinar was. Olgar stopped pacing, drawing Aeden's attention to him across the room.

"Reinar thinks he can exile one of our own. My one and only heir. It is unacceptable. We will not continue on this way. We will no longer live in fear of his judgment. You," he pointed around the room to each family, "have come here to offer your support. We do not have a lot of time. The hunters are coming for you. Each and every one of you. Yet Reinar deems the greater threat to be my son? It is an outrage." There were a few angry murmurs in the crowd, and then Olgar continued, "Today, we gather our strength.

Sharpen our arms and our fangs. At nightfall, when the full moon reaches its peak, we move on Reinar."

Aeden rose as he asked, "Why risk it? Let me speak with him. Allow me the chance to explain that the only way for us to stand against the turned is if we unite. Save your strength for the real enemy. For the Sons of the Six. If they come, you will need all the willing and able Vampyrs you can get."

Olgar's mouth twisted into something menacing. "This fight will happen with or without you, boy. Reinar's reign here is finished."

Aeden clenched his teeth, wanting to argue further. But it wouldn't do any good. His father had made up his mind long before Marcos was killed. He wasn't truly fighting for Aeden or for the revenge of his nephew. This was a long time coming. Running far deeper than Aeden ever could have imagined.

It was true, he could leave. He could accept his exile gracefully and hop a ship to another mortal kingdom. See the world. Keep moving and never look back. But that would leave Tessa caught in the middle of this feud. His father might see fit to dispose of her, too. Even if he allowed her to live, what would happen when the hunters came? She was a capable fighter, but she wasn't at her full strength. It was too big a risk.

His gaze drifted to Balis. He hadn't spoken much since Marcos' death. Long gone were the easy smiles and eagerness of youth. If Aeden had stood by his family—done what he'd been sent to the Downthorns to do—then Drake would have died days ago and Marcos would still be with them. Grief twisted like a dagger in his gut. Regardless of how he felt about the turned or his father's plans, he owed it to Marcos to stand with Balis now. To make sure no harm fell to him.

Accepting the impossible position he was in, Aeden raised his chin. "Fine. What's your big plan?"

His father loved his secrets. More than that, he loved to weaponise them. Whether blackmailing a wealthy family into serving him, or only sharing parts of his plans with his allies so they wouldn't try to stop him, Olgar reveled in the power of a good secret.

This was one of those instances. Aeden stood outside of the barn where their horses used to be kept. It no longer smelled of fresh hay and dusty fur coats. Instead, the powerful stench of rot filled his nose.

But it paled in comparison to what his father revealed as he dragged the creaky old barn doors open. Dilated, hungry eyes blinked wildly at him from the shadowy corners of the stables. The turned were crammed in like fish caught in a net. Bodies pressed together to keep away from the sunlight slipping through the open door and the cracks in the wooden roof.

A few hissed at him, and he did his best not to react. The attack was too fresh in his memory. He would never forget the brute strength of the beasts. Or how their claws slashed into Tessa's body as if she were made of the same silk fabric she had been wearing. It turned his stomach, and he struggled to level his racing pulse.

His father stood proudly beside him, boasting like a showman at the circuses the mortals loved to put on. Aeden tried to contain his disgust as Olgar introduced the families gathered around them to the turned mortals in the barn. "They didn't come easy, but here they are. Each marked by a witch. Blessed with power and strength to rival our own. But a human body can only maintain such gifts for so long without consequence."

Aeden swallowed the lump in his throat. "Where did you find this many?"

Olaf scoffed. "They hunt in groups. Found them snooping around the tree line before they'd fully turned. From what we can tell, using the power they've been granted consumes them from the inside out. Most are able to survive the transition." He frowned. "Only problem is they're sensitive to light."

Through clenched teeth, Aeden added, "And that they're highly volatile."

"We're working on that," his father snapped. "With compulsion, we may be able to control them. Turn them into the ideal soldier."

Aeden shook his head. His father was insane. From his own experience, Aeden knew the Sons of the Six could not be compelled. Not without great care and effort. This experiment of his father's put them all in danger. Even if it worked, what if the compulsion wore off? They should have been focusing on eradicating them. On finding any others who might be following in their stead. There was no telling how many more there were. They were like pests—just when you thought you were rid of one, three more came in its place.

Olgar continued to rile up his audience. "Reinar allowed these creatures to come into existence. He was weak and preferred to hide rather than conquer. If I'd had my way, the Six would have been wiped out. Their sons and the sons of those sons never would have been born. They never would have had the chance to band together."

Aeden wanted to argue. If his father had his way, then no humans would have been safe. He would have killed The Six along with any of their children. Innocents who hadn't done anything to them yet. Although Aeden was willing to go to great lengths to protect the ones he loved, he never would have been willing to go that far.

But as he looked around at the awe on the loyalists' faces, he could see there was no changing their minds. They'd been trapped in their cage for too long. They craved freedom. A fleeting rush of adrenaline told him that some small part of him still did, too. But in his heart, he knew this wasn't the way to achieve it.

If the bloodthirsty creatures could be controlled, then his father would use them as a weapon. Not just against the other witch-blessed hunters, but against Tessa and her people, too. Olgar would recklessly wield them to suit his needs. And after that, the world would be his for the taking. The prospect of it made bone-chilling dread wash over him.

Tessa needed to know what was happening. It didn't matter how angry she was with him. That could wait. Right now, they needed to think of a way to deescalate their people. There was no one he trusted more than her to help him. Emotions brewed like the beginning of a storm and Aeden turned away. Excusing himself, he pushed through the crowd. But Rose stepped in front of him and he scoffed, "Not now. I'm not in the mood."

With brows raised and eyes wide, she placed a freshly manicured hand on his chest. "I just came from the lake."

"So?" Aeden didn't care what she was doing or who she had likely snuck off to meet. He just needed to get out of there. To put distance between himself and his father.

"It's Tessa." Rose's expression gave nothing away, but his heart leapt into his throat none the less.

Had Tessa found Rose and spoken with her? Had she sent Rose to him because she wanted to meet? With a small glimmer of hope, he nodded, encouraging her to go on.

Rose pressed her lips into a hard, thin line, then said, "It's *about* Tessa."

With his heart beating as fast as a hummingbird's wings, he snapped, "What is it? Just say it."

Dread seeped in, filling him to the core as she said, "There is a funeral pyre."

Aeden clenched his jaw, scraping his fangs against his bottom teeth.

Impassively, Rose added, "Tessa lays upon it."

"You're lying." Aeden's nose flared in a fleeting fit of rage. Rose was jealous of Tessa, that much was clear from her behavior since the courtship started. But making something like this up was going too far.

"I'm not." Rose stuck her stubborn nose in the air. "It's the truth. I saw it with my own eyes. The Downthorns and their folk are gathering as we speak."

"Then you saw wrong." He clenched his fists. He had seen Tessa yesterday. She was in perfect health. Had received no injuries in the horrible confrontation between the cousins. It didn't make sense. If there had been an attack of some sort... If she had died, Aeden would have known. He would have felt it. There would have been a change in the forest or a stir in his heart.

After all the danger they had faced together, she couldn't be gone. No. Rose was mistaken. Or playing some mean trick. Right? When he met her eyes—cold and unmoving—he realized the latter was wrong. She was serious.

His mouth went dry and his words came out weak. "How? How did she die?"

Rose's eyes darted to the left as she said, "I didn't stay long enough to hear everything. But there was the mention of poison." When she looked back at him, she frowned. But there was no pity there. No grief for the loss of Tessa. Only irritation danced in her eyes.

Poison? Aeden gripped his jacket. In all the chaos since dinner with his family and the Downthorns, he hadn't grabbed a fresh one. The poison should have been in his pocket. Reaching roughly inside, he dug around for the deadly vial. But there was nothing there. No glass, no glittering, dark purple liquid. The poison was gone.

He muttered to himself. "Where is it?"

"Where is what?" Rose placed a hand on her chest as if concerned.

Aeden ignored her. He tore the jacket off, shaking it out as if by some miracle it would fall to the ground, and he would know that this was all a big misunderstanding. Still, nothing appeared. His breath hitched in his throat and he pinched the bridge of his nose, trying to recount the events leading him to this moment.

Dinner at his family's estate. The vial had been in his pocket then. That night, he had every intention of getting rid of it. Had his father suspected that? Realized he could swipe the vial from Aeden without being noticed? But Aeden couldn't think of a moment where he would have had the chance. Then there was the attack in the forest. His jacket had been torn, but the pockets remained intact. Had it slipped out in the woods without him realizing?

His heart sped. Rose was calling out to him, but it was as if he had plunged underwater. Even the sounds of the forest were muffled as he recalled the intimate night between him and Tessa in her room. His jacket had been discarded on the floor. The poison could have fallen from his pocket, then. But why would Tessa harm herself? She was a fighter. A survivor...

The jacket felt like heavy steel in his hand. He let it slip to the ground. "I need to go."

"Aeden, you can't. Reinar won't allow it. You're supposed to be exiled. If you show your face there, especially now, then they will kill you."

"I need to see her." If he saw with his own eyes, then maybe it would all make sense. If she had been poisoned, then he needed to understand the circumstances. Whether it was his father's doing. Or whether it was Tessa who had placed it on her lips by her own hand. A pang tore through his heart. She wouldn't have... she couldn't have... He couldn't say it. Not even in his own mind. She had little affection for Drake. But had she been so consumed with guilt that she thought there was no other escape?

Rose reached for him, but he slapped her hands away, unable to bear anyone's touch aside from Tessa's. A touch that he may never again have the chance to feel. Rose reached for him once more, and he caught her wrist with a firm grip.

"Don't," he warned.

Her eyes narrowed. "Let her go, Aeden. You are back where you belong now. That is what matters. Let. Her. Go."

He released her wrist with a hiss. Behind him, Olgar's boastful words filled the air. Bragging about how he was strong enough to cage the monsters and how—once Reinar was out of their way—nothing would stop them from taking their place in the world. Promising his people that nothing would hold them back from making the mortals submit to them. The crowd grew more rambunctious as his father's promises grew louder and more urgent.

Aeden stormed away from them, but Olgar called out to him, "Where are you going?"

When Aeden refused to answer—too consumed with the need to reach the lake—Olgar rushed up behind him. He grabbed Aeden roughly by the shoulder and turned him, so they were standing nearly nose to nose.

Olgar spat. "Don't you turn your back on me, boy."

"I am not your boy." Aeden shoved his father's hand off him.

Olgar's face reddened and his gaze shifted around the crowd, who had inched closer to them. If there was one thing his father hated more than not having power, it was being embarrassed in public. But Aeden didn't care. He never had. Perhaps that was why his father had treated him so callously. Knowing that his only son had no desire for fame and power must have grated on him all these years.

But Aeden would not allow his will to be bent any longer. It was Olgar's callousness and greed that put the poison in his hands in the first place. It was his father who had been adamant about using it. Aeden narrowed his eyes, "Just tell me one thing. Did you decide to use the poison when I made it clear I would not?"

Olgar's full cheeks jiggled as he shook his head. "What in the star's name are you talking about?"

"Tessa. Rose claims she is dead. *Poisoned.*" Aeden clenched his fists. "Tell me it wasn't your doing."

A smug smile spread across his father's face. "It wasn't me. But I shall reward whoever it was."

He was gloating. Glad Tessa was gone and out of the way. It was like lightning had seared through Aeden. With his fist still balled, he reared back and struck Olgar. His father stumbled back, wide-eyed. He rubbed his jaw and moved it around before speaking. "Seems you got your strength back."

Aeden glared at him. He was right about that. Feeding on the vein again had given him the gifts that came with the curse. And right now, he was willing to use those abilities on anyone who got in his way. He was heading to the lake to see Tessa, and no one was going to stop him.

Silently, Aeden turned on his heel and headed for the water. Footsteps followed him and he looked over his shoulder to find Olgar stumbling behind. Still heated, but also a little confused, Aeden asked, "What do you think you're doing?"

Olgar shrugged, still rubbing at his jaw where a considerably large bruise was already forming. "We're coming with you. If the Downthorns and their lot are gathered for the funeral, then it is the perfect opportunity to confront them." A mixture of excitement and malice sparkled in his eyes.

Aeden closed the gap between them and grabbed onto his father's jacket. His fingers twisted in the rough fabric and there was venom in his voice as he warned, "You will not come anywhere near that funeral pyre. Do you understand me, old man?"

For the first time in his life, hesitation flashed across his father's face. Carefully, as if trying to keep a rabid animal from attacking, Olgar said, "Son, if she is gone, then there is nothing else to hold you back. Think of your family. Of those you have left."

"I *am* thinking of the ones I have left." Aeden thought of Flora and the way her face lit up when she gave one of her true smiles. And of Reinar doting on Tessa with genuine fatherly love. Again, he warned, "You will remain here."

Without waiting for his father to respond, Aeden shoved him. The force of it was so strong that it sent him flying a few feet back into the crowd. Several Vampyrs tumbled to the ground under the weight of Olgar and gasps filled the air. Aeden had made his stand. And that, perhaps, was more surprising for everyone than the monsters sitting behind them in the barn.

Blinded by his determination, Aeden turned his back on them all and began to run. The lake would hold the answers he needed.

But what would happen when he got there? The tiniest, hopeful voice in his head told him that Rose was, in fact, wrong. That it was all a misunderstanding and he would find nothing but gentle lapping waves and an empty clearing when he reached the water.

Twenty-Six

Aeden

N ight never looked so bleak. The forest itself seemed to tremble as Aeden marched away from his home. From his people. The lake, being set in the heart of the woods, was where their funerals were held. Ceremonies like the one he attended less than a day ago for his own cousin. He hoped his father would listen to Aeden's command to remain behind. The Vampyrs who supported Olgar were eager. Too eager. When his father made his speeches about conquering the realm, there was a hunger in their eyes that went far past the point of craving blood.

Aeden had other motives, however. And they didn't involve Olgar and his plans. He needed to see Tessa. To feel her under his touch. Only then would he know the truth.

He was so lost in his thoughts that he didn't sense Rose before she sidled up beside him. "Aeden, don't do anything foolish." She grabbed him by the elbow, but he shrugged her off.

It was too late for that. He had already made all the wrong choices. The worst of all was leaving Tessa alone with her guilt. Alone to face what she had done. If he had been there to protect her, then maybe she wouldn't be... He shook his head, trying to clear it of thoughts of what her last moments must have been like.

Rose continued to push. "You grieve for that spoiled, self-righteous brat?"

Aeden stopped in his tracks, grabbing Rose roughly by the sleeve of her dress. "Don't you dare speak of Tessa as if you know anything about her."

"I know that the two of you didn't belong together." She raised her chin and bared her teeth. "You belong with *us*. Don't you dare think that I will allow your recklessness to ruin everything we have been working for."

Aeden narrowed his eyes. How much had Rose been involved in his father's plans? What did he promise her? There was no doubt about how far she was willing to go in order to get what she wanted. After all, it was she who went running to Drake during the masquerade. She was the one who had attempted to push Aeden and Tessa apart during that damned dinner.

With a heated warning, he said, "Stay out of my way. Worry about yourself."

He released his hold on her, picking up his pace to leave her far behind. But her words carried to him as she shouted, "Oh, you don't have to worry about that!"

Reinar and the other families were already at the lake when Aeden arrived. Flora was swathed in white lace, standing beside a wooden pyre. The slat of wood, stacked on branches, stood as high as her shoulder. When Aeden locked eyes with her, she turned as white as the mourning clothes she was wearing.

"Aeden," she said his name like a whisper on the wind. Much like the water witch had often spoken. It was wraith-like and Aeden wondered for a moment if the heartache the woman endured in her lifetime would turn her into one of the spirits who wandered the forest. Eternally cold and alone.

Reinar's voice bellowed next. "You! You can't be here." He took several strides toward Aeden, but stopped before reaching him. Dark circles surrounded his eyes and his face was more gaunt and thin than the previous day.

Aeden held his hands out to show he meant no harm. "Please. I need to see her."

"Leave now, Aeden *Ashbane*." Reinar spat his surname as if he couldn't bear to have it linger on his tongue.

Aeden glanced at the shroud resting on the wood. From here he couldn't make out the face of the woman lying on it because of the thin muslin covering it. But he spotted strands of silky dark hair and that alone was enough to feel as if a knife were being plunged into his chest. He started, "Reinar—"

"*Count* Reinar," he corrected. "You are not welcome here. It is only because of the love my niece bore for you that I do not strike you down where you stand."

Men from the other families slowly began to close in around him, trapping him like a lone wolf. He was outnumbered, but the bitter stench of fear and uncertainty filled his nose. They had to know that in the starving state they were in that he would out-match them in strength. That he—in true Ashbane fashion—had fed the way the curse intended.

With the pyre only a few yards away, Aeden took his chances, sprinting and dodging past the men who were too slow to grab onto him. When he reached the wooden slab, only Flora stood between him and the shroud. Unlike Reinar, her face softened at him. She tilted her head to the side as she studied him. Then, as if convinced by whatever it was she was searching for, she stepped aside.

No one followed him now. Indignant shouts turned to an eerie hush as Aeden climbed onto the branches so he could lean over the resting body. The shape was one he was familiar with. Soft curves he had memorized over the last few weeks. And dark hair he ran his hands through not so long ago.

He took a few strands between his fingers and shut his eyes tight, willing away the tears burning his eyes. Sucking in a deep breath, he opened them and gently removed the muslin veil. Tessa's eyes were closed. The heavy lashes kissed the tops of her cheeks. Aeden's heart plummeted, and he shook his head in denial. If she had been on a bed, he'd have sworn she was only sleeping.

Unspeakable pain lanced through him as he placed a hand on her cheek and sobbed softly. It was bitterly cold, and he took her face in both hands now. He grazed his thumbs along her lips as if he might warm the life back into her. Another sob escaped him as he noticed the purple stain on her once rose-red lips.

"Tessa," he pleaded, "come back to me. Please. I can't do this without you."

Flora stifled a cry behind him, but he couldn't bring himself to look at her. He couldn't handle seeing the grief he was feeling on another's face. Instead, he stared down at Tessa, silently begging the fates to change their minds. To bring her back to him.

"I'm sorry. I'm so sorry, Tessa." His voice was pinched as he cried out, "I failed you. You were the wolf all along. The strong one. The fierce one. I was a coward. I should have told you everything the moment I started to care for you. We could have faced this together."

Reinar cleared his throat. He sounded close enough to pull Aeden down, but no one touched him. As if not daring to move him before he was ready. Aeden couldn't stay there forever, though. He didn't have the strength to remain as they lit the pyre. So, he did the only thing left to do... say goodbye. Leaning over Tessa, he pressed his lips gently to hers. If only the poison still lingered there, as the stain of its color had done. Then he wouldn't have to face the consequences of his deceit—of his part in his father's plan. When he lifted his lips from hers, anger bled into despair.

The world around him spun as he stepped down from the pyre. With one hand on his stomach, he turned, expecting to throw up. He bent over with both hands braced on his knees and sucked in a heavy breath. The land beneath his feet looked the same as it ever had. Brown dirt with little blades of rich, green grass. He shut his eyes tight, unable to stand the sight of it. How could the world carry on as it always had with Tessa no longer in it? Animals should be wailing in mourning. The trees should be withering where they stood. How could it all carry on when Aeden felt as if he might crumble to pieces?

This was his fault. It was all their fault. His father forced him into Tessa's life, and he had stupidly agreed. Reinar had failed to keep his son leashed. Had allowed his past with Aeden's family to seep into the next generation. The humans and their hunters had forced them into the forest to stew on their bitterness, with nothing else to do but allow it to fester.

To Reinar, he asked, "How? How did it happen?"

"Poison in her wine." There was hatred in Reinar's eyes as he spoke. "We fear the pain of yesterday's events was too much for her. That she sought a way to end it."

The poison. Was Aeden right in thinking that it could have fallen from his pocket during their night together? He wanted to deny it. To tell them they were wrong. Believing his father had somehow done it was easier to accept and understand. To believe Tessa had been taken from the world by her own hand was unbearable.

Aeden's ears perked at the sounds of leaves shuffling in the forest. Footsteps. A lot of them. Each one deadly silent—unnoticeable to Reinar and his people who had not fed properly, if at all that night. Adrenaline jolted him into motion as he took a few steps and gestured to Reinar.

Tessa's uncle whipped his head around just as Olgar and the others came into view. Aeden wanted to be surprised that his father hadn't listened to him, but he wasn't. How could he be? Olgar would never pass up the opportunity to keep the upper hand.

The head of the Ashbane family and his followers were dressed for battle with thick leather jackets protecting their chests. It was the weakest spot on a Vampyr—where their hearts were. Aeden cursed at them under his breath as his father led them around the bank where the borders collided.

Shining moonstones gave light to Reinar and his men. They were lightly armed, with their weapons tucked away. There for a funeral, not a battle. To Aeden's relief, his father's men had their weapons sheathed. A small part of him—the part of him that still cared—hoped they would attempt to talk. To make a deal that kept anymore blood from being shed.

Olgar held a fist in the air, signaling for his people to stop before crossing the border into Downthorn territory. Each man stood face to face. There were dark shadows around Reinar's eyes, and his face sagged. His age was showing through his grief. Which did he grieve for more, though? Drake, his callous son or Tessa, his darling niece?

Aeden stepped between the separate groups, hoping to be the buffer to keep them from tearing one another apart while Tessa's shroud stood watch over them all. Reinar's eyes scanned the crowd and settled on Aeden. His frown deepened with a hint of sadness, and Aeden's shame grew. It was not the reaction Aeden deserved. If anything, he wanted Reinar to look upon him with murderous intent. Allowing Tessa's uncle to retaliate against him would be a far more befitting punishment.

Reinar finally spoke, but not to Olgar. Instead, he looked Aeden in the eye. "You have wrought heartache on this family. Enough is enough. Take your family home. Do not ever show your face on our land again and I will rescind the exile. If you all turn back now, there will be no need for further conflict."

Aeden stiffened. "Why would you do that?" Why would he be willing to bend the rules? The ones he had been ready to fight in order to enforce.

Reinar sighed. "I have no desire to go to war with your family. I know it was not you who killed my son. And although I believe your treachery is to blame for all of this, I will do what I must in order to ensure my people's safety."

Aeden furrowed his brow. Reinar knew the truth. Was that why he was so quick to believe that Tessa had ended her own life? More than that... If Reinar had found out the truth, then maybe the shame and guilt of taking his son from him *had* been too much for her to bear on her own. Through his teeth, he asked, "Who told you that I didn't kill Drake?"

Reinar's eyebrows raised, and confusion flashed across his face. Perhaps he was surprised Aeden cared more about that than the fact that he had been spared from exile. But Aeden didn't care about that. He would have taken a thousand exiles if only to see Tessa one more time.

Regardless, Reinar answered, "Viscount Peitor came forward."

Anger flared like lightning flashing in the sky. He found Peitor in the crowd, just a few feet away from Reinar, and the edges of his vision darkened. If he had kept his mouth shut, then Tessa would still be alive. Then Aeden wouldn't feel like a piece of his soul had been torn away.

Olgar, in his usual cold-hearted fashion, huffed. "Enough of this. Sparing the boy from exile means nothing." He pointed an accusatory finger at Reinar. "You had your chance to take care of our people. To decide what was best for the forest. And you failed. The Sons of the Six will only become more emboldened. You may not be able to protect the Vampyrs in these woods from hunters, but I can."

The crowd, which doubled with his father's folk there, turned to approaching footsteps. One of the brothers, who had been there to witness the death of Marcos and Drake, ran to them with Scarlet in tow. They were both drenched in blood and breathless. "T-the," he stuttered, "the hunter. He escaped. And he's brought more."

Scarlet stepped from behind the Steelhelm man and sobbed when she met Aeden's eyes. "They killed them. Like they were nothing more than pests to squash beneath their boots."

Reinar's voice trembled. "Who? Who did they kill?"

The Steelhelm man's nostrils flared and the pain in his voice made him appear smaller than he was. "My brother, Ricard and Lord Angus."

Aeden barely knew the men in question. But the pained look on Scarlet's face was enough to tug on his heart. This was Tessa's best friend. These were Tessa's people. And if the hunters had come for them, then *his* people were in danger as well.

The Steelhelm man wiped at his blood and grime streaked cheek, "The man we had in our custody. He transformed into a beast. The others that came for him... they're the same."

The blood seemed to drain from Reinar's face, but Aeden didn't have time to try to figure out what man they were referring to. As if the fates saw fit to play a big cosmic trick on them, spine chilling shrieks echoed through the trees. He would never forget that sound. Not after what they'd done to him and Tessa. Aeden searched for the source, but the turned mortals were blended well within the shadows. The Sons of the Six had found them. And they were there with a vengeance.

Olgar beamed as he commanded, "Accept my terms, Reinar. Bend the knee to me and my people will protect yours from what's coming. Decline, and you will not only have to face the Sons of the Six on your own, but you will have us to contend with as well."

Reinar shouted at Flora and Scarlet to remain near Tessa's body. They obeyed hastily. Fear for Reinar and his family flooded Aeden's chest. They wouldn't survive on their own. Not when they were on the brink of starvation. Silently, he urged, *Agree to my father's terms. Give him control in exchange for his protection. Save yourselves.*

Reinar did not balk. Instead, he nodded to his men. In perfect harmony, they unsheathed their weapons. It was all Olgar needed. He snapped to his own men and chaos erupted in the forest.

Grotesque creatures descended from the trees and Vampyrs from the Downthorn side of the lake whipped their heads around in confusion, as if wondering who the greater threat was. Olgar and his men, or the witch-blessed monsters. The two sides—long separated by their strict borders—clashed against one another. Fighting both neighbor and foe. Moonstones were scattered, trampled, and crushed beneath heavy boots, blurring the lines.

Aeden was knocked into his father. His anger sparked, and like a bonfire, it rose. He straightened and his vision reddened. This age-old family feud had brought them all nothing but grief and heartache. How had they not seen that sooner? Nothing he could say or do would stop his father and Reinar. Perhaps the fates had already decided what would happen. If that were the case, then Aeden could do nothing but allow the night to take its course.

Flames kept the beasts at bay before when they attacked him and Tessa. Perhaps they would do the same now. He grabbed hold of a branch, breaking it in half with the heel of his boot. Kneeling, he pulled a dagger from his side and struck the blade against a stone. Sparks flew, catching quickly on the dry leaves of the branch. With torch in hand, Aeden rose.

If the world did not share in his pain, then he would make it. If his father and Reinar wanted war amongst themselves even in the midst of a greater enemy, then Aeden would join it. But he would not choose a side. Instead, he would stand in the middle of it as they burned it all to the ground.

Twenty-Seven

Tessa

Time no longer existed. At least, not from where Tessa was standing. Trapped in an endless fog that she couldn't navigate, she realized there was no way out. The muffled sounds of those she loved echoed through the bleak darkness above.

At first, Tessa cried out for them. Relentlessly trying to catch their attention. Praying to both the stars and the fates that someone would reach down and pull her from whatever prison she was trapped in. It wasn't long before she realized it was no use.

Something like moonlight gave way to her surroundings, though there was no moon in sight. She sat down on the strange, reflective ground. At first glance, one would have thought it was shadowy water. But Tessa was completely dry. She shivered and hugged herself tightly. In Elfhame, her people told stories about the fabled afterlife beneath the hollows. An unearthly place where Fae spirits lived on for eternity in harmony with the land. But this place... The *waiting place*, as she had coined it, was not at all what the stories foretold.

A soft voice echoed in the darkness, jarring Tessa from her musings. It rang out clear and was nearby. "You are not far off. It is the *in between*, Lady Tessa."

Tessa scrambled to her feet. "Who are you?" And how had they read her thoughts? The hairs on her neck stood on end and her nerves vibrated with anxiety. It was the first being she had encountered since falling into the dark black night of death.

"You are not dead, dear child," the woman cooed. "You are simply caught between. Unable to enter the land of the dead because of the sickness in your blood."

The curse. Tessa inhaled sharply through her nose. She was trapped because of the monster she was. Unwelcome in the land of the Elders. Unable to rest. Squinting in the darkness, Tessa caught sight of a gorgeous pale woman drifting closer to her. She seemed to float along the reflective ground, and it rippled around her. A cool rush swept over Tessa, like water being poured over her head. And for a moment, she thought she would pass out.

Instead, she stayed frozen in place as the woman approached. Tessa's heart raced faster the closer she came. Droplets of water fell from the woman's dress and onto the floor, sending waves lapping around them. Still, Tessa remained dry.

Tessa flashed her fangs. "Who are you?"

Whatever this creature was, she was no mortal. Nor was she one of the Vampyrs from the Crimson Forest. There was a deadly, eerie quality to her. Like something that rarely surfaced in the realm of the living. But judging by her ethereal presence, she had come from Elfhame. It had been a long time since she'd encountered a creature of her family's homeland. She'd grown so used to the Vampyrs—her people—that she'd forgotten how startling the Fae could be. Though the woman was unearthly in her beauty, she also had a dangerous aura. One that made Tessa's flight instincts kick in.

She took a step back, but the woman didn't flinch. Instead, she spoke softly, like the faintest whisper in the night. "You do not know me. But I know you, Tessa Downthorn."

Tessa's heart felt like it might fly out of her chest. "Then it seems the polite thing to do is to tell me who you are."

The woman smiled, but it did little to settle Tessa's nerves. Rows of sharp, curved teeth lined her mouth. "I am called many things. Witch. Water Spirit. Lady of the Lake. But you may call me Ava."

Tessa gulped, ignoring the scorching pain that still lingered in her throat, though she shouldn't have felt anything in the waiting place, right? Overlooking the many questions she'd had since falling into her slumber, she asked instead, "What do you want?"

Ava looked Tessa up and down, as if assessing her. "It is not about what I want. Rather, it is about what *you* want."

Tessa's mind was reeling. How had this woman gotten here in the first place? Was she the ruler of this realm? If she had gotten in, then surely she could get back out. She could help Tessa escape. For that, she would indulge the strange creature. "I want out of here. I want to save them." Again, her ears perked at the muffled voices above. The ones that grew more urgent by the minute. She even thought she might have heard shouting, but it was difficult to tell.

With a mischievous smile, Ava suggested, "You want to save the boy. The one who stole your heart."

Heat rose to Tessa's cheeks. How did she know about Aeden? And what business was it of hers to speak to Tessa about matters of the heart? Ava's insinuations lingered between them. Rather than acknowledge them, she said, "I want to stop this insanity between our families."

"Then do it." The woman ran her finger along Tessa's hair. Her lips twisted in curiosity as if she hadn't touched another in quite some time. When she said *Lady of the Lake*, did she mean she quite literally lived in the lake? Is that where Tessa was? She glanced up again, hoping to see something—anything—to give her a hint, but found nothing.

Tessa quipped, "Get me out of here and I will."

Ignoring her, Ava mused, "You are nothing like her. I didn't expect that." With a tsk, she added, "You are as determined as she was, but far fiercer."

"Like who?" Tessa couldn't ignore her piqued interest.

"Ayana." Ava said it so matter-of-factly, as if they were discussing the weather and not Tessa's ancestor, who had brought the curse down on them all.

"What do you know of her?"

"I know plenty." Ava's eyes flashed with anger, and she snapped, "I know that I made a promise long ago. One that I intend to keep. It is why I've been helping to speed things along."

Tessa eyed her, noting Ava's razor-sharp, talon-like nails and the tiny seashells that adorned her fingers. "What do you mean by that?"

Ava sneered at her. But it appeared far less human and more feral. "The Sons. They were desperate, and your people needed a reason to come together."

Tessa's breath caught in her throat. "The witch. It was you who blessed the Sons of the Six."

"I simply tossed the pebble that started the ripples."

Tessa snarled, "Well, now the waves are about to crash in the forest. Whatever promises you made to Ayana are no good here. You have wrought havoc on us all."

Ava snapped her teeth. "Do you remember Ayana and Byron?"

Tessa set her shoulders back, trying to maintain some sort of defiance in the face of the know-it-all woman. "No. I was a child. But I am familiar with the curse. The King wanted to marry Ayana, but she loved Byron. We were cursed because of that jealousy."

"But do you know *how*? When the Elders would not grant him the power, the malevolent King took matters into his own hands." She made a motion with her hands as if wielding a dagger in the direction of Tessa's chest. Heavy emotion was in every word as she continued, "Carving the young lovers' hearts from their chests whilst they were still bleeding. Blood magic is powerful but combine that with the strength of their love and, well... you've seen the result."

Tessa had beheld the depictions in the paintings hanging in her home for years. Art that showed the King casting his spell. She didn't need another history lesson. Not when every minute she wasted with Ava was a minute that Aeden and the others were at risk. "Why are you telling me this? Why are you here?"

"Because all curses have a weakness. A thread to be pulled that can unravel it all. It is the law of our magic. And things have changed in Elfhame. This is your chance to set things right and return your people to where they belong. Then, and only then, will my promise to Ayana be fulfilled."

That got Tessa's attention. "Tell me how."

Ava smiled genuinely now. "The blood of the lovers—Downthorn and Ashbane alike—created the curse. Binding your people in an existence of both blood and sorrow. And it is only a love by the same ancestral line that can break it."

Tessa scrunched her face. There wasn't an ounce of love between her family and the Ashbanes. And although she knew she *could* have loved Aeden, that was broken now. Shattered by the lies and deceit between them. But if Ava thought that was the answer, then she would not argue. At this point, she would agree to anything to get out of the place between worlds.

Facing Aeden again would be painful. Knowing what their feelings for one another had done to their families was too much to bear. But broken heart or not, she needed to stop them. With a curt nod, she said, "Alright then. Get me out of here."

Ava placed her hands on the sides of Tessa's face. Her palms were damp and felt like old leather that had been left out in the rain too long. Tessa tensed as Ava leaned in and placed her lips against hers. This was no kiss, though. Ava blew softly, filling Tessa's lungs. It was painfully cold, like jumping into a frozen lake. Before Tessa could pull away, her vision darkened and the sounds of battle filled her ears.

There was a bitter taste in Tessa's mouth. But that couldn't be right. One wasn't able to *taste* in death, right? With a moan, she slowly felt the sensation return to her toes, then to her legs, and upward until finally she was able to open her eyes. But that wasn't right, either. She'd been poisoned. Of that much, she was certain. So why was she staring up at the blood red leaves of the Crimson Forest?

Her arms trembled as she rose to rest on her elbows. The glistening lake caught her eye, and memories of a woman with strange beauty speaking of curses and how to break them flooded back like a tidal wave. Tessa pressed her hands to her throbbing head.

Hard wood creaked beneath her movement and bile rose to her throat as she realized she was on a funeral pyre. *Her* pyre. How close had she come to losing her earthly form? To being trapped in the *between* for eternity?

There was a small squeak from below, followed by a squeal on the other side of her. Before Tessa knew it, her mother and Scarlet were leaping onto the wooden slat. Before she could get a word out, they began poking and prodding at her.

Her mother spoke in a hushed tone, "By the fates. It's not possible. How? What do you remember? Is there any pain?" Questions poured from her mouth and Tessa winced.

Scarlet brushed Tessa's hair from her face. "We thought you were lost to us. *Why?* Why did you do it?"

Tessa's stomach somersaulted. Did they know about Drake? With a burning throat, she replied hoarsely, "He was going to kill Aeden. Had already killed Marcos..." She grimaced, remembering the mortal women in his mother's room and wanted to add, *who knows how many countless others he'd harmed?*

Scarlet's long silver hair cascaded over one side of her face as she shook her head. "Peitor explained everything after we found you. I'm talking about the poisoning."

Tessa's mother helped her sit up and Scarlet grasped both of Tessa's hands tightly.

Flora bit her lip and tears welled in her eyes. "I can't imagine the pain you must have been feeling. The guilt... but to take your own life..." her voice cracked. "How are you here right now, my sweet girl?"

Tessa tore her hands from Scarlet's and scooted away from both of them. Battle cries filled the forest, but the pain of her mother and Scarlet's accusations overwhelmed her. "You think I poisoned myself? I would never!"

Neither woman looked as if they believed her. Instead of pressing the matter further, they backed away. Tessa appreciated the space, but she was still struggling to understand. How could her own mother and best friend think that she would hurt herself? As heavy as her guilt was for her role in Drake's death, it wasn't enough to leave the ones she loved behind in such a terrible manner.

Bile rose in her throat. Though she wasn't sure if it was from the after effects of the poison and coming back from the between, or the pitying looks she was getting from her mother and Scarlet. Throwing off the thin muslin someone had placed over her body, she turned and pressed her feet on the rough branches below. If Peitor had revealed the truth, then her uncle knew it was she who had taken his son from him. She needed to talk to him. To apologize. To beg for his forgiveness.

Her mother put a firm hand on her shoulder. "Tessa, we need to get you out of here."

She ignored her and asked, "What's happening?" The scene playing out before her eyes was a blur of bodies colliding in battle.

"Olgar. He ambushed the..." she paused and wrang her hangs uncomfortably, "funeral. And the hunter the Steelhelms captured yesterday escaped. War is upon us, and you are too weak to defend yourself. We need to go." Flora's face flushed with panic.

Tessa gazed out at the wreckage. Bodies were slain on the ground. The majority of which were Vampyrs. Why were her people losing if they vastly outnumbered the turned? With Olgar's supporters there, they should have had the upper hand. Should have been able to use their strength and vitality from feeding on the vein to their advantage.

Nearby, Peitor slammed his head into Aeden's uncle. She furrowed her brow. "Why are they fighting with each other? Why aren't we standing together?"

There was an almost sinister shadow across her mother's mournful face as she explained, "Olgar gave us an ultimatum. Hand control over to him, or fend for ourselves."

"We're not strong enough," Tessa argued. "We need to help one another. Where is Aeden?" she asked with dread. He should have stopped them. Why hadn't he made them see sense? Terror sank deep into her bones. Maybe he had chosen his father's side after all. Or had he taken the exile? Had Reinar killed him if he hadn't?

"He's out there." Flora patted her arm. "He came looking for you." Tears drifted down her face. "He was so distraught by what he saw. And when the turned descended upon us, he rushed into the fight."

The revelation that Aeden had come for her sent butterflies fluttering in her stomach. If only she could squash them like the pests that they were. She and Aeden could never be. That much was clear. But she needed to get to him and make sure he was safe.

Tessa clenched her shaking fists. "I need to find him. Olgar and Reinar as well. They are putting everyone at risk. We don't have time for infighting." She jumped down from the branches, ignoring the jarring sensation in her bare feet.

Flora reached out and grabbed her arm. "You can't, sweetheart. I can't bear to lose you again."

Tessa's heart ached when she turned to her mother. The woman had lost so much already, and she didn't want to be the cause of anymore heartache. But there was no other way. Not when the pained cries of her people were breaking her own heart at that very moment.

Tessa pleaded, "I have to go. We have to stop them." Neither side would win this battle. Instead, it would destroy them all.

Flora bit her bottom lip and tears poured down her sunken cheeks. "You are every bit your father's daughter," she said it wistfully, and a proud smile graced her lips. She slipped away from Tessa, backing up slowly until she reached Scarlet. The women embraced one another, watching Tessa wearily.

Each step was accompanied by searing pain. It racked her entire body and cast dizzy spells over her. Men knocked into her, too engaged in battle to realize she had awoken. Aeden was nowhere to be found. What if he was injured? Or dead. Lost in the same waiting place she had just been in? Her legs shook, nearly giving out beneath her. She was still weak from the poison. And although her stomach rocked with hunger, she knew she wasn't starving. Someone must have tried to feed her when she was found unconscious. Perhaps thinking it might fight the poison that coursed through her body. Yet it still wasn't enough to give her back her strength.

Weakly, she shouted, "Aeden!"

Each fallen body she passed tightened the knots in her stomach. Every head of auburn hair was like a dagger to her heart. But each time she realized it wasn't Aeden, a small flicker of hope grew brighter. He had betrayed her, but he had saved her life, too. He would help her fix this. Of that she was sure.

She called out for him repeatedly. Relentless in her search. And barely dodging the blows of battle-blinded men. Then she saw him. Aeden Ashbane. Covered in inky blood and shrieking savagely at a turned mortal as he tore its head from its body with his bare hands. She shouted his name again, and he blinked rapidly as if coming out of a war hungry trance.

But it was not her he was looking at. It was her uncle. Reinar stood yards away from Aeden. Separated by a sea of turned mortals and Vampyrs tearing one another apart limb from limb. Both men's shoulders rose and fell rapidly. For a moment, Tessa thought they might approach one another to speak. Might agree that they needed to band together if they were to survive this attack.

Except neither made an indication of a truce. Instead, Aeden made a beeline for Reinar, killing any who stood in his way with ease. It was like watching a stranger. This was not the Aeden who had laughed easily with her. It was not the man who had stopped her from killing the majestic stag. Or the kind soul who had helped Drake's victims. This was a man who did not care what happened to him. One who had nothing to lose.

Twenty-Eight

Aeden

W ar cries filled the small clearing. It was a sound that matched Aeden's own agony. There was no turning back now. Relenting to his fate, he stormed through the forest, which had become a battlefield. Heat flared, spreading across his skin like armor as he ripped the turned mortals apart piece by piece. Fueled by fresh blood and anguish, he fared much better than the Downthorns and their followers.

Smoke drifted through the air, making several Vampyrs cough at the outer edges of the clearing. It seemed others had caught onto his defensive maneuver. The turned were sensitive to the flame. But the heat filling the forest was more powerful than what a few lit branches would put off.

Aeden gritted his teeth. If the fates had already decided how their ending would unfold, then so be it. He charged through the crowd, dodging Vampyrs engaged in battle. They slammed and shoved into him, but he didn't let it deter him. If this was going to be his end, then he would at least take down as many of the cursed hunters as he could. He paid little mind to the Vampyrs, who were simultaneously battling one another while defending themselves against the hunters. It was time for everyone to pay for their sins.

A turned mortal with an endless row of fangs threw itself in the direction of a Vampyr. Aeden shoved the Vampyr out of the way and, in a blind rage, tore the turned creature apart. When he was finished, his senses returned, and he locked eyes across the field with Reinar.

The patriarch of the Downthorn family was covered in blood. Whether it belonged to the hunters or Aeden's folk, he wasn't sure. All he knew was Reinar's eyes were filled with battle-rage. And they were boring into Aeden with a savagery that was only spoken about in stories. This was the Reinar who had been a warrior. Terrifying in all his glory.

For a moment, Tessa flashed through his memory. The moments they had shared and the time he'd spent with her and the Downthorns. Easy laughs and open smiles. But she would never laugh again. Not in this world. He took a tentative step in Reinar's direction.

Aeden wanted to blame his father and Reinar for pushing him and Tessa together. But it was time for him to take accountability. He had willingly gone into the Downthorn's home with ill-intent. It was Aeden who had accepted that poison and then carelessly misplaced it. He hadn't been strong enough to save Marcos. Nor had he been there to ease Tessa's pain—to tell her that everything would be alright.

She had paid the price for his mistakes and now it was his turn to do the same. If Reinar wanted to punish someone, then Aeden would accept. His feet carried him faster than his racing heart. Not once did he break eye contact with the vengeful warrior. When he reached Reinar, Lord Peitor grabbed Aeden by the collar and spun him to face him. He was wounded in the shoulder and Aeden almost laughed at how easy it would be to put the arrogant man down.

Before he had the chance, something slammed into Aeden, hard as a boulder. He rolled toward the lake's bank. Sand burned his eyes and choked him. Before he could clear himself of it, a fist connected with his face. It jarred him back. Then another hit came. Again and again.

Instinct screamed at him to shield himself. To fight back or protect his face. But his heart said, *This is what you deserve.* Relaxing his muscles, Aeden accepted the brutal blows. His attacker grunted, letting go of Aeden's collar. He dropped to the ground, his head rolling with the threat of losing consciousness. Why were they stopping?

Aeden groaned, pushing himself up to his knees. His eyes were swollen, but as his body tried to heal itself, he caught sight of the attacker. Reinar breathed heavily above him. His fangs glinted in the moonlight. They could easily tear through Aeden's throat if he allowed it. He tilted his head to the side, exposing his neck for the taking.

"Do it," he snarled through a mouth full of blood. "End it."

Reinar grimaced, a look of regret shadowing his face. Still, he pulled a dagger from his belt and raised it in the air. Aeden locked eyes with him. His pulse was steady. Would he see Tessa soon? Was it possible they would be reunited in death? Maybe they would be welcomed into Elfhame's land of the dead together.

He closed his eyes, ready for Reinar to plunge the dagger into his heart. As he did, he imagined the soft tresses of Tessa's hair beneath his fingers. The full curve of her body pressed against his. And the easy smile she reserved for times when she was truly free to be herself.

Nothing happened, though. There was no sting of the blade. No more blows to the face. He growled, frustrated with Reinar's hesitation, and opened his eyes. A woman with long, rich brown hair loosened down to her waist stood with her back to him.

A wave of nausea rolled through him. It couldn't be. Was he already dead? He glanced around to see that the Vampyrs closest to them had stopped fighting amongst themselves. Distant echoes of the others who were still fending off the hunters rang in his ears, but it hardly felt real. All eyes were on the woman. She stood straight backed with an air of strength he would recognize anywhere.

Aeden's voice quaked, "Tessa?"

She turned to him. There was color in her face, as if she had not been dead only moments ago. Her long lashes cast shadows on her cheeks. And there was a sad smile splayed across her lips. "Aeden." A relieved sob escaped her, and she knelt down beside him. Her hands were warm and solid on his face. Not that of a wraith. She was here in flesh and blood.

"You were dead." Broken, he leaned forward, resting his forehead on her chest. "I thought I lost you."

With one hand on the back of his head, she soothed him with a soft caress. "I'm here, Aeden. I'm here now."

Twenty-Nine

Tessa

T essa held Aeden tightly on the bank of the lake. He shuddered beneath her, and she ran her hand through his disheveled hair. She was grateful for his head buried against her. The sight of his battered face would have made her crumple into a million pieces... A face that was beaten at the hand of the uncle she loved.

As if recovering from the shock of her reawakening, Reinar fumbled with his words, "You... We thought..."

Tessa wasn't sure how to begin to explain. Ghost white faces loomed in the corners of her vision. A line of defense had formed around them as Vampyr supporters of her family kept the turned at bay.

She opened her mouth, unsure of what would come out, but one of the men grunted as Olgar pushed his way through. He was covered in blood and what appeared to be ash. It coated his hair in a fine gray layer. Sniffing at the air, her stomach twisted. The scent of burning leaves blew by with the breeze. If someone had started a fire, then the danger had elevated to new heights. The Crimson Forest would never survive uncontrolled flames.

The crowd thickened beside Olgar. They were all streaked in soot and their bodies sagged from the wear of fighting. Tessa flinched, grabbing tighter to Aeden as shrieks intensified. Olgar smiled sickly. He was burning the creatures alive. That had been his answer. And now the only thing left standing between him and his plans was her family.

Reinar's eyes darted between Olgar, Aeden, and her. He clenched the dagger so tight his knuckles turned white. His voice rang out surer than he looked as he said, "It is time for the Ashbanes to pay for their traitorous ways." Even as he spoke, Tessa caught the hint of hesitation. He did not want to be there any more than she did.

With a firm shake of her head, she announced, "That is enough. All of you." She looked around at the bystanders. Vampyrs from both sides of the lake. Her folk were staring down at her and Aeden with confusion twisted on their faces. Meanwhile, the Ashbane's loyalists watched her as if she were a wraith who had appeared from thin air.

She addressed both sides as she continued, "Haven't you done enough?" She peered through the crowd where the fire bit at the trees. It scorched through the turned mortals like they were nothing more than parchment. Tessa shook her head in disgust. "Look at us. Even as our foe burn, we are *still* here ready to kill one another. Lives have been lost today because you were too busy blaming each other for your misfortunes." She glared at her uncle. At the man she had looked up to and cherished like a father. "Or too busy condemning your neighbors because they chose a different path than you. This isn't right."

When she directed her gaze to the crowd, a few glanced down at the ground as if embarrassed. Even Olgar, who was covered in blood, panted as he looked between his battered son and the dagger in Reinar's hand. Tessa rested her hands gently on Aeden's face and encouraged him to look at her.

His eyes were so dark they looked almost black. But still, she could see the shine of tears in them as she said, "Aeden, I was wrong. Wrong to be mad at you for doing what you thought you needed to in order to honor your family."

He shook his head. "No. I was weak for not standing up to them. For waiting so long to tell you the truth."

Together, hand in hand, they stood to face their people. There was no sign of Ava. Tessa glanced at the water, wondering if she had slipped back into her domain during the commotion. She had honored her word and gotten Tessa there. If they had been even a moment later, Aeden would have been killed. Dread sent the hair on her arms standing on end.

Tessa pleaded with the crowd—addressing both sides—as she declared, "We are only strong when we stand together. It is not about how we feed. Nor is it about what happened in the past. We are not the monsters that the Unseelie King tried to force us to be. Not unless we choose it."

At her words, Reinar dropped the dagger. It sent a rippling effect through the crowd. Each Vampyr who had brought a weapon with them let it clamor to the ground. Even Olgar relaxed his shoulders and unclenched his fists. The gruesome witch-blessed mortals no longer cried out in agony, but a bitter scent filled the air, mixed with thick smoke.

Tessa continued to grip Aeden's hand. Afraid that if she let go, she would lose her courage. This was working. But if she faltered for even a moment, then they could all change their minds. A hush had fallen over the forest. All except for the shuffling of one set of footsteps.

Rose pushed her way through the crowd with malice, ruining the beauty of her delicate face. "Bullshit! All of it." She charged at them. Jabbing a finger in Tessa's direction, she declared, "You just couldn't stay out of the way, could you?"

Aeden took a protective step in front of Tessa and said, "Look around, Rose, it's over."

Rose's words were deadly as she seethed, "It's not over until that bitch is cold and dead where she belongs."

Tessa's veins turned to ice. Recalling the single rose left in the basket, she guessed, "It was you. You're the one who sent the poisoned wine."

Rose snarled, "You were ruining everything. He wasn't going to let go unless you were gone completely."

Aeden's grip on Tessa's hand tightened. With disgust, he said, "The vial was in my pocket. You took it the night of the dinner when you bumped into me, didn't you?"

Rose neither confirmed nor denied the accusations. Instead, she reached down slowly, picking up the dagger Reinar had discarded. Before anyone could stop her, she lunged with the blade pointed at Tessa's heart.

Tessa grounded her feet, ready to dodge it, but Aeden leapt in front of her in a blur. There was a terrible cracking sound as the dagger landed deep in his chest.

Rose screeched and stumbled back as Aeden fell to the ground. Tessa dropped to his side, pressing her hands around the wound, careful not to move the blade. Through the blood, it was impossible to see where the point landed. She prayed to the stars that it had missed his heart.

Olgar grabbed Rose as she tried to flee. He held her roughly as Balis tied her arms behind her back. Tessa focused her attention back on Aeden, whose eyes had glazed over. His breathing was ragged and uneven. It became more and more shallow by the second.

This wasn't how it was supposed to end. Tessa wiped away hot, angry tears. Her hands were covered in his blood and a lump in her throat rose. Someone had to help him. The crowd closed in around them. Every one of the Vampyrs looked horrified, with gaping mouths and wide eyes.

It was like they were already mourning him. Already admitting defeat. Tessa had no such intentions. She glanced back at the lake and begged, "Ava! Please save him. Please! You made a promise, remember? So, honor it. Save him."

Although she knew the promise Ava made long ago, did not mean she had to protect Aeden in particular, she hoped it would be enough to entice her back from the depths of the water. If her promise meant getting their people back to Elfhame, then surely she needed Aeden alive to fulfill it.

The water rippled and with it, murmurs spread through the crowd. A few gasped as the ethereal woman rose above the lake in a shimmering light like the first sign of dawn. Her skin began to lose its luster, the further she drifted from the water's surface. It was replaced with a gray-blue pallor, and Tessa noted the strange shells and barnacles embedded in her skin.

She ignored the nausea that came from the sight of it. Instead, she focused on keeping pressure on Aeden's wound, and called to Ava, "Save him. Please."

Ava cocked her head to the side and pressed her lips into a thin, hard line. "I have done my part." She gestured around them at the battle weary Vampyrs still left standing and the flames licking up the trunks of the trees. "Now it is time for you both to do *your* part."

Tessa squeezed her eyes shut, willing the answer to come to her. Recalling Ava's story in the between, she whispered to herself, "Every curse can be broken." Her eyes shot open with panicked realization. She whispered to herself, "Bound by blood and... *Blood*. That's the answer."

With a curt nod, Ava drifted over the water and onto the shore. She left no footprints in the sand as she walked to Tessa and Aeden. Towering above them, she gestured to him. Tessa bared her fangs and bit into her wrist. It wasn't a fatal wound. Just deep enough to allow a few drops to fall into Aeden's mouth. If the blood of Vampyrs could heal mortals, then maybe it could heal him. And if Ava was right about unbinding the curse, then maybe this would save them all.

Light—similar to that of a rainbow—drifted down from her wrist like a waterfall. As the blood reached his lips, the light settled on Aeden's chest where the dagger was still plunged deep, with only the hilt showing.

Slowly, the dagger rose, drawing away from his body, until it lingered just above his chest. Tessa took hold of it and threw it into the lake. There was a small splash. One far too small for something that had nearly wrecked her entire world.

The wound began to close, healing itself at a speed much greater than their Vampyr abilities were capable of. Aeden let out a pained choking sound and his eyes fluttered open. Tessa didn't bother to look at the crowd's reaction. Nothing else existed at this moment but Aeden.

Until Ava spoke, that is. Tessa tensed; afraid she had done something wrong. But Ava simply said, "Now it is time for the two of you to reveal what is in your hearts."

Tessa felt a tug in her chest and a cool rush like water circled around her heart. It reminded her of the magic she once held before the curse. A faint whisper of memory. With a decisive breath, she leaned down, kissing Aeden softly on the lips. They were tender, broken and bloody from the blows he'd taken to his face, but she didn't care.

When she pulled away with his blood on her lips, her voice cracked as she proclaimed, "I love you, Aeden Ashbane. With all my heart, I love you."

Without hesitation, he responded, "I love you, too, Tessa Downthorn. A wolf in doe's clothing." The dimple on his cheek deepened as he referred to their first meeting at the masquerade.

Tessa's heart soared, and the tug in her chest turned to a tearing sensation. She clutched at it and gasped for air. Aeden grabbed her as her knees weakened. Reinar took a jolting step forward, but Ava waved him off.

Gleefully, the water witch said, "It's working. Don't fight it."

Tessa nearly fell as Aeden pulled one of his arms away from her and clutched onto his own chest. He groaned, then shouted, "What is happening to us?"

"Magic." Ava's response was so quiet, Tessa thought she might have heard wrong.

Agonizing pain ripped through Tessa's mouth and she touched her gums. It was like a blade being drawn through them. If Ava was right, then it was happening. They had done it—broken the curse through the blood of her and Aeden. The hint of magic that had encircled Tessa's heart burst. It flooded out of her chest, slamming into the Vampyrs around them. The cursed people who once called themselves Fae—who had been cursed for so long that they had forgotten who they truly were—gasped in unison as the magic washed over them like a tidal wave.

Tessa felt it, too. The hunger was torn from her belly and snatched away from her mind. And the scorching pain tearing through her mouth subsided. She reached for her fangs to find that they were no longer there. In their place were two perfectly normal canines. Ones meant for tearing into food, not flesh.

With a shaking hand, she reached for Aeden. He beamed at her, revealing a mouth free of fangs as well. The crowd was a mixture of pained and joyous cries as the curse unwound itself through each and every one of them. A few wept as they embraced their neighbor.

Aeden grabbed Tessa's face and pressed his forehead to hers. His eyes were no longer filled with red—a reflection of their bloodlust—instead, they shimmered in the approaching morning light with rings of brown. They were rich like the soil in the Autumn Court.

She gasped, "Your eyes."

He pulled away slightly with a deepening grin. "You did it. You saved us."

"*We* did it," she whispered back.

Then together, they rose to face their people. Tessa's heart rejoiced at the sight. No longer were they Vampyrs cursed to live on the blood of others. They smiled openly, flashing fangless teeth, and their eyes glistened in deep browns or frosty blues. It was too incredible for words.

Aeden must have thought so, too. With a warm embrace, he drew Tessa in close. No one seemed to mind as he kissed her. It was deep and fierce. One that said more than words ever could. It was full of promises. Heat bloomed in her chest.

When they parted, she opened her eyes to find the fire had been snuffed out. Like a veil had descended over the trees to defeat the flames. She gazed up at the sky, reveling in the sun shining full and free on her face. Looking up, she found that the trees were no longer tainted with crimson. The leaves had returned to their original green. Everything, it seemed, had been set to its natural order. Just as it always should have been.

Epilogue
One Year Later
Tessa

The hall was aglow with candlelight. It shined brighter than any flame in the mortal realm, as if fueled by the very magic of the palace itself. Tessa kept her hand on the wall as she walked. The Winter Palace was a mischievous place—its halls constantly shifting and leading visitors to rooms they had no intention of venturing into.

Tonight, she needed to get to the ballroom, and she didn't want to be late. So, with a hand placed firmly on the deep purple wall, she walked. Finally, she came to a door gilded in gold. She sucked in a deep breath. This was the first ball she had attended since returning to Elfhame. And she desperately wanted everything to go well.

Before daring to enter the room, she turned to a mirror on the wall. Even after a year since the curse broke, she couldn't get used to her appearance. Her eyes were returned to normal, free of the deep red that resembled fresh blood. Now they varied in shades of blue. Frosty on the outer rings and deepening into a glittering crystal lake near the pupils.

For days after the curse, she couldn't stop smiling. Simply for the sheer pleasure that sharp fangs no longer peeked out when she did so. But tonight, she smiled for a different reason. This was the night Aeden had been dreaming of.

Smoothing down her gown—a deep midnight blue with white winter roses embroidered on the bodice—she took a steadying breath and pushed through the doors. The room was filled with Fae from all over Elfhame. Ava hadn't been exaggerating when she said much had changed during their time away.

The King, for starters, seemed to have met a well-deserved fate. And for tonight, the new master of the palace had pulled out all the stops. He declared it to be a celebration for her people's perseverance in the face of the late King's wrath. Tessa was honored by the gesture. And surprised by his kindness. He and his husband had welcomed her people back to court with open arms.

A few men and women blocked her path, embracing one another in celebration. She side-stepped them with a grin. Even after all this time back home in Elfhame, her people still reunited with their former friends and neighbors as if seeing them for the first time. Even the men who had been left behind—cursed in another way by the late King—embraced their friends and family with teary eyes tonight.

There was still much healing to be done. Adjusting to their former lives was no easy task. But together, they were doing it. Olgar and her uncle kept their distance from one another. But they were amiable when attending functions that put them in the same room. It was easier for them to remain apart in day-to-day life as Olgar returned to his old home in the Autumn Court and Reinar to the Downthorn estate near the mountains in the Winter Court.

Her mother, however, had become quite close with Aeden's. They stood now, in the corner of the ballroom, huddled together like young girls. Flora's face had filled out over recent months. The color in her cheeks brought warmth to Tessa's heart. She smiled softly as she waved to them, but she did not join them.

Talos and Scarlet fluttered around arm in arm, chatting with other guests. Talos rarely trembled or quaked since returning to Elfhame, and seemed to have a permanent beaming smile on his face as of late. Scarlet winked at her as they passed by and made her promise to find them for a drink later.

Tessa agreed and inched to the back of the crowd that was gathered around a small stage. The palace had spared no expense, crafting the set up with beautiful birch wood. It stood well above the crowd, allowing Tessa a full view of Aeden.

He was already seated and biting his lip with concentration. She noted the slight furrow in his brow and silently cheered him on. It was impossible for him to hide his nerves from her. These days, it was impossible for them to hide anything from one another. Not that they even tried. It was a quiet agreement between the two of them. For there was nothing that the other could do that would ruin what they had. Not so long as they were always open and honest with each other.

Aeden rested his chin on the violin. It was the same one he'd played in the Crimson Forest. Although Reinar offered to have a new one crafted for him—a way of making up for the strife that had been between them—Aeden politely refused. As far as he was concerned, there was nothing more to forgive. Breaking the curse had given them all a clean slate.

Fate had *indeed* played a part in their lives. Through the love of Tessa and Aeden—two descendants of the lovers whose blood had bound them to a bloodthirsty existence—the curse was broken. None of their people had any intention of bringing the bad blood between all of them back to Elfhame. The only thing Aeden brought was his violin. And tonight, he would finally have the chance to play it in front of an audience.

He raised his bow to the strings, pressing it down gently. The first few notes were careful. Guarded. But as his eyes lifted to Tessa's, his face smoothed. With a dimpled smirk, he released the music, stringing it out in a lively melody. The Fae gawking at the stage began to sway to the tune and a few even took to the ballroom floor to dance.

Tessa, however, stayed firmly in place. Just as she'd done over the last few months while he practiced. They'd been preparing for this moment. He had even played for her when they took their trip into the mountains to see the fierce wild horses gallop through the heavy snow. That song—one filled with wishes fulfilled—is what he played now.

It was his song to her. A sweet, but untamed tune that told their story. As he played faster, coming to the crescendo, his eyes stayed locked on hers. The rest of the room seemed to fade away from her, leaving only the man she loved. This was everything she could have dreamed of and so much more. This was what made life truly worth living.

Acknowledgments

First and foremost, to my readers. Without you, none of this would be possible. Each time that pesky imposter syndrome creeps in, I think of you and all the love and encouragement you have shown me and my books. I would never have made it this far without the community I have built with all of you.

To my husband who has supported me in every new endeavour that has popped into my head. If I had to choose one person to spend a cursed eternity in a forest with, it would be you.

To mom and Catherine. Thank you for always lending an ear to my ravings, responding to late-night texts, and being my number one fans!

To my street team. Thank you from the bottom of my heart for sharing in the fun and for showing so much love to my books.

And to Ardena who has been beta reading for me since the very beginning. From creating incredible pieces inspired by my books, to sending me encouraging messages... it's friends like you who drag me out of that pesky imposter syndrome.

Finally, to my Chaos Corner: Danielle, Emily F, Emily H, Samantha, Jes, and Kate. You are seriously my rocks! Without all of you, I genuinely would not make it through the messy first drafts, rough edits, and bad days. I am incredibly grateful to each one of you.

About the Author

J.M. Wallace (Jordan) is an author of Fantasy Romance, with strong leading ladies and their supportive (albeit a bit morally grey) love interests. She is a proud stay-at-home mom of two and writes about magic, mayhem, and romance in her spare time (often with cartoons blaring in the background). When she's not writing about far-away worlds and the villains who haunt them, she can be found relaxing in the nearest local coffee shop or exploring her favorite bookstores.

www.jmwallaceauthor.com

Follow J.M.'s author journey!